T0037125

THE
DECOY
GIRLFRIEND

A Novel

LILLIE VALE

G. P. PUTNAM'S SONS
NEW YORK

PUTNAM
— EST. 1838 —

G. P. Putnam's Sons
Publishers Since 1838
An imprint of Penguin Random House LLC
penguinrandomhouse.com

Copyright © 2022 by Lillie Vale

Library of Congress Cataloging-in-Publication Data

Names: Vale, Lillie, author.
Title: The decoy girlfriend: a novel / Lillie Vale.
Description: New York: G.P. Putnam's Sons, [2022]
Identifiers: LCCN 2022029867 (print) | LCCN 2022029868 (ebook) |
ISBN 9780593422021 (trade paperback) | ISBN 9780593422038 (ebook)
Subjects: LCGFT: Romance fiction. | Novels.
Classification: LCC PS3622.A42526 D43 2022 (print) |
LCC PS3622.A42526 (ebook) | DDC 813/.6—dc23/eng/20220624
LC record available at https://lccn.loc.gov/2022029867
LC ebook record available at https://lccn.loc.gov/2022029868

Printed in the United States of America
1st Printing

BOOK DESIGN BY KATY RIEGEL

For Gaby, who rolled out the red carpet
and always makes me feel like a star

THE DECOY GIRLFRIEND

With two huge secrets, Freya Lal is the exact opposite of the open book she always considered herself to be.

She stares at the laptop on the counter of her aunt's bookshop, Books & Brambles. The blinking cursor at the end of the page mocks her. Grimly, she rereads her words until she has no choice but to come to the conclusion that she is, in fact, a one-hit wonder who will never be published again.

She holds down the Delete key until every single awful word is obliterated. The pinching band of tightness around her chest eases the moment the Word doc is blank again. Yesterday's words are gone, and she already can't remember what they said. It feels like Freya's chased away a bogeyman, one that's been Frankensteined together with ugly words stitched into unflattering sentences.

The more she thinks about it, not only does her imposter syndrome become more plausible, it becomes more obvious: her first book deal—when she was a teenage wunderkind—was obviously a fluke. How the *hell* is she supposed to turn in a first draft of her second book to her publisher when she can't even write two paragraphs before self-doubt creeps in? She's been keeping her lack of progress a secret from everyone for so long that the only thing that will help her now is to—

No. That's secret number two, and she swore that she was cutting back.

After throwing her long brown hair into a high ponytail, she shoves her oversize electric-blue plastic-framed glasses up her nose and holds back a groan. The only thing she has going for her right now is the fact that absolutely no one in Books & Brambles knows that the twenty-three-year-old girl slumped next to the register is in the throes of an existential crisis.

The indie bookshop is a few minutes away from its 9:00 a.m. opening, and two other employees are putting the finishing touches on the themed window display. Freya can catch snippets of conversation regaling all the gory details of her coworkers' terrible Tinder dates drifting down the aisle, too quiet and far away for her to take part in, even if she were dating right now (which she isn't) and even if she wanted to (which she doesn't).

"Are we sure these should be here?" Cliff's voice is strained, like he's lifting a tall stack of books.

With a confidence far greater than her few weeks of working here, Emma authoritatively replies, "If Stori left them up here, then yeah. Left window is for summer swoons, and right window is for summer slashers."

"I *know* that." Cliff's words are punctuated with a solid thump that Freya can only imagine is him setting down the books until the confusion is cleared up. "I *meant* are we sure because it's an old title."

"That can't be right. Let me see that— Oh. Just put them there."

"Should we double-check with Stori?"

"You mean Freya's *aunt*? Of course not," Emma snorts. "Didn't the name on the cover ring a bell?"

"Oh shit." Cliff's voice drops. "This is actually her? I thought she was a writer in the same way that you're a model."

Like Freya, Emma was another East Coast transplant who came to Los Angeles with big dreams. She had yet to book a modeling gig but had added *influencer* to her Instagram bio after her third DM from a brand that didn't care she hadn't cracked a thousand followers.

"I *am* a model." Emma's indignant and forgets to whisper. "*She* hasn't published a new book in years."

Mortification stings like fire ants down Freya's neck. They haven't said anything that isn't true, but it still hurts to hear the confirmation that she's already considered a has-been. In a city that makes dreams as often as it crushes them, it's not a lonely club, but it's not the life she'd envisioned for herself, either.

Compared to her debut novel, writing book two has been a completely different experience in every way. In high school, Freya—a self-professed neutral evil on the alignment chart—was entirely consumed by her writing. She woke up thinking about her characters, went to bed excited to write the next day's words, and jolted awake at 3:00 a.m. to jot down fragments of dialogue or scene ideas in her iPhone's Notes app. She spent every study hall reading the latest YA novel and asked for writing books and summer workshops every birthday and Christmas to level up on her craft.

The difference is Freya's mom had been around to cheerlead back then. Anjali Lal had a fierce optimism in all things but especially in this: if her daughter wanted to publish a book, she had every faith that it was a *when*, not an *if*. As Freya's first beta reader, her mother knew this was *the one* with a certainty Freya doubts she herself has had about anything in her entire life.

Freya never had to look for her own inner validation because she knew she always had her mom's.

Until she didn't anymore.

"Look, forget about it. It's Stori's call, and we're opening in, like, five minutes," Emma says finally. "Take the new Riley Sager novel and finish the other window before she notices we're running behind."

"Seriously?" Cliff complains, voice back to normal. "I helped you unbox the new Tessa Bailey, set up the sandbox, *and* used my superior stamina to inflate the beach ball and flamingo floatie."

Emma makes a bad joke about blowing, but Freya's already tuning them out.

The blank white page on her screen stares damningly back at her, so she fixes her gaze on the mountain of Steph Kirkland's books on the display stand closest to the register. All Freya has to do is get through the rest of the day, then it will all be better. Her best friends, who started as Twitter critique partners and turned into real-life besties, are all flying out to celebrate Steph's book signing at Books & Brambles tonight.

They're the only ones who know her second secret.

Even the best writer can have a bad writing day—or, in Freya's case, bad writing *years*—but this is the one thing she is always, *always* good at: impersonating the actress Mandini Roy.

The first time it happened was back in New York a year after her mother had passed, and it had been a complete coincidence while she was out on a date (back when she actually dated). It was with a guy from her building, and they didn't have a reservation for the trendy new rooftop bar he thought he could schmooze his way into. But by some strange stroke of luck, simply because Freya had parted her hair a certain way and worn a dress that looked *kind of* like one Mandi had worn to Cannes Film Festival, security had waved them through without even a blink.

That first time had been a total accident.

But every time after that hadn't been.

A free mimosa at a trendy new bistro off Madison Square Park; skipping the queue at an upscale lounge in Chelsea, the kind of venue where they wouldn't let you in if you were wearing sneakers, shorts, or sandals; rooftop bars frequented by the Wall Street crowd, offering sweeping skyline views.

Since her mother's death, Freya had lost all motivation to write. None of her usual tricks—people-watching, rereading her dog-eared and well-thumbed favorite books, taking up a new hobby—worked.

But the first time she was mistaken for Mandi, she couldn't wait to end the date so she could go home and write. Freya couldn't justify doing it often enough to finish her second book, but when she did, the novelty and, frankly, *danger* of it all fed her writing inspiration like nothing else could.

Maybe she wouldn't feel the temptation if she were good at something else, but after college, getting that external validation proved a lot harder. But studying was always an area where she excelled, and it didn't take much to talk herself into just *one* more experiment. She devoured every picture and interview of Mandi's until she had the actress's style down pat. Though there was no way she could afford the thousand-dollar-plus price tags of Mandi's favorite designers, Freya's copycat outfits were just as fashionable, for a fraction of the cost.

Successfully getting away with being Mandi broke the monotony of impending deadlines, the stress of her dwindling bank balance living in a city she could barely afford while attending NYU's undergraduate Creative Writing Program, and of the plunging guilt in her stomach that reminded her that with every night out, she was letting down her mom's memory.

Freya felt her mom's absence so keenly that she didn't think she could handle smelling the scent of her mom's perfume or seeing bits of her unfinished business around her childhood home: a bookmark stuck in the middle of an unreturned library book; a recipe she'd ripped out of a magazine, stuck to the fridge, and never got around to making; the clothes with price tags still hanging in her half of the closet.

So when her aunt invited Freya to come live with her in LA to focus on her writing, she'd leaped at the offer. Freya returns Stori's generosity by helping out around the bookshop every day.

"Good morning, everyone!" Stori sweeps onto the bookshop floor. She's wearing a smart short-sleeved mock turtleneck and brown houndstooth trousers. "Thanks for holding down the fort, Freya. I just got off the phone with the caterers for Steph's event tonight and sorted out the canapé situation."

"We're all done with the windows, too!" Cliff calls out.

Emma makes a sound of agreement.

"Perf! And you?" Stori turns to Freya with an expectant look on her face.

Aunt Astoria, who insisted on going by Stori, was her father's half sister and the only child from Freya's grandfather's second marriage. She's closer in age to Freya than she is to Freya's dad, but that doesn't stop her from occasionally slipping into a persona where she thinks Freya's her own child, instead of the adult who's basically her sister.

Stori has no idea what Freya's going to get up to tonight, and Freya's going to keep it that way.

Freya pastes what she hopes is an *I have my shit together* smile on her face as she removes her glasses. "I, um, got a lot of writing done, too."

Stori beams with pride. "I *knew* moving out here was exactly what you needed."

"Oh yeah. Absolutely." Freya nods, half-guilty and half-proud that she's gotten away with her little white lie about her huge blank page. She lowers the top of her laptop, hiding her shame from view.

"Don't forget to wear your store name tag!" Stori flashes an encouraging smile. "Today's going to be a busy one."

Tuesdays—book-release day—always are.

The next few hours go by in a blur of Books & Brambles's regulars and a few random walk-ins. Through some determined handselling, something that once filled Freya with awful anxiety but got easier every time she did it, she sells several copies of Steph's book and talks up tonight's signing.

By now, Freya's spent enough time away from her keyboard to start missing it. Her fingertips hum with the need to clack some keys and see her words take shape. She's glad Stori and the staff are out to lunch so she can work without distractions.

"Oh my god, this place is so cute!"

At the giddy squeal, which rings extra loud in the first quiet lull of the day, Freya glances up from her half-eaten Cup Noodles still steaming away in its Styrofoam cup.

Two wide-eyed teenage girls, presumably sisters, have entered the bookshop, followed by their tired-looking mother. They all share the same dirty-blond hair and I LOVE LA shirt in different colors.

Books & Brambles had made the same magnificent first impression on Freya. The orange-brick facade of the bookshop looks storybook charming, blanketed with yellow climbing roses and curlicued gold lettering on the windowpanes that hinted at the wonders within.

The girls' gazes follow the floor-to-ceiling bookshelves wrapping around the walls and old-fashioned wooden gliding ladders that remind everyone of the enchanting library in *Beauty and the Beast*. Freya knows they pick up on the feeling of magic coursing throughout the shop, from the rich polish of the cherrywood shelves and the inviting green glow of the banker's lamps adorning the quad of antique study carrels used by readers and writers seeking bookish ambience and cozy vibes.

"I *told* you coming here was a good idea," says the younger girl in a triumphant tone. "Browsing books is *way* better than waiting around trying to catch a glimpse of Taft Bamber filming. They cordoned off that part of the street, anyway."

"Sure, books are great, but we have bookshops back home. Only LA has *the* Taft Bamber."

Taft Bamber isn't just any Hollywood actor. He's the star of last decade's cult classic *Once Bitten*, the guy Freya's been thirsting after ever since she was a teenager writing angsty fanfiction well into dawn. While most of her friends credit teachers and authors as the reason they became writers, Freya's a little embarrassed to admit that for her, it was Taft.

She's always wanted to write books that made readers feel the way his characters made *her* feel: Magically transported. Swept away. Believing in happy endings and epic love triumphing over all.

But Freya isn't fangirling—she's freaking out. *Because Taft Bamber is filming right down the street.*

Which wouldn't be a big deal, except . . .

He also happens to be dating Mandi Roy, Freya's doppelgänger.

The girls haven't seemed to notice her yet, so Freya leaves them to browse, her writer's mind conjuring up dozens of hypotheticals, worst-case scenarios in which she runs into Taft on the street and he recognizes her as a dead ringer for his girlfriend.

She counts backward from one hundred. By the time she hits fifty, her heartbeat and anxiety still haven't steadied. She knows Stori would scold her for not greeting the customers—after she was done scolding her for not putting on her name tag—and that she really *should* ask them if they're looking for something in particular, but hearing Taft's name has rattled her.

Both girls are eyeing her and whispering furiously as they approach. The younger teen immediately asks, "Hey, do you know where I can find the gays-in-space graphic novel that's all over BookTok? Sorry, I forgot the title."

"I told you, she doesn't work—" the older girl begins, but her sister shushes her.

Freya grins. She's so glad Stori let her set up a trending-on-TikTok book display; her friend Hero's book has been selling like hotcakes. "I know exactly the book you mean. It's right over there."

While the girl wanders off in that direction, the older one gives Freya an apologetic smile. "Thanks. Sorry about my sister. *So* embarrassing she didn't recognize you. I *tried* telling her that you don't work here." Without missing a beat, she asks, "Killing time while you wait for your boyfriend?"

Mildly offended that anyone would think that's the only reason to be in a bookshop, Freya gives her an unsure smile. Her fingers self-consciously fly to her baby-doll camisole, wishing she'd worn her name tag this morning.

Before she can say anything, the younger girl rushes over, clutching novels to her chest. "I found it!" she squeals. "I can't believe it's autographed! And I also found *this* in the bargain bin!" She thrusts one of the books at her sister.

Freya glances down. It's *her* book. With a bright-yellow bargain sticker plastered on the cover that reads 50% OFF!

Mortification sears her neck, making her hot and sweaty. *That's where Cliff thought her books should go?*

"This was one of my faves." The older teen idly flips through the pages, reaching Freya's glossy picture on the back flap.

Be cool, Freya, be cool. Pretend that you get recognized every day and this hasn't made your day.

Freya's heart cartwheels in her chest. "Oh my god, really?"

"Yeah. I reread it, like, a million times." The girl tears her gaze away from the pages and hesitantly gestures at Freya with her phone. "You're probably sick of people asking you all the time, but could we get a picture together?"

This hasn't happened to her in *years*. Forget making her day, it's made her entire month.

"Absolutely," Freya says, trying and failing at nonchalance. Talking to one of her readers is amazing and totally makes up for the conversation between Emma and Cliff she overheard this morning. Maybe she isn't a has-been, after all. "Do you want me to sign the book for you?"

"No, that's okay." The girl tosses it on the nearest shelf. "Someone can put it back in the bin later."

Stunned, Freya follows its trajectory with wide eyes. It takes her a moment to connect what she saw with the casual dismissal, and when she does, it punches through her mind like fog.

"You're nicer than I thought you would be," the older teen comments. "Way more down-to-earth. You know, considering."

Um, considering what?

Freya stares at both girls in confusion. "Pardon?"

"Mom! Can you come take our picture?" The older girl flashes Freya a grin. "My friends won't believe that I met the *real* Mandi Roy without a photo. This is seriously so unreal."

Freya's stomach feels scooped out. "Yeah. Unreal."

CHAPTER TWO

Well, *that* cemented today as an official shit day. And it's not even over yet. The only silver lining is that no one was around to witness Freya's utter humiliation posing as Mandi, forced to share the girls' annoyance that they couldn't buy the books they wanted because no one was working the register.

The second the girls and their mom left, she dug around to find a former employee's name tag to wear and slipped her blue reading glasses back on. She is absolutely *not* getting mistaken for Mandi again.

Compounding Freya's run of bad luck, not long after finishing her Cup Noodles, now bloated and cold, an email notification pops up on her laptop screen. There's only one person it can be, only one person who even contacts her through her author-specific email anymore—her literary agent, Alma Hayes.

> Hi, Freya!
> Checking in on how the book is coming along. I know it's part of your process to keep your first draft close to your chest, but your editor is champing at the bit to read! It doesn't need to be perfect, it just needs to be done. I'm more than happy to run my

eyes over it for some light edits, too. Let me know how I can help. We're all still so excited!

The email is light and breezy, but to Freya, Alma's subtext is clear: *You're out of time, and soon your contract won't be worth the paper it's printed on. And just in case your first draft is absolute crap, I need to read it first and potentially run interference before your editor's poor eyeballs have to suffer it.*

Okay, that's probably the imposter syndrome talking, but *still*. An overdue book is *not* a good look.

Freya can do this. She *has* to do this.

Maybe it's time to go old-school; in the past, handwriting on scraps of paper sometimes helped unclog her creativity. Inspired, she seizes a ballpoint pen from a pink moth-printed Etsy mug and poises it over the back of an envelope she ripped into earlier.

Freya *should* use one of her numerous notebooks—she has enough to open her own stationery store, her mom always said, though it never stopped her from buying yet another pretty one for her daughter—but Freya can't bear to deface them with scribbles of ink. If she was putting pen to paper, then her words had better be the kind of stuff worthy of permanence. Nothing less than perfect. A Final Thought, not something she would want to cross out later, marring the clean, crisp pages and filling her with guilt.

Freya presses the pen into the envelope, willing the words to flow, but her brain is full of soft static.

Why is writing so hard? She wishes she could just fast-forward to the point in her life when everything is okay and her word count doesn't make her want to cry. Clenching the pen between her fingers, she lets the ink swirl mindlessly, daydreaming about how she *wished* her interaction with those teenagers had gone: that they recognized her for *her*; for her book, which meant something to readers, once upon a time.

Stori's fingers, glittering with stacked silver rings, snap in front of Freya's slack face. "Earth to Freya! *Please* tell me that dreamy look on your face means you were lost in thought while working on your book. Or daydreaming about a hottie," she adds thoughtfully. "Sam Heughan comes to mind . . ."

This joking around is kinda their thing. Last week it had been Regé-Jean Page of *Bridgerton* fame. Today, apparently, Stori was obsessed with *Outlander*.

Freya grins. "Natalie Dormer, actually. And I just wrote the best paragraph of my life, I'll have you know," she informs her, forgetting that Stori is blessed with the preternatural gift to see through any lie.

Lofting a perfectly arched eyebrow, Stori tugs back Freya's laptop screen, revealing a blank page. "You just deleted the best paragraph of your life, you mean, Queen of Delete."

Freya snorts. "Only if 'best' is synonymous for 'garbage.' And I know you're teasing me, but if that's the only royal title I get in my lifetime, I'll take it."

"*Freya*," Stori groans. She sounds as resigned as Alma. In a second, she's going to repeat one of the writerly quotes she picked up from the authors who do events at her shop.

Here it comes: "If you want the joy of having written, you must first *write*. You've been staring into space and doodling your signature on the back of that envelope for two straight minutes with your usual thirsty-for-Henry-Cavill smile on your face."

"What?" Freya sputters. "I wasn't—"

She glances down. Ah. Yes, she was.

In her defense, blank white envelopes are just begging to be scrawled upon and throwing away perfectly useful paper is just wasteful.

"And you've let your tea get cold. How many times have I re-microwaved this for you?"

Freya presses her lips together and mentally scrolls back through the day. "Two?"

Stori gives a long-suffering sigh and reaches for the forgotten mug. "Try three."

"Oops?"

It's always been like this with Stori: their close relationship shifting based on the setting and how much of a role model Stori feels like being. Party Girl Stori will join Freya and her friends in Jell-O shots and table dancing in Atlantic City; Sister Stori loves Freya like breathing, like a pulse; Boss Lady Stori will hire her part-time when book two is going nowhere fast and Freya isn't quite ready to call it quits on her dream just yet.

Taskmaster Stori is easily Freya's least favorite, especially when she shames her deplorable, non-writerly tea-drinking skills. Still, Freya adores her. Even when Stori's helicoptering drives her nuts.

Stori takes a tentative sip of the brew, eyeing Freya over the rim. She pulls a face. "Make that four."

Freya's tempted to remind her that she doesn't actually like tea all that much, but ever since she moved to her aunt's city and into her apartment over the bookshop, Stori's gone out of her way to make Freya's environment as writer-friendly as possible so she can finally finish her draft. Freya doesn't want to disappoint one of her last remaining cheerleaders, so she'll gratefully accept the micromanaging.

"At least tell me you sent those poor unfortunate words to the Graveyard," Stori says, reaching out to comb her fingers through Freya's hair. It's a habit of hers, but unlike her aunt's silky black hair, Freya's coarse, oft-tangled waves aren't meant to be played with.

"Um. Fresh out of plots. These went straight into the incinerator. Fiery annihilation."

Freya doesn't dodge Stori's hand in time, wincing as it catches on a snarl in her locks. It's unbelievable she was once so precious about saving lines, copying and pasting them into a separate Word doc saved as "The Graveyard" in some kind of childish optimism that they'd be resuscitated one day. But like her career and her love life, everything she's written in the last three years is dead on arrival.

Freya's critique group calls her ruthless for killing her darlings, but she knows she's not.

She's *terrified*.

She can't remember the last time that she wrote a sentence she cared about enough to advocate keeping, and part of her thinks that after so long, maybe that means she's out of things to say.

Stori untangles her fingers from Freya's hair. "I'm reheating this writer fuel, and then I'll be back to make sure you get it down your gullet. Try to rewrite that paragraph while I'm gone."

"You do remember I'm not your kid to issue commands to, right?"

"You do remember you're on the clock and I'm your boss?" Stori says with a smirk. "The only acceptable reason for fingers not being on keys is if a customer needs help. Deal?"

"Deal. Want me to pinkie promise on it?" Freya's only half joking.

Stori eyes the lapel pin with an old coworker's name on Freya's camisole. The real Randy quit last week.

"When I said wear a name tag, I meant maybe one with your actual name?" she says, barely holding back an eye roll. "You know that's a synonym for 'horny,' right?"

"I mean, considering my dating drought, it's technically not wrong," Freya drawls, giving her a teasing jackass salute, the kind she can give Sister Stori but not Boss Lady Stori, and her aunt doesn't turn away fast enough to hide her grin.

SOON AFTER, WHEN Stori disappears into the stockroom to get things ready for tonight, Freya turns to the hard stuff—the entire contents of a six-cup Bialetti, which comes to one giant mug's worth. Illy espresso is vastly superior to quadruple-microwaved tea, which frankly tasted a little toxic.

Freya's fresh coffee is piping, but her new paragraph is every bit as insipid and lukewarm as the many that came before it. She hesitates, scraping her teeth over her full bottom lip, then presses Delete with a hard-heartedness that her best friends would have envied.

With each letter and each word disappearing in a slow-moving trickle, it looks like something's swallowing up a scurrying single-file line of ants. Instead of selecting the entire paragraph and deleting it in one go, it's just so much more satisfying to see each letter wink out of existence.

"Freya, m'dear. How's the writing?"

She looks up to see a familiar patron, Mrs. Skye McKenzie, totter up to the counter with her usual stack of hardcovers, which almost reaches her chin. Freya loves Skye, and knows she means well, but it's her least favorite question.

"Oh my gosh," Freya squeaks, thrusting her arms out to take the weight from the older woman. "You should have asked me to carry these up for you!"

"Nonsense. I'm sturdy as an ox. Fit as a fiddle." Skye gives Freya a look as she perches her glasses on her nose, Pride flag–colored beaded chain swaying. "Those are similes, you know."

"I did know that," Freya says every bit as gravely.

Before she even arrived in LA, Stori had bragged about her "famous" author niece to all the Books & Brambles regulars, which was super sweet, but now that she's here they all think they have to impress Freya with their knowledge and inquire about her writing, her love life, and her good health—in that order.

"Any men in your life?" Skye glances at Freya's open laptop. "Ones who aren't fictional?"

"Nonfiction and I are amicably separated."

"Life isn't nonfiction." At Freya's eyebrow raise, Skye concedes, "All right, it is. But you're not going to find love standing still with both feet on the ground and your nose buried in a bo—well, computer. One day you'll be as moldy and decrepit as me, you know."

"'Moldy and decrepit' are about the furthest words I'd associate with you," Freya says, scanning the topmost book in her pile. "We're talking North Pole far."

And it's true: Skye McKenzie, of indeterminate age, is as spry and sharp-tongued as ever, with a shock of electric-blue hair and bright floral dresses her wife sells at their co-op.

"That's true," she agrees. "I was exaggerating to make my point. But don't forget, summer is for falling in love and being swept off your feet. That's what my mother always said."

Freya fights back a wry grin. Lately the only men capable of even an ounce of dialogue that might elicit feelings of love, or even lust, only exist in books, TV, and 300,000-word fanfiction that keeps her up until 5:00 a.m. The chances of her meeting anyone of any gender this summer are zip, zilch, and zero. Especially with this deadline hanging over her head like a guillotine waiting to drop.

Sure, love would be nice, but the timing is all wrong. Freya's disastrous luck with men aside, she has a career to get back to. If she doesn't have something to give her publisher soon, she'll have to return her advance. She doesn't have that kind of money in her bank account these days.

And even if she scraped it together, the shame of having a canceled book will follow her like the worst sewer stink. Every single publisher out there will know that Freya Lal, former literary darling, isn't good for it. Even thinking about the possibility makes Freya want to hurl.

Actually, no. Freya takes it back. She categorically does not want to hurl. Regurgitated tea would taste *more* dreadful than the usual stewed-lawn-clippings kind.

"You know," says Skye, "there's so much going on in LA during the summertime! Listen, why don't you come to the barbecue my wife and I are throwing next weekend? You might hit it off with someone." She snorts. "Unless, of course, you're waiting for someone to waltz through those doors."

After her epically humiliating morning, Freya can't deny the warm fuzzies making a home in her chest when someone's taking an interest in her for *her* and not because they're mistaking her for her more glamorous look-alike.

"You never know when opportunity will knock," Freya says agreeably. "Sure, if the right person walks in here, I'll be so swept off my feet, I'll practically fall over."

"Oh, I'm not a sadist," Skye says gaily. "I'll settle for you going a little weak in the knees."

ele

CHAPTER THREE

Opportunity doesn't knock so much as bowl into the bookshop. Before Freya can even finish scanning the second book in Skye's pile, a tall and willowy guy with panicked eyes—and a tall iced coffee in his hand that sloshes dangerously at the rim—beelines straight for the register.

He's not quite a regular; she's seen him here only a handful of times, usually with aviators perched high and an Oakland baseball cap slung low over his face. Today he's dressed a bit smarter in chinos and a zip-up gray hoodie with just the barest hint of his rust-colored V-neck peeking out.

He's always felt familiar, but with so little of his face visible, name recognition had always evaded her. Today is the first time Freya truly recognizes him: the actor Taft Bamber. *Well, shit.*

The temperature increases ten degrees, and Freya almost chokes on her own spit. Her mind slingshots her back to sneaking into exclusive clubs, getting reservations with just a flash of her (*Mandi's*) smile in Rouge Dior 999, and the tiny opal earrings currently sitting on her dresser, ones she couldn't refuse in time before the box was pressed into her hands at a local boutique.

Dread drenches her from the top of her head to the tips of her toes, pooling in her mouth with the acrid tang of shame. As he approaches, paranoia becomes her new best friend. The day is already terrible. Of *course* this would happen.

"Hi, I'm here for a book," Taft says without preamble.

She's sure her eyes widen a fraction, but she swiftly schools her expression. That is so *not* what Freya thought he'd lead with. She was already rehearsing her speech, wondering if she was half as good an actress as his girlfriend, would she be able to sweet-talk him into not giving her away?

He's regarding her with frank, assessing eyes, but nothing about his demeanor hints that he's here to bust her.

"Feel free to browse." Freya tilts her head in Skye's direction, still holding her breath. "I'm with a customer."

He blinks like he isn't sure he heard her right. "I can't wait. I need it *now*."

"Yeah, well," she snaps. "This is a bookshop, not stream-on-demand. You'll have to wait your turn." She thumps down the book she's holding and reaches for the third, pointedly ignoring him.

This is the weirdest fight-or-flight response she's ever had. She knows she should *probably* be nicer to him. Hell, it'll still be a miracle if he doesn't eventually catch on to the resemblance, and baiting him further won't help her cause. But after the morning she's had, she's fresh out of patience.

Who does he think he is, storming in here and all but demanding she set everything aside to cater to *his* wants?

Thorny irritation prickles up her arms. It doesn't matter how handsome he is, with those Aegean-blue eyes that beg a woman to sink into them like Poseidon's seas and sexy two-day scruff that would cause the most delightful friction along her jaw when they kiss . . .

Stop it, Freya! You may impersonate his girlfriend from time to time, but that does not *make you the girlfriend he kisses, even in your horniest daydreams!*

In the awkward lull where her imagination runs rampant, Taft rakes his hand through his brown waves, drawing attention to the streaks of stardust silver. He's way too young to be considered a silver fox, but damn, he's making that look *work* for him.

Though there's still a trace of boyish charm about him, he's nowhere near as preppy as he used to look. Even on his most recent show, *Banshee of the Baskervilles*, another supernatural period drama that just finished airing its final season, his hair wasn't this long, silvery, and temptingly tousled.

Even years later, *Once Bitten* is still one of Freya's beloved comfort watches; Taft played a cynical vampire who had been turned and abandoned by the love of his life, a mysterious woman he's chased through the centuries, consumed only with thoughts of revenge and a closed-off heart. He'd nailed the tortured, emotionally unavailable spurned lover like no other actor has been able to do since, spurring a thriving fanfiction community even so many years after its cancellation and only one season.

On *Banshee*, he plays a stuffy-but-sweet Victorian occult detective whose cases are usually crashed by a socialite with a secret   she's a banshee. Played by It Girl Mandi Roy, her character's particular skill (other than butting heads with Taft's) is her bloodcurdling wail, which heralds imminent death, but they're usually able to avert disaster.

Filmed on location in Dartmoor, England, the fourth-season series finale ended with her banshee scream for Taft's character, pegging him for death just as the two realized their feelings for each other. It was the worst kind of unceremonious cliffhanger. Freya's watched each movie-length episode—of which there are only an infuriating six (!) per season—twice, and it's still not enough. Apparently the production budget was way too high for a fifth season, and the show was canceled, but thanks to dedicated fans, it's getting a movie instead to bring the beloved series to a more befitting end.

Freya yanks her gaze away from Taft, even though her thoughts determinedly cling on. If she ignores him, he'll go away, she reasons, so she does her best not to look at him as she continues scanning the books in Skye's pile.

I will not be weak for rude men. I will not give him the time of day, and I will most certainly not ogle him. I will pretend he isn't the most hot and provoking man I've ever met.

Taft seems to take her silence as a call for more information, so he propels into a long-winded explanation. "You don't understand," he says, trying and failing to keep the edge from his voice. "I'm filming a cologne commercial on the street behind you, and I literally have fifteen minutes before the next take. I called a while ago and spoke to someone who said they'd set it aside for me. This is my only chance to grab that book before they notice I'm missing."

Still not looking at him, she suppresses an eye roll. Everyone's an actor or a model or a yoga instructor or something else *très California*. The glossy, rosy sheen of celebrity has long since faded from her eyes.

Celebs are either people who give new meaning to the expression "never meet your heroes" or they're so next-door normal that they're happier going about their life as incognito as possible and *not* name-dropping just to skip ahead in line, unlike *someone* Freya could mention. Freya's had a lot of time to practice the tactic herself in her Mandi getup.

"Oh, it's fine," says Skye. "Honey, you go on and help this *handsome* young man."

Freya shoots her *Are you kidding me?* eyes. "That wouldn't be fair. You were here first."

"Thank you, ma'am," he says. Then, to Freya: "She said it's fine. Please?"

She refuses to be swayed by his surprising show of manners. Brandishing the price scanner in his general direction, she bites out, "Sir, I'm not sure who you think you are, but you can't just—"

"I could tell you, if you want." He sounds plain amused by his offer, like there's no end to the things he'd delight in telling her.

She gapes, forgetting for a second that she's pretending he isn't there. "Excuse me?"

"Who I think I am," he clarifies.

Freya runs her eyes over him, hoping her gaze sears. "Oh, I think I've already got a good idea."

With a little smirk, his eyes flick to her chest. "Look, *Randy*, I'm willing to bet there's a book under the counter with my name on it."

There's a freeing anonymity with being able to give as good as she gets when no one knows it's her, Freya, giving it. It's nice to have a conversation with someone who isn't gouging a new wound or picking at an old scab.

She smiles through clenched teeth, scanning another book. "Not unless you're the author."

Taft's smile, on the other hand, is flagrantly genuine, his dimples resembling parentheses popping up on either side of his mouth. "What, you don't think I fit the author aesthetic?"

Skye's gaze volleys between them like she's watching a tennis match.

Freya leans in, her voice dropping conspiratorially. "*Maybe* I'm not even sure you can read."

It doesn't put him off. If anything, his eyes have the temerity to blaze—*like he's having fun!*—as he gears up for another serve.

"No drinks allowed," she declares swiftly before he gets a chance to respond, pointing to his iced coffee. "You look like a person who spills."

He brings the drink to his mouth, smiling around the straw. "Wrong again. Once something's in my hands, I don't let it go easily."

She narrows her eyes and tries not to notice that his lips are shaped into a perfect Cupid's bow, giving him the impish appearance of a naughty child about to accept an unintended challenge.

"I don't see a sign anywhere." He holds her gaze as he takes a sip with an unnecessarily loud slurp that she's positive is done *entirely* to provoke her.

She makes up her mind to laminate several signs to hang around the bookshop just for him.

They both simultaneously open their mouths, but before Freya can beat him to the punch with a line of banter so winning she might actually write it into her book, Stori arrives in a gust of honey-lemon tea, balancing two blistering mugs and a plate of fancy cookies on a tea tray.

Taft eyes the tea. "'No drinks allowed,' huh?"

Damn it. "No *outside* drinks," Freya clarifies. "You can buy something at the bookgarten."

She points to the flung-open doors leading to the back garden that Stori started landscaping in spring, transforming the unused space into an outside reading and hangout space. Trailing roses the colors of a summer sunset spread over the orange-brick back wall of the bookshop and twine enchantingly around the all-weather drinks gazebo. It looks like something from a fairy tale and is one of Freya's favorite spots.

"I'm so glad I didn't miss you!" Stori exclaims, shoving everything into Freya's arms instead of on the counter, which is *right there*. She crouches to root around under the counter, her voice muffled as she says, "Your book is here . . . somewhere."

Taft sends Freya a victorious grin, the parentheses on his cheeks popping.

She refuses to acknowledge it.

"If I can *find it*," she mutters. "When was the last time you cleaned under here, Freya?" She glances up with a puckered forehead. "You've turned my counter into the equivalent of your dad's junk drawer."

"Stori," Freya hisses, thunking the tray on the counter.

Now Taft knows her name *and* thinks she's some kind of feral pack rat who can't bear to throw anything away. Which, fair. But *he* doesn't get to know that about her.

And he doesn't get to know about her dad, either. That the man who used to be the most fastidiously tidy person in her entire universe now couldn't bear to throw out the generic customer holiday greeting cards that still came addressed to Anjali Lal or her half-finished to-do list with tasks that he promised were *up next, sweet pea*, but that he never got around to. It's still pinned to the fridge with the BEST MOM IN THE UNIVERSE magnet, filled with the bubbly half-cursive handwriting that Freya shared with her mom.

This stranger—this entitled, insufferable, handsome stranger—shouldn't know that her dad squirrels away jagged bits of paper Mom tucked between pages because she could never find a bookmark when she needed one. Or that Freya's still hanging on to Hunka, short for Hunka Junk, the high school MacBook Pro her mother bought her, a connection even more tangible than the book dedicated in Anjali Lal's name.

And as she's consumed by the memories, Freya's rational mind points out that this stranger doesn't actually know any of these things, but she still feels strangely protective anyway. Of Dad, of the under-counter mess that Stori admonishes, but mostly of herself.

"Here we are!" Stori surfaces triumphant, holding up the book.

She has no idea where Freya's thoughts have spilled. What she's inadvertently caused.

It's not her fault. She's probably forgotten what she said. Freya knows she should move past it, too, but even years later, it's hard.

With a stiff, robotic arm, Freya takes the book but almost drops it on Stori's head when she sees the yellow Post-it slapped to the cover of her friend Steph Kirkland's book.

More to the point, the proof-positive name on it: *Taft Bamber*.

He lofts exactly one eyebrow, simultaneously smirking. It's the move that immortalized him in about a thousand GIFs, some of which she's even *used*.

Oh no. Her stomach loop-the-loops. How *mortifying*.

Stori puts an arm around Freya's shoulder, squeezing her to her hip, which is kind of a feat while Freya's bagging up Skye's books.

"Oh, not that one, dear," Skye says as Freya reaches a young adult novel. "It's for my niece. Could I get this gift wrapped?"

Freya wriggles free of Stori's embrace and brings out all the wrapping paper. "You took my recommendation! Trust me, your niece will *love* it. Pick whichever pattern you want."

The author is Mimi Díaz, who has relentlessly amazing covers and multiple six-figure deals. She's more established in her career than Freya and Steph and the rest of their cohort, and has perpetual looming deadlines, but she's always the first of their friend and critique group to reserve her flight whenever there's a book birthday, and she *always* springs for celebration Moët. Freya makes a point to recommend her books to all her favorite customers.

As Freya starts to shear off a sheet of the magenta paper dotted with corgis tangled up in streamers and party hats, her skin goose bumps like someone's got their eye on her.

"You should come back at eight," Stori tells Taft. "We're staying open a little later tonight because we have the author flying in from New York to do a reading of her latest book. You can get it signed!"

Taft makes his "Really?" sound interested.

Stori's voice drops conspiratorially. "She's friends with my niece, Freya. You remember I told you about her the first time you came here? She's here to finish writing her book."

"Right, Freya the author," says Taft, widened eyes betraying only the tiniest hint of surprise.

Another customer who knows all about her. A very handsome, very famous one who now knows her name, and suddenly, hearing him say it again is all she can think about. Is there anyone left in LA who Stori *hasn't* talked her up to?

His eyes search her face. "You know, you look eerily similar to—"

"I know," says Freya, cutting off his train of thought. "I get that a lot."

The corners of his eyes crinkle when he smiles. He doesn't smile like that on camera. At this distance, his eyes are kaleidoscopic with partial heterochromia, both rimmed in a brilliant blue that pops on the big screen but flicker with a glow the exact shade of a Jarritos lime soda.

"I read your book," he says with the supreme confidence of someone who absolutely has not and doesn't think they'll get called on it. "At JFK. And only, like, the really popular ones are sold in airport bookshops, right? My mom's a big reader, and I'm pretty sure she mentioned you were one of the best debut books?"

Maybe Freya's being petty, but after her memorable-for-all-the-wrong-reasons day, she's not in the mood to chat about the success she fears may never happen again.

So maybe she should be flattered he cares enough to lie—and not just lie but lie with a detail about the airport specific enough to give him the benefit of the doubt—but his attitude makes her prickle, and she can't resist teasing him.

In an offhand tone, Freya asks, "So what did you think about the part with the eleventh-hour plot twist when her lover comes back into the picture?"

Stori and Skye give her flummoxed frowns.

Taft goes still and contemplative, eyebrows scrunched. Then his face smooths back into handsome indifference. "I thought it was outrageous and contrived."

He's on to me.

Freya rips and sticks little bits of tape stuck on each finger of her right hand before deftly folding the wrapping paper over Skye's book tight and neat. "You're right; it would have been completely 'outrageous and contrived.' That's why my editor had me ax it and rework my entire third act."

A startled laugh escapes him seemingly before he can stifle it. In other circumstances, she would have quite enjoyed the sound.

Eyes narrowed, he says, "I figured. Things like that don't happen."

"Then why is it a beloved romantic gesture in movies?" she counters, sliding the book into Skye's tote. "The man bursting into the wedding chapel to fight for the woman he loves?"

"Key word: 'movies.' Not real life." He grimaces. "Since I've filmed that exact scene three times in different productions and attended over a dozen real-world weddings where it didn't, I think you can take my word for it."

"Take your word for it?" she scoffs. "After that bald-faced lie about reading my book?"

The receipt printer cranks out paper long enough that it starts to curl under itself into a scroll. Freya snatches it and hands it to Skye without asking the usual "In the bag or with you?"

Taft winces. "Sorry. I shouldn't have said— Sorry. I didn't read it so much as, uh, flip through it. I had a flight to catch, and there were just so many choices that I couldn't pick. I always get indecisive when I browse."

Finally, some honesty.

"That happens to me all the time," Skye says sagely as she heads for the door. "My advice? Buy them all. When it comes to books, you can never be too greedy or go too wrong."

Freya doubts Skye has the faintest inkling of who Taft is or that he probably *could* buy them all. But Freya does and is suddenly reminded of the reality of the situation. Of who exactly Taft is. And who he's dating.

Which is why she studiously avoids eye contact while she rings up his book, almost jumping out of her skin when her fingers graze his as she returns his credit card.

"What if I want mine gift wrapped, too?" he asks.

Freya pauses. "Are you asking? Or was that a hypothetical?"

Stori's drifted away to straighten an endcap, but even from the back, Freya know she's still paying attention. *Be nice,* Stori mouths over her shoulder.

I'm always nice, Freya sends back telepathically.

And to prove it, she squashes down her tart reply that if he'd wanted it gift wrapped, he should have told her before she swiped his credit card. Now it's a second transaction of $1.50.

"And would you like a bow on it, too?" Freya asks, still looking downward and suppressing an eye roll.

"Naturally. The biggest one you have."

"It costs extra."

Taft doesn't ask how much, like a normal person, just waves a hand for her to get on with it. Freya unrolls more of the corgi wrapping paper, about to cut into it, when he clears his throat.

"Could I see all the choices you have?" he asks.

Do not glare at customers.

"Since you asked so nicely," she says sweetly, smiling with her teeth.

The corner of his top lip gives the tiniest twitch upward. "And could you do one of those twirly ribbon things with the scissors?"

She glares, but he doesn't scare easy. If anything, he's getting better at standing his ground.

With a few swift swipes, the ribbon races along the scissor's slant.

It's the smallest of things, something she's done a hundred times in the last couple of months she's lived and worked here without even thinking about it. But Taft leans down to stare at the perfect coils of sparkly silver and gold like they're something exquisite, as if *she's* created something magic.

The awed look on his face stirs a pathetic sense of enchantment in Freya's chest. A whole day spent on her book—a day of deleting detritus that's put her writing progress in the red, of disappointing Stori, of being bad at tea—and *this* is what gives her warm, fuzzy satisfaction?

Something that anyone can do. With their eyes closed, though she wouldn't recommend it where scissors are concerned.

The exalted feeling rushing through her is the way she used to feel when she smashed her daily word-count goal, no sticker motivation required. The fireworks in her stomach as her email dinged with an invite to a book festival and they flew her out first class and comped the hotel. The cramp in her hand as she signed thousands of preorders, enough that her literary agent was convinced Freya was a shoo-in for bestseller status months before either of them actually saw it in the *Times*.

It's the energy she once felt when sprinting with her friends on Zoom for half an hour and managing a thousand words by the time the timer went off. Red-eyeing her deadline, reworking the third act with only drive, desperation, and a deadly amount of coffee, triumphantly-slash-hastily emailing the manuscript to her editor a minute before the midnight deadline without a salutation or a subject line.

How the mighty have fallen. Freya slips the wrapped book into one of Books & Brambles's recyclable brown paper bags. If only she could do the same thing with her thoughts. Let them walk out the door with a customer, heading far away from here.

Stori was wrong—the change of scenery moving from New York to Los Angeles wasn't a fix, it was just more failure. And Freya is so sick of the taste. She's had a mouthful of it the last three years, as much as she can stand. But she can't backspace on the wrong turns of life, no matter how much she wishes she could. She has to keep moving ahead, like she's on a deadline and every word counts.

Shit. She *is* on a deadline.

Freya gets a grip on herself. "Will that be all?"

Taft takes the bag, letting the twine handles dangle off his thumb. There's a pause as they both watch it sway before he says, "Yeah. Thank you."

"Don't forget about tonight!" Stori calls out from deep within the stacks.

Freya cringes, praying to whichever deity might be listening in for this embarrassing interaction to be finally over and for him to go away.

"Yeah, maybe!" he calls back. Then, to Freya, at regular volume, "I'll see you?"

Technically, with his eyeballs, for Steph's signing tonight? Yes. But it's hard to translate his subtext. It sounds like he's trying to gauge . . . something else. Something that, if she didn't know any better, she suspects could pass for flirtatious.

His tone fills her with uncertainty, but still feeling a little contrary, she shrugs. "Will Mandi be joining you?"

Taft's face slackens with surprise, and his fingers squeeze into a fist around the handles.

It takes Freya a minute to get it—until that moment, he didn't realize that she knew who he was all along. And for some reason she can't place, he's disappointed.

CHAPTER FOUR

Taft knows he shouldn't have flirted with her. He'd known from the moment their eyes had met over the blue-haired woman's shoulder that this girl was absolutely his type, and therefore very, very off-limits.

Which made it hideously inconvenient that Freya—barbed-tongue, chemistry-goggle-glasses-wearing Freya with the lightning fingers— was the only thing he could think about as he got on with the rest of his day: wrapping the commercial; going to the post office to mail the book he'd just purchased to his mom; taking a cold shower that had more to do with her than the heat; cuffing his classic black blazer to mid-forearm as he got ready to go out, still uncertain if he was attending the signing at Books & Brambles or not.

In a way, Taft was kind of glad that he probably pissed Freya off for good with the way the inelegant words fell out of his mouth—*I'm here for a book*—because there was no way anything could come of it as long as his manager, publicist, and contract explicitly prevented it.

Fuck, it wasn't just inelegant. It was rude. And then he'd just kept right on digging his own grave, needling her just to watch that flush of red crawl up her pale, svelte neck. He'd done sex scenes that didn't do it for him as much as that cross look on her face did.

Bantering with her, he'd heard his heartbeat in his ears, soft and petering at first, and then everywhere all at once. Hours later, he was still a little stunned that he could pull off verbal foreplay without some woefully underpaid writers' room providing the script for him.

It was second nature when a camera crew was crowding a few feet away and a beautiful woman's jaw was cupped in his palm. It was the kind of feeling that was easy to feign with the right angles and dialogue, a feeling that his *characters* felt all the time but which he rarely did.

Hell, his talent for intense chemistry was the reason he was in this situation in the first place. His ability to make a love scene smolder with Mandi in *Banshee* was what started the rumor that they were secretly dating off-camera, and when season three started to go the way of all once-great shows, the studio had reached out to their publicists to float the idea of a staged relationship to boost ratings. Since they weren't dating anyone else and the audience was loving it, they kept the showmance going for season four, too, because they were at risk of losing their primetime time slot to another buzzed-about new show.

Everyone agreed that the showmance would only last until *Banshee* got renewed for season five, but it wasn't enough to save them from an early death thanks to the exorbitant production costs. He was grateful that viewers petitioned to save the show, and it was because of their passion that there was a movie happening at all.

The only fine print? Give the fans what they want—Taft and Mandi are a package deal until the premiere.

It didn't matter to the studio whether the relationship was real or not as long as everyone else believed it. And of course they did, because Taft and Mandi were damn good at their jobs.

Selling love was the easy part. He was fond of Mandi, and she of him, he hoped. Spending so many months of the year together in Dartmoor, it was hard not to bond. At first, he'd been a little in awe of her, but she was surprisingly easy to talk to, and she always said yes to spending time with him, whether it was running lines or going sight-seeing. But it was abundantly clear to both of them that they didn't feel romantically toward each other, so a contractual relationship didn't seem like a big deal. There was no chance of a messy fallout that would derail their winning strategy. And it lifted their profiles, which meant both their managers and publicists were on board.

But thanks to the past couple of years of his scripted showmance, he was woefully unpracticed at flirting with a stranger. Which, in retrospect, was a good thing, considering that he *shouldn't* have been flirting with anyone who wasn't his costar and girlfriend, Mandini Roy.

And Taft Bamber is nothing if not loyal, showmance or not. He could never quite detach himself the same way when it came to the people he'd let in, even when it seemed like those people were living their lives just fine without him in it.

So after putting on the finishing touches on his going-out ritual—wearing his watch and dabbing a drop of cologne at the base of his throat—he reaches out to his best friend and former roommate, Connor Kingdom. This video call is another ritual—spaced out each month so Connor doesn't realize Taft is keeping track of the growing distance between them.

"Hey," comes Connor's disembodied voice. His phone screen is aimed at the ceiling of his house before the angle is adjusted and his face comes into view.

Taft recognizes the coffered ceiling and recessed lighting from Connor's Instagram Stories and the double-door steel refrigerator plastered with huge plastic number magnets and Polaroids of his one-year-old. The houses in his zip code are all new and gaudy, shamelessly *I have arrived*, and nothing like Taft's taste at all. The Kingdoms haven't had people over to their new house yet, but they love a good party, so a housewarming is imminent. Taft's already picked out the perfect gift from Williams Sonoma.

"Sorry, we just got back from Joshua Tree," Connor continues. "Lemme just put this shit down and— Do you have *any* idea how much baby stuff we have to travel with?"

A swift yearning hits Taft. Connor's life is *real*, so solid and complete, while Taft is . . . alone. When he's not doing something *Banshee* related with Mandi, he doesn't know where he fits, or with who.

"Hey, man. Can't say I do." Taft laughs, because why would he? "How's it going?"

A yawn pulls at Connor's mouth, quickly morphing into his usual winsome smile. "Can't complain. Hey, Holly. Holls. Say hi to Taft."

"Conn. I'm sweaty and gross after the drive."

"You're gorgeous," Connor proclaims, swiveling the phone to show off his wife, a stunning woman wearing a sundress that looks like a picnic blanket, and their sleepy-eyed daughter, Kora. The camera pans over an entire set of Louis Vuitton luggage piled on the white marble floors before turning back on the family. "And Taft doesn't care."

"I don't care, and you're always beautiful," Taft confirms.

"You're such a charmer," says Holly, blushing, as she hands Kora off to her husband.

"Hey! He's just repeating what I said first," Connor says indignantly, adjusting his grip on the baby trying to scramble up his shoulder.

It blows Taft's mind a little, seeing his best friend as a dad. Connor's good with Kora, rubbing her back and not even caring that she's trying to chew his car with a mouth that's more gums than teeth. A rush of affection courses through Taft for this little person in a pink dress and matching bow gathering her wispy black hair into a sweet Troll doll up-comb.

Would it be presumptuous to wiggle his fingers at the screen and say *Hi, Kora, it's your uncle Taft*? Every time he sees her, he waits for Connor to introduce him, but maybe too much time has passed. Would it have been different if he'd been at the hospital when she was born—like their other friends—instead of filming *Banshee* in Dartmoor?

He doesn't want to make it weird by trying to form a bond that hasn't been offered, but then he can't stop wondering why it hasn't been. He's known Connor for years; he and the guys rented an apartment together for the entire short-lived first season of *Once Bitten*, and even for a few years after that. He *should* be an honorary uncle, damn it.

"So when are you going to let me set you up with one of my friends?" asks Holly.

Never, mouths Connor, affecting an innocent expression when she almost catches him.

"Um, pass," says Taft, with a short, awkward laugh. "You know I'm seeing someone."

And honestly, after the *pleasure* of bantering with Freya, being set up with someone from the industry doesn't exactly hold an appeal. It's always more homework than fun. If his checkered dating history is any indication, he fully expects any future date with an actress to go like this: they'll both show up having googled each other, but she'll still feign surprise to learn he's originally from Texas and ask him where his accent went, as if they both don't know he wouldn't have gotten as far as he has if he'd kept the drawl.

She'll probably wear emerald green, which he'd once told *Teen Vogue* was his favorite color, in a romantic but misguided attempt to curry attraction, and he'll hold her hand while leaving the restaurant because there's bound to be paparazzi lurking around the corner and the last time he didn't hold a girl's hand, the unflattering headline read: BAMBER MAKES A BREAK FROM BAD DATE.

Mortifying. Needless to say, no one's publicist had been happy. If there's one good thing that's come out of "dating" Mandi, it's that he can give bad first dates like that a miss. He tries not to think about whether a first date with Freya—off the table for the foreseeable future—would be as divertingly delicious as he suspects it would be.

"Holls," says Connor. "He's with Mandi, remember?"

At least until the premiere.

But Taft withholds that part, since his contract also forbids him from disclosing any showmance specifics with friends who can't keep a secret from their wives.

Holly tilts her head. "Oh, sure, but it's been a couple of years and we haven't even properly met her."

Taft humors her. "You've met her. I introduced you at that rooftop party last month."

"Yeah, for all of five seconds before that producer pulled her away," Holly says with a pout. "That's not even remotely the same thing." She snaps her fingers. "I know. We should go out. Grab a meal. Maybe invite her up to Joshua Tree next time the gang all gets together?"

"Oh, man, you should have come," says Connor. "Jakey's new place is *sick*."

Taft's smile slips, ice water trickling over his head and into his ears. For a split second, he thinks he misheard. Steadying his voice, he asks, "Wait, did you say you were at Jake's?"

"You know he's vegan now? He served us shiitake steaks for lunch with no sides and *no beer*." Connor makes a face like he's not sure which is worse, putting a hand to his stomach. "Listen to the grumbles. I'm fucking ravenous."

Taft did not know Jake was vegan or that he'd bought a house in the desert, but he keeps a look of polite interest on his face as though he had. "Oh, wow. Vegan. Hard to keep track of what everyone's up to these days."

Which is true. Lately he's had to rely on social media to keep him up to date on his old castmates, and even then, it's not always the full story. Like everything else—brand image, friendships, and even who he *dates*—their lives are just as curated. But he's sure he didn't see anything online about this.

Later, he'll identify the blocky lump forming in his heart as the lead weight of knowing the answer before even asking the question. But now, as casually as he can, he asks, "Refresh me, when did that even happen? He told me but I completely . . ."

"Oh my god, I know, right? It's like we're all so fucking grown-up these days." Connor laughs. "Shoot. I've got to stop cursing around the kid. Holly's on me about that."

"Probably a good idea. Unless you want 'fuck' to be Kora's first word."

Connor chuckles. A beat passes. Taft rides it out, raising his eyebrows.

"But yeah," Connor says, "it was last week. At our housewarming, I think? Totally stole our thunder, by the way, but that's Jakey. He dropped the pics in the group chat if you want to see. But listen, man. I'm sure everyone understands. You've had a lot on your plate. You're so busy being Mr. Big-Shot Movie Star these days, dude." A short laugh. "Next time, all right?"

Taft's chest caves in as he struggles to get up to speed.

Connor had a housewarming. And he didn't tell Taft. He feels silly now, remembering all the tabs left open on his iPad, full of overpriced housewares he thought the Kingdoms would like.

There's a group chat?

Not the one they started back in the *Once Bitten* days—a different one that doesn't include him. He's taken aback when he sees his face in the small front-facing camera screen. Nothing about his expression gives away that his teeth are gridlocked and his heart is Olympic sprinting for some invisible finish line that he's not sure he'll ever reach.

"Well, we've gotta eat some real food. We're dying for some broccoli beef and veggie lo mein. And it looks like you've gotta jet, too? Lookin' snazzy, Bamber." Connor wolf-whistles.

Even though Connor is talking him up, Taft feels his heart sink. This is how he always does it, Taft realizes. As though Taft is the one too busy to stay on the line, to catch up. When really it's Connor who has other, better things to do.

Things that don't involve Taft, like housewarmings and group chats and, fuck, probably even Kora's christening. Thank god he didn't call himself Uncle Taft; there's probably already a godfather-to-be waiting in the wings. Probably fucking Jake.

"Kinda jealous you're living the life while I'm covered in baby drool and whatever *this* unidentified stain is." Connor flashes an end-of-call smile. "We'll let you go. Talk soon?"

Taft opens his mouth to say, *No, it's fine, I'm in no rush*, or even *My life isn't as glamorous as you think it is; I was actually thinking about going to a bookshop.*

But Connor doesn't wait, and a second later, Taft's phone reverts to the home screen. He stares at the brightly colored icons until they dim to black, and his phone turns to a brick in his hand. Of all the roles he's played, the one of unreciprocated friend is the worst.

He and Connor came up together. Got their first big break together. They'd shared the most Icarian of highs and the most heartbreaking, hellish Hollywood lows.

They'd gotten shit-faced after bombed auditions, after pilots not getting picked up, after being unapologetically replaced by someone with bigger name recognition and star power—they'd been through the trenches, chewed up and spit out by the same people who dangled the golden tickets. Survived the hailstorm of noes before hearing that first yes.

Taft had even cried in front of him when they'd landed their first roles in *Once Bitten*, Taft as the lead and Connor as a supporting character, and then cried again when it got canceled before the first season even finished airing. His performance was scathingly called "paper-thin" and "as shallow as a kiddie pool" by more than one critic. Only a couple of reviewers acknowledged that his story lines and dialogue didn't give him a lot to work with. But particularly cruel had been: "Throw the whole show away—one bite is all it takes to spit it out," followed by a targeted breakdown of his weak acting chops.

Through sheer grit and hard work—and a couple of failed pilots that in retrospect he was glad hadn't gone forward—he'd dug himself out of his career grave. He'd gotten a guest spot on other supernatural teen dramas, and a few times, the viewers loved his characters so much that the showrunners had decided to expand his role.

He's grateful, but despite catapulting to a new level of fame with *Banshee* and the anticipation for the movie, he can't wait to move on from it. He's got some scripts for indie films waiting for him, any of which he'd be happy to attach his name to. He's not looking for something with big names and an even bigger CGI budget—just the chance to reinvent himself from his typecasting as the lead's hot boyfriend.

Taft wants to shed this reputation but not his friendships. He knows some A-listers who drop their friends when they "make it," but that's not him. So why does it feel like *he's* the one being left behind?

Sometimes, Taft can't shake the feeling that despite knowing Connor's worst fears and biggest dreams—and even the way he snores like a trash compactor when he's drunk off his ass—they're still strangers in the ways that really matter.

Then again, maybe he's being too hard on his best friend. Maybe Connor genuinely assumes Taft is just as busy as he is. That they're all leading these fast-paced lives, squeezing in friends during the gaps in their schedules.

But Taft's slipping through them, and no one's noticed.

So when Mandi calls him a few minutes later to see whether he'd be up for hitting the clubs tonight, he doesn't tell her he's planning to go to a bookshop. He can imagine what she'd make of *that* on a Friday night. She probably wouldn't come right out and call him boring, but the subtext would be loud and clear. And Taft's a reader; he's good at reading between the lines.

"We have to make at least one appearance this weekend," Mandi reminds him. "Come on! It'll be fun! You weren't doing anything else, right?"

"Yes, I was, actually. You've interrupted a wild orgy I'm hosting," he deadpans.

"Sarcasm is one of your *least* endearing qualities, dear boyfriend."

"Are you looking forward to this being over?"

Taft prides himself for always thinking before he speaks, so at first he's surprised that this slips out. But then he gets it; if he and Connor are friends out of habit, then maybe that's how Mandi feels about him, too. With him because she has to be, for both their careers, not because she gives a shit.

But Mandi knows exactly what he's talking about and doesn't pretend to misunderstand or obfuscate. "You mean when we mutually break up and tragically announce it to our millions of followers in a carefully captioned Instagram post crafted by our publicists?"

There's no mistaking the bite in her voice.

He almost smiles. "Now who's being sarcastic?"

"I'm not being sarcastic, Taft. I know it's not real, but you're the best 'boyfriend' I've ever had."

If Taft isn't one to vomit out his every thought, Mandi isn't one to say what she doesn't mean. She doesn't claim to love her cold brew when it's just okay at best, and she takes to Twitter to lambast whoever slims and shrinks and sculpts her magazine covers even when her manager would prefer if she'd just gush about how much she *loves* the way the final product turned out.

Product, not person.

"First rule of Hollywood: pay attention when people reveal what you are to them," Mandi had said the morning after that magazine cover reveal and the resulting argument with her manager.

Taft had stayed the night for emotional support and slept on her sofa with an arm slung around her German wirehaired pointer. She'd passed him a cup of coffee, and then she'd tossed the magazine in the trash. She made sure to throw her used Keurig pod on the cover, letting it bounce off her face.

They've been friends for five years, ever since that first chemistry read for *Banshee*. They've never slept together, obviously, but from time to time they faked spending the night. Her apartment has a doorman, but Taft knows that she sometimes likes having another person stay over, especially since Kurt, one of her more dogged paparazzo stalkers, has started getting more intrusive.

"If you totally hate the club, we can leave," Mandi offers. "But, um, if you're up for it, I'd really love to blow off some steam."

Words matter to her. So Taft knows he can take her at her word. But at the moment, he's more concerned about *why* Mandi needs the night out so badly. "Is everything okay?"

"It's just—I've been having the weirdest day," she says. "My manager's been fielding some pissy calls from some local business owners saying that if I don't shout-out their store, they want their stuff back? And I was like, I don't *have* their shit."

Mandi does get unsolicited freebies for promo sometimes, and if she wears the items publicly, she's conscientious about acknowledging the generosity. Most people understand that all name drops are solely at her discretion, though, so it's strange that there are suddenly pitchforks aimed her way.

"Gareth's a shark," says Taft. "He'll figure out whatever's going on."

Her gusty exhale is loud in his ear. "A shark who never lets me take a break. 'If I'm always "on," so are you,' remember? He once told me he sleeps about four hours a night so he can keep up with all the time zones."

Taft frowns. "Did you ask him about taking some time off before the premiere?"

"Yeah. He scheduled me a two-hour massage. Said it would work everything out."

Taft is pretty good at masking his emotions, but he's suddenly glad he's not on video with Mandi. He's sure his expression would give away that he could cheerfully strangle her callous manager. "Tense muscles, maybe," he scoffs before he can stop himself. Then, with more diplomacy, he says, "I guess his work ethic can work for some people. But if it isn't working for you, maybe it's time to have a conversation."

"You *know* the last time I tried he implied that I wasn't as invested in my career as he is," snaps Mandi. "You know what? It wasn't even an implication."

"I'm sorry."

She takes a breath. "No, I'm sorry. It's not you I'm mad at."

He tries a joke. "Don't worry about it. What else are emotional-support boyfriends for?"

She sighs, and he can practically *hear* her worrying at her lower lip. "Yeah."

If any part of him was torn about the risk of returning to Books & Brambles to see Freya again, Mandi's need for a night out with him makes the decision surprisingly easy. "Just so you know," he says, "I'm doing this for you, not because of that ridiculous contract they made us draw up."

"*YOU ARE THE BEST!* Okay, our names are already on the list. I'll meet you inside."

CHAPTER FIVE

"To our very own tour de force!" cheers Mimi, holding up a flute full of Moët and gently clinking it against Freya's.

Steph pretends she isn't totally loving it as the friend group toasts her. "Oh my god, y'all," she says with a Texas twang, no less accented after moving to the Upper East Side as a teen. Her hands move to play with her twists before she remembers she's swapped them for braided Bantu knots.

Her high-voltage neon-yellow nails pop against her brown skin as she grips the stem of her flute, raising it high. "To the best friends a girl could ask for. Thank you all for flying out here for this. And special thanks to Mimi, for keeping the champers flowing." She gestures her glass in Freya's direction. "And to this babe, for having the courage to move to such a fabulous new city and finding this sick club."

"And don't forget getting us in," adds Ava Capshaw with a giggle, doing a little tipsy twirl in the strawberry-pink baby-doll dress that got a slight eyebrow raise from the bouncer. She's easily the most modestly dressed person in here. *"Thanks for having Mandi Roy's faaaaace."*

"Shhh!" Freya hisses, casting a glance around them. "This is the last time."

"You always say that," Mimi says with a wink. "And it never is."

The lie comes easily. "Well, now that the writing is flowing, I don't need the high anymore."

"Proud of you, Freya," says Steph. "And I'm knocking this one back for Stori—who sadly couldn't join us—for drumming up a full house at her amazing bookshop and organizing the best event I've had all year."

"We're supposed to be toasting you!" Freya protests, bumping Steph's shoulder with her own while throwing up a mental thank-you to all the gossip sites that listed this place as the hottest It Spot, because despite what her friends think, she's barely stepped outside Stori's neighborhood the whole time she's been here.

"Yeah, Steph, let us have this," says Hero—from Shakespeare, not Fiennes—Crane with a laugh. "When was the last time *Kirkus* called any of us a 'tour de force to be reckoned with'?"

"Or how about 'an auto-buy author at the top of her game'?" chimes in Ava. "'An utter delight from the first page to the last page'?"

Mimi taps her chin, pretending to think, showing off nude almond nails with just a hint of sparkle. "Oh, that's right. That would be *never*."

"'Scorching, sizzling, spicy.'" Hero recites the words like she's reading them off a Google search. She blinks, ignoring Steph's groan. "'They're really running out of ways to say you write the best high-heat sex scenes in the biz, huh."

Freya grins, sipping her champagne. "Don't forget that reviewer who said Steph wrote the most satisfying climax she'd ever read and swore on national TV that's how she and her husband got pregnant."

Steph huffs. "Okay, now I *know* you're trying to embarrass me."

Mimi giggles. "If that was ever in doubt, we weren't doing a very good job."

"Okay, can we talk about how cringey it is that men say 'We're pregnant'? Like they go through even a minute of the agony of their body changing?" Ava makes a face. "I can't believe I married a man who thinks that is in *any* way an appropriate way to make a birth announcement. *Twice.*" She pats her still unnoticeable baby bump before reaching for her mocktail. "Maybe the third time's the charm and I've successfully purged the phrase from his vocabulary."

"Wouldn't bet on it," teases Steph. "Jonah's a giant dork."

Ava sighs in pretend defeat. "You're right, so I won't even gasp in outrage."

Mimi's thirty-two and went through a zen Mother Earth–like pregnancy last year, reveling in the size of her belly and glowing like a goddess, no Instagram filter required. When she's not writing bestselling middle-grade fantasy-adventure series, she runs a popular parenting blog.

On the other hand, this is Ava's third with her high school sweetheart, and she's borne none of her pregnancies with grace, swearing each one will be her last as she screams for the epidural she always thinks she won't need. She's Freya's age, but she's already a whole adult in a way Freya feels she never will be.

Ava never makes it a secret how impossible it is for her to write book-club women's fiction with two kids under four. She's always run ragged, barely squeaking by on her deadlines. Last year, the turnaround for her copyedits was so tight that Mimi and Hero split the pages between them while Steph and Freya took over her social media promo.

At some point or another, they've all leaned on the writing group for help. So why is it like pulling teeth for Freya to be honest with them about her—*oh lord, even saying this hurts*—writer's block?

"Freya, you've barely touched your drink," says Mimi. "Everything . . . okay?"

Four pairs of eyes slide from the flute held loosely in Freya's hand to her face.

The implication is obvious, especially after Ava's segue.

"*So not pregnant!*" Freya yelps. "If I was, don't you think I would have led with that?"

And the thing is, she would. These girls are her sisters, her family. They found one another through Twitter pitch contests, critique-partner matchups, and fangirling over sneak-peek snippets, Spotify playlists, and dream casts of their characters. They made it through the query trenches together, sharing solidarity screenshots of agent form rejections, impersonal batch rejections, and *this close* passes so specifically brutal they made them want to quit their daydreams.

The only thing stopping them was one another. Their strength, their support. It's held them together like superglue through Freya's grief when her mom died; the breakdown of Mimi's first marriage and the IVF struggles during her second; Hero's gender-affirming breast implants; Ava's book-promo burnout and gargantuan to-do lists in her too-short days; Steph's growing pains as she founded a mentorship group for new writers at the same time she was getting her farm-animal sanctuary off the ground.

Freya tells them everything. Which makes it even harder that she can't tell them how impossible, how unsustainable, the dream has become for her. Calling it a nightmare might be too strong, but what else can she call the bottomless pit of dread in her stomach that never seems to go away, even though Mike's Hard pink lemonade, Haribo gummies, and buttercream donuts love to try?

Her muse is missing. Or her motivation. Or *something*.

She's ashamed to admit that writing is hard for her because it never used to be. She's not the same writer she once was, and she doesn't know how to get that girl back. If she tells them, they'll all want to help. In fact, they'll probably lovingly (read: bullyingly) insist on it. And the last thing Freya wants is to be another to-do on Ava's Medusa-like list: *Ask*

Freya about writing tucked between *Schedule kids' annual checkup* and *Shave for weekly scheduled sex with hubby.*

Freya is already Stori's project. If she becomes theirs, too, she'll lose the last shreds of her pride.

"She'd need to have sex first," Ava says with an evil little glint in her eye. "And the last time you shared anything about a guy in the group chat was . . . Remind me when, exactly?"

"Nope, no way, not happening. This is Steph's night," Freya says pointedly.

"And that means you have to do what I want." Steph smirks. "And I really want to hear the answer to that question."

"I *could* just scroll back and try to find it," says Hero. "But I don't think Facebook Messenger will go back all the way to the Dark Ages."

Mimi's face is the kind of innocent it's never been for as long as Freya's known her. "Did you even *have* Wi-Fi capability in your ancient cave dwelling?"

"I hate you all," Freya states, pointing her finger at each of them in turn. "Unequivocally."

"Let me hook you up with my little brother," says Mimi, not for the first time.

"My brother is single again, too," says Hero. "He always has the best lollipops. And all the floss you could want! Mouthwash in tiny bottles!"

"I cannot fathom that man's sweet tooth," grouses Ava. "He's a children's dentist!"

"If she dates him, she'll *need* a dentist," mutters Mimi.

Freya winces. "Please stop pity-throwing brothers at me! I'm focusing on my career right now. And for the foreseeable future. I'll date when I meet a man who isn't going to be a distraction."

"Um, hello, that's all men," Steph quips with an indelicate snort. "It's their blessing and their curse. *Speaking* of your complete and total avoidance, when are we going to get a look at those chapters you keep promising us? You've missed the last three critique swaps."

Freya's teeth lock behind her Rouge Dior 999 lipstick. Great. She'd done so well keeping them at arm's length all night, even though they tried to corner her at the bookshop with questions about how far she'd come on book two. The only thing worse than talking about her non-existent love life is talking about her nonexistent writing progress, but somehow they're two for two.

"How am I supposed to find a boyfriend when my standards are supportive, bookish, cinnamon-roll *fictional* men written by women?" Freya demands—quite reasonably, she might add.

"You could start by turning a little to your left," suggests Steph. "You've got an admirer. He's been looking over here for a full minute with a glazed expression. Don't stare."

Naturally, all of them crane their necks at the same time to stare in his general direction.

Hero is the first to spot him, releasing a low whistle.

Mimi pretends to fan herself.

"I said 'don't stare'!" Steph hisses.

The throbbing music recedes. Freya's friends' voices dull to a low buzz.

Because there is no mistaking the man staring at her like she's the only person in the room, even though there are four jaw-droppingly beautiful women next to her.

Steph squints. "Hey, isn't that the dude from *Banshee of the Baskervilles*?"

Taft Bamber is staring at her with obvious recognition. Freya's heart slingshots straight for her throat, and she teeters in her heels, which are several inches too high for her even on a good day, which is pretty much any day other than this one.

Oh my god. What are the chances? Running into him twice in one day.

Her heartbeat is so loud that she hears it over the pulsing music. Goose bumps prickle all over her exposed skin, making her shiver in her red cutout dress.

She thought she was in dangerous territory with her friends before, but this is . . . She doesn't even know how to describe the vulnerability she feels when he looks at her like that. For the millionth time today, Freya doesn't have any words.

"He's even hotter in person! And he's totally staring at us!" squeals Ava.

"Calm down, married lady," says Hero with a laugh.

"Crap." Mimi gets there first. "Freya, I'm so sorry! We should never have asked you to pose as his girlfriend to get us in here tonight. You should—"

Freya interrupts her. "Get ready to run like Cinderella before the clock strikes twelve?"

TAFT'S SO RECOGNIZABLE that he blows past the bouncer at the club, swapping the sticky press of humidity for the air-conditioned tundra inside. He can feel a hundred hungry eyes on the back of his neck as he enters, heading straight for the bar.

He hesitates a moment when the bartender approaches, a stunning redhead wearing a MY PRONOUNS ARE THEY/THEM pin and the same classically timeless black-and-white blazer and shirt combo as he is, in line with the club's mandatory dress code.

His father's voice rings in his ears: *Real men drink whisky.*

Fuck it. He orders a Tom Collins.

It goes down like a fizzy, grown-up lemonade, and he gestures for a second one before he realizes Mandi is a solid ten minutes late. And since she considers showing up ten minutes *early* as being right on time, something's up. He scans the club, and for just a moment he thinks that he spots her in a group of women. His brow furrows in concentration, but his line of sight is swiftly blocked by grinding bodies.

"Thanks," he says distractedly to the bartender when they slide his drink over.

He checks his wrist again; his manager got him a black Zenith watch for his twenty-sixth birthday after he landed the *Banshee* movie with Mandi. When he'd looked up the cost, his heart almost popped out of his chest like a cartoon character. But he had to admit, there's something powerful about a good-looking watch; Bruce Wayne could wear it all day in the boardroom *and* when he transitioned into busting bad guys.

Taft doesn't feel powerful now. Just a little forlorn, claustrophobic in this loud, pulsating club, skin flushed from gin. The event at Books & Brambles probably ended about an hour ago, he estimates. Did Freya search the crowd for his face? Or had she known what he hadn't yet— that he wouldn't show up tonight after all? No, of course not. That's . . . preposterous.

He sighs and downs what remains of his Tom Collins. It's a good thing Freya's recognition earlier jolted him out of the fantasy he was indulging in, that he could unashamedly flirt with her without the repercussions that came with being part of his world.

If he did anything to jeopardize the success of the movie—which apparently hinged on everyone shipping "Raft" (his and Mandi's celebrity portmanteau for Roy and Taft, thanks to several fans showing up on set to scream, "We will go down with this Raft!" during the third season)—his team and Mandi's would both fight to the death for the right to kill him.

He knows Mandi wouldn't lead the charge, but he also knows she needs the good publicity as much as he does. Just as he's about to text her, his phone lights up in his hand. Her name flashes on the screen and he answers at once.

"And the day keeps getting weirder!" she shrieks in his ear.

"What happened? What's wrong?"

"So *apparently*," she says, voice thick with sarcasm he knows isn't aimed at him, "I was already let in half an hour ago. They think this is some hoax and I'm impersonating *myself*."

"What?" He cups his palm over the phone. "I don't think I heard you."

He could have sworn she said— But that can't be right.

"I'm out front. With everyone else." Her voice lowers. "I'm afraid these unfeeling creeps in line will start filming this any second. It's so embarrassing. Please come get me."

"I'm on my way." He slips through the sea of sweaty grinding bodies like an eel.

No one tries to stop him as he makes his way back to the entrance, though he does get several appreciative glances from all genders. If anything, his recognizability has increased since he started sporting the silver. The premature grays are another thing he gets from his mother, along with her taste for fruity umbrella-topped cocktails and her love of reading, yet more things his dad doesn't relate to.

That's when he sees her, in a slinky red cutout dress that shows off tantalizing glimpses of bare skin. Sexy enough for the club but still tasteful, showing off an open back and a long neck adorned with a dainty gold choker.

His brow furrows. Didn't Mandi say she was stuck in line?

Her earrings catch the light as she turns, their eyes meeting across the room. Long legs, nude pumps. Wholly and completely, she dazzles him.

Taft freezes. He's never had this reaction to Mandi before.

His phone goes off in a frenzy of beeps.

Mandi: Hurryyyyy

Mandi: Where are you?

Mandi: I SWEAR, IF THIS ENDS UP ON TMZ . . .

Mandi: WHOEVER'S FUCKING WITH ME, THEIR
HEAD WILL ROLL.

Whoever the mirage in red is, she's not Mandi.

Feeling returns to his limbs as her earlier words come back to him: *impersonating myself.*

His head shoots up, clocking the girl in the red dress. Her face blanches into an *Oh shit* expression when she notices him. Definitely not Mandi, Taft decides. She would never let her mouth drop in horror like that, not even in her early acting days, when she was doing too much work with her face.

The Mandi look-alike sticks around long enough to murmur something to the people she's with, and then with one last panicked look over her shoulder at him, she makes a break for it.

Without even thinking twice, Taft takes off in pursuit.

Because here's the thing: like all the characters he's played, Taft *always* gets the girl.

HER LEGS WOBBLE like unset Jell-O in her absurdly high heels, but she makes it a gallant distance of all of twelve feet before Taft—and her guilty conscience—catches up to her.

She bobs to the left; he blocks her. She switches to the right; he mirrors the action.

Freya's friends start forward. She shakes her head subtly, and they drop back, but she knows they'll keep an eye out.

If she thought Taft looked sexy from across the room, he's even more unfairly attractive from two feet away. Hot even in his obvious confusion.

His waves are more defined than they were at the bookshop, like he just hopped out of the shower. And his rolled-up blazer, exposing a pale forearm with fine brown hair just a shade lighter than the scattering of freckles darting up his elbow . . . Freya's mouth goes dry.

"You look so . . ." *Familiar.* A furrow deepens across his forehead. "Who *are* you?"

Washed-up writer? Check.

Pathetic imposter? Also check.

Liar? Well, that's the one thing she seems halfway good at.

For one wild, throwing-caution-to-the-wind moment, Freya considers telling him that she *is* Mandi. Testing if she can pull it off, striking the right note of anger and exasperation. Watching the confusion fade into embarrassment as he realizes this is totally his bad for not recognizing his own girlfriend. And Freya, being the benevolent and forgiving sort, will let him off the hook.

"We know what you're up to," Taft says, voice pitched so low she has to strain to hear him over the music. "Posing as her all over town to get free stuff. You had a good run, but the jig is up. You need to stop. Come with me."

Freya's blood thrums hot under her skin.

He's going to call the police. He's going to get Mandi involved. The whole thing is going to come out and everyone will know—Stori, her dad, the whole goddamn Internet—that the best thing Freya Lal has going in her life is pretending to be someone she isn't.

When Freya makes no move to follow him, Taft reaches out, hand closing around her wrist. On these jelly legs, one, two tugs is all it takes to flatten her against his chest.

His entire face slackens with surprise as she stumbles closer than either of them expected.

Taft doesn't lose his balance as embarrassingly as Freya did; instinctively, he braces her, hands circling her waist. For such a slender guy, his thighs are surprisingly strong and steady on either side of hers. She kinda hates that she notices. With their hips and chests flush, she has to tilt her chin up to look at him.

At this angle, with his mop of tousled dark curls, one flopped endearingly over his forehead, and his rosy lips parted, he could be Prince Charming's double.

Okay, at any angle.

"Whoa," he says on an exhale. "I've got you."

Yes, he certainly does, her lizard brain whispers. During Freya's spill, her hands had flattened against his chest, bracing herself. She can move now, but her body isn't cooperating. And he's making no effort to let her go, either. His hands rest lightly on her waist, a reminder that he wouldn't let her fall even when he didn't have a reason in the world to save her.

An electric thrill ricochets down her spine. Is it the whole club that's slowed down or just them?

Freya swears that she hears the erratic *pump-pump-pump* of his heart against her palm. If she moves her hands up just a few inches, they'll glide across his collarbones and curl around his neck. From there, it's just a whisper-thin distance to his lips.

No, Freya, from there it's jail. *He's probably already signaled security and he's just distracting you with his masculine charms until they get here.*

Well, he's not going to succeed. She jerks away, rocking out of his arms in her haste to put as much distance between her and the solid feel of him as humanly possible.

Taft's eyes are flared as wide as hers, mouth open with the start of a *Sorry*.

Freya overcompensates trying to collect herself, struggling with her own two feet. He swoops in, hands settling on her waist again. Their faces hover so close she can feel the warmth of his breath, second only to the coil of heat pooled low in her belly.

A crowd is starting to gather, the tension between them noticeable.

She sucks in a breath, willing the rising panic back down. "You're making a scene."

Taft's jaw drops. "*I'm* making a scene?"

"Yes." She places her hands on his upper arms. *Oh.* He's slender but his muscles are well defined.

"Did you just feel up my biceps?" His voice is one-quarter amused, one-quarter annoyed, and two parts solidly confused.

Freya's face is as straight as can be when she responds, "No, I don't think so."

Taft's eyes narrow a fraction. His eyes disconcertingly map her face, as though he's seconds away from figuring out that she's Freya from the bookshop.

"Trouble in paradise, Mandi?" someone jeers, closer to Freya's ear than she's prepared for.

She flinches violently. As if on cue, a blaze of phone camera flashes go off all around them. The last thing Freya sees before she bolts is her panicked expression reflected in Taft's burnished-gold eyes.

CHAPTER SIX

I expect this kind of bullshit from my other clients, Taft, but you?"
Moira Lord frowns at Taft across the length of the conference table,
more sad than mad. "What were you thinking?"

The sun glares mercilessly through the floor-to-ceiling windows of
the eighth-floor office Taft and Mandi were hauled into, thanks to
early-morning wake-up calls from their frantic managers. Taft takes a
desperate sip of his water and tries not to make it obvious that he's not
looking at her but at the 3D words popping out from the wall behind
her that read LORD & FINE MANAGEMENT, instead.

He also tries desperately not to think about the girl in the damnably
sexy red dress who got them into this mess to begin with, but she's been
invading his daylight thoughts with the same ease as she'd slipped into
his dreams.

He's finally placed her, but he's keeping her name to himself. He
doesn't trust Gareth with it, especially because the man won't care if a
random, nameless girl gets doxed if she's outed as a fraud. A part of Taft
thinks he shouldn't care, either, after everything that's happened, but
then he remembers he does know her name: Freya. Bookshop Girl. Absolute menace.

Think about how much trouble you're in. Think about your reputation circling the drain.

Her face punctures through every attempt to distract himself.

Think about the paparazzi—mostly paunchy, graying, middle-aged dudes—in their underwear. No, don't think about nudity, because that leads to . . .

Taft digs his blunt fingernails into his palm, the sting almost as intense as his dreams last night. Think about *anything* other than the girl in red and the way she'd felt against him, sending his impulse control off-kilter. How he'd ached to bend his lips to hers and discover her body like a secret. The heat of her mouth, the softness of her inner thighs, the leaping pulse at her throat.

It's useless. His resolve is made of butter. No matter how much he implores, cajoles, and bargains with himself, Taft can't think about anything else other than *her*.

"He *wasn't* thinking," corrects Gareth Binghamton. "And now his drama is rebounding on my client."

All four of them stare at the laptop open to TMZ, at the appalling headline and the damning picture of "Mandi" wrenching herself away from Taft like he's a stranger.

Which technically he is. But he's not going to mention that.

Because for some reason, after driving down Melrose Avenue this morning in silence—spines ramrod straight and excruciatingly awake even without coffee—Mandi turned to him from the driver's seat with that look on her face that he could never say no to.

"Hey, Taft," she said. "What if we *didn't* tell them it's not me in the picture? I mean, if they can't tell the difference . . ."

Then, before he could even fill her in on the dots he'd connected, she rolled her Audi into a parking spot in front of Lord & Fine's Constellation Boulevard address just a minute before their appointment, ending with only a whispered "I wouldn't ask if it wasn't important."

He still doesn't know what Mandi's up to, but he'll follow her lead. And he can always divulge her look-alike's identity after the meeting.

Taft tunes back in, catching Gareth mid-insult.

"He's not in his soapy CW shows anymore," says Gareth snidely. "He's in the big leagues now. He has to act like it."

Taft's jaw ticks, and he stares at Gareth until the older man breaks eye contact first.

Mandi flushes before flicking her eyes Taft's way. "That's not fair."

"What's not fair is you two fucking up a good thing," says Gareth. "You're being paid ridiculous money for one of summer's biggest tent-pole movies, and all you have to do is pretend to date until those first-week box office numbers hit."

Taft crosses his arms. "What happened to 'All publicity is good publicity'?"

Gareth gives him an evil look. "Whoever said that wasn't part of the Internet era, where everything lives on forever to be mocked and memed."

"Look," says Taft. "We're done with postproduction. Nothing we did is going to jeopardize the release. What happened last night was regrettable, but I promise you that won't happen again."

Gareth snorts. "Really? You think you can make it until the July-first premiere?"

Mandi nods emphatically.

"It's just a month," Taft bites out.

Gareth continues as if he didn't even hear him. "You're both attractive people. Surely it isn't such a hardship for you to be seen having a good time in each other's company? Spotted kissing and grabbing ass somewhere with good lighting and plenty of people? You didn't use to be this prudish with other boyfriends, Mandi."

"Classy, Gareth." Moira scowls. "We all know the optics are bad. What's done is done."

Whatever else she thinks, whatever other choice words she has for Taft, she's keeping it to herself until they're in private. Despite her reputation as a straight shooter, Moira doesn't believe in public dressing-downs. Two of her best qualities, other than being a savvy manager.

Gareth operates differently. When Mandi reaches for one of the glazed donuts that Moira's assistant left next to the bottles of cold water, he clears his throat in a meaningful way.

Mandi smoothly changes direction, plucking a Red Delicious— arguably the least delicious apple—from the fruit bowl like it's what she'd been going for all along.

Taft follows the motion with narrowed eyes and hates Gareth even harder.

"I know you think I'm being hard on you because you weren't my first choice for the male lead in *Banshee*. But your chemistry doesn't lie. It's off the charts on-screen. It's why you got the role. But for you, this upward trajectory is pure fucking luck. Mandi, though? I have been conscientiously crafting *her* brand from the second she signed with me. She got top movie parts fresh out of the gate. Do you know how rare that is? She's going places, and I'll be damned if it's downhill because of a weak link."

Jesus. Taft's aware that Gareth's never exactly thawed toward him, but he's never chucked the gloves off and gone straight for the jugular. He's a load of hot air, but he's still managed to make Taft feel horribly guilty. Gareth's right—Taft hadn't been discreet. He'd reacted purely on instinct when he confronted Mandi's look-alike last night. He didn't stop to think about the fallout. He should have anticipated that there would be dozens of hawkish eyes watching their every move.

Taft stares at the space between Gareth's eyebrows, wondering if he's leveled up his telepathic murder skills enough to at least give the man a headache.

A second later, Gareth's cheek twitches and he rubs his forehead.

Lukewarmly satisfied, Taft uncrosses his arms and takes another swig of his water. "So we'll just lay low for a while. Stay out of the limelight. They'll get bored and move on when they see there's no story here."

Gareth grabs for a clementine that he doesn't peel, just squeezes in his hand like it's a stress ball. "That is the exact *opposite* of what you need to be doing. As long as you two are holed up, you fan the flames of speculation. We need *more* public appearances to counter the rumor that you broke up."

Moira has a strained look on her face, as if agreeing with Gareth on anything brings her pain. "Let's figure this out together," she says with a forced smile. "We're not leaving until we have a game plan for the next month. Let me just cancel my eight-o'-clock."

The rest of the meeting passes in a blur. By the time Mandi and Taft are excused—leaving their managers behind to hash out the itinerary—Moira's nine- and ten-o'-clock appointments have all been pushed forward.

"Think they'll kill each other?" Mandi asks as she steps through the front door Taft's held open for her.

"Moira knows better than to commit murder in a room that doesn't have blinds."

She adjusts her metallic-blue sunglasses on her nose. "Darn."

He throws her a quick glance but doesn't push. When it comes to Gareth he has to tread carefully, like he's walking on eggshells instead of warm, California-sun-dappled pavement.

The man's great at contracts, but taking care of his clients' mental health? Not so much.

But Mandi's loyalty runs deep. Taft should know; he's one of the few people privileged enough to have it. Which means he also knows she won't find it easy to dump the man who jump-started her career.

It's easy in this business to feel like you owe someone for saying yes, easy for the power dynamic to shift from two equals in a professional relationship to a client who feels indebted, worried that they'll never get another yes again. It's total bullshit; if Mandi left Gareth right now, there would be two dozen managers ready to take his place, all of them dying to work with her. She seems to be the only one who doesn't see it.

"You look tired," he says in lieu of what he really wishes he could say but knows she isn't ready to hear. "How late did you stay up?"

He can't quite tell, but he gets the feeling she's rolling her eyes behind her Ray-Bans.

"Don't think the circles under *your* eyes have gone unnoticed," she informs him, digging in her purse. "I'm just polite enough not to mention it. Here, this'll help."

He accepts the little pot of Glossier Stretch Concealer he's bummed off her a few times before. "Thanks. I'll buy you a new one."

"No rush. The dark circles will remind me I'm human." A gusty laugh escapes her.

Eyebrows scrunched together, Taft tries to make sense of her statement.

"So are you ever going to explain why we couldn't just tell them the truth?" he asks. "Would have saved us getting chewed out." Him more than her.

"Soon." She scrolls her phone, eyes lighting up as though she's got good news.

"Okay, Little Miss Cryptic," he drawls, letting a hint of his Texan accent come through.

Mandi looks up with a sheepish smile. "I'm sorry. I know you got the brunt of it. Gareth was a bit much back there."

"I don't need you to apologize for him. He doesn't deserve it. Doesn't deserve you, either."

She bumps his shoulder with her own. "There you go being a caring, supportive boyfriend again. Tell me how I'm supposed to break up with you?"

"According to every news outlet in the known universe, you already have." He screws up his face, letting the bitterness seep into his words. "Everyone thinks we had a blowup because I cheated on you."

She leans her head against his shoulder for a brief moment. "I can't understand why that's the story they're running with. How do they not see what a decent guy you are? You'd never do that."

He flashes her a grateful smile. Then it occurs to him that while he and Mandi were in the doghouse, the Mandi look-alike got off scot-free.

She didn't get dragged out of bed at an ungodly hour to get yelled at. She's probably still in bed, blissfully unaware that she made our world implode.

Taft doesn't realize he said any of that out loud until Mandi gives him a startled look.

"Don't be too sure about that 'blissfully unaware' part," she says lightly, raising her hand to hail a passing taxi.

"What do you—?" The taxi pulls to a stop in front of them. "Wait, what about your car?"

Her smile speaks of secret things, the insouciant shrug not half as subtle as she thinks. "Mind making your own way home? I need my car for . . . something else."

That's pretty vague. He eyes her as she shepherds him into the taxi's hot leather back seat. She's definitely up to something. There's no mistaking that self-satisfied crow to her voice.

Taft's stomach growls as he hangs his head half out the window. Since Mandi didn't get to eat a donut, in solidarity, he hadn't helped himself to one, either.

"Right now? Do you have to? I'm ravenous. I could eat . . . I could eat . . ." He genuinely can't think of an animal large enough to convey just how hungry he is; even *elephant* falls short. "There's something I have to tell you. I thought we could grab brunch at Loupiotte Kitchen," he finally settles on.

"Come to mine tonight. We can talk, and I'll make you dinner," she promises. She rattles off Taft's Los Feliz address, then bounds back to the curb. There's a look of determination on her face he usually only sees when she's running lines before a scene.

"You're cooking?" She's *definitely* up to something.

"Hey, I cook on occasion."

"Only when you want to impress a guy or demand a favor," Taft says with a snort. "You don't have to butter me up, Mands. Just ask." That's what friends do.

Mandi gives him a genuine smile. Briefly, he wonders whether anyone has ever said that to her. He knows they're friends because they have to trust each other so much, but he doesn't know if she would choose him on her own. Their relationship had started out transactional—what if that was all it would ever be to her?

"I'm still feeding you," she insists. "But first I have a . . ."

Whatever else she said is swallowed up as the taxi merges into traffic, but over the whoosh of wind in his ear, Taft could have sworn she'd said she had a doppelgänger to find.

He sits back and laughs under his breath.

Yeah, right. What are the chances of Mandi running into Bookshop Girl in a city this big?

CHAPTER SEVEN

You've got this, Freya. She waits for the boutique owner, fingers tightening around the small jewelry box she's been clutching for the last five minutes, trying to wipe her slate clean.

After last night's catastrophe, she'd made up her mind: no more impersonating Mandi Roy.

Never again. Never ever. Not in a million years. Last night cut it too close for comfort. And even though Freya had been able to make a break for it in the confusion of camera flashes going off—Taft's attention distracted just enough to lose her in the crowd—it's time to stop.

It's been fun, but it doesn't make Freya feel good about herself anymore. It's like overdoing it at drinks with the girls; the third sparkly cocktail feels like a good idea, but the next day she's full of regret. Sure, she'll miss it. But it's for the best.

Every part of Freya's life is in a rut right now—romantic, social, professional—but one day, she's going to be her again. The Freya Lal that she was before.

And it's going to be amazing. Once she hands in this book, she's finally going to explore the city and meet new people. Date without feeling guilty and find a guy who puts all her book boyfriends, past and present, to shame. Her life will be back on track and getting caught as a petty impersonator does *not* fit into her life plan.

Which is why Freya got to the boutique right when it opened for the day, in her Mandi masquerade for the last time so she can return the gorgeous earrings she should never have accepted in the first place. She had tried her best to shake off materialistic freebies, but sometimes salespeople are so insistent that saying no would seem unconscionably rude, and she never wanted to hurt anyone's feelings. At least getting into clubs without waiting in line or getting a dessert comped on her lunch bill was pretty harmless.

It's not as though Freya would swan into places saying *I'm Mandi Roy.* If she looked the part, people tended to draw their own conclusions.

A few feet away, browsing a jewelry case full of minimalist gold jewelry, a young woman around Freya's age glances up. She does a double take, recognizing "Mandi."

It's nothing short of magical how an extra hour spent dolling up can transform her into Mandi's mirror image. A swipe of Dior Rouge 999 on Freya's lips is the razzle-dazzle of the magic wand; the white pumps that make her legs go on for miles and lend her those extra few inches of height are the vaunted glass slippers from the fairy tale.

Freya offers the other shopper a small smile, because that's what Mandi would do. She's known for her warmth toward her fans. The girl squeaks and resumes browsing, eyeing Freya every few seconds. She looks as though she'd like to ask for a selfie but can't summon up the gumption.

"Mandi!" The owner emerges from her office in a pantsuit that has big boss-babe vibes.

"Hi, Elena," Freya says, slipping into the Mandiest smile in her arsenal to greet the middle-aged white woman. She pops open the jewelry box to show her the two shimmering studs. "I was just telling one of your associates that I came to return these opal earrings."

"Oh, sure! No problem. Want to swap it for something else?" Elena moves to a countertop carousal, spinning it slowly. "I have these turquoise teardrops that would look gorgeous on you!"

The employee whom Freya unsuccessfully tried to explain the situation to, a handsome, willowy Black man, whispers something in Elena's ear. Her bright smile fades.

"I think there's been some misunderstanding," Elena says slowly, glancing between the box and Freya. "You don't want to exchange the earrings. You want to give them *back*?"

Freya tries to keep from wincing. Elena sounds so insulted. She was probably banking on the publicity. "I appreciate your generosity," Freya says. "But it's too much. As beautiful as the gems are, I can't accept them."

"You already did accept," Elena argues. "Mandi, please. The earrings were a gift."

Freya holds the jewelry box out, and when Elena doesn't take it, she gently places it on the counter.

"Wait! Maybe there's something else you like better?" Elena casts a wild eye around all her glitz. "Maybe a crystal choker? A diamond solitaire? This fourteen-karat white-gold ruby ring?"

Oh my god. Freya's eyes widen. Each item Elena rattles off is more expensive than the last.

"No!" Horror rises in Freya's throat. She backs up, bumping into the young woman behind her, jostling the phone in her hand. Freya hadn't realized she'd drifted so close. "Oh my gosh, I'm sorry."

The woman hastily drops her phone into her purse, looking squirrelly. "Don't worry about it."

"May I?" Elena approaches, her dentist's-wall-of-fame smile even more dazzling than the choker she's brandishing. "I remember you admiring this one once."

Oh no, that must have been the *real* Mandi.

Freya tamps down her panic. "Really not necessary!"

"It would be more like your gift to me!"

Freya looks at Elena.

Elena looks at Freya.

The boutique owner's face is pink, agitated. Freya has a sudden frightening image of Elena taking her chances lassoing it on Freya like a little kid playing a game of ring toss.

Shame sticks her to the spot. It's different from the usual swift stab of regret when she lies to Stori or her friends about her writing progress, which has lessened over time the way guilt often does when you get a bit too used to it.

The wounded confusion on Elena's face makes Freya want to tell her the truth: *The earrings are stunning, but I can't accept them because I'm not who you think I am. I'm not Mandi.* That would definitely make Elena stop thrusting freebies on her.

But she can't admit that. To Elena or anyone. The woman is friendly and earnest, but it's easy to be nice to famous people when you're angling for their goodwill or a red-carpet shout-out. If she knew Freya was an imposter, Freya's pretty sure she'd call the police.

And Freya Lal's fantastic future? Down the drain. Like *that*.

Worse, it's also Mandi's reputation at stake. She doesn't deserve to be bad-mouthed because of this.

Mandi Roy has no clue she exists. Nonetheless, Freya owes her.

At the very least, she owes it to her not to fuck up her reputation as Hollywood's golden girl. So Freya spends the next ten minutes doing damage control to assuage Elena's worries that she hasn't somehow offended "Mandi," ensuring she has no reason to trash-talk the actress.

It's a miracle that she manages to leave without having another bauble foisted on her. On her way out, she sidesteps the other customer, the girl who still hasn't bought anything even though she's been browsing for as long as Freya was there.

As Freya heads for Stori's car—borrowed without asking since she'd definitely want to know where Freya was going dressed like *this*—parked across the street, she exchanges one nightmare situation for another.

Or rather, the nightmare perfectly parallel parks in one smooth move, cutting her off.

"Watch yourself!" Freya shouts, leaping back to the safety of the curb.

The window of the white Audi rolls down.

The driver, a girl with wavy chocolate hair, lowers her sunglasses. "Oh, I am. And I've gotta say, it's like looking into a mirror." She tilts her head, studies Freya. "Almost."

Oh no. It can't be. Heart jackrabbiting, Freya asks, "What are you—"

The girl calmly slides her glasses off her nose and lets Freya get a solid look. An unmistakable look. At the same time, she checks Freya out: the white ruffled maxi H&M dress Freya's wearing is a known dupe for something that Mandi has in her closet. The white pumps and the sliver of a gold anklet complete the signature look.

Freya's heartbeat rampages, a cold sweat breaking out on her brow. Her feet are doing that thing again where they can't seem to move even though her brain is screaming at them to do so.

The Mandi Roy gives a satisfied nod, as though Freya's passed muster somehow.

The ambient street noise peters away to a low hum. All Freya can focus on is the sheer horror of coming face-to-face with her mirror image.

This can't be happening. She mentally repeats it a few more times, but yes, it is. *Fuck.*

How did Mandi find her on the exact morning she'd sworn off being Mandi forever?

The actress smiles. "I think this conversation is better had in private, don't you?"

Freya blinks. *She's smiling at me. Why is she smiling?*

Mandi should be furious, ranting and raving about punishment and how Freya won't get away with this, how it's totally *beyond* her how *anyone* could think for a second—for a millisecond!—that Freya is anything more than a discount Mandi.

Freya hovers on the edge of the sidewalk. "You want me to get in?"

"Yes. I just want to talk. What happens after that is up to you."

Freya's pedicured toes curl into her sandals. The words sound ominous, threatening even.

It's Mandi's smile that throws her. It speaks volumes; that by some eerie stroke of bad luck, everything has worked out according to plan. It's a Cheshire grin if Freya's ever seen one.

I'm not falling for her friendly charm. There's no way it's not a trap. She may not be shouting about jail time, but she doesn't have to. It's there in the subtext.

"How did you even find me?" asks Freya.

"Tagged Instagram post."

It clicks at once: the woman from the boutique. *Guess she got her selfie after all.*

Nervously, Freya rubs her lips together. Fuck. Big mistake with this matte lipstick.

She can tell from Mandi's wince that it's probably already feathered outside her lip line. There's nothing about this day that's anything short of woefully horrific, so why not add one more thing to the list?

It's painfully obvious to Freya how dissimilar the two actually are. Mandi would never mess up her lipstick, never show how nervous she is, no matter how caught off guard she might be. Must be nice to be that poised.

But Mandi Roy has had enough of waiting. She leans over and pushes the passenger door open, arching one perfectly plucked eyebrow. "What's it going to be, 'Mandi'?"

CHAPTER EIGHT

Freya doesn't get a lot out of Mandi on the drive to the actress's apartment. They spend most of the journey in silence, without even the radio to break the tension. It's on the tip of Freya's tongue to apologize, but what would be the point? Mandi would think it's only because Freya got caught. She wouldn't believe a word out of Freya's mouth.

Under California penal code, are Freya's crimes a felony or a misdemeanor? Does it violate her book contract's morality clause? Should she shamefacedly loop her agent in? Alma's probably going to drop her—after this, there's no way Freya isn't her *worst* client.

Yikes. The fact that's even a question running through her head right now . . .

Freya bunches her knees together, coils into herself, and tries not to wonder how badly she'd be injured if she threw open the car door right now and flung herself out into the street.

Mandi glances over as though she senses Freya's skittishness. "We're still a few minutes away. You should check #Raft on Twitter."

Freya taps her phone screen awake. She doesn't even need to type anything into the search bar—the hashtag is already trending. She gasps when she sees the first image that pops up and the accompanying caption, guilt stirring in her gut.

Freya wanted to be in the news again, yes, but definitely not like this.

She and her friends had all FaceTimed for an hour last night, still a little buzzed and shaken after the close call in the club. Too close, everyone had agreed.

None of them knew then how the story would break this morning, that Taft would be called a cheater when it was really Freya who was the fake. For such a heartthrob actor, he's got a great reputation in the media. But now he's the one getting the blowback for something he didn't even do.

Guilt curdles in Freya's empty belly. *I've messed up more lives than just my own.*

"Mandi, I had no idea," she says, throat dry and words sticking in shame. "I didn't know these pictures went viral. I'm so, so sorry. I tried to put it right this morning, but I know it's not enough. If you need me to publicly come clean, tell everyone that your relationship isn't in trouble, that it wasn't you last night—"

"Are you kidding me?" Some of Mandi's composure breaks. "That's the *last* thing I want."

Parsing that confusing declaration is giving Freya a headache, and she doesn't think she has the right to ask Mandi a question. It's only 10:00 a.m., and her friends are probably still fast asleep in their swanky hotel room. She consoles herself with the thought that when her friends wake up, they'll check Twitter and see the headlines. Just like with a messy revision or a sticky plot point, they'll help her get through this.

The trip passes in silence until they arrive at Mandi's building, at which point Mandi, whose silence has had Freya catastrophizing the whole ride, deigns to tell Freya how they're going to get past her doorman without him seeing double.

Mandi scrounges in the big beach bag behind Freya's seat. "Here, you'll need this."

She throws something at her, and it catches Freya in the face before falling to her lap. She looks down in disbelief. "A bucket hat? I haven't seen anyone wear these in . . ."

Unprompted, an old memory pops up, all soft and hazy at the edges: a photograph of Freya in a matching lavender bucket hat and elastic pants, no more than two years old. Squirming in her mother's lap, Freya's small, eager fingers frantic to turn the pages of her board book on the rug in front of them.

Tears spring to Freya's eyes, washing away the film of sepia going back two decades.

"Oh, come on," says Mandi. She jams it down on Freya's head, tugging it low over her eyes and ears. "It's not that bad. It's very nineties." She tilts her head and smiles. "I look good."

"Then you wear it," Freya mutters under her breath.

Mandi smirks, then pulls out another hat for herself, this one far more in vogue.

"But that's a straw hat! Yours actually looks cute!" The indignant words are out before Freya remembers that she's trying to stay on Mandi's good side.

"Hmm, straw?" Mandi adjusts it in the rearview mirror, slightly angled, while humming under her breath. "I had no idea. Thank you for illuminating me about this newfangled chapeau."

Freya didn't expect her to be this funny. Or this petty. Or know French.

Mandi gets even more hilarious (!) inside when she ushers Freya past the doorman, a youngish white guy who pauses the financial podcast he's listening to when he sees them. He's fine to let them just walk straight to the elevator, but Mandi makes a point of stopping right in front of his desk. He doesn't seem surprised when she greets him like a friend, as though they have quick chats quite often.

"This is my cousin," Mandi proclaims without being asked, pointing to Freya.

What is she *doing*?

"It's her first time visiting LA, and I promised her parents I'd take good care of her."

Freya shuffles her feet, hanging back.

"Geraldine, say hi to Doug."

It takes hairline eyebrows and a pointed stare for Freya to grasp that Mandi's addressing *her*.

"Hi, Doug," Freya repeats dutifully.

How is this her life? At some point between the car and the lobby, she's become Geraldine, Mandi's gawky cousin with truly abominable fashion sense.

To complete the disguise, Freya's also wearing Mandi's sunglasses, which look sexy on the actress but, coupled with this hat, embarrassingly touristy on Freya. Sweat crawls over every inch of Freya's skin, her arms also having been stuffed into the sticky skintight sleeves of Mandi's exercise pullover.

Wicking, my ass. Freya's chest, almost a cup size larger than Mandi's, strains against the fabric, giving her an unflattering uniboob.

"Gerry's not used to the sun, poor thing." Mandi clicks her tongue sympathetically. "*Skin condition*," she adds, sotto voce.

Freya's face flames even hotter. Mandi's clearly enjoying this.

"That's too bad," says Doug. "It's gonna be a hot one today."

"Taft will be by later," Mandi says with a sweet smile. "You can send him on up."

"Sure thing." Doug grins. "Happy to see that crap about you two breaking up was a whole lot of nothing."

"Taft is the best. You know those media vultures." Mandi rolls her eyes. "Happy couples just aren't as exciting to write about. They're in the wrong business, honestly. If you want to make things up so badly, go write fiction."

Doug nods in sympathy. "You've got that right. Well, it was nice to meet you, Geraldine. Hope you get to enjoy the city while you're here."

Mandi barely holds it together until they're in the elevator. She punches the button for her floor—the penthouse, naturally. The second the doors shut on Doug, she dissolves into giggles. "You were incredible! You totally pulled off that scared little-girl-in-the-big-city act! I *knew* you could handle yourself!"

Freya gives her a tense smile. It wasn't an act.

"Shouldn't you be mad at me?" Freya asks, struggling to peel the extra layer of clothing off. "Yell at me or something! Put me out of my misery, please."

"I am mad," Mandi says mildly. "Look at this face. It radiates fury."

"You're still smiling," Freya points out, frowning. "Were you . . . testing me?"

"It's my villainous evildoer smile. And don't frown. We'll get premature wrinkles."

We? Freya scowls harder until she realizes that Mandi's partially right: of the two of them, only one has easy access to ridiculously spendy skincare. She also doesn't miss that Mandi sidestepped the question.

"'Villainous' and 'evildoer' are synonymous," Freya grumbles.

The elevator dings. Mandi's already stepping out. "Oh, look, we've arrived at my lair."

Freya finally manage to wrench off her pullover. "Ha ha."

Mandi throws a wink over her shoulder.

This whole situation is confusing and absurd, but Mandi's so charming that it's impossible to stay mad at her, Freya quickly realizes. It's also impossible to get a bead on her.

"You can come in, you know!" Mandi shouts through the flung-open front door.

"Uh, Mandi?"

A very large, very woolly-looking dog has just bounded into the foyer, blocking the door. It barks twice, daring Freya to come closer. Is it a friendly bark? A warning bark? She has zero clue.

The dog studies her, head inquisitively cocked to the side. At least she think it's looking at her; it's hard to tell when its wiry eyebrows are falling into its eyes. Its coat is a lovely milk chocolate–cinnamon color, carrying through to the whiskery, shaggy mustache and beard.

They stare off as Mandi flits about inside, doing god alone knows what, leaving Freya to deal with this behemoth of a dog. Whose eyes she can't even see. Plonked in front of her like a hairy barrier.

Freya swallows. She didn't grow up with dogs. That's not to say she's scared of them. She just has a healthy appreciation for their size and teeth. That is absolutely *rational* in a situation like this one.

Mandi cranes her neck out and takes in the scene. "Hen's friendly. Just give him a firm no and push his face away if you don't like licks."

Freya's jaw almost drops.

Putting her hand anywhere near his mouth is the *last* thing she's going to do. If this dog's wet tongue wants to lick her to death, she will simply sit back and let it.

Freya chooses to focus on the least terrifying thing Mandi just said. "You named him Hen?"

"That's *Sir* Hen to you."

"You expect me to believe that this dog is in any way a chicken?"

Mandi's laugh is a silvering tinkle. "It's short for Henry, and yes, while he's a wonderful watchdog, he's actually a huge softie at heart, so get our cute little derriere in here now."

There she goes with *our* again. Freya cautiously inches forward, cringing when Henry gets too close. He pokes his nose against her thigh, nuzzling her through the fabric. In return, Freya tries not to do anything that could be construed as a threat, like moving. Or breathing.

Mandi's perched on a pale pink sofa in the living room, a tall glass of soda in hand. There's another waiting on a coaster on the modern center table.

Except for the sofa, all the other furniture is the same bright white as the walls. There's nothing homey about the kitchen tucked behind her, all recessed lighting, white marble counters, and sleek white cabinetry that blends into the background, elongating the dimensions of the space. It's an expensive apartment with nothing out of place, much like Mandi herself, but that's where the similarities end. Devoid of charm and warmth, there's nothing to indicate that the actress actually lives here.

"You've helped yourself to everything else, so I half expected you to look right at home here," Mandi says after Freya sits down opposite her. "But you don't."

"Neither do you," Freya counters, taking a sip of her drink. Diet Pepsi, ice cold and crisp.

A micro expression of surprise crosses Mandi's face. "The only thing in this whole sterile apartment I got to pick was the sofa. Didn't even get a say in the neighborhood, but that's the price for 'moving up in the world,' I guess."

It explains why the whole place looks like a showroom, but why would *the* Mandi Roy do anything she didn't want to do?

Freya isn't sure how to respond to Mandi's weird honesty, so she just takes another tentative sip, keeping one eye on Henry and the other on her trembling hand. The last thing she needs is to dribble on a sofa that probably costs half her book advance.

She still doesn't understand why she's sitting in Mandi Roy's apartment like they're friends, and Mandi doesn't seem to be in any rush to tell her. Maybe she wants to watch Freya squirm.

"Are you going to tell me why I'm here?" Freya finally asks when it becomes abundantly clear that Mandi isn't going to break the silence. "Why you're not threatening to turn me in?"

"Do you want me to do that?" Mandi sounds genuinely curious.

"No, of course not!" Freya blurts out. "I just don't get why *you* don't want to."

Mandi sets her half-empty glass down on the table with a hard clink. "Okay. Cards on the table. I've had all of last night and part of this morning to scroll through thousands of my tagged photos. And I had about a million thoughts, most of them not so flattering about you, but the one that stuck out the most was, *Damn. This girl is good.* So yes, I was testing you."

Freya coughs on the Diet Pepsi. Her eyes sting a bit by the time her throat clears.

"I get asked for selfies so often that they all bleed together," Mandi continues. "Even so, it was tough to separate the pics that were me and the ones that were you. You nailed my look. Even our voices are kind of similar. I bet underneath it all we could pass for sisters, if not twins."

Freya flushes at the compliment. She'd done her homework: When she started to rely on being Mandi more often, she had scrolled Mandi's Instagram to see what affordable brands she favored and watched Mandi's old *Vogue* "Get Ready with Me" YouTube video to perfect the makeup. She knew all the products Mandi used and the way she applied them, and the way in which she spoke—cultured and confident, never cocky. Mandi's every word was thoughtfully considered. Her elegance, on the other hand, was unmistakably her own and not easily imitated. Which wasn't an issue, since the people who mistook Freya for Mandi were never inner circle; club and restaurant interactions were quick and impersonal.

Freya takes a deep breath, the kind that unclogs the words from her throat and gives them life. "I'm sorry for falsely impersonating you. It wasn't intentional. I mean, it didn't start that way. It was just a case of mistaken identity the first time. And after . . . it was just a bit of fun when I needed it. And I tried not to need it."

She throws a glance Mandi's way; her face is impassive, but Freya can tell she's listening.

So Freya keeps going. "But my mom had just—" No, Freya refuses to use her death as an excuse. "I was going through kind of a bad time. I was only thinking about myself. And eventually it became easier to re-create on purpose what first happened by accident."

Mandi looks sympathetic, but Freya doesn't know how real it is. Whether even Mandi's friendly charm is an act. The *Los Angeles Times* didn't call her a "silver-tongued silver screen sylph" for nothing, after all.

"Mandi, I want you to know, I have never—not once—said 'I am Mandi Roy.' I know you're living your best life and have probably never felt this way, but I just wanted to temporarily step out of mine. It was never about the swag or defrauding anyone. I know you don't have any reason to believe me, but it's the truth."

"Okay," Mandi says slowly, and Freya doesn't have the first clue what part of her explanation she's acknowledging, but Mandi looks contemplative now. Henry's cozied up at her feet, and the actress weaves her hand into his mop of fur, scratching his head until his pink tongue lolls out.

The silence is oppressive, and Freya does her best not to fidget. She respects that Mandi wants to sit with this, but if she could say something *before* Freya stress vomits, that would be amazing.

"It just occurred to me that I don't even know your name," says Mandi.

"Freya Lal."

"Can I see your ID?" There's no hint of recognition on Mandi's face.

"Sure." She hands over her driver's license and tries not to flinch when Mandi's iPhone's camera shutter takes an extra-loud click.

"No offense," says Mandi, not sounding at all apologetic. "Had to be sure it's your real name."

Freya blinks. It hadn't occurred to her to lie. About this.

"Listen, Freya. You might know what it's like to pull off being me for a couple of hours. Maybe even a whole night. But you have no idea what it's like to actually be me. What you do is like . . ." Mandi casts around for the right words. "You're playing Cinderella. When the clock runs out, you get to be you again."

Her whole *life* is a fairy tale, and she's calling *Freya* Cinderella?

"So," Mandi says coolly, still on her phone. She taps at the screen before saying, "You've probably figured that I'm not going to turn you in. But you *are* going to pay me back."

The ominous words shoot goose bumps down Freya's arms. "I don't have—"

"I don't want money," Mandi bites out. "No, Freya, you're going to pay me back in *time*. Every second you stole from me over the past few years. You're going to play the role of a lifetime." She steeples her fingers together. "Shall we say it adds up to around four weeks?"

"I'm sorry?" Freya doesn't know whether she's apologizing for what she's done or for not having the first inkling of a clue what Mandi's talking about now.

But honestly? Both.

Mandi's triumphant smirk speaks volumes: *You're not sorry yet, but you will be.*

The tingles are running rampant over Freya now, and they have very little to do with the arctic air-conditioning or Hen's unblinking bull's-eye stare, like she's a human-size chicken nugget he wants to dip in slobber sauce.

Mandi elegantly crosses her legs. "I need to get away from my life for a while. How would you like to be me for the next four weeks, until the *Banshee* movie premiere?"

That's a trick question if ever Freya's heard one. Sure, playing pretend for one night is fun, but she knee-jerk knows for a fact that she has zero desire to fake it for a whole *month*.

Besides, it's one thing being mistaken by a bouncer or hostess who she sees for all of two minutes! Rubbing shoulders with the elite in Mandi's circle is a new, undiscovered circle of hell—there's no way she could get anything past the people who pretend for a living.

Freya's mouth goes dry. Including Taft, Mandi's boyfriend, and the whole reason the pictures went viral in the first place.

Mandi must obviously be kidding. *Ha ha. Good one, Mandi. Almost had me.*

Freya has to deescalate. Handle this smart. Show no fear, but back away from the situation in a nonthreatening manner. Mandi's just an actress. She's no scarier than a grizzly in Gucci. Actually, scratch that— the imagery *is* a bit scary.

Be brave, Freya.

So, naturally, a hysterical *How is this happening?* giggle slips out. "Uh . . ."

Sir Henry eyes her. At least Freya thinks he does. It's kind of hard to tell.

Her tongue feels like sandpaper, and it takes forever for her lips to unstick. "You can't be serious. There's no way I could pull it off."

"Have some confidence in yourself, Freya. You already have."

Acrid shame bubbles in her gut. Sure, at this point Mandi is probably the one character Freya knows the best, but now that she's met her, Mandi isn't a character anymore. She never was.

She's a woman waiting for an answer, and Freya swallows past the lump of regret. "Do I have a choice?"

"You *always* have a choice," Mandi says, tone waspish.

Yeah, two bad ones. Play along or face exposure. Put like that, the answer is obvious. Still, Freya tries, "I'm a literal rando off the street,

Mandi. You're willing to leave your career in the hands of someone you don't even know? How do you know you can trust me?"

Mandi's answering smile is somehow both sweet and grim at the same time. "Oh, I know I can."

"What does that—"

Mandi holds up her phone, showing a browser search of Freya's name, accompanied by a headshot and book cover. "Because if our little secret gets out, your reputation will be ripped to shreds just like mine." Her smile is all shark. "I think this is what they call leverage?"

CHAPTER NINE

In the days that pass after Freya leaves the apartment, Mandi doesn't contact her. It's just long enough for Freya to almost entertain the fantasy that the whole meeting was a deadline nightmare that didn't actually happen. That would make a lot more sense than the golden girl of the silver screen blackmailing Freya into taking her place *or else*.

Freya's working the register at Books & Brambles, laptop optimistically open on the counter, and is sucking down the dregs of her iced coffee when an iMessage notification slides across the screen. She automatically opens it, assuming it's one of her friends.

Unknown Number: Your homework. Study up, Freya. You WILL be tested.

A document accompanies the message, titled "MANDI_DOSSIER."

"Great," Freya fumes; just when she thought she was off the hook and that Mandi had talked herself out of this epically bad, no-way-it-can-work idea, *this* happens. Her hands clench around the plastic cup until the ice rattles.

A few feet away, Cliff and the customer to whom he's selling Steph's book look over. Even Emma pauses in rearranging the stationery and bookish gifts table until Freya waves a hand in apology.

She doesn't add Mandi to her contact list, as if that will make it less real. It's a futile stand to take, because the last thing she wants to think about swiftly becomes the only thing she can think about.

Which really fucking sucks at a time when she has a book to finish that trumps all else.

Maybe it's the word "homework" that does it, or the reminder that Mandi expects her to memorize a novella's worth of her life history, or just the fact that Freya was a former honor roll kid, or *all* those things, but she does as she's instructed. There's a little burn of jealousy that an undoubtedly super-busy Mandi wrote all of this in three days.

She minimizes Mandi's doc with a yawn, satisfied with what she's retained on her first read-through, and reopens her manuscript. She scrutinizes her words, but spying Stori stacking shelves nearby and watching her with a hopeful expression, she refrains from her first instinct—deleting everything.

Before she can congratulate herself on her willpower, both Freya's laptop and phone come to life with her literary agent's FaceTime call.

Thinking fast, she props her phone up on her laptop screen, answers the video, and starts tapping away furiously on the keyboard. She pauses, trying to give the impression she's just finished a long bout of uninterrupted typing and needs to clear away the brain fog.

"Oh my gosh, Alma! Hi!" Freya chirps.

Oh yeah, she's nailed it.

"Were you just fake typing?"

Freya whips forth an innocent look. "Of course not!"

Alma peers at her through the screen. "You *were*."

"I categorically deny it."

Some people make the mistake of thinking that with such an

old-fashioned name, Alma Hayes is as dusty as they come, but they couldn't be further from the truth. She's sharp as a paper cut. With her pixie-cut mop of ginger curls, Peter Pan–collared shirts, and ever-present cardigan, no one sees her coming: she's a fierce negotiator and looks out for her clients to the nth degree.

It's because of her that Freya still even has a book two at all. Freya doesn't want to disappoint her.

Alma's voice turns sly. "Then you won't mind turning your phone around so I can take a quick peek at all your progress, right?"

Oh god, Freya's already sweating nervously. Again. "You know I don't want to jinx anything by showing anyone before it's ready for eyes. I've had too many false starts."

"And things are going okay this time around? Not another dead end?"

Freya hates lying to her. Hates wondering if Alma's buying it. It's even harder to dodge when Freya can see her agent's face on the screen. Sometimes she thinks Alma does it deliberately so she can try to get a read on Freya in return.

"Never mind coming up with something, Freya," says Alma. "You're a terrible actress."

If she only knew . . . Despite the fond tone, for a half second, Freya's almost affronted. Almost. Then her ridiculous feeling of wounded pride is replaced by something far more worrying.

"Wait . . . what's up?" Freya bites at her lower lip before catching herself on the screen. "We didn't have a call scheduled. It's not— They said I still had time! They're not canceling my contract, are they?"

Alma's face goes so still that Freya thinks the Wi-Fi is on the fritz. "No," Alma says finally, the word drawn out in a way that tells her that whatever Alma says next won't be good. "You still have your promised four weeks. But that's it, okay? You know I'll go to the ends of the earth for you, but they've demonstrated an enormous amount of grace, and I can't make excuses for you forever. I *know* you know this, but the wolves are at the door. You're running out of time."

There are a few more euphemisms and an aggressively perky *I believe in you!* before Alma hangs up. Freya doubts she's put her mind at rest, and despite Alma's best intentions, nor has she Freya's.

APPARENTLY ONE DAY to cram is all Mandi thinks Freya needs, because barely twenty-four hours after receiving the dossier, between bouts of snail-pace progress on her manuscript, Freya is summoned to an address in Los Feliz.

Parked in Stori's Civic in the driveway of a charming little bungalow on Melbourne Avenue, late-afternoon sun warming her thighs, she tries to rally herself with Stori's favorite (but least useful) affirmation: *You've got this!*

"I so don't 'got this,'" Freya says with a groan, slumping over the steering wheel.

In hindsight, she should never have given Mandi her contact details, but she'd been too stunned to refuse after that bombshell of a proposition . . . taking Mandi's place for the next four weeks.

Freya's had some time to get her head around it, and even though she's tacitly agreed by showing up to the address Mandi texted her, it still feels surreal.

Her phone goes off in a barrage of incoming text chirps from the group chat.

Ava: I Google Earthed the house. It's in a REALLY nice neighborhood.

Hero: I can't believe you agreed to this preposterous idea! There's only about, oh, a

MILLION ways it can go wrong, AND HOW ARE
YOU GOING TO CONVINCE TAFT THAT YOU'RE
HIS GIRLFRIEND?

Ava: Like it would be a hardship kissing that
face haha. I wouldn't mind "convincing" him lol
lol lol.

Mimi: UGHHH I wish we were still in LA! Tell us
everything! Did you go in yet?

Steph: You should have told Stori where you were
going. This feels sketchy. If we don't hear from
you in an hour, we're telling her.

Affection glows warm and soft in Freya's chest. Mandi would be
furious if she knew she had spilled the scheme, but if her friends were
able to keep the original ruse a secret for the past few years, she trusts
them to hold on to this one. Besides, if her best friends can't be here in
person, this is the next best thing.

She types back a response.

Freya: Mandi was pretty cryptic, but it should be
fine! She probably just wanted to meet
somewhere else. Less eyes. BYEEEE, heading in!

Bright yellow dandelions peep through the gaps in the stone walk up
to the front door, which is painted the same shade as the Italian basil in
the windowsill herb garden. Smaller and pointier green leaves sweeten
the air with the scents of lemon and anise.

As she reaches for the lion's maw door knocker, her thoughts turn to Hero's very valid question: Just *how* is she going to fool Taft into thinking she's Mandi? Of all people, *he* would be able to tell.

She doesn't need to dwell on it long. Because seconds after she drops her hand to her side, nervously scrunching the cuff of her black denim shorts, the man himself answers the door.

"You!" tumbles out of Freya's mouth even as the rest of her goes rigid.

"Bookshop Girl," he says calmly.

He doesn't seem in the least surprised to see Freya gawking at him like a starstruck fan. She gets it now: she doesn't need to convince him, because he's already in on it.

Five years ago, at the height of *Once Bitten*'s popularity, she would have promptly swooned into his arms if they had ever come face to face. Nothing short of bamboo under the fingernails would get her to tell anyone that she'd once spent an entire New York Comic Con prowling the Javits Center hoping to accidentally-on-purpose bump into him between his panels, but security wasn't letting anyone get close.

Little did that sweet little Taft Bamber–stan Freya realize just how close she'd be to him one day, now for the third time. Her bones liquefy just thinking about being pressed against him again, his palms warm against the curve of her back and his eyes hungry with longing. He may not have known who she was at first, but there was no mistaking what was going through his mind when he'd caught her mid-fall.

Should have swooned when I'd had the chance. What a missed opportunity. She's almost rueful.

His hand flexes against his thigh. "Coming, Freya?"

"Excuse me?" she squeaks.

"Mandi's inside." He opens the door wider and lifts a gently rounded brow. Just one.

It's an enviable gesture that shouldn't look as hot as it does, and yet the simple invitation lightning strikes straight between Freya's legs. Unlike her, he has no trouble making eye contact.

Proximity to this man is a dangerous thing, she's starting to realize.

"Oh. Yes. I'll just—" She sidles by him, sucking in a breath as though that will somehow minimize any overlap in their personal-space bubbles, but not before getting a tingling whiff of his Acqua di Parma that's almost as heady as the fact she's in *the* Taft Bamber's house. Considering he answered the door, it's a solid assumption, and one that proves correct when she sees the slim entryway table with a picture of his family at a backyard barbecue. She tries not to stare, but it's hard; pre-fame teenage Taft was cute.

He's barefoot and there's a shoe rack next to the door, so she slips off her black slingback block heels.

"In the daylight, you look—" He stops himself.

"Less like her? And now an inch shorter?"

It's not surprising. Freya's makeup is minimal, just enough to make her look awake.

"I was going to say," he says, throwing her a sharp look, "that you look different. More like yourself."

Taft leads the way from the foyer to the living room. The polished hardwood flooring continues throughout the open-concept house, along with the herby, welcoming scent of sweet basil and citrus fruits. As they go deeper inside, he closes all the windows and draws the gauzy white curtains.

Unlike Mandi, Taft is practically a poster boy for soft furnishings.

Plump, squashy pillows line the back of the three-seater emerald velvet sofa, the rolled arms looking like something out of a London library. Faded Persian rugs overlap on the floor, anchored by a toffee-colored leather ottoman and, endearingly, a pair of ragged house slippers.

The mid-century modern teak and walnut furniture is warmly finished, popping against the white walls almost as much as the brass-framed Klimt prints and the enormous square mirror propped against the wall opposite the sofa. The decoration is minimal but welcoming.

In short, Taft Bamber's living room is nothing short of a West Elm wet dream.

Mandi's perched on a wide, squarish white armchair with rattan-embellished arms. She looks effortlessly cool and chic in a floral wrap dress that Freya recognizes from the Anthropologie website's latest summer arrivals.

Freya's gaze drops to Mandi's lap.

Mandi's wielding a pair of barber scissors and a wicked smile. "Welcome to *Mandi's Next Top Model*."

Freya is too stunned to move until Mandi whisks a nylon cape around her shoulders and beckons for her to sit on the barstool Taft's carried from the kitchen.

She stares at the scissors and then shoots her eyes straight up to Mandi's face. "You want to cut my hair? I agreed to memorize your study guide, not put my literal neck on the line!"

"You've been lucky so far that no one's noticed your hair is a teensy bit longer than mine and a couple shades of brown too dark," Mandi says breezily, snapping the scissors open and close. "It's one thing fooling a bouncer or a maître d', but you're going to be in rooms with my manager, my friends, pretty much anyone in Taft's and my social circle. You have to be ready, *and* you have to be convincing."

She's not wrong. But it still rankles.

"Can't we go to a salon?" Granted, Freya won't be able to afford any stylist Mandi goes to, but if it has to look flawless, box dye isn't going to cut it.

"Not if we want to be discreet. Don't underestimate the speed of the gossip network. Now *sit*."

"Have you ever cut hair?" asks Freya. "Because, no offense, yours is no home hack job."

"I'm not your stylist," Mandi says, nodding to Taft. "He is."

The alarm must show on Freya's face, because Taft laughs under his breath. "Believe me, this is not how I thought my day would be going, either," he says, rolling up the sleeves of his loose-fitting white linen shirt. "But I used to do this all the time, so I do know what I'm doing."

Freya suspects they think she's being a big baby. Losing a few inches and pigment isn't nearly as risky as Mandi trusting Freya with her entire career, for mysterious reasons that she didn't divulge to Freya.

"Okay," Freya says, the word tugged out and reluctant and filled with fervent prayers to the hair deities, but it's all the permission Mandi needs to step aside and let Taft take her place.

The heat from Taft's chest and abdomen warms Freya's back, and while he and Mandi talk quietly about what needs to be done, Freya zones out.

Not the smartest decision, especially when the stink of bleach tingles her nose, but she can't keep up with words like "color developer" and "levels" and "toning shampoo." She has virgin hair because her mom was convinced that coloring your hair makes you go gray faster, and Freya thinks it'll keep her anxieties to a minimum if she doesn't overanalyze what's happening behind her.

"I'll be in the kitchen," says Mandi, pressing a hand to her temple. "The peroxide always gives me a splitting headache. Tell me when her hair's all foiled so we can go over logistics."

Taft's breath ghosts over the shell of Freya's ear. "Hope you studied."

Goose bumps sprinkle down her neck and upper chest. He's being politely friendly, but the words hold a warning.

"What happens if I fail?"

If he notices the faint wobble in her voice, he doesn't let on. "Don't fail."

She scoffs. "Real helpful advice. Look, you're her boyfriend. Can't you talk her out of this?"

His lips quirk as if he's amused. "When the people I love want something, I will do everything in my power to help them get it."

It's a disarmingly honest answer, and one she didn't quite expect. But then, Taft seems full of surprises. "Is that why you're playing along?"

His fingers gently touch her scalp, and it takes everything Freya has not to jump. "I do need to touch you for this part, if that's okay."

"Yes, you can touch me anywhere you want."

She thinks the strangled sound behind her is a cough.

"Er. What I mean is—" Freya squeezes her eyes shut, positive she's already failed.

Mandi would never be this indecorous. And if she were, it would be coy and charming, not has-this-girl-ever-spoken-to-a-single-other-human-being awkward.

"Good to know." His fingers start to trace through Freya's hair. His voice barely holds back a laugh. "You don't have to close your eyes. I haven't started yet."

She sighs and turns to look at him. "You sure you know what you're doing?"

He angles her back the way he wants her with a soft click of his tongue. "If you're going to be Mandi for the next few weeks, you've gotta have more faith in me."

"Right. Sorry. Right." She tilts her head to look at him. "How do you know how to do this, anyway? Did you do a stint at a Great Clips in high school or something?"

He hesitates. "My mom used to color her hair at home. She couldn't reach the back, so she had me help out. I watched enough YouTube videos that I learned how to cut and layer, too."

"Not a lot of sons would go to that much effort."

"I guess not." His voice returns to coolly professional and not at all like he's about to intimately bury his fingers into Freya's hair. "Is this how you normally part your hair?"

She can readily imagine how many girls would kill to be in her place right now, continuously being touched by one of Hollywood's hottest. Distracted, she mumbles, "Yes."

He adjusts her head again. "Are you tender-headed at all?"

Even Freya's actual stylist never asked her that, she just yanked away. She tries not to let the surprise show on her face when she answers, "Yes, but it's fine, my hair is usually a little tangly, especially in the back middle."

"I'm going to comb your hair out, but if it yanks on your scalp, let me know. I'll do my best to be gentle."

And to her astonishment, he does. Every time the fine-toothed comb hits a snarl, his nimble fingers tease it out. Not one single hair snaps the way it would have if Freya was the one doing it, far too frustrated and impatient for such a tedious task. But Taft doesn't complain once, even though it takes him forever to get through her thick mane.

Halfway through, her eyes flutter shut. She never considered before what a small yet mighty pleasure it was to have someone run tender fingers through your hair, followed by the slow, rhythmic strokes of a comb. Most of her ex-boyfriends treated foreplay and affectionate gestures as precursors to be endured rather than enjoyed, always with sex as the end game.

Freya hopes that she isn't looking like she's enjoying this too much, even though she totally is. "So . . . ," she broaches hesitantly. "The silver in your hair. Natural? Or is it for a role?"

"Natural." His nails gently scrape against her scalp, working through a particularly nasty knot. "Sprung up out of nowhere, but the movie execs liked it so much I'm contractually forbidden from coloring it. Apparently it went over really well in focus groups."

"I can see why," she says before she can think better of it.

His fingers still. "Good to know."

Mercifully, he can't see her face, and Freya's fine to let him have the last word.

Taft is thorough and methodical as he brushes the cold paste on her hair, covering it in foil to separate the highlighted sections and keep the heat in. "Are you nervous?"

"About how my hair is going to turn out? Yes. About everything else? Also yes."

He laughs under his breath. "At least you're honest."

"Sometimes," Freya acknowledges. She wouldn't be here otherwise.

He takes an extra-long time to start the next section of hair, wrapping it around his finger like he's thinking something over. Finally, he asks, "Why do you do it?"

There's no point pretending to misunderstand. "It's the only thing I seem to be good at lately."

"That's . . . disappointing."

"To you and me both," she mutters.

"I meant because you don't seem to count your writing as something you're good at. It's a shame, if you ask me—which I know you didn't— but I'm not really one to hold back on a compliment. Especially when the other person is so damn in the dark."

Freya's skin prickles under the cape and beneath her beige cropped cami. *Finally*.

She knew he'd recognized her from their encounter at Books & Brambles when he called her Bookshop Girl at the front door, but he turned away before they could acknowledge it. This time, Taft lets her get away with swiveling around on the barstool to look at him. "You're not seriously telling me that you read my book," she demands.

"Bought the e-book the second I left the shop." His lips twitch. "Funny story, it wasn't under the name 'Randy.'"

Taft's tone is so dry that Freya balks for a second before getting the joke. "Ha ha. Just so you know, whenever anyone tells me they like my book, it takes everything in me not to make them give me an oral review right on the spot."

"Oral, huh? I could do that."

Dear god. She makes a small sound that sounds like a croak, then spins herself around before he can see the full-blown lust in her eyes. *What the fuck, Freya. You* cannot *go after Mandi's man.*

He hums under his breath, returning his attention to Freya's hair. Her scalp's starting to feel a little warm, and it wouldn't surprise her one bit if the bleach fumes were making her lower her inhibitions a frightening degree.

"Just about done. And for what it's worth, Freya is a prettier name than Randy," he comments, a hint of humor in his voice as he crinkles a piece of foil around the last section of hair. "What does it mean?"

"It comes from the Old Norse name Freyja, the goddess of love and beauty." Freya gives him a wry smile. "Also war and death. My mom got her master's in Viking and Medieval Studies at the University of Oslo, then came here for her PhD in Scandinavian studies. My paternal grandfather was her thesis adviser here. He'd invite her for family dinners and holidays because she was so far from home, which is how she met my dad. He wasn't a folklorist like Mom, but they both loved the name Freya."

His fingers slide to her neck, ostensibly playing with the baby hairs on my nape. "Where does the 'Anjali' come from? I noticed 'Freya Anjali Lal' on your book cover."

"Um, well, it's not part of my legal name. My mom, Anjali, passed away shortly before my book published. I would never have believed I could write a book if she hadn't encouraged me every step of the way. She never let me forget that I had magic in my fingertips."

His idle touching stills. "I'm sorry. It's a beautiful name."

"It is," she agrees. "It's Sanskrit for 'divine offering.'" Freya cups her hands together, palms out, to show him the pose. "I wanted to honor her memory by using her name."

"I know it's not the same, but I kinda get it? I got some funny looks for my name when I started out. Agents and managers said shit like 'I'll consider signing you if you change it to something less weird.' It was made pretty clear that it had to go if I was going to make it as an actor. But our names aren't just ours, they're the history of everyone who came before. I'm proud to be Taft Bamber, even if I did get teased in school for my first name being the same as a president who's known for getting stuck in the tub."

Freya stifles her smile, even though he can't see her face. "I like your name. And I like it more knowing how hard you fought to keep it when it would have been easier to give it up."

She's not sure what it is about him that makes her this earnest, especially given their more combative exchange at the bookshop. Maybe because he's being the same way with her. She should really, really not like him as much as she does. And yet . . .

"I'm so sorry this is taking forever," she babbles. "If you think it was bad today, you should have seen it in high school, when it was waist-length and thick enough to smother someone."

"Freya." He moves to stand in front of her. Taft doesn't touch her, but her name in his mouth caresses her skin in one shivery syllable. "I wanted to take my time with you."

Oh. *Oh.* She throws her eyes to the ceiling as if it's more interesting than the frank, disarming expression on his face.

Are there aphrodisiacs in the atmosphere of Los Feliz? Because that's the only explanation for this proximity crush. So then, naturally, it would follow that the air at the club was similarly tampered with. In fact, she's starting to think that whenever Taft is in the vicinity, entire neighborhoods turn dangerous.

"Are you done flirting yet?"

Mandi's complaining voice makes Freya jerk, almost toppling off the stool.

Taft's hands are there to steady her, but he releases Freya way faster than he did at the club. It looks like he's painfully aware of how they got into this mess to begin with.

It's hard to tell whether she's grateful for his restraint or grumpy about it.

"Just finished, actually," Taft says blithely, taking the mixing bowl to the kitchen sink. His voice sounds careful and professionally neutral. "She's all yours. It still needs a few minutes for the color to lift, and then I'll tone and trim two inches."

Mandi's eyes, so like Freya's own, but far more suspicious, dart between his back and Freya's flushed face. "Did you tell her what Gareth and Moira came up with?"

His shoulders stiffen, and he runs the tap at a full flow instead of answering.

"Mature!" Mandi yells. She settles down on a leather wingback chair. "Guess he didn't. Okay, doppel-Freya. Don't freak out."

"Whenever someone says that, it's never followed by anything other than impending disaster," Freya points out, not loving the new nickname. "I reserve the right to freak out."

Mandi casts an irritated look at Taft, clearly wishing he had done the hard work of breaking the news. "Fair, but just know that we're adults here and this is *so* not a big deal, because *someone* has more than enough space for two more and is just being ornery about the most practical living situation."

She seems to be expecting more pushback than Freya gave her about the cut and color.

"Thanks to you two and that stunt at the nightclub, our managers have decided that we, well, need to be managed better. And that means a *lot* more public appearances to sell that we're the perfect couple and definitely neither of us cheated." Mandi crinkles her nose. "There's an itinerary of events I'll get them to scale back on, and, um, a few strong suggestions that are less suggestions and more . . . edicts."

Taft's been washing the bowl a lot longer than necessary. Even as she tries to focus on Mandi, Freya finds herself taking notes like he's a character she's later going to pirouette into prose: good at domestic tasks, unwilling to break bad news, and possibly an ally against whatever bananas plan is about to be proposed next.

Freya blinks. "And your managers know about me taking your place?"

"God, no." Even Mandi's snort sounds sophisticated and succinct. "Gareth would lose his shit."

Taft nods. "There is no known *or* unknown universe in which involving them would be a good idea."

"Okay," Freya says, drawing the word out. "So what does that mean for me?"

"Taft and I have been 'dating' since season three," says Mandi. Freya's not sure why there's a slight inflection. "So Gareth, my manager, thinks that it's time Taft and I took the next step."

A shocked laugh lurches out of Freya. "Marriage? Your *manager* is dictating that?"

Mandi rolls her eyes, as though that isn't 100 percent what her words implied. "No way. But you and Taft *are* moving in together. Welcome home."

The sentence lands like a wrecking ball.

"Ha ha." Freya waits for Taft to say something, but he just turns off the tap and comes over with an indecipherable look on his handsome face. "Wait, you're serious?" she yelps.

"Yes, Gareth insists it needs to happen ASAP to combat the bad press. But the public appearances are what's most important. Just a couple of parties and club invites I've already accepted," Mandi says in a voice that is not soothing, not at all. "Moira and Gareth want us to do a photo shoot for movie promo, and a few excursions around the neighborhood to really sell you settling in. The paparazzi are pretty obsessed with me and Taft, which is why you'll actually have to move in here so they can catch 'us' together. But I'll be back in time for the premiere!

You'll both need to share some pics on social media together, be spotted in public, something low-key . . ." She trails off thoughtfully.

Freya wants to point out every single reason why there is no way this will work, except, she realizes with dismay, her own actions have repeatedly proved that it *will*.

"I got you a phone case that matches mine," says Mandi, evidently nonplussed by Freya's less-than-enthusiastic response. "Luckily we have the same iPhone model."

"*Lucky*," Freya repeats faintly.

"Well, yeah. So if you have any personal photos as your wallpaper, you'll need to change that. There are eyes—and cameras—on us all the time. If we don't get every detail right, down to our accessories . . ."

The implicit consequence is obvious: one false move, and all their cards come tumbling down.

"I'll log you into my Instagram on your phone so you can post pics, but I'll handle all the comments." Mandi waves her hand with a confidence Freya doesn't feel. "This is all stage direction, nothing to worry about. While I exit stage right, you slip in stage left without anyone spotting the difference."

Mandi clocks the overwhelmed expression on Freya's face and hastily adds, "Trust me, you'll be fine. Taft is with you. And you already look and talk like me, plus you'll have access to my wardrobe, so that's not a problem."

Freya is still hung up on the part where Mandi thinks Freya taking her place isn't a problem, let alone the million-and-one logistics she just threw at her. As though a sunny smile and a can-do attitude are all it takes to pull this off.

"'*Not a problem*'?" Freya pinches herself. Unfortunately, this is all too real. "*All* of this is a problem!"

For the first time, she sees a genuine smile from her doppelgänger.

"Yup," Mandi says cheerfully. "But now it's yours."

CHAPTER TEN

"Worst moving day ever," Freya declares to an empty bookshop the next day, sleep weighing down her eyes and a migraine pressing against her temples as she opens her laptop, Hunka Junk, to a throwback background circa four years ago. Her friends beam at her with sparkling-grape-juice smiles and empty flutes, Books & Brambles in the background looking nearly the same as it does this morning.

Freya's family crowds around her: Her grandfather, black hair and thick mustache long turned white, and his second wife, the blond Southern belle who has never been *step*grandma or *step*mom to Freya and her dad, but simply Grams and Mom. Stori, the coolest person Freya's ever known, who was going through a phase where she dressed exclusively as nostalgic style icons like Margot from *The Royal Tenenbaums*, all smudged eyeliner and barrettes in bobbed hair and preppy polo dresses. Dad, unshaven and haggard, looking unmoored without Mom, but it's the fierce pride in his weary eyes that Freya chooses to focus on.

People talk about looking at the past with rose-colored glasses, but that night was pure LA in all her fizzy-champagne, bubblegum, neon mirage. No matter how many bookish celluloid daydreams she sifts through, this is always the one Freya comes back to like an anchor.

There's a faint stirring of regret as Freya takes in her younger self, so full of promise and a thousand and one ideas to send her agent, sure she was shitting gold. If she could reach into the screen and scream some sense at that Freya, she would do it in a heartbeat.

Maybe, then, *this* Freya wouldn't have been up until 2:00 a.m. with Mandi, being quizzed on everything from her first on-screen kiss (terrible); the directors she would never work with again (even more so); and all her interviews regarding her personal life, upcoming projects, and previous filmography.

At some point during the inquisition, when Mandi moved on to her ex-boyfriends—a topic Taft presumably already knew way too much about—he turned in with a mumbled good night. But not before first brewing the girls a fresh pot of coffee to see them through the night and washing up all the dinner bowls. Even though she tried not to be aware of it, it was impossible not to be: Taft was a cute host.

Because while Freya was getting a deep dive into Mandi's friend group, Taft had tossed together a delicious microgreen salad the color of a summer sunset, with slivers of rainbow carrots and watermelon radish, jeweled pomegranate seeds, and sweet, bursting navel oranges. She and Stori mostly relied on takeout and three-ingredient, ten-minute meals, so his home cooking was the best thing she'd eaten in a long time, and Freya had gratefully devoured it while Mandi breathed down her neck to finish faster so they could get back to work.

If Freya thought Mandi's Wikipedia page was thorough, it had nothing on the dossier she had to study. And like every test she'd ever taken in school, she'd aced it.

Freya's next test is going to be astronomically more difficult. How is she supposed to tell Stori about moving out, without revealing where? Without mentioning the blackmail and that she's living with a movie star's boyfriend because *she's* supposed to be the movie star?

Mandi was emphatic that Freya couldn't tell anyone—anyone who didn't *already* know at least, once Freya came clean about her friends' preexisting knowledge.

If Freya tells Stori, though, she doesn't put it past her protective aunt to get involved. And that's the last thing Freya wants, her flesh and blood knowing the mess she'd made.

If she were still here, Mom would be so disappointed.

"Morning, Freya," says Stori, hiding a yawn behind her cup of tea as she comes downstairs. She's already enviably put together. "Didn't hear you come in last night."

Freya takes in the faint half-moons under Stori's eyes with a flicker of guilt. Making sure she came home safe is something Mom would always do. "I'm so sorry, I should have texted. Did you wait up?"

"Don't worry about it. I'm just glad you had a fun night out. Tea?"

"No, thanks," Freya says quickly, holding up a shot of espresso.

"You're definitely your father's daughter," Stori says, smiling around the rim of her cup. "I've never developed a taste for coffee. Looks like something from an oil change."

Freya quickly winds her hair into a low bun before Stori notices the change in color, and forces a light and bright tone to her voice. "Don't let him hear that! He gave you that Bialetti three Christmases ago, and it was *still* in the box until I showed up."

Stori snorts. "There's no way you're guilting me when Jay hasn't even cracked the spines of any of the books I've sent him."

"Dad hasn't even read *my* book yet," Freya points out. Same as most of the family to whom she gave free copies, but that's author life for you.

"But your mom and I read every draft, the advanced-review copy, and the final version. Speaking of, if you need an alpha or beta reader . . . hint, hint."

Freya cups a hand around her ear. "What was that? You were being too subtle."

"Fine," Stori says with a long-suffering sigh. "If you don't want to talk about your book, then at least satisfy my curiosity about where you were last night. And with who. And did you do something different with your hair?"

Freya gives the bun a self-conscious pat. "I was . . . working."

Not technically a lie. Delicious dinner and Taft's deft fingers aside, Mandi's quiz had been nothing short of brutal. She was a way more unforgiving taskmaster than Stori ever could be.

"There's nowhere in LA conducive to getting writing done at that time of night." Stori's eyes sparkle like the New York City skyline Freya misses so much. "Wait. Were you with a guy?"

"No!" Lie. "I have a deadline!" True.

"One does not preclude the other," Stori says dryly. "A girl's still gotta get some."

"Okay, I love you, but never say that again," says Freya. "And it does if you're me. The only body part I need to be thinking with"—she taps her forehead—"is this one."

"And these," says Stori, making a crude gesture with her fingers. "Don't forget these."

"I *cannot* with you," Freya groans. She could have gone her entire life without that allusion to masturbation. Sister Stori she loves and Boss Stori she appreciates, but Talking-About-Sex Stori is one Stori too many.

"What? Get your mind out of the gutter. I was totally talking about typing." Stori smirks. "But since you mention it . . . Marcus has a work friend—" her aunt starts to say, but Freya cuts her off with a scoff.

"Stori, your boyfriend only knows tech bros. I love that he tries, but I *cannot* be set up with another guy who makes conversation like he's giving a TED Talk."

"What's wrong with a guy who articulates himself well?"

Freya rolls my eyes. "Believe me, I could enumerate the ways."

"I would love to argue more about this with you, but it's almost nine, so I'm going to open the store and then get started on our online order mailouts." As Stori walks away, she turns around and yells, "And get rid of Randy's name tag! I swear, you're going to get in actual trouble one day!"

Once Stori disappears into the storeroom, Freya taps open her manuscript.

Unlike her usual writing days, today there's a happy hum in her fingertips—she's ready to type. Even though Stori would love to know that Freya has a new book idea, she's keeping it to herself, just in case it doesn't go anywhere. She's used to several months of failed starts, but after meeting Mandi, she's finally unearthed a story she's excited about.

Ironically enough, seeing Mandi with a pair of scissors yesterday had jump-started her imagination in an unexpected, pseudo-murdery way. Even though she was already exhausted from their quiz session, Freya stayed up half the night pulling together a new pitch: a young adult thriller about a teen starlet who ropes a look-alike runaway into taking her place at a performing arts academy on the Upper East Side for sinister reasons, not least of which are the two bad boys who are currently pursuing her.

The similarities to her own situation aren't lost on her, but she's in no position to turn down inspiration when it strikes. Not only is the timing serendipitous, this one just feels *right*, already half formed in her mind, title and all: *Kill to Be You*.

It's a bit strange to have a spark of story so new and precious to safeguard. Even if it goes nowhere, at least she's doing something this morning instead of typing "THE END" just to feel something. Which, sadly, has been happening more often lately.

Freya keeps typing as the morning meanders slowly into afternoon, right around the time post-lunch she starts getting bored and drowsy. She knows how lucky she is to work here, and the last thing she wants is for Emma and Cliff to catch her sleeping on the job, but Freya wouldn't mind a continuation of last night's dream, which had drifted into hazy memory all too quickly. All she remembers is Taft was there.

And now he's very much *here*.

"You!" Freya finds herself accusing him for the second time in as many days.

His lips twitch. "You really have to work on your customer service."

Her eyes slink from a curl messily draped over his forehead to the drinks in his hand. "Kinda like how *you* should work on your listening skills. You brought another iced coffee in here? Seriously?"

He's unrepentant. "Technically, I brought two. And I still don't see a sign up, *Randy*."

"You're lucky I don't have the power to ban you for life." But she accepts the coffee with a blush. "Thanks. How did you get in here without me noticing, anyway?"

He gives the bookshop a quick once-over. "Is there somewhere we can talk privately?"

The store isn't crowded, just a mother-daughter pair out in the bookgarten and an elderly man who buys and reads a new book every time his wife drops him off to run errands.

"Um, I can step away from the register, but I can't leave the floor." She hesitates. "We could go into the stacks?"

He nods and follows Freya among the shelves, where they're hidden from any prying eyes.

Today he's dressed in a gray V-neck tee that looks like it would be soft to the touch, and well-fitting jeans that sit snug on his hips and taper down the length of his long legs. Freya passes dozens of guys dressed like him on the street every day, but no one could ever mistake Taft for being commonplace.

With the tall bookshelves bracketing them, he feels impossibly close. Butterflies stir low in her belly, wings fluttering faster and harder with every second.

"So, why are we skulking around like two teenagers about to make out in a library?" she asks.

Taft's entire body jerks. "That's not what we're doing," he says hoarsely, tightening his fingers around the coffee cup. "Wait, are you speaking from experience? In an actual library?"

She crosses her arms. "I'm not telling you that. I could have been talking in hypotheticals."

"Yeah, but you weren't." His tone is mildly scandalized. He sets his cup on the shelf ledge, and she follows suit. "You're an author. Shouldn't a library be, like, your holy ground?"

A laugh startles out of Freya. *Please*, there's no way he's such a Boy Scout. She's seen the indecent things he's done with his mouth during on-screen kisses. And it's no secret that Mandi is a fan of PDA.

She raises an eyebrow. "I'm sure you and your girlfriend have gone further than kissing in *way* more public places than this. Besides, I'm only your decoy girlfriend, remember? We don't actually need to discuss our exes. *Pretty* sure they don't run in the same social circles."

His lips part as though he's about to argue, but then he clenches his jaw. "We have a birthday party to attend tonight, and Mandi overlooked something. If we don't resolve it, it's going to give you away before we even get started. So that's why I'm here."

Freya tenses. Not only does she have to move into Taft's place tonight, but they have to do their first appearance together, too? Mandi did warn her that their managers wanted to move fast on the action items, but in no way does Freya feel ready for the lion's den.

"Okay," she says, trying not to freak out. Striving for blasé and cool and not at all like proximity to him might make her erupt in spontaneous fangirl. Or, worse, change her name and flee LA so she won't embarrass everyone. "What's so worrying that you had to come *here*, where anyone could catch us?"

"It occurred to me that, um, people act differently around each other after they've been intimate."

What feels like a century of awkward silence inches by.

"I mean sex," says Taft, flushing the prettiest shade of pink.

Freya swallows. "Yeah, I did get that."

"I couldn't stop thinking about it after I got in bed."

"Oh?"

Taft gives her a *look*, guessing where Freya's thoughts have taken her. "There's a familiarity in the way they touch, look at each other. We won't have that."

The smile drops off Freya's face. *He's not suggesting that I . . . that we . . .*

The space between the stacks narrows until everything fades and it's just him and her. His chest didn't seem quite as broad yesterday, nor his curls so messy.

"Listen, Taft, I know that this is really unfair to you," she says, hoping her voice doesn't leap about like her jackrabbiting heart. "Why don't you just tell Mandi that you're not comfortable faking it with me? You're right, we're strangers, and there's no chance we can get away with this. They'll see right through this absolutely unhinged con, and that'll be embarrassing for all of us."

He ignores Freya's not entirely selfless advice, worrying at his bottom lip until it turns as red as his cheeks. "Actually, I was thinking . . . more along the lines of getting to know each other a little better."

She snorts. Somehow, his embarrassment has the exact opposite effect on her. Exuding a confidence that her heart doesn't reciprocate, she asks, "Vocal cord–wise or carnally?"

"*Freya*," he hisses.

It really is too easy to embarrass him. "Calm down, I'm kidding."

Taft runs a hand through his hair, presumably trying to smooth it, or maybe it's just a nervous habit, but either way, it only musses it even more. "Aren't writers supposed to be shy?" he asks, a bit grumpy, as though he's somehow been misled.

"I think you mean introverted, not shy," she corrects. "And not all of us."

"You're right about that," he mutters.

"So how do you want to do this? Strip down? Lay bare our vulnerabilities?"

He works his jaw. "You're using those words on purpose."

She can't help but tease him. "As a writer, yes, I am very purposeful with my words."

"Speaking of words," says Taft, apparently deciding a change of topic is safer ground. "I also wanted to offer my support. You had some very justified reservations about moving in, and believe me, I get it. If you want me there when you talk to your aunt, I'm here for you."

The crackling energy between them pivots to something distractingly caring.

She blinks. "Oh, that's . . . sweet. But, um, to be honest, I still have no idea how I'm going to tell her. Mandi was pretty clear about keeping our arrangement a secret."

"Screw that," he says firmly. "Stori's your family. You shouldn't have to lie to her for us."

"I've been lying about a lot of things for a lot longer than you've known me. And yes, I realize that doesn't speak in my favor, but sometimes a lie is preferable to the truth."

He scowls, dark brows almost touching. "I have never found that to be the case."

"You're an *actor*. Your tradecraft is in lying."

"Says the fiction writer. Who isn't exactly a stranger to wearing a mask herself."

Pot, meet kettle. He's not wrong, but the words still bring a surprising sting.

Somehow their bodies have instinctively angled toward each other, and even though they're not touching, his minty breath warms her face, and she's close enough to count the smattering of freckles across his exposed collarbone. Close enough to push his back against the shelves and tilt up to kiss him.

But he's taken—off-limits.

Taft is the first to pull back before the moment boils over. "When enough of your life is fake, you start to value what's real all the more. Trust me. Be honest with Stori before she finds out some other way."

Freya shakes her head. "I don't get you."

He said he'd do everything in his power to help the people he loves get what they want. While part of her thinks it's super weird he's *this* devoted a boyfriend, the other, bigger part admires him for his loyalty. It explains why he's willing to get to know a random girl wearing his girlfriend's face just so the aforementioned girlfriend can get a "break" from her charmed life. But it doesn't explain why he's going out of his way to help *Freya*, to whom he owes nothing.

His crooked grin makes her stomach spin faster than a tumble dryer. "What's to get?"

"You and Mandi. She's willing to leave you to some opportunist's clutches?"

"You shouldn't talk about yourself like that," he says with a frown.

"I can be self-deprecating if I want." Freya rolls her eyes. "'Honest with Stori,' ha! The guy who's about to embark on a fake relationship with a decoy girlfriend does *not* get to judge me."

"Why not? It's not like it's any more fake than my 'real' one," he shoots back.

There's that inflection again. The same one Mandi had.

His face drains of all color. "I didn't mean . . ."

A wave of understanding washes over Freya. "Taft." She waits until he makes eye contact. "Are you and Mandi in a fauxmance?"

His unblinking stare is horror-struck. "We've been calling it a show-mance," he mumbles.

Oh hell. This is infinitely more convoluted than even the most chaotic, unhinged ghosts of Freya's first drafts past. She and Taft are a fake relationship hidden within another fake relationship.

He doesn't need to ask her to keep it a secret, because at this point the ever-growing list of things they aren't allowed to tell is far more than what they can. Besides, with all the leverage they're holding on each other, it's mutually assured destruction. Not the greatest start to a relationship, she has to admit.

"So everything you were saying about 'people act differently' after they've had sex?" Freya asks, a little cautious and a little jealous about the answer.

"I've never slept with Mandi," Taft says tiredly. "But we're friends. It makes it easier to pretend. I don't really enjoy casual touching with most people, but in my line of work it's kinda unavoidable. She and I don't cross any lines."

Freya's suddenly exceedingly glad she squashed any impulse to kiss him.

As though he's read her mind, Taft says, "I like it when you— That is, I mean— I don't mind if you— And you did give me an open-ended invitation to touch you. So."

She laughs under her breath. "It's cute that you're more awkward in-person than you are on camera."

"And you're less shy than you were at my house."

"Yeah, well. I was a guest then. Now I'm your roomie."

His kaleidoscopic eyes are unreadable. "Girlfriend."

"Decoy girlfriend," Freya replies, perhaps too glibly, because he looks like he's biting back whatever he really wants to say. She takes a step closer with her hand outstretched. "Can I?"

At his answering nod, she slides her hand up the softness of his tee, the bony jut of his collarbone, and, finally, his neck. He's holding himself rigid, but after a minute, the tension ebbs out of him. When that happens, she cups the side of his face, *feeling* the exact moment he relaxes.

"So you and Mandi have never slept together, but you've obviously kissed, right? That's something that's probably expected of us, maybe even tonight at the party? So should I . . . ?" She lets her words linger, letting him grasp the meaning in her pause, just in case it's not what he wants.

"*I* was going to suggest chatting over coffee, but your take-charge method works for me."

At his throaty words, confidence spurs her into motion. Freya closes the gap between their bodies until she's nestled into him, her face in the crook of his neck and shoulder. His hands skim the waistband of her jeans, warm thumbs finding the cool sliver of skin between the denim and her emerald puff-sleeved satin blouse.

"You look good in green," says Taft, voice deeper than before. His irises glow gold.

A gasp tumbles out of her mouth before she can thank him. His right hand reaches into her hair to pull it out of its bun. His handiwork spills over her shoulders in perfect glossy waves. Fingers tighten into her scalp, a pleasant prickling reminiscent of his slow, steady strokes with the comb. Freya chases the sensation, arching against him just a little.

He visibly swallows. "You know, I never thought I had a librarian fantasy until I saw you."

She gets the feeling he'll kiss just like he acts. With single-minded focus, a commitment to what's right in front of him, and a driven desire to make it good.

Unfortunately, she doesn't get the opportunity to find out.

"Freya, do you know where I left the—"

Later, Freya will realize Stori's tone was already frustrated, as though she'd been calling for Freya a few times already, but she'd been too wrapped up in Taft to notice. Before she can disentangle from him and put a respectful distance between them, Stori rounds the corner.

It takes two seconds for her eyes to bug out at the sight of Freya in Taft's arms. Whatever she was going to ask wilts on her lips. Her mouth opens and closes multiple times, guppy-like.

Then Stori's stunned gaze lands on him, and Freya sees her connect the dots.

Stori nods in their direction. "So this is what we're calling 'work' these days?"

Taft manages a shamefaced, dimpled smile, coupled by biting his lower lip.

Yes, it is work, *actually*. Freya tries not to ogle him. And also yes, there are some great perks.

She's tempted to make up something on the spot about how they hit it off the first time he came into the store and they've been keeping it quiet because he's in a staged relationship with his costar, but then she remembers his advice.

"Stori, can we talk upstairs?"

"Why not? It's not like there's anyone working checkout, anyway," she says acerbically, eyebrow pointedly raised.

Freya winces. Okay, she deserved that.

"I'll watch the store for you," offers Taft. "I've worked register before."

Stori is entirely unimpressed. "In real life or on a set?"

"Perfect, thanks, Taft," Freya says hurriedly.

"*Fine.*" With one last daggered look at the both of them, Stori stalks out.

"I'm sorry about that," Taft says after a long, excruciating silence. "Don't get me wrong, this was hot, but our first kiss should be . . . I don't know, special?"

Freya drags her teeth across her lower lip.

How special can it be when we're both pretending I'm someone else?

"No worries, I've got this." She grabs her cup. "You were right, before. About honesty."

He nods, but the set of his mouth is a little dejected. Whether it's about their kiss being interrupted, Stori finding out like this, or even how tonight's going to go, Freya has no idea.

To be fair, she wouldn't blame him if it was all of the above. Because, same.

But she still has confidence strumming through her veins, so she's not going to leave it at that.

"And for the record," Freya whispers as she extricates herself from him and their *almost*, "call me a writer cliché, but I *do* love libraries. There's always something about things that should be untouchable that make you want to violate their sanctity more, isn't there?"

CHAPTER ELEVEN

The girl reflecting back at her in the side mirror looks about as far from a librarian—even a sexy one—as possible. Freya tries to pick out one feature that looks distinctively like herself, but can't. It's oddly disappointing, even though that's the whole point. If she and Taft get busted tonight, it won't be because of her makeover skills. Everything is on point.

She's no stranger to becoming Mandi for the night, so why does this feel for the first time like she's giving up something? Something valuable?

"You're thinking too loudly," says Taft. He's driving them to Mandi's friend Jennifer's house in West Hollywood, just a few minutes away from Sunset. "Sure you don't want to talk about how it went with Stori?"

"I told you she was fine with it."

Well, as fine as she could be when Freya hadn't given her much of a choice. Stori had been intent on trying to talk Freya out of it, even threatening to talk to Taft herself, but Freya knew it was no use when *Mandi* was the one in charge and had every intention of holding her to it. So she assured her worried aunt that her promise to Mandi wouldn't interfere with her novel deadline or picking up the occasional shift at the bookshop.

Taft makes a noncommittal sound. "You know, you *can* tell me real stuff, too. It doesn't all have to be fake."

Freya gets the feeling he's trying to connect with her, trying to bond, but it'll be too hard to pretend to be Mandi if she shares too much about herself.

And tonight and for the foreseeable future, *Freya* is the one person she can't be.

Honestly, she probably shouldn't even mind that. It's not like she was able to open up about her writing struggles with Stori, Alma, or her friends, anymore. Sometimes it feels like making things up is her only talent in life. Freya's walls are so high that if those closest to her can't scale them, the guy sitting next to her has no chance.

But the more he says sweet shit like that, the more she wants him to try. Which is scary, because even though he isn't Mandi's for-real boyfriend, which still boggles her mind a bit, this is risky enough without complicating it with real feelings.

Which means what happened in the stacks can't happen again.

"I get what you're saying, but maybe we should just keep it professional tonight," Freya says tightly. "I can't afford to slip up. Maybe you can compartmentalize, but I'm not an actress."

"Freya—" he starts.

"Which means you should probably just call me 'Mandi' even when we're in private."

"Don't be ridiculous, you haven't signed your whole life over to become a clone. It's only a few public appearances."

On which Freya's whole real life depends. It's a difference without a distinction.

Without warning, his hand lands on her knee. She startles, thighs swerving away and an audible squeak escaping between her lips.

"You can't do that every time I chastely touch you," says Taft, voice ringing with bitter amusement. "As you so eloquently put it, Mandi and I have gone further than this in public."

He says "eloquently" like he really means "crassly." If he wasn't worried before, now he should be. She was pushing to become more familiar earlier, and now Freya's squirming and blushing like an untouched virgin, when all he did was place his hand on her knee, arguably one of the least sexy body parts.

Embarrassment wars with the sheer amount of want rampaging through Freya's shaved, exfoliated, and dewy body. Mandi had sent all her holy grail products over to Taft's, where Freya had gotten ready now that it was officially her home sweet home. With the managers breathing down their necks, the living arrangements were nonnegotiable, so she hadn't fought Mandi on it. But it's starting to sink in that while Freya may look the part, she's afraid that her unpreparedness is written all over her face.

"It'll be fine," Taft says, reading her silence for what it is. When they park at their destination, he pauses while slipping the keys into his pants pocket. "We'll be fine."

"I know," she lies.

It's not "we" that Freya's worried about—it's *her*. It's nice of him to treat them as a unit, but the success of tonight depends solely and wholly on her bad habit of being a damn good liar.

He glances at her. "You might want to tell your face that."

There's a flash of movement, a metallic glint from the street. She starts to turn toward it, but Taft steers her toward the front door. Her bravado isn't buoyed by his solid presence, not even when he wraps an arm around her waist and tucks her into his side as they pass through the open gate.

"Did you see that?" she whispers. "Someone's following us with a camera."

"It's an occupational hazard. Probably the same vulture who's been—" He stops abruptly.

Frazzled, she's about to demand he finish the sentence when the front door flings open.

"Happy birthday!" Freya blurts brightly to the stunning woman behind it.

The birthday girl, Mandi's friend Jennifer, is white, statuesque, and blond.

The stunning woman in front of them is . . . not.

Shit. Freya needs to backtrack. The mistake curdles in her mouth until the other woman laughs.

"Like Jen would ever get the door. Start drinking early tonight, Mandi? That's not like you."

Freya should deflect, say something light and witty. She *should* have a repartee at the ready. She should do literally *anything* else except stand here with all the charisma of a boiled chicken breast. But her Diored lips stick together as her brain goes on high-speed blender mode, trying to improvise.

Taft's fingers squeeze her hips, and instinctively, she knows he's going to cover for her. "My fault, Phoebe." He nails the *Sorry, not sorry* smirk as he teasingly adds, "We were celebrating with a bottle of Dom earlier. She's such a lightweight."

Freya understands his subtle cue. Immediately, she places the woman in front of her.

Phoebe Reid, one of Mandi's oldest friends, half Black, half Argentinean, is famous for being famous. Her dad plays a doctor on a popular medical drama and was named *People*'s Sexiest Man Alive last year, while her mom has her own line of athleisure, which her actress-influencer daughter is the face of.

Phoebe's eyes flit to Freya's bare ring finger. "Celebrating?"

Taft keeps firm, even pressure on Freya's hips as though he's trying to ground her. His touch is two-fold, a tumultuous cocktail of comfort and arousal. The former is fine, but the latter is, well, distracting.

But Freya has a role to play, and he's already set her up with the perfect opening.

"Oh, we don't want to steal Jen's limelight tonight. We both know she'd never forgive me," Freya says playfully, placing her hand right over Taft's heart.

It's a well-known secret that Jennifer James's jealousy went from passive-aggressive to aggressive-aggressive ever since Chanel chose Mandi to be the new face of No. 5. Where Mandi is undoubtedly the de facto It-Girl Heroine of Hollywood, Jen always plays the girlfriend, sister, or best friend.

Taft takes the affection a step further, tugging Freya against his chest and nuzzles his nose behind her ear. It's a ticklish spot, and she hopes the tiny tremble that wracks her shoulders is mistaken for a shiver of pleasure instead of surprise.

Phoebe grins and steps aside to let them in. "So, no ring, but there *is* something. The rumors of trouble in paradise have obviously been greatly exaggerated."

Taft winks. "Don't believe everything you read."

When Phoebe's back is turned, Freya whispers, "Thanks for the save."

Taft doesn't reply, but his eyes are soft as he nods. They don't need words to convey that they have to be more careful if they're going to get through tonight unscathed.

While Jen's two-story Tuscan-style white stucco with a red clay mission tile roof is all charm on the outside, it does a complete one-eighty inside. Glass and chrome are everywhere, a sunken living room with oversize white leather sectionals, and a back wall with floor-to-ceiling windows that lead out to a huge balcony overlooking a pool. It's a big house by any standard, but especially by LA's.

"What was that earlier?" Freya asks, raising her hand to self-consciously touch her neck.

Taft subtly herds them away from a group of people trying to get their attention. "That, sweetheart, was improv. Good job not jumping out of your skin."

The casual endearment throws her, but not as much as the phantom tickle of his skin against hers. "You didn't tell me you were going to do that!" she protests.

"I won't always be able to," says Taft. "We have to sell this. You do know what 'improv' means, don't you?"

She smiles between gritted teeth. This is *not* amusing. "I'm not struggling with the definition. Just the . . . application. I'd appreciate some warning next time."

"Because I found one of your erogenous zones?"

Freya snags two flutes of champagne from a passing waiter. "You are being very . . . distracting."

"Most girls don't tell me that it's working this soon," he says with a wink.

Still a bit flustered, she glowers and thrusts the second flute at him.

Taft leads them in the opposite direction of a group of well-dressed young men calling Mandi's name. To Freya's surprise, it seems like Taft's skirting anyone who actually wants to talk to them. He and Mandi had warned her that their friends would see the sensational headlines for the garbage they were and *probably* wouldn't say anything to their faces, but this is getting ridiculous. They can't be unsociable all night hoping to avoid possible unpleasantness.

Throwing a glance over her shoulder, Freya asks, "Aren't we supposed to mingle and casually let people know we're living together? Rub it in their faces that they got 'us' so wrong?"

Taft makes a sound that is neither agreement nor disagreement. "Mandi's strategy is a bit more bull by the horns, but I think this calls for a gentler touch. Let's see and be seen. Notice how effective it is already?"

She sweeps the room and hopes the wispy falsies Mandi made her wear don't poke her in the eye. He's right, there are a lot of eyes on them. Some are daggered, some are open and curious, and others are undressing her like she's barely even a person, just a hot mannequin wearing a dress.

Without thinking about it, Freya presses closer to Taft as they stroll around the perimeter.

While the Reformation dress hits her ankles, the hip-high slit makes her feel exposed, and every eye in the room is hungry. Freya knows it looks gorgeous, but it's far too daring for her comfort level, and it takes an extreme force of will not to bunch the edges together to cover her upper thigh.

"I feel like we're in a Regency romance novel taking a turn around the living room," she admits, drawing a laugh out of Taft. "Or, like, *Bridgerton*. Or am I confusing that with the Victorian era?"

A ripple of warm breath curls around her ear. "I suck at remembering all the eras. But I bet the Victorians would be scandalized if they saw those stunning legs. Luckily, your current audience is far more appreciative. Everyone's eyes are glued to you," he whispers.

She scoffs. "You mean the dress. It's wearing *me* instead of the other way around."

"Sweetheart, it's all you."

Earlier that day, Mandi had commandeered more than half of Taft's walk-in closet with her jaw-dropping wardrobe, including a shoe rack and jewels that resembled a dragon's hoard, accompanied by a look book of how every item should be paired and worn.

Freya had wanted to wear a statement necklace, but Mandi insisted that the dress *was* the statement.

She hadn't really understood what Mandi meant until she clocked the enraptured looks at the party. This dress is the equivalent of an exaggerated, insouciant eye roll to anyone who thinks for even a second that Mandi and Taft are on the outs. The shape of the fabric contouring snugly to Freya's body and the high slit all scream one statement: *No secrets here.* This dress is power.

Freya throws back her champagne in one gulp.

Wordlessly, Taft exchanges his untouched drink for hers. "Try to nurse that one for—"

Freya lowers the second, now-empty flute, shooting him an apologetic look over the rim.

"Longer than two seconds," he finishes, fighting a grin.

"Oops? In my defense, that was *excellent* bubbly."

Taft plucks the flute from her hand and leaves both their glasses on a tray. "I wouldn't know," he says dryly. Then, in one smooth move, his hand cups her jaw. Freya can't hold back her gasp in time when his pinkie travels an electric path down her lobe.

"W-what are you doing?" Her eyes hold his, unblinking.

In a low, teasing voice, he asks, "Do I need to keep an eye on you?"

"Two eyes, preferably." Freya allows herself a flirt, leaning into his warmth.

He was right about seeming exclusive and cozy—it was a good call. She's still a little jumpy after what happened with Phoebe, and if she messes up on the first night, Mandi's going to think she wants to get caught.

If that happens, our deal is off and she'll report me.

Freya may have gotten used to it the last few years, but failure is not an option here.

"I lost you for a second there," he murmurs.

A spidery shiver slinks down her spine as his hand skims her back in precisely the right way to make her tremble against him. Her breathing goes shallow. "Just thinking. See, there are some touches I can resist, and others are a bit harder. I'd like to know which is which before I do something unforgivable."

He bends his forehead to hers, and the entire room floats away like cloud. "Oh yeah?" he rasps. "Like what?"

Like lean up a few inches and close the gap between our lips. Like run my hands over your surprisingly broad shoulders and dive into your messy curls, molding myself into you even more than I already am. Like maybe fall in love with you for real.

All things Freya can't do because no matter who she looks like tonight, no matter that they're going home together, underneath the makeup and glamour, she will always be Freya. Playing pretend is one thing, but she needs some distance before she lets herself get devoured by him and something that can never be real.

Swallowing the regret-shaped lump in her throat, she asks, "Is Mandi really such a lightweight?"

His brows scrunch, and his eyes laser into Freya's with an expression of disbelief. "You really want to talk about her right now?"

There's a hint of warning in his voice that they shouldn't be discussing "her" in the third person with so many people around, but there's also confusion.

"Yes." *No.*

Oh, she doesn't know anymore.

It's always been electric when she's near Taft, but something tonight has shifted. Life was simpler when all she had to worry about was losing her contract, not her heart. The undivided attention of his stare makes her feel a little unfocused and fidgety. Not how she felt before in the dress, but in a new and different way.

Taft takes a half step back, hands dropping to his sides. "She's mindful of how our lifestyle can lead to excess."

"Smart. I should probably cut myself off, then," Freya says, not totally convinced she's just talking about the booze.

"Probably a good idea," he agrees. "That's how slip-ups happen."

"Are they still looking at us?"

"They're looking at *you*. They have been all night." He hesitates, and then adds in a voice so quiet it's meant for her and her alone, "Freya."

Startled, her eyes shoot to his. "They see what they want to see."

Taft's voice is a low caress. "Maybe them. But I see *you*."

CHAPTER TWELVE

Taft misses the feel of her at his side. Soft curves pressed against him, trusting him.

Somehow—and he still can't figure out how—he spooked her. Been too earnest, too real. After they paid Jen all the requisite birthday niceties, Freya muttered something about working best on her own, splitting them up to divide and conquer, and jetted off to drop more bread crumbs of their happiness around the room.

Celebrities are faster than the Internet when it comes to hot gossip, and right now #WeWillGoDownWithThisRaft is seconds away from trending on Twitter. And it was all thanks to the girl across the room, fake-laughing at some probably inane witticism from a familiar tanned action hero–looking dude with a square jaw and three inches on Taft.

Keeping Freya to himself had been a damn good plan. He hadn't been *entirely* selfish. Using their coziness as a lure to smother all rumors of his alleged cheating worked like a charm.

Unfortunately, any good lure relies completely on the bait. And in this case . . .

He narrows his eyes at the growing group of men paying court to the girl they think is Mandi. If he wasn't so irritated, he'd snicker at their transparency. Going by the expressions on some of their faces, they clearly forgot he exists and are plotting how best to woo his girl.

Hold up. *His* girl? Since when has he felt like that?

Taft tries to triangulate the origin of that thought: the club, his house, the bookshop.

Somehow, in all three places where he's had significant meaningful interaction with Freya, she's become someone he wants to hold on to. She's reckless, somewhat morally dubious, a complete and *total* threat to his career, and . . . the most exhilarating woman he's ever known.

It doesn't help that Mandi insisted Freya wear that dress tonight. He's always been an emerald-green man the way some men are ass or boob men, but he's starting to reevaluate that.

He's a *Freya*-in-emerald-green man.

He knows she thinks it's borrowed from Mandi's closet, one of the many outfits that haven't yet been repeated, and he hadn't corrected the assumption. Mandi had actually purchased the gown specifically for Freya, and maybe a little bit for him, too—she knows how much he loves the color. She'd asked him to send full-length photos of Freya wearing the dress for her approval. Mandi might have been the one to send back a wall of heart-eyes emojis, but he knows Freya saw the stars in *his* when he lowered the phone.

Taft didn't agree with adding more pressure on Freya on her first big night, but Mandi thinks Freya will take it more seriously if she thinks Mandi has already hightailed it out of LA to her North Carolina Airbnb rental. In actuality, Mandi's staying nearby for a few more days, just in case. She believes Freya can do this, but she doesn't trust her not to mess up as a way out. If Freya gets busted, Mandi needs to sweep in to pretend this was all an amusing publicity stunt so she and Taft can save face.

Granted, he doesn't know Freya *that* well, but Taft doesn't think she'll screw them all like that. He suspects that, despite evidence to the contrary, when she gives her word, she doesn't give it lightly.

He's so in his own head that it takes him a moment to realize Freya's wiggling her fingers at him as if to say, *Yeah, that's my boyfriend over there.* She's holding her body taut, like she's primed for flight, and the muscles around her fake smile are strained.

The guy she's talking to follows the movement and sizes him up.

Taft manages a brittle smile before walking over. He's sure he didn't miss the look of blatant relief on Freya's face. He drapes his arm across her shoulders, letting his hand dangle possessively over her chest, a breath away from touching. "Mind if I steal my girl for a second?"

He sweeps her away without waiting for an answer.

"Thank you," she says through an exhale. "He was such a creep. Came onto me *so* obviously, ugh. Up close he looks even more plastic than a Ken doll. I think he was trying to feel out how monogamous we are."

A prickle of heat roots in his chest. Fuck, this is his fault for not keeping a closer eye on her like he teased he would. He should have paid more attention to who she was with and anticipated some of the sleazier guys trying to make their move.

"Is my lipstick still okay?" She waves a hand at her mouth, pulling him away from his self-recrimination. "No smudging?"

Damn if she isn't adorable even when she's using him as her compact mirror.

He pretends to study her. "Mmm, maybe a little."

"Oh no," she whispers, looking a little flustered. "This always happens."

"I've got you." Taft takes the golden opportunity to gently trace the dip in her Cupid's bow. He doesn't rush, his thumb brushing slowly but deliberately over sensitive flesh.

Even with her heels, he's almost a head taller than her. He doesn't miss the way Freya stiffens, but she doesn't pull away. The space between their bodies disappears. Nothing about this moment is meant for an audience, and suddenly, Taft hates that they have one.

Freya's whiskey-colored eyes swallow him whole, her red lips parted in something that looks a lot like wonder.

He has to try not to frown. Has she never been touched this reverently before?

"Are you done?" she asks, words scarcely above a whisper.

Oh, baby, not even close. He honestly can't imagine a world in which he'd ever have enough of her.

His voice is almost as hoarse as hers when he responds. "Yeah. You're all set. So, uh, guess he didn't succeed in charming you away from me, huh?"

Freya draws herself up, looking a little offended. "Gross, no. I don't fall for dubious charms."

That seems to satisfy the spiky monster in his chest. "Oh. Well. Good."

"Fending off unwanted advances is ravenous work." Somehow, her smile still manages to sparkle. "Accompany me to the hors d'oeuvres table?"

I'd accompany you anywhere perches on the tip of his tongue, but he holds back, pretty sure she doesn't want to be hit on right now.

"I could eat," he says, letting her tug him in that direction.

He relishes the feel of her smaller fingers curling around his forearm, and he wonders what would happen if he took her hand in his, instead.

"You know," she says conversationally, "I can never type 'hors d'oeuvres' right on the first try. In the new book I'm working on, I call them 'canapés' to get around spelling it."

Her admission catches him off guard, and he chuckles. "'Appetizers' would be an even easier work-around."

"Yes, but can I even call myself a writer if I don't find a prettier word to use when a simple one would suffice?" She stuffs a caramelized mushroom-and-onion tartlet in her mouth, puff pastry crackling. "Oh, and if you see me reaching for anything that has Brie, any kind of baby animal, or goat cheese on it, please stop me. I *will* projectile vomit."

Taft smiles. "Consider me warned. And at your service."

He places extra emphasis on the last word just to make her blush, maintaining eye contact until she's the first to look away. Color rises from her upper chest, crawling up her neck in a wild-strawberry flush. He desperately desires to follow it to see how far down it goes—he hopes it doesn't show on his face.

"Speaking of, thanks for playing my white knight earlier." Freya nibbles a chocolate-dipped mandarin slice sprinkled with coarse sea salt. Her tongue darts out to the corner of her mouth just in time to catch a piece of salt.

Taft wishes his hand were there instead. *Fuuuuuck.*

"Thankfully you understood my SOS," she continues. "Every time I tried to come up with a reason to leave, he asked me another question. He was super keen to get me on his show."

Taft clenches his jaw. *Yeah, I'll bet.*

"That's not happening," he growls, grabbing at a watermelon-and-prosciutto skewer. He holds it like he wants to stab it into someone and he has a damn good idea who.

Freya surprises him by grinning. The anger immediately dissipates when she looks at him like that. She reaches up on her tiptoes to whisper in his ear, "Oh, I know. I handled it. Mandi would have been proud."

He cocks his head, lips pursing in question.

Her grin turns into a devious smirk. "I told him his show wasn't a good fit for my brand."

Taft busts out laughing. "That's cold. And perfect."

She seems inordinately pleased with herself, tossing her head back in a giggle. "I thought so, too."

Taft flicks his gaze to her slender neck before he can stop himself. He forces himself to smile like everything is normal and he isn't about to combust. "A devastating comeback. Do you always go straight for the jugular?"

She winks at him. "Let's just say writers are *really* good at finding killer inspiration."

Pride and arousal awaken, unspooling low in his gut. He savagely stomps them down.

What the hell was Mandi thinking, giving her this dress? Freya-in-emerald-green is his kryptonite in the best-worst way.

He's never believed in love at first sight, but he suspects he's been a goner ever since he saw her behind the counter at Books & Brambles, scowling at him behind her big blue glasses.

Jesus, he needs to lock his shit down, and fast.

CHAPTER THIRTEEN

"Our Instagram post got more likes than Jennifer's," Freya says around an enormous yawn, padding into Taft's kitchen the next morning with a laptop under one arm and her phone in the other. She flashes him the screen, covered in a wall of messages. "Mandi's thrilled—" She breaks off in another yawn.

She doesn't cover her mouth, which is sweetly endearing, until he realizes her tank top has slid up a few inches. He catches a tantalizing but all-too-brief glimpse of a toned stomach before she drops her arm.

With supreme force of will, Taft drags his eyes back up to her face. "I made breakfast."

"The amazing smell woke me up," she admits. "I'm still so exhausted I could have slept until— Shit, it's already noon?"

Her sleep-rough groan goes straight to his cock. "Okay, not a big deal. Call it brunch."

"No, I had *plans*." She sinks into a chair, propping her elbows up on the kitchen table.

"If you're talking about you-and-me plans, we're good until this evening."

"Are you sure we can't get out of going to Phoebe's 'cerebral' thing tonight? I mean, she *called* it art house, but let's be honest, it sounded like a home movie."

Taft slices into the still-hot Spanish omelet—filled with potatoes and a little onion—and plates it, along with ripe raspberries and a few sprigs of mint from his windowsill. "How is it that you've known Mandi's friends all of five minutes and you're already just as petty about them as she is?"

"I'm not— Sorry, am I?" Freya winces. "Phoebe's lovely. Really. I suppose I just had an idea that this would feel less like, well, work. Which I already had quite a lot of, frankly."

"Hey, no skin off my nose," he replies easily. "Mandi's friends, not mine."

She pushes her laptop away to make room. "Do I get to meet yours next?"

"Uh." He thinks about Connor and the other castmates he hasn't caught up with in person for a while. Weeks. Months? What kind of adult man doesn't have friends? "Maybe," he hedges.

If she noticed his brief hesitation, it's forgotten the second he slides her plate over. Her eyes widen with delight, and she immediately lops off the pointy tip of the omelet with her fork.

But unlike him, she doesn't eat it first.

"The tip of literally everything—cheesecake, frittatas, cake—is the best part," she explains, pushing it to the side of her plate when she sees his curious, amused smile. "I want to save it for last."

"Just call me the nonjudging breakfast club," he jokes. She's fucking adorable. Saving it for last. Hell, he'd chop off the tips of all the other slices and serve it to her if she wants. Should he offer? Would that be weird? "Er. Brunch club."

Impish humor lights up her eyes. "That movie had nothing to do with breakfast, but I won't quibble with any man who makes me potatoes for breakfast."

He hides his smile with a strategic sip of fresh-squeezed orange juice. "And I know better than to even attempt verbal sparring when my partner uses 'quibble' in normal conversation."

"I have a vast vocabulary, and I refuse to be verb-shamed," she says, straight-faced.

"Yeah, I'm familiar with your particular lexicon," he drawls. "You were swearing up a storm last night. Did you manage to get out of your dress okay?"

Freya pinks immediately. "You mean you didn't take it off? I'm a little hazy."

She's eyeing him so worriedly that while his first inclination is to tease her, he knows they're nowhere near there. Yet.

"You asked me to help undo the back zip," says Taft. "Then you changed your mind and said something about setting boundaries."

Relief blooms over her face. "Oh good. *That* I remember."

"Then you tried to kiss me." He smiles at the memory. "You fell over."

She blanches and drops her full fork on her plate. "Those damn heels."

"May have had more to do with the champagne fountain," he says wryly.

"I overdid it," she realizes, covering her mortified face with her hands. "I swear, I meant it when I cut myself off. I just got so nervous with everyone asking questions about us, and obviously there *is* no us, or rather there is, but—" She takes a deep breath. "I just kicked one bad habit, I don't need to add another. I promise it won't happen again."

"Freya, you're not in trouble," he says a little incredulously. "I left you to it and eventually—after a lot of cursing, and at one point I think you stubbed your toe—you clearly wriggled out of the dress."

He wonders if it's puddled on the floor next to his bed. Not *quite* the way he'd wanted to divest her of it, but still, the idea of Freya fast asleep, his sheets wrapped around her, is heady.

"We didn't get back home until after two a.m. You were wiped but not that drunk. Eat, it'll all come back to you. You didn't lose sight of our game plan. We did a good job."

She nods and sits up a little straighter. "Oh, I didn't realize until I woke up that you gave me your bedroom. You didn't have to do that, I can totally take your guest room."

"Oh, um, you'll be more comfortable in mine." Quickly, he adds, "*Eat*. You need sustenance after last night. Boyfriend prerogative."

Freya picks up her fork and *finally* takes her first bite. "Best boyfriend ever," she moans around a mouthful. "Where did you learn to cook?"

"My mom. She was determined that her sons know their way around the kitchen. I guess she got fed up with my dad pretending not to know how to do anything to get out of helping."

There's a hint of a frown on Freya's face, but she just nods. "So you have brothers?"

Taft swallows a mouthful of soft, succulent potato and egg. "Three."

"I actually already knew that. Wikipedia." She glances down at her plate and mutters, "Great. Waste of a question." At his curious look, she explains, "I was thinking we could try getting to know each other for real. Like you suggested. I know you don't really have to know *me*, but—"

"I'd love to." He chews thoughtfully. "Might help if you ask me things you can't google, though."

"Well, it seemed like an organic way to segue into it." Freya spears another piece of omelet and wraps her lips around it in a way he's quite sure she doesn't intend to be seductive.

It's just egg and potato, nothing to get excited about. He directs this to his groin.

"Tell you what, there's a technique my mom told me to try when I was younger and had some trouble making friends," Taft says when

Freya starts to roll a raspberry up around her plate with a slim pointer finger. "She said it was impossible for someone not to like you once they know ten secrets about you."

"Uh, hate to break it to you, but you already know my biggest one." She pops the berry in her mouth with a loud smacking sound. "Hi, I'm Mandi!" she chirps in a comically bad falsetto.

He hides his smile. "Small secrets. Familiarities that no one would know about you unless they *really* knew you. And it has to be stuff that isn't the same for everyone. No generic bullshit. Like no saying you love finding a lost bill in your jeans pocket or getting an extra nugget in your ten-piece."

Freya tears a mint leaf into shreds over what's left of her omelet. "Isn't that cheating? Fast-forwarding through the getting-to-know-you fun stuff?" She hesitates. "But I guess we aren't really dating, so . . . Yeah, I guess we can try. Can't hurt to arm ourselves with more info, right?"

Taft ignores the twinge in his heart. "I'm willing to bet it wouldn't even take ten things to make someone like you."

She gives him an awkward little smile, like she highly doubts that likelihood. "Oh, you know, this is a lot like how I develop my characters."

"Yeah?" He can't lie, he's interested in the overlap.

"When I'm still in the sandbox stage, figuring out all my pieces and how they fit together, one of the first things I do is come up with ten interesting things about them. But like you said, it has to be really personal to them." Freya makes a face. "No favorite colors—that is a terrible icebreaker—but I know yours is green."

"Ah, see, now there's something specific." He grins. "You have strong feelings about icebreakers."

She plays along. "And what fascinating insight into my psyche does that tell you?"

"I don't know you nearly well enough to psychoanalyze you, but I'd probably infer that you're someone who doesn't do bullshit. You don't want perfect, practiced answers. You want to wade through all the ugly and get it wrong ninety-nine times so you can find the right one on the hundredth. That's why you haven't written your second book yet, right? You're committed to getting it right."

For the longest moment, Freya doesn't say anything. She just looks stunned. Taft's horrified that he's said something to offend her, something that it's now too late to take back, which is the exact opposite of what he'd intended.

God, what had made him think he knew her enough for an on-the-spot dissection? And the *way* he'd just babbled all of that, as though he were trying to impress a teacher with the right answer. No *wonder* she's looking at him like she can't quite believe it.

The weight on his chest lifts when she gifts him with an open smile. "You're right. I'm the Marie Kondo 'I love mess' meme personified. I may not use everything in the story, but the backstory percolates in my brain. Grounding technique to make them real. The important stuff will find a way." She laughs somewhat self-deprecatingly. "Sometimes I don't even see how it finds its way in until my fifth read."

He's aghast. "You read your book five times? And you don't get sick of it?"

After *Once Bitten*, he stopped watching his scenes. There's a cognitive dissonance he can't escape when he watches himself be someone else on television, and unlike his football-obsessed father and brothers, he can't watch the same plays over and over for research. He doesn't even like rereading books, but he can bet that Freya does.

"Five *at least*." There isn't a hint of exaggeration in her earnest voice. "Trust me, when you're an author you never sit down to write a book without being completely in love. It's torture sitting your butt down to write if you resent every minute of it."

He's still wrapping his mind around reading your own words that many times. "Does that happen to you a lot?"

She hesitates, seeming to weigh something. "I haven't been able to write my second book. I've tried, like, so many times. Changed my habits up. I went to a different New York coffee shop every day. I changed my manuscript font from Times New Roman to Comic Sans—which was *horrific*, by the way. I seem to always hit this threshold beyond which I lose all motivation to continue, and I start over. Delete everything. I stopped counting my drafts a long time ago. Pretty sure I give my agent nervous shits, although of course Alma's way too nice to say so, and— Wait, why are you looking at me like that?"

The question falls from his lips before he can stop himself. "How are you so okay letting things go?"

She snorts. "Once biggies like your career circle the drain, it's easy."

He doesn't want an easy answer, he wants a how-to manual. Her offhand attitude runs contrary to absolutely everything Taft believes. He slowly blinks. "Doesn't it hurt? Those words were part of you. Something you created."

Freya nibbles her lower lip like she's giving it serious thought. "I mean, yeah, of course. It's supposed to hurt. If it didn't, it would be meaningless, and isn't that worse? Think about it like this: Yes, I worked hard on those words, but if they weren't working for the story, they're keeping me stuck someplace where I can't grow. I'm always going to be rooted exactly where I am, trying to work around what's already there instead of finding a new way forward that's the right fit for me."

He sits with that for a second. He has to revise his earlier assumption: she's not cavalier; she's pragmatic. He could admire it more if he didn't find her just a little bit terrifying.

What must it be like to be that all or nothing? Freeing, he supposes, but he can't imagine that mindset for himself. Compromise is how he got where he is now.

Freya pushes her empty plate away. "Um, I guess that counts as one of my ten things?"

Her expectant face tells him it's his turn.

Taft strives to think of something personal that isn't too heavy. "I love when dogs have people names."

Her eyes light up. "Me too! It's adorable. My turn again?" Her nose scrunches in thought. "Why is it so hard to come up with something that I want to share that isn't, like, too revealing? We *do* have to live with each other after this, so you can't know all the juicy things about me, like that I think Funfetti is basically the best cake ever and I eat it with no frosting like a heathen."

"I'll count it," he says with a grin. "But Funfetti? Really? I need to refine that palate."

"Shut up, it's the cake of my childhood," Freya grumbles good-naturedly. "My family isn't big into baking. My mom was an amazing cook, but the gene didn't exactly—" She stops. "Your turn."

"Uh, okay. I haven't told anyone this before . . ."

"Are you sure you want to tell me?"

He keeps his tone as light as hers. "Do I need to swear you to secrecy?"

"My lips are sealed," she quips, flashing a smile.

"So, filming *Banshee*, both the movie and the show, it was such a massive production, you know? Which was great, and really humbling, to be part of something that had *that* kind of scale. When I was working, the energy was great, but it was also a lot of waiting around for them to need me. The hours were . . . frustrating. And since I always had to be on set and we were on location in Dartmoor, there were opportunities I couldn't pursue here at home."

Freya hums in acknowledgment, so Taft continues. "I'd love to get into indie films, find a script I really believe in. Get back to my craft. Do something with less CGI. But that's basically all I get to audition for lately. I just want to change people's perceptions of what I can do as an actor. I want to be more than the 'hot teenage boyfriend'—I have range, but I'm never going to be able to prove it unless I do something different. At least on *Banshee* I'm more or less playing my age."

"No more supernatural stuff," she says succinctly. "You want to redefine your career?"

"I mean, I'm twenty-seven. It's already a stretch playing a teenager, and I'm only getting older."

"When has that ever stopped a show?" she jokes. "But, seriously, good for you. Life's too short not to do the things that move you."

"Like you and writing. We wouldn't do these jobs if we didn't love it, even when it's the worst."

"I do love it," Freya says with a smile that Taft can only interpret as bittersweet. "Sometimes I feel like even though I have the only job in the world I'd ever want, I haven't earned it. Like a better writer who'd earned their stripes more than I had wouldn't feel so stuck all the time. I got my first book deal young—really young. And everything was different then. Now that it's just me on my own, I feel like . . . like I'm rowing out to sea in a shabby rowboat that's leaking water, and all I have to paddle with is a broken oar, and I'm desperately trying not to go under before reaching land."

Taft turns her phrase over in his mind. She has a way with words that he envies, but he gets the feeling that if he tells her that, she'll assume he's just saying it to cheer her up. "You're not alone in feeling that way. Your friends . . . do they understand? Do you have other writers you can talk to?"

She seems to have people in her life. Family in LA. Does she really think she has to struggle alone?

Her expressive face shutters. "It's your turn," she says in lieu of an answer.

She doesn't owe him one, so Taft doesn't push, understanding that maybe she's said more than she intended to. It makes his heart race, knowing that he has that effect on her.

Reciprocating her honesty, he says, "I don't really know how to talk to my dad." A micro-expression of sympathy flits over her face. "I know he was disappointed that I chose acting. He never really came out and said it, but . . . My older brothers are all pretty macho straight dudes. They're the sons he knows how to talk to, all cut from the same cloth. I know he loves me, but sometimes I can't shake the feeling that he would have preferred if I'd failed out here and had to go home to be an assistant coach or something."

"You deserve to know he's proud of you," she says quietly. "But your mom? She's supportive?"

"Of everything I've ever wanted," he says without needing to think about it. "So it's not like I have it bad or anything. It would be nice if he watched something of mine and said he enjoyed it. I don't know."

She levels a *You do know* look at him. "I've watched everything you've ever been in. Not in a creepy way, I swear! I was literally a teenager, and you happened to act in all the shows I loved. Your characters have always been my favorites."

His heart swells. "Yeah?"

Suddenly, she can't meet his gaze. "Yeah."

"I cling to things too hard," he says after a centuries-long moment. "People, too. I put them first, and I don't always get it back. Instead of cutting my losses, I hold on tighter."

Other than Mandi, I don't think I have any real friends is what he doesn't allow himself to say. *Are you and I friends?* is even more humiliating.

How do you ask the girl you're (fake) dating if she wants to be friends with you for real?

Freya frowns. "What you want out of a relationship—romantic or platonic—doesn't matter any less than what the other person wants."

No one has ever told him that before. He isn't sure he agrees, but she says it with such confidence that he really, really wants to.

A sharp bark breaks into his reverie.

Freya's eyes are wide. "Why did that sound like it came from our house?"

"Uh, about that." He scratches the back of his neck. "Mandi did say my place had enough room for two more, remember?"

Her eyebrows furrow. "Yeah, me and yo— *Nooooo*," she breathes, realization crashing into her eyes. "Hen?"

"He's in the backyard. He's a good boy, but he's probably missing Mandi. She brought him by an hour ago. I'll bring him in so you can take him for a walk and get acquainted."

"I—a walk—alone—with him?" She sputters. "Taft, wait!"

He halts halfway in getting up.

"Mandi's dog hates me," she says flatly.

"No, he doesn't. He just doesn't know you yet. Give him some time to—"

"I understand why she left me her boyfriend and her wardrobe, but I draw the line at inheriting her pet, too!"

In response to Freya's high pitch, Henry barks again with twice the gusto.

"He's a German wirehaired pointer," says Taft. "Generally speaking, as a breed it does takes a while for them to warm up. Hell, Sir Henry didn't even like *me* much at first."

She shakes her head, still unconvinced. There's a mutinous set to her mouth.

"You're the girl who walked into a nightclub wearing a fuck-me dress like there was no doubt you belonged there," he reminds her. "Don't tell me you're scared of a standoffish dog?"

She stares at him. "So . . . Secret number four. I have a healthy respect for dogs."

Shit. That's code for scared of dogs.

"Okay. Well, we're going to have to do something about that." Taft gets up, aware her eyes follow him as he heads for the rattan side table by the front door where some of Hen's stuff is stowed in a drawer. "It's going to look weird if you don't spend time with him."

"I can't take him for a walk," she says as she follows him to the foyer. When she crosses her arms, Taft is treated to a lovely view of her pushed-out breasts. "I have work to do."

"Babe, you have to remember that you have two men in your life now," he says, trying not to laugh as he rummages around.

The endearment just slips out, but it feels right. He wonders what she might reciprocate with if she was in an affectionate mood, if she has a favorite already or needs to try each one on for size. He can't wait to find out.

"Cut the crap, Bamber," Freya grumbles.

"Funny you should say that . . ." He turns around with the leash in one hand and a blue plastic baggie in the other.

She zeroes in on the baggie, wrinkling her nose. "Aww, babe," she says in a Splenda-sweet simper, batting her thick black lashes at him. "You are so full of shit."

CHAPTER FOURTEEN

I t isn't lost on Taft that Freya does not take Henry for a walk that day or any of the next. He picks up her slack, walking Hen himself, and chooses to find her stubbornness lovable instead of exasperating.

Instead, every day, she diligently settles herself down at his dining table or on the green velvet sofa with her laptop, rather adorably nicknamed Hunka Junk, and types in such a ceaseless stream that it crosses his mind once or twice that she might be getting paid by the word.

She shoos him away every time he tries to peek at her word count, but he notices that if Hen claims the opposite end of the sofa, paws almost touching her feet, she—after a few frightened glances over the top of her screen—doesn't withdraw her toes. Progress, Taft thinks with pride. Both on her book *and* with the dog.

With her imagination, the other stuff comes a lot easier to her: she's bubbly and charming in their practiced Instagram Live "We Moved in Together!" living-room tour. To Mandi and their managers' glee, their movie-date pics rack up a ton of likes and comments when Freya's camera timer catches her tossing caramel corn in his mouth. But none of that holds a candle to the way their notifications blow up at the cuteness of their soggy appearance on a sunny afternoon giving Hen a rather disastrous bath. Clearly, pet pics are always a winner.

She insists on doing the dishes every time he cooks and alternating buying groceries at the farmers market, even though he doesn't think it's necessary. She'd blistered something about not being a burden when he'd tried to broach it, though. If it makes her happy, he will happily let her pitch in for whatever her heart desires.

They've fallen into the picture of domesticity ever since their first breakfast together, which was possibly the nicest morning-after Taft's ever had. Not that he's had any lately with a contractual commitment hanging over his head, but still. Having Freya there is nice.

Even though he wakes up on the couch each day with a stiff back, he doesn't mind. He enjoys making the coffee every morning, knowing the nutty aroma of freshly ground beans brewing will lure her out of sleep like a beacon.

"Taft!" she almost shrieks now when she sees his feet sticking out over the arm of the velvet sofa. "I thought you were sleeping in the spare room?"

He blinks blearily at her, waking up an entirely different kind of stiff. This Freya seems to be yelling at him, while the one in his dream was doing other, far more pleasurable things with her mouth. "Go 'way," he mumbles, grateful that he's conscious enough to adjust the blanket over his hips. "Sleeping."

"Yes, and very uncomfortably from the looks of it."

He barely registers the note of censure in her voice before the cushions dip and the warmth of her backside presses against his ribs as she wedges herself onto the sliver of the sofa's edge.

His eyes fly open. "What are you doing?"

She's scowling down at him, and he immediately holds his breath in case it's gross.

"Taft, I assumed the spare room was a guest bedroom. Or at least had a futon!"

"Until now, I've been so busy in Dartmoor that I haven't had the chance to furnish it. Anyway, no one's visited me here, so . . . There's just some boxes and weights in there."

"I *shudder* to think what this is doing to your back. I would never have accepted your bedroom if—"

His hand shoots out to grasp her wrist. "Let me stop you right there. There is no way I'm making a woman spend the night on the sofa while I sleep in a bed."

Freya opens her mouth, presumably to argue some more, but he surges up, now fully awake. Whatever she was going to say is swallowed by a squeak as her hand comes into contact with his bare chest. "Are you *naked*?"

He can't decide if she's horrified or interested. Either way, she hasn't blinked for at least twenty seconds. He grunts and readjusts the blanket with his free hand. "I'm wearing boxers."

Her palm smells like the coffee she's probably just finished stirring, the botanical face serum she uses every night, and, curiously, the faint woody muskiness he associates with libraries. He wants to distill it into a bottle that he can carry around with him always.

Rosy from sleep and fresh-faced like this, she looks more like herself than she has in days. Her eyelashes are naturally long and curled even without those ridiculous falsies.

I want to wake up to this woman every day.

He glances down. "Um, would you mind?"

Freya's cheeks flame. "You'll need to let me go, first."

"Right," he says hoarsely.

That makes sense. That is reasonable. That . . . would require his muscles to cooperate, first.

She stares at his fingers lightly clasping her wrist. "You still haven't—"

He lets her go.

Without her warmth, he feels cold and bereft, even though the temperature is perfect. He can't shake the urge to press his lips over her pulse point and make her squeak again.

To inhale the scent of her skin like he has every right to. Resentment seethes in his chest that he doesn't. He wants her, but he doesn't get to have her.

He's never hated that ironclad contract binding him and Mandi together more.

"Actually, I have an idea." Freya tilts her head, considering him for a long moment before offering her hand. "Do you trust me?"

His head gets stuck pulling on the shirt he tossed on the back of the sofa, hiding his smile. She could have extended a man-eating crocodile and he would still have latched on with a thank-you. "Yes," he says simply, surprised to discover how very much that's the truth.

There was no other answer, and yet he knows it's the right one when a pleased flush steals over her cheeks. "Come to bed with me?"

"*Freya*," he chokes out.

"You're the one who said Gareth thinks we should be more affectionate in our posts."

She yanks him to his feet. He barely maintains his hold on the blanket.

Taft trails after her into the bedroom, still trying to work out what the fuck is happening, when she launches herself on his unmade bed, crawling on all fours to the headboard.

Sweet baby Jesus. He screws his eyes shut, but the image is burned onto his retinas.

Freya props both pillows against the headboard, unnecessarily fluffs them with vigorous fists, then pats the rumpled space next to her with one hand. Her phone is already in the other.

Gingerly, he joins her. "I know for a fact that filming a sex tape was *not* on Gareth and Moira's list," he states.

Besides not being his style to begin with, it wouldn't fit with his homespun golden-boy image, which was why the cheating rumors in particular were so damaging.

"That's a shame," Freya says casually. "It should have been."

Visuals flood his mind. He snatches at the sheet that's tossed at the foot of the bed, pulling it up to cover himself. This girl is going to short-circuit his brain if he's not careful.

"Think about it," she continues, oblivious to his suffering. "People *will* be scrutinizing our public appearances, dissecting every look and touch, no matter how convincing we are. But sweet little intimate moments are so much harder to fake. We're missing an opportunity here."

He blinks. She's never initiated an idea like *this* before.

"I know, I know," she says with a sigh. "I can't believe I'm suggesting this, either. In fact, self-preservation is screaming at me not to. But I'm part of this, and maybe it's the academically gifted kid in me, but I'm going to do a good job. All of this is happening to you *because* of me, anyway."

He gets that she's apologizing, but he can't bring himself to share her remorse, not when her actions brought her into his life in the first place.

"Go on, then," he says, waving a hand and affecting an expression of boredom. He will simply lie back and think of England. He will be stoic and self-controlled. He will ignore his raging boner and the soft, warm body of the gorgeous girl next to him. He will—

Freya's fingertips gently ghost over the hem of his shirt as she scoots closer.

The "Shit!" flies out of him in a sibilant hiss. His thoughts turn to honey, syrupy and slow, and his teeth ache with want. Scalding desire shoots through his entire body.

She rolls her eyes, but she's blushing. "I barely touched you, you big baby."

He huffs. If it wasn't for the hard-on making movement a bit difficult, he would have leaped out of bed and dashed straight for the bathroom to take care of the problem.

But that wouldn't resolve the bigger issue—the woman in his bed, the same one working her way determinedly into his heart. The one he'd love to call him *baby* without any less flattering adjectives before it.

She brushes her lips over his jawline, a bit scruffy from not shaving, but she doesn't seem to mind. If he turns his head just slightly, she would be kissing the corner of his mouth.

A thrill of pleasure races down his spine, but she breaks their connection the second she gets the picture. She hunches over to edit it, increasing the brightness and contrast. She'd snapped the shot from a height, giving her vaulted cheekbones and a plunging neckline.

And that's when he registers something that had been totally and utterly lost on him before. His gaze traces the contours of her shoulders and arms with possessive interest. "Are you . . ." He pauses when he hears the rough rasp of his voice. "Wearing my shirt?"

She's left it unbuttoned, revealing a creamy upper chest and a black bralette that offsets the white button-down to perfection.

Freya doesn't look up from the phone. "Yes. It helps sell it."

Taft throws his eyes to the ceiling and counts backward from ten. She's sadistic. She's trying to kill him. Slowly.

"You don't mind, do you?" She looks at him over her shoulder, worrying at her lower lip as she fidgets with the collar. "Sorry, I should have—"

"I like you wearing it," he interrupts.

There. It's out there now. All caution has been thrown to the wind.

He can't bring himself to regret it.

She hurriedly returns her attention to the phone. "Any idea for a caption?"

Without thinking about it, he lazily runs his knuckles over her spine. "I'm drawing a blank. Maybe ask Mandi?"

She tenses as if the suggestion annoys her. "Actually, I think I've got it."

"Perfect." He dances his fingertips higher up her back. Her shoulders tremble when he reaches the clasp of her bra, but he skims past her shoulder blades, reaching his final destination.

"Oh," she breathes when his fingers cocoon into her hair. She doesn't have to tell him to be careful of tangles, because he already is. *"Taft."*

Has anyone ever said his name like that before? It's impossible, but he hardens further.

It's not just physical attraction. He relishes the quiet intimacy, the precariousness of their situation. Dangling over a cliff's edge, teetering toward a fall.

And he can't deny that it's a heady triumph having a little payback right now, to know she's as affected by him as he is with her mere existence. He *yearns* to take them both over the edge.

Taft closes his eyes, savoring these seconds before the connection is severed. His breath hitches as his heartbeat takes off at a wild gallop. Careers are on the line. Nothing more can ever happen between them as long as he's fake-dating Mandi. If Freya's identity comes out, the headline fallout would make what happened at the club look tame in comparison.

There's always *after*. A near future after the premiere in which he could date Freya out in the open. But the more he rolls it around in his mind, the hope sours into dry-mouth fear.

His staged relationship with Mandi isn't uncommon. Lots of celebrities do it to spark a little intrigue or for a promotional boost, but as soulless as it might be, at least the contract held the safety of certainty. With Mandi, he's never worried about any messy emotional feelings—his feels-too-much heart has been kept safe.

If he pursues things with Freya, she will be the first girl in years who has been *his* romantic choice. Taft will be vulnerable in a way he hasn't been with any other date since moving to LA.

He knows he's not a barnacle person, someone who everyone wants to stick with. He's never inspired clinging, not even when he was in school. His friends had always liked one another more than they liked him and graduated from Taft like he was a stepping-stone meant to be outgrown. There are times he sees it happening with Connor and, without *Banshee*, maybe even Mandi.

If Freya discards him, too . . .

As hard as it is, he fortifies his resolve and retracts his emotional drawbridge.

Freya's impromptu wake-up call was nice, but that's all it can be. *He can't do this.*

So what if Freya Lal is the woman who made his heart feel like that magical hold-your-breath moment before turning on the Christmas tree lights? Like recognizing the first five seconds of his favorite song playing somewhere totally random? Like untangling himself from a hug he isn't ready to let go of yet?

The day she entered his life, she changed the filter through which he viewed everything. The only problem Taft had with that was . . . did he want to feel that way?

These days, he isn't sure he's been *happy*, exactly, not like the carefree days when he was little and thought strangers were friends who had yet to meet him. But he was comfortable in his loneli—isolation. In his solitude. Where he was protected from the possibility of getting hurt. Protecting himself from possibilities, period.

And he suspects that once the haze of lust defogs her eyes, Freya's going to realize this isn't any more than a proximity crush for her. It happens on set all the time. He's seen on-screen relationships between costars break up the most solid of Hollywood marriages. It can be hard to untangle feelings when you spend so much time together every day.

Freya knows how to be Mandi, but he isn't sure whether she's ready to enter the fishbowl as herself—whether it's even *fair* for him to subject her to everything that comes with his life.

He decided on his path before he turned eighteen. He went into it, mostly, with his eyes open. Freya never did. Taft wants her, but he can't be selfish with her.

He desperately wishes he'd asked someone what would happen if he fell for someone else while he was in a showmance. What would happen if he fell for a non-celeb? He knows some of those relationships have stayed under the radar, but how? He wishes he'd even *thought* to ask.

If he's being honest, he wishes for a lot of things.

"You were right," Freya murmurs. "About what you said at the bookshop before I moved in. Getting closer, being friends for real. Needing to be more comfortable with each other. It was a good idea."

The reminder burns him. He's jeopardizing both his career and his heart for a girl he hasn't even *kissed* yet.

A girl whom he shouldn't even want to kiss, but he does, and what's more, it's all he can think about. The untapped desire lingers inside him, its very own level on Maslow's hierarchy of needs right up there with food and water.

He drops his hand, ignoring her soft whine and his own sense of loss.

"And as friends," he says stiffly, "we should set some ground rules."

She twists around to face him, sitting cross-legged. Her warm brown eyes are filled with surprise. "Rules for what?"

He gestures between them. "Getting through this."

With our hearts intact.

Taft glances down at the phone she still loosely holds, screen tilted to face him. The Texas-size lump in his throat grows. The caption reads: *Feelin' flirty this morning.*

Followed by a string of flower and heart emojis. It's sweet. Moira would lap it up and congratulate them for the thousands of comments and followers they're sure to get. Gareth would be impassive, which for him was as close to praise as they'd ever see.

Freya's unpracticed initiative is a masterstroke.

That's the worst thing about this, Taft realizes with a sinking heart. That together, they're actually *good* at the fakeness. Strategic, even. The dream team.

But his dream girl can stay only that—a dream.

CHAPTER FIFTEEN

So let's say I have this character," Freya says offhandedly a few days later. She waves her virgin Bloody Mary at her laptop screen, hoping it conveys how airy and hypothetical her question is.

Staring back at her from Zoom, her friends look exhausted from their own deadlines—is that spit-up on Ava's blouse?—but they all perk up, excited that Freya's finally letting them in.

She still has time before Taft and Hen get back from their walk, but she says the next words in a rush, just to be safe. "And she's into this guy, and she thinks he feels the same, but then he starts icing over after he lays down ground rules for their relationship. How should she, um, approach that? Without looking needy?"

They all start talking at once, until Mimi's voice cuts through. "What do you mean he 'lays down ground rules'?" She leans in, intrigued. "Are you writing alpha hero romance?"

"And can I read it?" Ava pipes up.

"*God*, Ava," Hero groans. "Freya, is it possible your protag misunderstood his signals?"

"No, there's no way I did!" The defense blasts out of Freya like cannon fire. She knows what she felt, and she's willing to bet the balance of her advance that he felt the same way. "I mean, I hope I didn't? Um, I mean, I hope I didn't write him unclearly. The love interest. In my book. That I'm writing."

Very natural, Freya. Not suspicious at all.

Something about the other morning scared Taft off, and not only can she not figure out what it was, but he doesn't even want to discuss it.

Right after she'd posted the Instagram photo—which worked *perfectly*, she might add—he'd abruptly insisted that they needed some ground rules: He emphatically stressed that casual intimate touches were forbidden unless it was for the benefit of an audience. They're strictly platonic roommates who don't share the same bed.

For any reason. Ever.

Also, clothing is to be worn at all times. *Our* own *clothes*, he'd added as an afterthought.

He didn't appreciate Freya shrugging off his shirt in annoyance two seconds later, or, if the smolder in his eyes had been anything to go by, he appreciated it maybe a little *too* much. It was a petty win, but she'd take it.

Steph frowns. "Why the hell would she let him decide this unilaterally? A relationship has two people. He has the right to make up his own mind but *zero* right to make her choice for her."

"Oh my god, yes. Thank you!" Mimi vigorously waves her glass of red wine at the screen. "Steph just put into words what my mind was too sloshed to come up with, and she is absolutely correct. Strong, independent women wouldn't take his shit without giving him a piece of their mind." She makes a fist and pretends to pop the screen.

Hero nods. "Is this for your new book? How far along are you? When's it due?"

The last two questions are often directed at pregnant Ava, so it takes Freya a second to realize they're all looking at her expectantly. She doesn't need to consult her phone calendar because the date is engraved into her brain, mentally circled in red as she counts down to D-Day: deadline day.

"I'm at the twenty-five-thousand hump, and I still have almost two weeks," Freya informs the Zoom group. "And before anyone asks, no, you can't read it. I'm keeping this one to myself for now."

"I thought we were your accountability buddies," Mimi says with a pout.

"No, I actually think it's smart you're trying something different," says Steph. "Shaking up a routine never did anyone harm."

"She literally moved from New York City to Los Angeles!" hoots Hero. "How much more shaking up does she need?"

Mimi smirks. "She def needs some sense shaken into her. Talking about her *fictional* love interest when she's cohabiting with a real one." She tsks at Freya.

"Yeah, right." If Freya's smile looks a little wooden, they'll probably just assume Zoom froze for a second, right? "He's not *my* love interest. He's with Mandi." Her friends know that she's the decoy girlfriend, but so far she's kept Taft and Mandi's fauxmance a secret.

This is a prime window for Ava to make one of her trademark horny comments, but for some reason, she refrains. Maybe her hormones are returning to baseline, or maybe it's her kid clamoring for attention, the sounds of his childish babble turning everyone's smiles a little gooey.

Steph notices, too. "Ava, are you growing up?" she teases.

Ava throws back her head and laughs. "Never," she promises, scooping her oldest into her lap, quieting his attention-seeking noises with a cuddle against her baby bump.

Freya lets out a discreet breath that she *totally* knew she was holding when the subject shifts to focus on her friends: Ava's and Mimi's upcoming books, Hero's latest graphic novel pitch and gorgeous sample illustrations, and the skin-loving goat's milk soap from Steph's sanctuary she's promised to send them.

Safe topics that lead away from the quicksand of Freya's life. She should be happier about it.

"Oh, and my publicist should be reaching out to all of you sometime soon about scheduling some in-conversation bookshop chats with me," says Ava. "It'll be good promo for you to talk a little bit about your new book, Freya. You didn't do any at Steph's last one."

Freya loves them for thinking of her, but honestly, it's not like she doesn't already know she's a pity ask.

"Yeah, people need a reminder you exist," says Mimi. Before it can hurt, she adds, "Get your booty back online! Social media only works if you're actually social."

Steph snorts. "Um, did you not just say *yesterday* that you can't wait until you're famous enough to leave Twitter for good? Besides, since I went updates-only, my mental health has been way better. Being an online personality isn't for everyone. I kinda miss the days when authors were mysterious, je ne sais quoi figures who couldn't be perceived."

"*Yes,* but when I said it, I didn't think anyone would remember," whines Mimi. "At least get on Instagram. It's way more chill, and the reader engagement is better."

"Look, we all know that except for a few TikTok wunderkinds who make me feel impossibly old and crusty, none of our hustle moves the needle as much as a publisher can," says Hero. "Kudos to anyone stepping away. That includes you, too, Freya. Being antisocial can be a form of self-care, too."

What? Startled, Freya chokes on a gulp of peppery tomato juice. "I'm not antisocial."

She guesses she can *kinda* see why they might think that. Since moving here, she hasn't exactly made any friends. Except Taft. And even that's looking iffy right now.

She knows they're all looking out for her, but it's like pulling teeth to be consistent on social media when she doesn't have any exciting news of her own to share. Freya will happily celebrate and share other people's milestones, but she can't wait for the day when it's her turn again.

Acknowledging her professional jealousy is healthy, but she never wants to corrode with resentment. All the good things she wishes for herself, she wants for her friends, too.

The group finishes their writing session with minimal interruptions—Freya's word count actually holding its own against her friends' for once—and before they all click out, they set their next group video chat. They used to have one regularly every Saturday, but with half of them busy with family stuff and encroaching deadlines, it got harder. Now it's just whenever they can all swing it.

Ava and Freya are the last to leave the virtual room.

Ava hangs back, fussing with the items on her desk with too much concentration to be anything but purposeful dillydallying. "Babe, I didn't want to put you on the spot by asking this before, but . . . you weren't asking us to help you work through a character problem, were you? It was about you and Taft."

Her voice is gentle, but it lands like a sledgehammer.

Here it is. Freya's chance. Her opening to let her friends in. "I . . . I don't know what you could possibly be implying."

"I'm not 'implying' anything," Ava says frankly. "Maybe Hero, Steph, and Mimi don't stalk his Instagram, but I have nothing better to do at three in the morning except raid the fridge with some serious pregnancy cravings and catch up on celebrity gossip. And I'm telling you, the way that man looks at you is not just for show. The pictures with Mandi are completely different. He looks at you like I look at pickles."

"He's an actor," Freya protests. "He's good at faking bedroom face."

But not with you. Before his total one-eighty, you could have sworn he wanted to—

No. Don't go there. That way lies more crushed dreams than Hollywood Boulevard.

Ava snorts, then says, a bit wistfully, "Something tells me if you're in the bedroom with him, nobody will be faking anything."

Freya completely has the same feeling. But her face gives nothing away as she says, "I'm going to pretend I didn't hear that, you absolute horndog!"

Ava's laugh is unrepentant. "What's it like being roommates with a celebrity?"

"Pretty much the same as living with anyone."

"He's a hot human male, so, uh, no, it's not the same."

"He has a girlfriend," Freya weakly points out, trying to keep up appearances.

Ava studies Freya like she's looking for a crack. "Freya, you're living main-character life right now. I can't say I'm not a little bit jealous. But now I can't help but think . . ."

Despite herself, Freya says, "Yeah?"

Ava's eyes are sad. "That whatever"—she waves her hands—"*this* is, it runs the risk of heartbreak for both of you. And when your role in this charade's all over and Mandi returns, you're going to have to deal with remembering that it was just a role for him, too."

Freya promised she wouldn't divulge this, but now it sort of feels like she has to. "Ava, this is for your ears only." At her nod, she tells her, "They're in a staged relationship to promote their movie. They're not in love with each other."

"So he's free to explore moments with you?"

Freya tries not to give anything away. "He's been . . . very respectful."

"Fuck that," Ava says without skipping a beat. "You should offer to run lines with him or something. In movies that always leads to sexy times."

"That's exactly why I haven't," Freya says with a groan. "We have this promotional photo shoot coming up for their movie, and I don't know how to tell him that the last time I was professionally photographed was my high school graduation pictures."

"Yikes. All the more reason to ask him to help you out." Ava waggles her eyebrows. "Maybe in more ways than one."

"I'm fake-dating someone who's fake-dating someone else! This is bad advice!" Freya yelps. "You're supposed to tell me not to be seduced by his charms because he doesn't know what he wants yet."

Ava snorts. "I think that ship has sailed. Anyway, I think he probably does know what he wants. That's why he suddenly wants rules, right? He's *scared* to want what he wants. But when his movie is out and he's a free man . . . maybe the two of you can get together?"

Freya's eyes widen. "He hasn't made me any promises. I don't *expect* anything."

Ava's knowing look pierces straight into her soft, squishy heart. They both know what Freya desires, even if she can't admit it out loud, not even to Ava. If she speaks into existence what she wants—who she wants—it'll hurt even more if she can't be with him.

"I don't know him the way you do," says Ava. "So maybe I'm talking out of my ass, but maybe he thinks keeping his distance is the smart call here. I mean, your situation is kinda like *Love Island*."

Freya's amused. "We're not walking around half dressed. Even before the rules, I wouldn't have."

"Not like that!" Ava snorts. "Think about it, in 'real life,' if either of you got the ick, you'd go your separate ways and wouldn't have to see each other again. But continuing to live together for weeks, even when it hurts to be around the other person . . . when you crave to kiss them and be with them again . . ."

Freya starts, mind picking up where Ava trailed off. That's a good point. She hadn't stopped to consider that her feelings would still be there even after she returned to Stori's. That *his* would be, too.

Taft is, she knows, above all else, a romantic at heart. Even in a contractual relationship, his desire to deeply know another person and be known in return is undeniable. He would hand over his heart in an instant—which is exactly why she can't take it. Because even though they live in the same city, they're worlds apart, and she doesn't want either of them to know what it's like to have their heart beating so far away, living lives that never quite intersect.

She's a writer, so, naturally, she knows the most eloquent way to respond.

"Shit," she says.

Ava's mouth tugs into a sympathetic smile. "It's scary to dive into something new when it might not work out and you'll still have to see each other every day. No one wants to be the lovesick islander moping around the villa," she imparts, all wise and sage.

As Freya absorbs Ava's advice in silence, the sound of the front door opening is shockingly loud.

The boys are back.

"Ava, I've gotta go," she says as she hears Hen's paws scrabble across the wood floor.

"I don't want you to get hurt. Seeing this through is going to be hard." Ava looks like she wants to say more, but in the end she settles for a long sigh. "I don't envy you."

Freya almost ask her what she means, but then she realizes she understands. She holds up two fingers in a pinkie promise. "I won't. Books over boys."

That's the way it has to be. She's convinced of it now.

TAFT CATCHES THE tail end of Freya's conversation when he returns home. He knew about the writing sprints and made sure to leave the house for a few hours to give her privacy. As he kicks off his shoes and puts away Hen's leash, his lips quirk into a smile.

"Books over boys" is such *a Freya thing to say*, he thinks fondly as Hen trots off to greet her. Her stacks of books have started to cover most of the surfaces in his living room, bookmarked with envelopes filled with her looping scrawl. No scrap of paper is safe.

He rather adores his charmingly frugal pack rat of a roommate.

Roommate. The word sticks in his craw, ill-fitting and not the way he sees her at all, despite his best efforts. Taft's mouth twists. But that's all she can be. His rules had made sure of that.

And he's regretted it every minute since.

Before, he might have jokingly announced, "Honey, I'm home!" The words still find their way to his tongue. He stuffs them back down his throat. Nope, not happening.

It's nowhere as easy to ignore how he feels about her, though. Especially when the evidence is everywhere. His eyes skip over the writerly paraphernalia: the mood-setting licorice-and-lavender soy candle, the motivational word count tracker filled with gold stars for every one-thousand milestone reached, and a nearly empty pack of Haribo gummy bears. She's saved all the green ones . . . for him?

Finally, his gaze settles on the moss-and-magenta-striped blanket Freya wraps around her shoulders on cool mornings, neatly folded over the arm of the couch. It was the last thing her mom ever crocheted, and it tugs at Taft's heart that it's the only way Freya can be hugged by Anjali Lal now.

"I'm back!" he calls out, following her voice to the kitchen.

Freya's sitting at the table, chin propped on her raised knee, looking thoughtful. When he enters, she looks up from her laptop with a welcoming smile. "Hey. Good walk? You were gone a long time."

Her smile hits him like a sucker punch. It's a hell of a lot better than the tentative ones they've been exchanging post-rules. Taft can resist a lot of things but not the temptation that is Freya Lal. He dares any human to try. Didn't even need all ten things in the ten-secret game to fall for her—hard.

"Yeah, we had fun. Hen introduced himself to everyone we met, including one very brave squirrel," Taft says, forcing a laugh as he crosses to the sink to rinse out his reusable Gatorade squeeze bottle.

Guilt cramps his stomach when he realizes these are the first words they've exchanged today. The last few days he's been starting the coffee for Freya, then slipping out the door for a crack-of-dawn run, returning rosy and sweaty only when he knows she'll be deep in her writing.

But not even all those miles can put distance between how he feels about her.

Not now that he knows exactly what his sheets smell like when she's slept on them.

"How's the writing going?" Taft asks, nodding to her open laptop.

Freya downs the dregs of her tomato juice, the tip of her tongue darting out to catch a stray drop on her lower lip. "It's going. I hit a little bit of a stumbling block, but, um, nothing I can't handle."

Hmmm, evasive *and* mysterious. He opens his mouth, not sure what's going to come out. Maybe *Tell me more about your manuscript.* Maybe *I take everything back, I didn't mean it, please forgive me.*

"What do you feel like having for lunch?" he asks instead.

Freya blinks. "Oh, um, anything's fine. Do you need help?"

He waves her back to her laptop. "Thanks, but nah. You and Hunka Junk should make the most of the day. Day after tomorrow's going to be pretty hectic with the photo shoot."

He swears she looks disappointed. Then her expression clears and she gives her screen a determined look, pushing her shoulders back and nodding.

"You're right," she says. "Thank you."

He whips around before he can take it back. Even though his shirt is sticking to him and he'd love to take a cold shower for *reasons*, he needs to save his wrist for chopping vegetables. He pops in his AirPods in an obvious *Do not disturb* and opens the fridge, rifling for lunch ingredients.

Ever since he was a kid, working with his hands has helped him relieve stress and anxiety. The days he cooked were the only times Taft ever felt like his older brothers were jealous of *him*.

And in the last few days, cooking has anchored him, kept him from being swept away or pulled under by the sheer depth of his feelings for Freya. The first day of his self-imposed rules, when he'd wanted nothing more than to sweep her hair away from her face, he'd busied his fingers with making hot honey wings and roasted corn; day two had been saucy pasta with summer vegetables and his favorite Michigan cherry wine, and he'd had a hard-on all through dinner thanks to her "yummy" noises.

Now, Taft hums as he plucks fresh herbs from his window box herb garden. Homemade Margherita pizza topped with plenty of basil and zingy mint lemonade sound like the perfect distraction.

Unfortunately, it doesn't work. Five minutes into rolling out the dough, flour dusted over his knuckles, it's obvious that ignoring Freya is statistically impossible. With every *click* and *clack* of her keyboard, he's reminded of the woman who has taken up a presence in his home—and in his heart.

Playing it safe has never felt so dangerous before, like Taft is a pot left boiling too long.

Be like Waffle House, he tells himself sternly. *No matter what crap befalls you, keep going. Stick to your plan. You can deal with temptation all day long, but you know you can't handle losing your heart.*

A little later, Taft pulls out his AirPods. "Lunch is ready! It's such a nice day, want to eat on the patio?"

"I could use some fresh air," Freya agrees, getting to her feet. Her hand lands on top of Hen's head, idly scratching as though she isn't even aware of it. "I'll help you carry everything outside."

"I've got it," he starts to say, but it's too late.

"*I've* got it," she insists, tugging the pitcher of lemonade out of his hands.

Her fingertips, warm from typing, graze his. He sucks in a sharp breath. Every single sense is magnified by her nearness, so he doesn't protest when she snatches the glasses and silverware, too.

Taft's backyard is a small oasis. The kitchen door leads out to a prettily paved patio with a teak dining set and just barely enough grass for Hen to run around. The tall privacy fence keeps out nosy neighbors, the view obscured even further with lemon and clementine trees. Hen races through the door ahead of them to sniff at a fallen fruit before determining it isn't a toy to play with.

"This is really nice," Freya comments as she pours the lemonade. "Stori and I don't do a lot of cooking, so I really appreciate, you know, all of this."

"Taking care of you is the least I can do." Taft's face freezes in a guilty expression. "While you're here, I mean. With me. Not with me, but living in my— Hey, do you want some arugula with that?" He gestures at the arugula side salad with a bit too much enthusiasm.

There's a nice breeze out, but maybe Freya's hot, because her whole face is pink. "Please," she says.

He gives her a serving, then, remembering the bag of gummy bears, adds another forkful.

She watches with amusement that he pretends not to notice.

Right as he's about to slice the pizza in half, Freya yelps, "Wait! We should take a picture."

He hadn't even noticed she'd brought her phone with her. "Sure."

It's a bittersweet reminder of the roles they're both playing. When she's done, she runs the caption by him and posts it to Mandi's

Instagram. Immediately, the likes start to climb. Within seconds, they're at two hundred.

Once the pizza is halved, Taft tries to remember every reason he had to keep his distance.

He can't.

Instead of what he really wants to say, he asks, "Do you want some spicy chili oil?" He offers her the bottle.

"On pizza?" She side-eyes him, clearly doubtful.

He sprinkles some on his half, grinning. "Olio di peperoncino is lip-tinglingly good. Trust me, you haven't lived until you have spicy olive oil on a Margherita pizza."

"Why mess with perfection?" Freya cuts a neat square with her knife and fork.

Taft takes a deep breath. "Because . . ." *WAFFLE HOUSE WAFFLE HOUSE WAFFLE HOUSE.* "Sometimes you think something is pretty good the way it is, because you've always stuck with what you know. But it could be better, and deep down you know it. If you add something new, something you could have never seen coming, your life could change."

He isn't talking about the food anymore, and he hopes she knows it.

Freya's lips close around the fork, pulling the pizza into her mouth. "Hmmm, yeah, that's true. But you could also ruin something good. And this is actually really, really delicious. Hard to see how it could be improved, and I don't know if I want to risk it."

"That's . . ." Not what he wanted to hear. "Fair enough."

He should have known better than to want someone he can't have.

THE NEW AND unwanted distance between them should have given her more time to focus on her book, but instead, Freya's motivation to write starts to wane around the thirty-thousand mark. By thirty-five-thousand she seriously considers scrubbing the whole thing. Three days of hating almost every word she types. Three days of wanting to fling herself into the sun. Three days of Hen draped over her legs, moving a little closer each time, somewhere between a woolly blanket and a paperweight.

And her writer's snarl is all *his* fault.

Now, as they sit in the dressing room on the set of their promotional *Banshee*-themed photo shoot, makeup artists fussing over them, Freya *aches* to tell Taft so.

This is the most high-profile item on their to-do list, one that will really sell their chemistry as a couple, and to her dismay, he only looks at her when he thinks she isn't looking back. She tries to keep her gaze steadfastly on Taft, hoping to catch him in the act, but her makeup artist keeps tilting her face back to him so he can touch up her lipstick.

The strokes tickle as his brush traces the sensitive outline of her lips, and Freya involuntarily squirms. Benji, a handsome Black man with waist-length locs, tuts as he fixes her smudged Cupid's bow for the second time.

"Stop nibbling your lips," he gently admonishes before stepping back to study his work.

For Freya, the photo shoot involves tight-laced corsets, laughably large hats with fake birds perched on the brim, and a dipping neckline that emphasizes her décolletage and the floral black cameo necklace hanging above the swell of her breasts. She toys with the dainty chain and delicate gold filigree around the pendant, letting her fingers dance across her collarbone, but annoyingly, even that action doesn't draw Taft's attention. She sighs. At least wardrobe nixed the voluminous hoop skirt after seeing her balk.

Taft, on the other hand, isn't buried under layers of fabric and looks sinfully good in his formal and elegant pin-striped pants and suspenders, wine-red silk shirt, and matching velvet Gothic tailcoat.

To Freya's supreme annoyance, whenever she catches him looking at her, he's the first to glance away.

Benji must have seen her eyeing Taft and mistaken lethal intent for lust, because after an embarrassing moment where he whispered into his colleague's ear, they both made excuses to leave the room. He stopped on his way out the door to toss her a bold wink over his shoulder, as if to say, *You're welcome.*

This room is way too small for the pressure cooker of awkward and wounded and confused that Freya is feeling. She takes a deep breath, inhaling the scent of all the hair spray it took to keep her pinned updo from tumbling apart the way *she* would in a second, if she wasn't careful.

"You're messing this up for us," says Freya, fighting to keep her voice even.

Taft looks up from his phone, a question in his otherwise carefully guarded eyes.

"The silent treatment is getting noticed," she says. "You're blowing my cover."

But it's more than that—he's making her miss memories that they never even got a chance to make.

He's quick to parry. "Unlike you looking at me like I'm on the menu, which is *so* subtle, by the way."

She didn't expect his quick comeback, the yearning in his voice that brings an ache to her throat, or for him to return his attention to his phone. Frankly, she's more than a little surprised he even noticed that *she* was noticing him.

After the requisite niceties with the makeup artists, he'd spent his time scrolling social media so fast that Freya highly doubts he was actually able to read anything. Now, his attention seems caught on one post in particular, but at this angle, she can't see what it is. A transparent avoidance tactic, and not one that she's going to let him get away with. Before, he stayed in the present instead of clinging to his phone, and she misses having his attention. She misses *him*, period.

Freya sets her jaw. "Are you being avoidy because you don't trust me to follow your rules?"

The answer is obvious. What's even more so is how *bad* he is at it.

But he surprises her. "No," Taft says after a long pause. "I don't trust *me*."

The confession hangs in the air long after he ducks his head, returning to whatever on his phone is oh so fascinating. He doesn't get to just *say that* and pull away again. Their makeup chairs are only a couple of feet apart, but the distance between them is even more vast. She can't take his remote expressions and this is for the best demeanor anymore. Not when she knows that it's all bullshit.

Ava's right. No one goes to this much trouble if they aren't into you a *ridiculous* amount.

She rephrases. "Then please stop avoiding me. I hate it. If you think any of this is making me think about you less, you're wrong. It's not. It makes me think about you more."

His eyes soften infinitesimally.

Freya takes his lowered defenses as an opportunity to snatch his phone. Maybe it's childish, but she has to meet him where he lives. "You're not getting this back until you talk to me."

And then her eyes land on the Instagram post staring up at her. It's a picture of the *Once Bitten* cast, and when she swipes, she sees that it's a photo dump of several selfies. Everyone is laughing and smiling—with one noticeable exception.

Taft is nowhere in these pictures. Not even once.

Love my OB fam!!! reads the caption, posted by Bowen Brennan, Taft's former on-screen love interest. She's tagged it with a hashtag, too.

When Freya clicks it, she's taken to hundreds of #OBReunion photos going back years. Premieres, meet-ups, someone's housewarming out in the desert . . .

Freya clicks one at random. It's Bowen and Connor Kingdom at Venice Beach, Bowen playfully mussing his hair while Connor's arm is outstretched to take the selfie. Below, a fan has commented, *How come you and Taft don't hang out?*

Bowen's response is accompanied by a kiss-blowing emoji. *HAHAHA omg what are you talking about!!!! I love Taft! He's such a good dude! We hang out all the time! We just don't always post about it!*

The lady doth exclaim too much, Freya thinks sourly. "Taft, this is such bullshit."

He shifts in his seat, face unreadable. "Can I have my phone back?"

"No."

"No?"

He gives her a blink that can only be described as disbelieving. "But . . . it's my phone."

She pushes the Power button, sending the screen black, then lets it land in her purse next to her own iPhone. "If I do, you're only going to punish yourself further. I've been living with you for how long now? There hasn't been a single time that you've spoken to one of them unless *you* reached out first."

"I don't keep track," he says stiffly.

She scoffs.

Taft looks like he wants to argue, and Freya's eyes dare him to so she can tell him what should be blatantly obvious, just how special he really is and *why can't he see that*, but the makeup artists return for the last finishing touches. Freya ignores the knowing smirks that seem to insinuate something quite a bit steamier than the argument that just happened.

The tension between her and Taft crackles when they're shepherded to the luxe living room of the restored Victorian house that they're using for the *Banshee of the Baskervilles* promo images. The windows are draped in swathes of opulent purple-and-gold brocade that puddle on the herringbone wood floors. Gold light spills from the true-to-the-period brass floor lamps, casting the room in an inviting, buttery glow.

Freya and Taft are instructed to stand in front of the roaring inglenook fireplace, hair and makeup artists fussing over touch-ups, and at some point someone thrusts a glass of Scotch-that's-really-iced-tea into Taft's hands. Between the heat from the fire and the crowd of set designers, prop managers, and photography assistants who all look terrifyingly competent, Freya's sure that she's sweating, but thankfully the setting powder on her face is truly a holy grail product.

Why do people always advise you to think of the audience in their underwear? It's terrible! It doesn't work! And it leads to an overactive writer's imagination thinking about how devastatingly handsome Taft would look in various stages of undress . . . Stop it, Freya!

She doesn't have long to fret, because August, their photographer, breezes over and introduces themselves with they/them pronouns and a disarming grin that immediately sets Freya at ease.

"I'm thrilled to be working with you," says August, giving Freya a firm handshake. "I'm a huge fan of *Banshee*. I can't believe the fourth season ended on that cliffhanger! I mean, your scream is the harbinger for his death. Literal *shivers* down my spine, Mandi. I can't wait to see how the movie ends."

"You and me both," jokes Freya, because she has no idea, either. She catches the way Taft's face tightens and telepathically sends him back some calming vibes. "The director wanted it to be a surprise, so we filmed several different endings," she explains.

She remembers Mandi telling her that, along with the advice that playing mysterious and coy was a good way of saying something without *actually* divulging anything that could get her in trouble. When in doubt, Mandi said, confirm nothing. Fan the flames of speculation—nothing was sexier than a secret.

Taft's jaw unclenches, and he gives an approving nod at Freya's save.

"Guess it'll be a surprise for everyone," says August. "So you two already know the aesthetic we're going for here. There's a couple folks from the production company here pushing hard for sultry clinch cover–type poses, but I'd like to experiment with something more understated, if you two are cool with it?"

"Sure," says Taft. "I'm happy to take your direction."

August grins. "Great! Taft, I was thinking you could start off by staring moodily into the fire." They raise their camera to their face. "Really look like you have a problem. Hint at everything to come."

He does *have a problem.* Freya holds back her snort.

Taft keeps the glass in his left hand but uses his right to brace against the fireplace, bending his head to look like he's transfixed by the flames. The fabric of his tailcoat stretches magnificently over his broad shoulders, and the photographer immediately makes a cooing noise of approval.

"Yes, yes, that's perfect, Taft. Hold that pose." August snaps a photo of just him. "You're really worried about whether you and Mandi are going to survive this movie. The bad guys are even bigger and badder than before. You're losing hope that you get to walk away from this fight. Mandi, comfort him. Do what feels natural to you."

Freya bites her lip and takes a step closer to him, lightly placing her fingers on his sleeve. Taft's head swerves to her, hand jerking just enough to slosh some of the liquid.

"Hey, talent, try *not* to make us pay damages!" the set designer barks, followed by some nervous laughter from the assistants. "On-location cleaning fees are a bitch."

"They're fine!" August shouts back, not pausing in their glut of photos. "Carry on!"

Freya ignores all of it. She nudges the glass out of Taft's hand, raising it to her own lips.

"Yes!" shouts August. They take a flurry of shots, moving closer to zero in on Freya. "I love that, Mandi. It's *inspired*. Why *shouldn't* a woman have a Scotch if she wants one? This is Mandi Roy's world, and we're all just living in it."

August isn't wrong, Freya thinks wryly. She mentally banishes the audience and takes a sip, just enough to wet her lips. It's the wrong kind of liquid courage, but it's all she's got. Emboldened, she tips the glass back for a deeper swallow, fingers wrapped tight and secure.

Taft doesn't look away. Neither does Freya. She parts her lips, tongue chasing after a stray bead of iced tea that clings to the rim. She watches him visibly swallow. Their gazes lock in a silent battle of wills.

When Taft doesn't make a move, August attempts to give them some direction. "Taft, at the end of season four, Mandi's character was in the middle of confessing her feelings for you but was cut off by her own scream. Can you take that current quiet intensity you're rockin' and add some pining in there? A dash of fear about your future together? There's something so scary about losing love before you even get a chance to have it, right? Can you channel that?"

Freya watches the flames and indecision reflect in his eyes and dance across her glass. She doesn't think it's *just* Bowen's Instagram photo that has him so rattled, but whatever has him frozen, he needs to snap out of it.

"Actually, hang on. The vibes are kinda off. Are you guys okay?" asks August. "I don't know, you were both great just a minute ago, but together, you seem a little . . . stiff? We can take five if you need."

The slightest suggestion that the sinking-ship rumors about Raft were right sets off a ripple of whispers among the bystanders. The *last* thing they need is a "source close to the couple" leaking gossip about their lack of chemistry at the photo shoot.

Freya presses her lips together. She's trying, but Taft is emotionally giving her nothing in return, the human equivalent of a frozen steak. "No, we're good!" she chirps, hoping August buys it.

"I'm going to touch you now," she then says in a voice low enough for only Taft to hear. Before he can even blink, she thrusts the glass into his palm. She's going to need both her hands for this.

With her right hand, she curls her fingers into his cravat, while her left snakes around the back of his neck so she can tug herself closer. The seamless synchrony of the move seems to stun him, because several seconds pass before Taft takes a ragged inhale.

"Scared, Bamber?" Freya whispers. "All these layers of irritating Victorian clothing will safeguard your virtue, if that's what you're afraid of." She's half teasing, but he doesn't crack a smile.

August must like the cravat grab, because they don't shout out any further encouragement. They're far enough away to keep the shots wide, capturing the glamorous ambience of the room. Over the flurry of snaps, Freya's sure she can hear her own heartbeat keyboard-smashing.

"That's not what I was afraid of," says Taft.

The first thing she registers is the use of past tense: *was*. The second is that he didn't deny being scared of *something*.

She peers into his eyes, trying to read him.

He slowly drags his hand up his chest until the glass rests against his heart. And then he waits, holding the pose as though it's for the photographer's benefit.

"The tender intimacy between you right now is perfect," crows August. "It's all about the subtext."

Freya struggles to keep her Mandi mask in place. What subtext? Did Taft's gesture mean that he was afraid of losing his heart? Afraid that *she* would be the one to hurt him? She's pretty sure she'd chew off her own arm before she willingly hurt him.

Stumped for a way to convey that to him while all eyes are on them, Freya bites her lip. His attention is immediately drawn to her mouth.

"Can we go for a kiss?" asks August. The other people in the room hum with approval.

Freya's eyes flick to Taft's in an unspoken question. It's not exactly how she'd wanted to share her first kiss with him, but she'd take any opportunity to thaw the awkward subzero situation between them.

"Can we?" Freya asks, skimming her fingertips over the angle of his jaw. If he's not okay with it, she'll respect his boundaries. She'll follow his rules. She'll bury her feelings, if that's what it takes.

When Taft hesitates, regret and uncertainty grip Freya's stomach. This isn't right. If this is the only kiss they'll ever share, it shouldn't be like this. She wants him, *burns* for him, but she doesn't want him backed into a corner—she wants him to melt with her.

His eyes are soft, but the rest of his face is unreadable. But then he nods, eyelids closing in tacit permission and body leaning forward as though in invitation. She waits for his lips to close the gap between them, even tipping her chin up a little to meet him. It's only been a few seconds, but even when someone impatiently clears their throat and August swiftly hushes them, Taft doesn't follow through.

So Freya does the only thing she can think of.

She kisses him first.

At first, she was going for just a peck, but she wants to prove something. Not to any of the onlookers, but to Taft. That there's something between them that is growing too big to ignore and he's not going to win any prizes for trying.

The moment their lips meet, she cuffs one hand around the back of his neck and lets the other curl around his jaw. The kiss is soft and sweet—full of everything she's forced herself to hide from him—and she's determined to keep it that way, until she feels him respond. For one searing second, she's furious—but not surprised—to discover Taft is an unparalleled kisser.

She'd hoped that with her initiating the kiss, she could show him everything he could have had with her if only he'd want it as much as she did. Instead, he'd turned the tables on her—again. It's getting to be a habit with him, she's realizing. But this one she doesn't mind at all.

When his hands frame her face, purposeful and sure, his kiss *devours* her. He takes her bottom lip in between his teeth, lightly pulling. It stings, but not enough to hurt, and his face blurs in front of her until she thinks she's gone cross-eyed. She's never been kissed like that, rough and a little bit feral, and she thinks she likes it, but it's over before she can examine it too closely.

They separate for a second, and Freya takes the chance to breathe, gratified when Taft takes a sharp breath, looking dazed and a bit like his lungs had stopped working. Vaguely, she hopes August captured those shots, because she'd rather like to see what she and Taft look like. Wonders if the goose bumps scattered all over her limbs and other places will show up.

She's just resigned herself that their one and only kiss has served its purpose, but to her everlasting shock, Taft dips his face to hers again, leaving no doubt as to what he wants. He kisses her with slow, tantalizing deliberation, and she rewards him with an impulsive nip at his lower lip. He makes an undone sound that's half growl, half groan, and she smiles against his lips.

Taft follows her every nonverbal cue as though this is their thousandth kiss, not their first. His tongue is impatient, teasing the seam of her mouth until she opens for him, and then claims her mouth completely in an all-consuming kiss that makes her body sing as though she's been fine-tuned for him and him alone.

As she nibbles at his lips, he pins her against the heat of his body. He's tall, but his frame has never had this sexy, looming quality before.

She arches her back when she feels the firm tug of his free hand plundering her hair with questing fingers, exposing her neck. His lips hover enticingly over her pulse point.

For this one moment, this man is all hers and she's all his.

"Taft, hold that pose!" August calls out. "Your profile is perfect."

Well, all mine, and everyone else's in the room, Freya thinks wryly.

Few things in life are perfect on the first try. Not first drafts, not first orgasms with a new partner, and definitely not first kisses when you're still learning each other and what you like. But kissing Taft Bamber is pretty fucking close.

It's hard to hold the pose, and she has to cling to his shoulders just to remain upright, a fact that isn't lost on him if the small, unruffled smirk playing on his lips is anything to go by.

She scowls back, frazzled and aching for him. "You did that on purpose," she whispers.

He sweeps his fingertips along her jaw. "I didn't want to lose something great before I even gave it a proper chance." When she grasps his meaning, he surprises her all over again. "Freya," he murmurs into the hollow of her throat. "The next time I kiss you, it won't be for an audience."

CHAPTER SIXTEEN

"D on't even think about it," warns Taft.

Freya yelps, the undignified sound only springing from her throat because he caught her by surprise. Her finger, poised over the Delete key, twitches at the same time Hunka Junk almost topples from her lap. She steadies it before it can crash to the floor.

Hen, rudely awoken, slopes away from the couch with a disgruntled look at the human disturbance.

Flustered, Freya glares at Taft. "How long have you been standing there?!"

He's holding a mug the size of a cereal bowl, the indescribable scent of his favorite brand of coffee from the neighborhood farmers market wafting over. He doesn't always drink it himself, but he brews it every morning for her. It makes the house smell amazing, particularly because he has this thing about grinding his own beans.

"Long enough," he replies cryptically. "Why is the last thing you wrote 'I'm pretty sure the actor is trying to kiss me'?" His eyebrows waggle.

"I typed '*kill*,' not 'kiss'!" Horrified, she brings the screen down.

Narrowing her eyes, she demands, "Wait, were you reading over my shoulder?"

One, rude. Two, he doesn't get to tease her about the kiss.

She can't stop thinking about their electricity at the photo shoot. When she'd felt his lips respond, kissing her back with a fervor that rivaled her own, Freya had thought for sure that when they went home that night, everything would be different. That he'd take her in his arms like he'd done at the shoot and quit pretending he didn't want her the way she wanted him.

But her anticipation had been forced to go on the back burner for *hours*. Under all the bright lights, her makeup had melted several times and had to be retouched. The multiple wardrobe changes and hours of posing until August was satisfied with the promotional stills. The stiffness in her back and shoulders, the migraine from the constant instruction and sensory overstimulation. By the time the shoot was over and they got home, she was too wiped to do anything but go straight to bed.

Now they're finally going to have to face the undeniable truth: he can't hide from his feelings anymore.

Taft hands her the mug, which is still spiraling with steam. "Is that hot guy based on me?"

"This is a gross invasion of privacy! It wasn't ready! You can't—! It's not—!" she sputters. "And who said he was hot? Now I *have* to delete it!"

"I mean, his character sure sounds like me. Looks like me, too. Wavy brown hair, fey-like eyes, impish lips made for—"

"You can't just shamelessly consume someone else's screen! This is intellectual property theft! This is—this is— *Stop smiling at me like that when I'm trying to be mad at you!*"

Taft shoots Freya an entirely unrepentant grin as he sits down at the other end of the sofa. "I couldn't resist. You've got me curious about what you've been working on."

"You and everyone else. But you're just going to have to wait."

"Fine, fine." He heaves an exaggerated sigh. "I'll join your legions of adoring fans."

Lips halfway to the mug's rim, she commends herself for holding back her snort—*barely*.

That pipeline has long dried up. She'd consider herself lucky if Nigerian princes or spam bots find her website's contact form these days.

She can't help but tease him. "One kiss is all it takes for you to adore me?" She takes a sip of coffee, unable to keep herself from humming with pleasure the second it hits her taste buds. Taft knows exactly how she takes her brew. One sugar and just a splash of almond milk instead of creamer. She likes her coffee to taste like coffee, not like milky, sugary rocket fuel.

"Of course I— Um, what I mean is, I'm sorry. I was a dick. I didn't mean to ice you before." A flush crawls up his neck, scorching his ears red. He scratches at the scruff on his jaw, still looking steadfastly anywhere but at her. "I don't know how to be just friends with you. I don't know if you've noticed, but you've basically knocked me out of my equilibrium."

Freya resists an eye roll. "There is a middle ground between ravishing me and treating me like I'm radioactive." Not that he seems to have found it. "I mean, you're not one of those guys who thinks men and women can't be friends?"

He looks mildly offended. "Of course I don't think that. I'm friends with Mandi."

"So then why the icicles?" She holds her arms out like bat wings, imaginary icicles hanging off her elbows.

The corners of his mouth relax, and he rakes his hand through his hair, oblivious to the way his casual tousling is making her mouth go dry, and her traitorous stomach muscles tighten.

What's more annoying is just how good he looks unshaven, a little bit of that apocalyptic disheveled look that actors on zombie shows always wear. He probably doesn't even realize how much it works for him, and Freya would have told him if not for his unwelcome rules preventing her from crossing the line between friend and more-than-friend.

Taft throws an arm over the back of the sofa, fingertips just shy of touching her shoulder. His fingers twitch on air. "Come on. You're not looking for any distractions right now, either. You have a deadline that comes first."

Freya tries not to frown. True enough, but since meeting him, being distraction-free wasn't her first choice. It was what she settled for being okay with when he made it clear nothing could happen between them. Maybe his rigidity shouldn't have surprised her. After all, Taft is a man with a scripted, synchronized love life, carefully choreographed for max career benefit.

"I heard you talking to your friend the other day," he continues. "'Books over boys'?"

It's Freya's writer dream to have a lover repeat her own words back to her, but this isn't quite the way she thought it would go. They both have entirely too many clothes on, for a start.

"Is eavesdropping your new thing now?" she asks wryly, straining to stretch her legs out as far as they can go without touching him.

Taft chuckles, but a frown of concern quickly takes over his face. "Are you okay?"

"Yeah, just stiff. I've been working all day."

Freya's gotten more used to Hen, but she's still nowhere near comfortable shoving him away when he claims his spot on the couch as her personal furry furnace, paw adorably draped over her typing hand like he wants a cowriting credit—and now her muscles are paying the price.

Taft starts to reach his hand out toward her calves as though he's going to give her a massage but lets it drop. "You shouldn't sit in the same position for long stretches of time."

As she watches his fingers flex against his thigh like he's restraining himself, a sense of loss fills her, but she breezes past it just like she's been doing ever since he friend-zoned her. It's gratifying that there's some part of him that craves connection, even if he tries to resist. Taft is thawing, but he's not all the way there yet. *Baby steps.*

She takes an extra-long sip, hiding her face behind the mug. "Tell that to the world's worst writing assistant ever. Or the best. I don't know how much I'm going to keep, but thanks to Hen, I did manage to get all this out."

"That's good." Taft stares at the laptop as if he can read the words within. "So you don't have writer's block anymore?"

She takes a moment to consider. "More like writer's snarl."

"What's that?" His fingers drum against his chino shorts.

"I made it up. It's when you have things to say, but they're tangled like yarn, so you can't say them to your satisfaction, and everything you write sucks, anyway, so what's even the point?"

"Let me read it, and I'll be sure to tell you why it doesn't suck," he says confidently.

This time she does snort. "As my 'friend,' you're going to be brutally honest?"

"Deeply honest, yes. Brutally honest? Never. Who told you that honesty had to be brutal? And can I kick their ass?"

She stifles a smile but has no control over the rush of affectionate warmth that his words bring. "This feels like something you have big feelings about."

Taft shrugs, like he's trying to downplay it. She's noticed he does that a lot, pretends like what he wants and feels doesn't matter.

"The rest of the world is more than happy to tell you everything that they think is wrong with you," he says. "Why would you expect it from friends who love you?"

"I . . . guess I never thought about it like that." Freya blinks at him, drawn to explain. "For authors, no matter how talented you think you are or maybe you actually are, a first draft is never perfect. You learn how to take critique and kill your darlings, and it stings, but eventually it fades and you're a better writer for all that work and heartache. It sounds harsh, but it's a good lesson: don't get attached to things that aren't permanent, that can get deleted in a keystroke."

"That sounds . . ." He seems to struggle for a tactful way to put it. "Like the kind of thing that can really fuck with your self-worth."

"Isn't it the same in your industry? Actors lose out on roles all the time, get every flaw thrown back at them, live their whole lives under the public's unforgiving eye. The list goes on."

"Yeah, of course. But it's not exactly the same, is it? We bring characters to life, but they aren't us. They don't come from us. Somewhere, a writer like you spun them up out of nothing, like magic."

If that was true, Freya could wave her wand, say an incantation, and her book would be done. Ugh. If she was a better writer, she wouldn't even *need* a magical solution to a nonmagical problem. She would persevere on her own merit and sheer force of will.

"I get what you're saying," says Taft. "And I don't know a whole lot about writing books or publishing them, but maybe thinking about everything *potentially* wrong with your work in progress is preventing you from seeing everything that's right with it."

Freya's words are automatic. "It's a first draft. There's nothing right with it."

A frown creases Taft's forehead. It's sweet how much he cares, but his voice of support can't silence the flagellating fear that she can't write anything real anymore. That she achieved her dream of being an author and that's it, it's all over for her. She's peaked, like a once-superstar actor whose breakout role defined the whole trajectory of their career and now that's the only thing they're remembered for.

"So you go into each book bracing yourself for the worst? It must be hard to write that way." There's no judgment in Taft's tone, but Freya bristles a bit anyway.

He doesn't get it, and she can't blame him for that, but he needs to understand.

"You put your heart in your book," she says, "and then you send it out to literary agents who basically decide if that book is good enough for them to represent. I can't begin to count how many seemed excited at first, then ghosted like I wasn't even worth a rejection."

She chances a peek at him. Most nonwriters don't care about publishing politics, feigning polite interest until a lull when they can change the topic to something they find more interesting.

Taft's undivided attention is on her.

"But that was nothing compared to the ones who picked apart everything I loved and told me how much they hated it, how it was unmarketable, that it wasn't even ready to query. Even though I never told them I was only eighteen, I was terrified they somehow knew, and someone would tell me I didn't belong."

Taft makes a disgruntled noise in the back of his throat that is both sexy and validating.

"Like, when Alma offered," says Freya, "she told me she fell in love with my book and could champion it. That she already knew the perfect editors to sub it to, which she did. But even so, every time you send part of your heart out into the world, it just means dozens of more chances to be rejected, a 'no' waiting to happen."

Now Taft's leaning a little bit into her voice, like he's listening extra hard.

"There's this thing people say, totally cliché but it's true. 'It only takes one yes.' Getting Alma's felt like winning the lottery, but the noes never stop coming, even for super-successful authors. It's probably the same for you?"

Taft whole-body nods. "I lose out on roles I want all the time.

Sometimes I don't even get a reason. Just a vague, unhelpful 'They decided to go in a different direction' or 'You don't have the right look.' There are times I think I've been counted out before I even step foot in the room."

Freya makes a face. "And, like, it's not even always something you can improve on. Sometimes it's just you they don't like. Publishers, readers, random people who are ready to tell you all the reasons why you suck. Even when it's constructive and tactful . . . And don't get me wrong. Art *should* be critiqued. Once it's out in the world it isn't just mine to love and protect anymore, but it doesn't make it any less brutal."

For creatives, a thick skin is a must. For every one incredible person who connects with an artist's work—with their heart—there are a dozen more who will happily tear it apart.

The truth is, honesty is rarely gentle. You learn to take what you get.

Taft steeples his fingers together, presses them against his lips. "When I first started acting, I was so excited every time someone had heard of me. I was so grateful that I *existed* to strangers. And as much as I will always love *Once Bitten*, as it got more popular, I wasn't just Taft, anymore. I was a target."

She knows. She remembers the reviews. And it doesn't surprise her that Taft felt each one.

"And on the day that the show got canceled, when I felt so shit," continues Taft, "I saw this Twitter thread about top-tier *OB* fanfic. And there was this one that I started reading, and it took my breath away. It felt like someone saw me. Understood my character. The writer said I inspired them, but the truth is, they inspired *me*. I'm so grateful they didn't abandon the fic, because sometimes I still go back to binge the whole thing."

Freya's heart squeezes. "But you never reread anything. What made this the exception?"

"This line." And then he quotes it: "'There is no greater magic in all the universes combined than someone who builds a home for you in their heart.'"

Goddamn it, he's quoting *her*. It may even be the sexiest thing he's ever done.

"And in their author's note," Taft says, "they said that some chapters end before you're ready, but it's only one chapter, and you can always change the ending, so they were going to keep writing what they thought season two would look like. I told myself if they could keep going, so would I."

"Of all the fanfics in all the world, he happened to click on mine," Freya says under her breath.

"I've always wondered what happened to them," he muses, looking a little lost in thought. "They haven't updated with any new fic in a while, but I hope they're still writing. Did you ever read it? It was called—" His eyes widen, and she can *see* him catching up. "Wait, what did you say?"

Her voice is deceptively neutral. "I have read it. At least five times."

It's a callback to their first breakfast together, and she can see the exact moment he gets it.

But she understands something now, too.

Her voice becomes choppy as she confesses, "When you create, your heart becomes fair game. And I guess I didn't realize how much of my heart was . . . *her* heart. My mom's."

Taft covers her hand with his larger one. His solid, unwavering presence anchors her, and his silence holds space for her to continue when she's ready.

"For me and most writers I know, our hearts are full of gratitude that we get to have this job, which is all everyone wants to hear. No one wants to know about the scabbed-over parts. For so long, I was sabotaging myself because I was scared to do this without her."

It has taken her until this exact moment to realize it, but it's why Taft's rejection was hitting her so hard: this relationship, fake as it is, is the first fiction Freya's poured her heart into in a long time.

The silence stretches, both of them sitting with what Freya's shared. She's the first one to break it. "If you don't say something eventually, I'm going to get anxious that I somehow broke one of your precious rules."

He huffs. "Freya, for what it's worth, I wanted to take back my dumbassery about rules pretty much ASAP. I tried to broach it over pizza, but . . . Anyway, I'm sorry for getting carried away at the photo shoot."

"You tried to take it back? When?" Light bulb moment. "Wait, we weren't just talking about pizza?"

He looks embarrassed. "I thought you'd read between the lines."

She tries not to groan. "You decided to back away without even asking me if I was willing to risk it."

"If we do, our time together might just be another scab one day."

Of course, sure, there's a real possibility of that happening, but if the alternative is an impersonal frozen tundra, Freya's not going to make it until Mandi returns in two weeks for the movie premiere.

"Maybe. Or maybe I'll write you into a book and it will live on forever," she jokes.

He laughs. "Haven't you already done that?"

Freya flushes, thinking back to the snippet he managed to sneak. "He's not you, trust me."

Considering the circumstances of how they met, maybe asking for his trust is too cheeky.

"I trust you," says Taft. Her eyes fly to his. "And if you'll let me, I promise I won't ever be brutal with you. I know you've had it rough lately, but whether or not I ever get to read what's on your screen, I will always be gentle with your heart."

———————

TAFT MEANT EVERY word. But he also knows that actions speak louder. Even though he knows it's not something Freya expects, he wants to prove it anyway. And he thinks he finally has the perfect idea.

A few days later, he's ducking into Books & Brambles—having shaken off a stealthy photographer and a group of giggling teen girls who weren't exactly subtle about trailing him—when he overhears Stori talking to Freya. Neither woman sees him enter.

Stori's draped over the counter where Freya's sitting with Hunka. Freya's hair is piled high in a messy bun, errant curls and blue glasses framing her bare face. Even though she's "off" when they're at home, she needs her time at Books & Brambles to recenter herself. He doesn't want her to lose herself completely in being Mandi, and he knows that's not what she wants, either. It caught him off guard the first time she went to work, how much he missed her presence, but now he's sure of it: Freya occupies the center of his universe.

But fuck, he can't help it. When she's not with him, he feels adrift. He misses her more than he ever thought it was possible to miss another person. So today, he gives in to his impulse to pop in for a visit.

"*You're doing it again.* Staring off into the distance with your thinking-about-Richard-Madden face," says Stori, reaching out to tug one of Freya's curls.

Taft half smiles. If Freya's a fan, he'll introduce them.

"You know me so well," says Freya. "All right, prove it. *Game of Thrones* era, *Cinderella*, or Marvel's *Eternals*?"

Stori sounds smug as she answers, "That's a trick question. He's equally hot in all of them."

"Lies! Robb Stark all the way! The right amount of stubble is, like, the sexiest thing on a guy."

"I didn't know you were into facial hair."

Freya's voice goes up a notch. "It's a . . . um . . . recent development."

"Hmm, doesn't a certain roommate of yours happen to have—"

"Taft!" Freya's shriek cuts Stori off. "What are you doing here?"

He gives her an amused smile. "This *is* a bookshop, isn't it?"

Freya bites her lip, glancing at the street visible through the window display. Seemingly satisfied by the empty sidewalk, she searches Taft's face. "Were you seen? I mean, were you careful?"

Amused, he nods. "Very. I took the long route to get here in order to lose anyone tailing me."

"Hmm, countersurveillance. Very sexy stuff," Stori says with a smirk. Freya shoots her aunt a displeased look, but Taft can swear he sees her fighting a smile.

"Aaaaand that's my cue to go rearrange some books and pretend I'm not here," announces Stori. "Try not to reenact any erotica this time?" She gives Taft a pointed look as she departs.

"I think I'm growing on her," he says with a shrug.

Freya snorts. "So, seriously. Why are you here?"

"Way to make a guy feel welcome," he drawls.

She arches an eyebrow.

Taft throws his hands up, flashing his palms in a silent mea culpa. "Okay, I know it's risky. I just . . . I really wanted to see you. And maybe pick up a book?"

It's a remarkably weak excuse, and he could kick himself for not being better at improv. They do *live* together—she hasn't been gone long enough for him to miss her. And yet. He swallows and tries not to think about whether Freya finds his following her to a totally different neighborhood romantic or . . . cringey.

Thankfully, Freya nods like it makes complete sense. "What did you think of Steph's? I never saw you read it around the house." When he just looks at her blankly, she adds, "You know? The first time we met? You reserved her book."

"Oh." He scratches the back of his neck. He reads, and he reads a lot, but it's mostly memoirs and lush, sweeping women- and queer-authored fantasies. "I actually didn't buy it for me."

"Right, the gift wrap . . . I guess it was a present for someone else?" She buries her face back in her laptop, flush crawling up her neck and tingeing her cheeks a lovely rose. "Sorry, you don't have to tell me."

Surely, he's imagining the tone of jealousy?

Freya's tapping away too hard and too fast to actually be forming any intelligible words. He's heard her in the every-finger-flying-over-the-keyboard-at-the-same-time throes of inspiration and he's heard her when the only click-clacks come from repetitive use of the Delete key—this is neither.

Freya, he realizes with pleased surprise, might actually be as posses-sive as he is. No one's ever reciprocated before, not really, and damn if it doesn't feel like a thundering, elated ovation in his chest.

She doesn't get that she's the *only* woman he wants to give pres-ents to.

"The book was for my mom," he says. "I tell her I get gift cards I don't need to bookshops, or anywhere really, because it's the only way I can get her to accept anything that isn't a birthday, Christmas, or Mother's Day present."

"So you gift wrap books you think your mom will enjoy just because?"

She really isn't letting this go, Taft realizes. He's going to have to give her something. And the first thing that comes to mind—the first thing that spills off his traitorous tongue—is, "The gift wrap was for me."

Freya's head jerks up.

"It got me a few extra minutes with you."

And it was worth it. He'd do it again.

Taft is out the door before she can say a word.

———

FREYA'S UNABLE TO stop thinking about the last words Taft said before he left the bookshop. Her shift isn't long, but it draaaaags until she's home again.

Hen greets her at the door with an enthusiastic *woof* and a cold nose. In the background she can hear the faint pop and sizzle of cooking. Whatever Taft's making smells good, but she can't let herself get distracted. Between the distance, then the kiss at the photo shoot, and now this middle ground they've developed, Freya's been unable to suss out how Taft truly feels. But today felt important.

It's a small but significant reveal: he liked her from the beginning. Even before he knew who Freya was, when he had to keep up the pretense of dating Mandi, Taft had tried to prolong their interaction.

Ava had it right, Freya thinks as she slips off her shoes. His guard is up because he's trying to protect himself. She only wishes she knew what it would take for him to see he doesn't need to protect himself from *her*.

"I picked up those sourdough rolls from the bakery that you asked for!" she calls out as she enters the kitchen.

Taft gives her a quick smile and sets down the knife he's using to trim the broccolini, stretching out a hand for the bag. Their fingers graze, shooting a spark of awareness through Freya that quickly turns to a surge of heat. For a split second, they both freeze.

With a flustered laugh, Freya steps away. "What smells so good?"

He makes a small humming sound. "Chicken marsala. I just finished frying the breasts and sautéing the mushrooms. You're probably smelling the marsala wine and chicken stock for the sauce."

She spots the red-skin potatoes on the cutting board. "Need any help?" They both like their mashed potatoes with the skin on, topped with a generous amount of cheese and salty crumbled bacon.

"I'd love that. But would you mind stepping into the spare room with me for a minute?"

"Did you finally get yourself a bed in there? Because you know I hate that you've been kicked out of your own room and relegated to the couch," she says, following him.

"I did buy some furniture, but . . . Well, you'll see. Go ahead and open the door."

Forehead scrunched with confusion, Freya obliges.

The first thing she sees is the desk.

To be fair, it's impossible to miss, massive and gleaming a rich walnut, surrounded by all the writerly things she could ever possibly want or need.

Her trusty laptop, Hunka Junk, sits next to a vintage black typewriter. Underneath a modern gooseneck lamp crouch a couple of succulents in cute pots—at this distance, she can't tell if they're real or fake. The "F" black-and-white Tiled Margot Monogram Mug from Anthropologie stuffed with an assortment of rainbow-colored gel pens. An unopened pack of sticky tabs and two stacks of bright Post-it notes, small and large. When she takes a step closer, she sees Taft's handwriting on one: *I believe in you.*

Next, she's arrested by a spiral-bound navy notebook with celestial bodies and the constellation she was born under, a dove-gray vegan leather journal, and a floral hardbound one with a pretty silk ribbon.

"I've never seen you use one, so I didn't know what you'd like," he confesses. "But I was worried you'd lose the notes you leave on all your little scraps of paper."

No one has bought her a notebook since her mom. Freya blinks back tears.

"Um, but just in case you don't want to get them messy . . ." Taft clears his throat as though he's a little uncomfortable. "Open the drawer."

She does. Inside she finds a neat collection of a week's worth of envelopes that he hasn't thrown away.

This time, she does let the tears fall. Struck speechless, all she can do is stare at him. A small smile curls the corners of his mouth as he scratches the back of his neck before shoving his hands into the pockets of his jeans, a bashful gesture that takes her breath away, too.

"You did this for me?" she says hoarsely, and of *course* he did, what a silly question, but he nods seriously.

"Do you like it?"

Incredulous, she repeats, "Do I *like* it? Taft, I . . . this is . . . I've never had my own office before." She swivels the mauve velvet chair, the back shaped like a shell. She scrapes her teeth over her bottom lip before saying, "No guy has ever done something this thoughtful for me before."

"I wanted you to have a place here that was all yours. Somewhere to work in peace without . . . distractions."

She glances up at him from underneath her eyelashes. "Distractions aren't so bad."

He laughs. "Let's see if you're still saying that the next time Hen's a space hog."

"He's sweet. I wasn't sure how living with him would go at first, but, uh, he knows just what I like."

Taft's eyes fly to hers, searching for something. Whatever he finds there, the smile he offers her next is new, one of a man who's laid all his cards on the table—or in his case, the desk. The faint parentheses around his mouth are a testament to how much and often he smiles, but this one shows her everything: vulnerability, yearning, and, above all, a desire to make her happy.

"The typewriter isn't new," he says when she runs her fingers over the keys. "It was my grandfather's. He used to be a writer, and when he passed away, this was one of the keepsakes I wanted to remember him. It's been boxed away for years, but, uh, I think he'd love that someone was using it again." His smile is wry. "Good luck deleting huge paragraphs on this."

"Taft, thank you." Freya bites her lip, touching the keys with even more reverence. "It's perfect. But it's too much."

Taft isn't her best friend or her aunt, and yet he valued her writing enough to give her an office to do it in. A typewriter to prevent her from moving backward. A reminder of his faith in her on a Post-it to keep her moving forward. All she can think is how he's the most comforting thing she's had in a long time.

He didn't just make place for her in his home, he *made* it a home for her.

"It's not too much, it's just a few small things," he starts to say, but she stops him by stepping into his space and putting her arms around him in a gentle hug.

She's breaking the rules, but she knows he doesn't care when he hugs her back. The longing in his eyes is second only to the thrum of his body, as though being this close to her will unravel him. He holds her like she's something precious, something he doesn't want to mess up.

"Thank you," Freya murmurs against his shoulder. "This is . . . everything."

"I told you," he says. "When the people I . . . care about want something, I will do everything in my power to help them get it."

CHAPTER SEVENTEEN

If Freya had thought the fancy New York City theaters were impressive, they have nothing on the downtown LA theater that Bowen Brennan rented for a private screening of her new film and directorial debut.

Buttery yellow light floods from the ceiling, giving the invitees a gilt-edged glow. Local craft beer and cocktails are being served out in the lobby, so hardly anyone is already seated.

"Do we need to go mingle with your old castmates?" Freya asks as they help themselves to crustless shrimp-and-watercress petit four sandwiches. Why something this delicious must be so miniscule aggrieves her.

"They don't really know Mandi well," Taft whispers in her ear, voice slightly strained. "We're fine."

It isn't the first time she's gotten the impression that he doesn't quite fit in with these people he calls his friends. After seeing Bowen's Instagram comment about Taft, it's clear to Freya that there just doesn't seem to be a lot of affection between them. He keeps updated on their lives, but they don't take the same effort with him. The imbalance doesn't seem noticeable to anyone but him—and now her.

"If they're pretty much strangers, then I don't have to worry about getting anything wrong," she points out logically. "And since I owe Mandi an update call tomorrow, anyway, she'll be filled in."

His shrug, elegant in his smoky charcoal tuxedo, is noncommittal as he pops in another not-so-satisfying swallow of sandwich. "The night is young."

"As long as you're not just trying to keep me to yourself all night," she teases.

Taft's answering smile sends a siege of butterflies soaring through Freya's stomach.

"Would that be such a bad thing?" he teases right back. Seemingly without thinking about it, he presses a tender kiss to her temple.

It's only when she gets a glimpse of the other lobby-goers sneaking glances at them that she can't tell whether it's for *her* or an act to sell Taft and Mandi's relationship.

But her body doesn't know the difference, even if her head tries to make the distinction. Goose bumps skate down her arms and legs. Freya's toes involuntarily curl in the silver heels her doppelgänger dictator insisted she wear when they video-chatted earlier about what outfit she should wear out tonight.

She's in a gold Carolina Herrera ball gown that clings to her figure and makes it even harder to walk. But it gives her an excuse to hang on to Taft's arm, and she knows that paired with the crystal collar necklace, the limelight is extra flattering, so it's not *that* agonizing.

"Everything okay?" asks Freya. "You've been kinda quiet and lone wolfy since we got here."

She wonders how much of that has to do with Connor Kingdom holding court with some of the other *Once Bitten* cast members at the far side of the lobby. The fact that he waved at Taft but didn't wave him over, a distinction that had her setting her teeth until her jaw ached. The way Taft's eyes keep flicking back to them with a longing he must be unaware of, a flash of insecurity that looks out of place on his handsome face. God, she knee-jerk hates his so-called friends.

She fixes a glare to the back of Connor's neck, hoping he feels it. Turns around. Realizes Taft is left out. A hypocritical part of her wants to tell Taft to just go over and insinuate himself into their group, but she gets how it's safer to just pretend it isn't happening. She never *was* good at taking her own advice.

Looking up at Taft is dazzling, thanks to the chandelier glittering above their heads, casting an almost disco-ball effect through the room. Not to mention the man himself, sexy as hell in his tux and well-defined curls. At an event full of hotties of all genders, Freya's smitten for only him.

Taft exhales. "Yeah, I just . . . didn't realize how much I wanted this for myself."

"Awwwww, you're getting all misty-eyed," she teases, nudging his side. "Your premiere is just two weeks away, and we'll—you'll—be arriving in *plenty* of style."

She hopes he doesn't notice her slip. Sometimes, it's easy to forget this life comes with an end date.

Taft gives her an indulgent smile, still a little bit dreamy as he takes in the ambience. "I don't mean the premiere. I mean"—he gestures—"all this."

His unhelpful sentence hardly illuminates Freya further, but the stars in his eyes are practically bounding.

"Really?" she asks. "You must have had a hundred nights just as glamorous as this one."

Maybe more. Cannes, Tribeca, Sundance. Met Galas and Paris Fashion Week. All those Best On-Screen Chemistry and Network Fantasy/Sci-Fi TV Show awards he racked up for *Once Bitten* and *Banshee of the Baskervilles*.

He comes back to himself with a self-conscious laugh. "Nah, I don't care about all the pomp. I mean, I'd like to do what Bowen does. This film was her passion project. Could you imagine if I could create my own stuff, not just wait and see what might come my way? I want to take risks and follow my heart."

Before she can tell him to go boldly after it, someone shrieks, "Oh, there's Mandi!"

Immediately, they're overwhelmed by a throng of people all dressed to the nines. Holly Kingdom pushes her way to the front, smile in full force. She's dragging Bowen Brennan, the blond bombshell on the theatrical release posters and the lady of the hour, behind her. Their voluminous evening gowns billow around them, ensuring people make room.

"Have you met?" Holly asks without ceremony. "Bowen, you know all about Mandi, of course. Naughty Taft, keeping her all to yourself! Mandi, I promise you have nothing to be jealous about. Bow only played his on-screen love interest." She winks. "As far as I know."

Seriously? A ripple of annoyance winnows through Freya. Taft stiffens, and she has to employ every facial muscle to keep from snarling at Holly.

Bowen looks uncomfortable. "Hi, please don't pay attention to Holly. Nothing happened, and I am very happily married to that man over there." She points at a lanky dirty-blond swinging his cocktail glass exuberantly while a handful of film critics furiously scribble notes.

Freya strives to be friendly. "No worries, even *I* was rooting for your characters ever since the pilot, so I get why Holly clearly mistook on-screen chemistry for more. At one point, I wanted to be you."

Well, more precisely, *she* wanted to be the one kissing him, but it never hurts to stroke an ego.

Taft startles, and Freya can feel the weight of his stare from the corner of her eye, but Bowen breaks into a grin, looking relieved. "I don't know whether to be flattered or embarrassed. I like to pretend that the show never happened, but I guess that's going to be hard from now on."

Bowen slides her eyes to Taft, as if she just remembered he was there. "Good to see you. It's been a while."

"It has," says Taft, as though they hadn't just seen her laughing with their former cast a few minutes ago. "Congrats on your directorial debut."

Bowen had been his love interest on *Once Bitten*, but because it was canceled so quickly, the will-they-or-won't-they between the couple had never been resolved. It had kicked off a lot of fanfiction, though, Freya's included, and the show had a huge cult following that rivaled *Buffy the Vampire Slayer* in its heyday.

Despite their scorching combined sex appeal on-screen, there isn't a hint of chemistry between them now. They're hanging about awkwardly, as if they hadn't once shared the same set or the same breath.

Freya gives Bowen a thousand-watt smile. "We're so excited to see the film. How cool is it working with your husband every day?"

Bowen beams, all too ready to gush.

Not only is the movie Bowen's directorial debut, but she and her husband, Charlie, also produced and starred in it. Since it's a tearjerker of a love story comped to *The Notebook* and *The Lake House*, naturally, Freya came prepared wearing waterproof mascara, fully committed to bawl.

"It was incredible," says Bowen, "but maybe you'll know what it's like for yourself soon enough."

Holly titters, and if it's possible, Taft tenses even further.

"Oh, I'm sorry." Bowen looks genuinely confused. "It's just I heard that you two were— But clearly they were unfounded rumors."

Freya recoils as the dots connect. *Engaged?* Her eyes widen. "We are nowhere near that yet."

Yet? Did I say that out loud? She almost chokes on her own spit. *Fuuuuuck.*

If she looks at Taft, she knows blushing is inevitable. And Mandi would never lose her composure. She wouldn't stammer and try to walk it back the way Freya instinctively wants to.

"People like to gossip," says Taft, saving her. He rubs his palm from her bare shoulder all the way down to her elbow like he's warming Freya up. She leans into his comfort. "And after we got a little passionate in a club a few weeks ago, we've been the topic du jour. You know how it is."

Freya cozies into his side, heartbeat instantly calming when she hears his, and tries not to think about how he feels like *home*. It's added up in quiet cups of morning coffee and reminders to stretch her muscles. Reading on opposite ends of the couch, Taft absorbed in his stack of scripts while she alternated between peeking at him and focusing on her screen. The gift of his grandfather's heirloom typewriter and the scratch-paper envelopes Taft saved for days to tuck into the desk drawer of her writing space.

Taft is the comfort of the childhood Craftsman her dad still lives in; the brownstone in New York where every impossible dream felt within reach; the two-bedroom apartment above Stori's bookshop that always smells of books and tea and reheated takeout.

But even in the softness of this moment, Freya can't escape the hard truth that she's just a fill-in for the actress who is supposed to be here, and though she's temporarily taking her place, nothing about Mandi's world is hers. Not even him.

Nothing here is for keeps.

"Though, of course, after tonight, everyone will only be talking about you," Freya says with a practiced Mandi smile, hoping this redeems her after that awkward slip. "All your buzz is well deserved."

Bowen is about to reply when her eye is caught by a middle-aged couple, who, despite being dressed in couture, look about as out of place as Freya herself currently feels. "Oh, my parents are looking a little lost. I better go rescue them. You should all probably start heading in."

As if on cue, her husband announces it's time for everyone to take their seats. Holly goes off in search of Connor, but Taft and Freya still linger in the lobby as though they're waiting for fresh drinks.

Despite the earlier tension, now that they're alone, Taft's smile is sweet and languid. "You wanna be the one to tell Mandi she better binge *Once Bitten* before someone asks her something she won't be able to answer?"

It never occurred to Freya that Mandi would *need* to. She winces. "She never watched the show?"

"A clip before the *Banshee* chemistry read. She wanted to be sure I was more than just a pretty face. I think she called my previous filmography full of 'disposable teen dramas,' and yeah, to some people, it was. I don't even think my dad saw the pilot," he says with a shrug. It doesn't look as offhand as Freya thinks he wants it to be. "But the show meant something to me. Even though it was canceled, getting my first big chance changed my life."

A rush of fierce pride fills her chest. His gratitude is one of the things she enjoys the most about him, she realizes. Taft isn't one of those actors who sneers at how he got his start once he "made it." Sure, she hasn't known him long, but she knows others in his position would have put themselves on a pedestal long before. He never has. He doesn't look down on anyone, not even himself and his start in teen dramas, and that's an attractive quality.

"It wasn't disposable to me, either," she tells him. "What I said earlier wasn't just flattery. You two were my favorite characters. This is embarrassing to admit, but for a long time I was more invested in your character's love lives than my own."

Taft grins. "See, now that's the kind of ammunition you're supposed to make me promise never to reveal to another living soul *before* you actually trust me with it."

But Freya doesn't need to extract any such promise from him. It isn't a trade-off or a transaction. It's just honesty.

"I trust you," she says recklessly.

Taft's eyes are soft. "Yeah?"

"Maybe I have astonishingly poor self-preservation instincts," Freya teases, just to watch him huff in annoyance. "Or maybe I'm a fan."

He reaches for her hands, brushing his thumbs over her wrists. "Of the show?"

Silly man. "Of you," says Freya.

TAFT WATCHES FREYA instead of the love story playing out on the screen.

She couldn't have shocked him more if she'd kissed him again. She's a fan of *him*. Not his characters, not his celebrity, but *him*. Like every single smile she's sent him since day one, this confession makes him feel like there's a sunrise in his chest.

He knows he should pay attention to Bowen's movie, but he can't tear his eyes away from the woman sitting next to him, red lips parted and hand limp in her bucket of popcorn. Her fingers are marinated in salt and butter, and she doesn't even seem to notice.

She would if he reached over and sucked each one clean, he thinks with a strange mix of possessiveness, lust, and curiosity.

It isn't the first time he's thought about giving in to his feelings for her. Of reaching out with both hands and taking what she's been offering him for days.

Freya's face flickers with every emotion she experiences. Despite the fact that she's started slamming her laptop shut every time he enters the room, she's an open book. It's refreshing to discover that, despite being a proficient liar, she's still guileless when it comes to what she feels.

And for some incomprehensible reason, she feels for *him*. She *trusts* him.

Taft thinks it's the biggest responsibility—the biggest honor—he's ever had.

"You're not watching," whispers Freya.

"Yes, I am. Ask me anything."

He hasn't been paying attention. He hopes she doesn't call his bluff. Can he help it if she's more fascinating and beautiful to watch?

Her voice sounds so close as she says, "If you were, you'd be tearing up right now."

When the glow of the screen hits her brown eyes just right, he's startled to discover that they gleam with tears. "Are you okay?"

She angles her neck toward him, but keeps her eyes fixed on the screen. "Oh no, is my mascara running?"

Taft stares for longer than necessary. She's still staring straight ahead, anyway, so he gets away with it. He wonders what it would be like to be openly spellbound by Freya without the cover of darkness masking his desire. "No, you're perfect."

That gets him her full attention. He can read the question in her gaze and he looks back steadily, willing her to peer into his exposed soul if that's what she wants.

Please want that.

"Don't," she says, glancing around like someone's about to shush them.

But thankfully, they're seated in the back, and the closest people are three seats away in either direction. Taft gestures to that effect, not surprised at all when understanding reaches her eyes. She can read him almost as well as he can read her.

"Doesn't matter." Her voice is pitched low, almost a plea. "We shouldn't do this. Not here."

It strikes him then that she isn't referring to talking during the screening—which is also forbidden, or at the very least frowned upon—even though they aren't disturbing anyone.

"I'm all out of reasons why we shouldn't," he whispers.

She sucks her bottom lip into her mouth, teeth biting down. "Taft?"

He loves the sound of her voice, the way she says his name, and the little lilt at the end.

She's said his name a hundred different times, a hundred different ways. Surprise and elation when she saw her new office for the first time; trepidation when Hen headbutts her to the front door for the walk she won't take him on alone; frustration on more than one occasion, usually because he's asking how her writing is going, which he's starting to realize is never a good question to ask a writer knee-deep in the weeds.

But this is the first time she's said it with a hint of reverence. Expectation. Hope.

Freya's eyes search his with all the force of a lighthouse beacon, and he can't help but be hypnotized. He's always loved brown eyes, and he suddenly can't remember if it started before or after he met her.

He's spent a lot of time soulfully gazing at women, coached by directors, photographers, and intimacy coordinators, but for the first time in years, this isn't a set and he isn't playing a role.

No one is watching. This moment is reserved solely for them.

When he looks at her, Taft is just a man looking at a woman he's falling for.

His mind erases everyone in the theater, silences the movie, and spotlights Freya with a beam so bright that the entire room turns to shadow. He takes everything he feels for her and lets it show through his eyes.

It's absolutely harrowing.

Relying on every tool and trick he's picked up over the years to convey emotion through a single look, he projects his heart into her hands as though Bookshop Girl hadn't already claimed it on day one.

He knows it's working when Freya's tongue darts out to wet the seam of her lips. "What about your rules? Because if you're going to blow hot and cold again . . ."

He cups her jaw, lets his thumb nestle into the soft part under her chin.

"Pretty sure that counts as touching without warning," she says with a Cheshire smile.

The air between them becomes more electric.

How had he ever allowed himself to believe all these years that compromise was the only way in which he could succeed?

The answer, he realizes, is obvious. Before, he didn't know Freya.

"Are you going to kiss me or keep me waiting?" Taft tips her mouth up and hovers an inch from her lips, eyes seeking hers. Letting her know in no uncertain terms what he wants.

Freya brings her hand up between them, tapping her chin as she pretends to think. "I mean, seems fair?" She shrugs prettily. "Wasn't me who was the holdout. I did spend a *lot* of lonely nights in your bed."

There's no way she doesn't know what a sentence like that does to him.

"Fuck the rules," Taft says vehemently, more growl than speech.

"I could have told you that," she says, voice surprisingly prim for a woman who is unrepentantly crushing the collar of his Tom Ford button-down dress shirt to bring him closer.

They're close enough to share the same breath. He'd swished with an aggressive amount of Listerine before they left, and he knows Freya brushed her teeth so they'd be extra clean and stand out against her Dior lipstick, but between them they've probably eaten the equivalent of two regular-size shrimp sandwiches, and what that means for their combined breath is . . .

Actually, he doesn't care. He's contrived enough reasons to stay away from her, there's no way he's going to talk himself out of kissing her tonight.

"So we're clear," he murmurs against her lips. "You've upended my entire life."

Freya, he notices, never looks so smug as when she's won.

"Good," she says. "That makes two of us."

Taft gently brushes her cheek with his knuckles. "I'd really like to kiss you."

Her eyelids flutter as she tilts into his touch, covering his hand with hers. "Now, please."

Can he deny her anything when she asks him so sweetly?

With a wolfish smile, he leans in. Just as he's about to give Freya what she wants—what they've *both* been waiting for—the overhead lights come back on.

CHAPTER EIGHTEEN

Worst. Timing. Ever.

Freya blinks owlishly as her eyes adjust to the brightness. The first thing to come into focus is Taft: brown hair curling over his ears; the faint pucker of his mouth; and a rounded, stubbled jawline begging for hands and lips. If anyone were to turn around, they'd spot Freya's and Taft's heads leaning in so close that there'd be no doubt as to what they were seconds away from doing.

Taft groans, a sound that could be mistaken for disappointment at the movie ending, but she knows better. They lock eyes and both unsuccessfully try not to laugh.

"Soon," he avows, and every inch of her leans into the rough rasp of his voice.

There'll be other chances, she knows that now, but she can't deny how much she wanted this one, both of them aglow from the screen, the thrilling juxtaposition of hushed secrecy in a public place heightening their desire and desperation. It isn't their first kiss, but now that they know what they mean to each other, it deserves to be special.

The murmur of the crowd grows as people start to move around, bringing Freya back to reality. A group of reporters make their way to the front of the theater to get some quotes from Bowen and her team.

"Let's stretch our legs?" asks Freya, shifting against the scratchy seat. "Grab a drink before our required after-party appearance?"

She doesn't know why she suggests it. She's already flushed and her dress is sticking to her skin, and alcohol will only exacerbate the issue, but it's something to do, striding toward a new scene instead of delaying in the cliffhanger of an old one.

"Sure." Taft stands and offers Freya his hand.

As he helps her up, she gives his fingers a squeeze to convey that this isn't over. To make her point, Freya's fingers chase his when he's about to let go. Surprised delight flashes across his face as she keeps them together. If they couldn't kiss, holding hands is a close second.

As they sidestep their way through the row, a voice cuts through the chatter with enough enunciated buzzwords that it's impossible to miss.

"Your former costar's name is conspicuously absent from this project. He's always spoken very fondly about the show, so can we assume that Taft had scheduling conflicts that prevented him from signing on to reprise his role in the *Once Bitten* reboot?"

Taft falters, coming to an abrupt stop.

Freya glances back at him immediately, clocking the uneven pink patches that have sprouted on his cheeks and the wild look in his eyes. His fingers dig into hers almost painfully, but she doesn't pull away. Her intestines tighten and twist like a balloon animal, blood rushing to her ears, as Taft's frozen body starts to cause a pileup in the aisle.

"There he is over there! Taft! Taft! Can we get a quote about—"

Instinct screams at Freya to take him and run, but it's too late, they're boxed in.

The big-shot industry names Freya's had to memorize edge past the pair with disgruntled expressions, leaving Connor, Holly, Bowen, and the other *Once Bitten* alums visible. They all wear stony masks, revealing nothing, while Taft's ambushed face shows everything.

Betrayal, devastation, and then, finally, steel.

Media outlets weren't allowed to bring cameras inside, so the inquisition goes analog as journalists and critics all reach for pen and paper. Within seconds, Taft and Freya are surrounded.

"With the first season greenlit, as production gets under way, do you think you'll choose to be more involved?" someone throws out.

The other questions follow in a barrage:

"Is it true that you're prioritizing film over television roles? Do you consider yourself infinitely in-demand? Can you tell us how many other roles you've turned down?"

"Mandi, did Taft's rumored off-screen romance with Bowen give you reason to doubt your boyfriend?"

"How do you feel about Connor, your former cast member and roommate, playing your—sorry, *his*—new role?"

"Even though you're the only original cast member not returning, are you on board with the new creative direction, including handing over the mantle of male lead to Connor?"

"Yes or no: Nostalgia-fueled cash-grab? Is recycling content everything that's wrong with Hollywood? Would you call repurposing IP creative cannibalism?"

Secondhand betrayal body slams into Freya. This isn't just invasive. It's *cruel*.

With every question, the situation clarifies itself even more and more. The *Once Bitten* reunion hashtag on Instagram wasn't just an inside joke among friends. It was literal.

They're bringing back the show, and Taft isn't part of it.

They didn't even reach out to him. No one else seems to realize that

Taft has been tossed into the deep end here, learning about this all in real time, and she can't tell if that's because she knows him so well or they know him so little. The cast hovers at the periphery of the crowd, looking like they're all holding a collective breath.

"I'm sorry, everyone, but this isn't the time or place," says Bowen, trying to mediate the situation. She looks at Taft with a trace of regret. "I have no idea where the leak came from, but you'll get all the details with the official press release."

"Yes, we're here to celebrate Bowen and Charlie tonight," agrees one of *Once Bitten*'s supporting characters.

"Come on, Taft, give us a quote," wheedles one of the journalists. "Unless . . . there's a reason you don't want to? A secret feud behind the scenes?"

Anticipation gleams in every one of those vultures' eyes.

The cast says nothing. Connor has the fucking gall to look annoyed by it all, the tempo of his foot tapping picking up with every question lobbed at Taft. Bowen catches Freya's daggered gaze and mumbles something to her husband before they make their escape. Holly hangs on to her husband's arm, for all the world a proud partner until Freya slices her attention the other woman's way. Holly's smile fades and she pretends to find something on the wall endlessly fascinating.

Anger and revulsion roil in Freya's stomach. *Cowards*, all of them.

Taft holds up his free hand, and the questions peter to a stop. His voice, when he speaks, is steady. "So, first of all, I just want to say that I am unbelievably thrilled for the fans, new and old, who will get to experience the magic of *Once Bitten* all over again."

Freya's brain screeches as she stares in horror. What is he doing?

"One of my favorite things about *Once Bitten* is that the lore is so rich that it can be retold from any number of angles and perspectives, as plenty of fix-it fics can attest to." Taft laughs, a little too well-timed and practiced to be anything other than fake. "While my shooting schedule is super busy right now, if we can make it work, I'd love to swing by the set."

We? Who is this *we*? The people who deliberately excluded him from his own show, threw him away like fucking garbage? He had no clue about any of this. No one from the show even approached him, so why isn't he throwing them under the bus?

She sets her jaw and tries not to look like she wants to telepathically murder his so-called friends.

From the way the cast members who are still hanging around flinch, it's clear she hasn't succeeded.

Good. She gets that Taft doesn't want to make a scene, but *she* doesn't have to be the bigger person, too.

"So, Taft," says a hard-faced blond woman, not looking up from her notepad. "To clarify, you weren't the holdout? Now that you've jumped to the big screen, do you ever see yourself returning to TV, or have you moved on to bigger and better things?"

Before he can answer, Freya presses herself into his side, their hands still held tight between them. "Oh, I'm sure you'll still see him on TV," she says in as pleasant a voice as she can muster, which, gauging from the look Taft shoots her, probably isn't very.

"Of course." The woman's smile doesn't reach her eyes, and Freya notices she stops writing.

Doesn't matter. Everyone else is hanging on Freya's words, and she's not done.

"With jumping straight from the most recent season to filming the movie, we've had a hectic production schedule. But we've been fortunate to work with a *supportive* team. And this guy"—she tips her chin up to give him a fond, adoring smile—"is such a wonderful, giving actor to act opposite, I honestly can't imagine how hard it's going to be not working with him on set every day. And I'm not just saying that because I'm dating him."

This gets the expected round of light laughter, but her speech isn't for them. She resents so much all her friendly overtures to Bowen when Taft is the one who deserves all praises, sung and otherwise. The crass allegations that he's sold out somehow to do a commercial film and international projects needs to be dealt with in a way that only a writer and decoy girlfriend can.

"I was so struck by his nuanced acting chops and the tremendous energy he brought to *Once Bitten*, it's why I knew he was the only possible lead for *Banshee*," says Freya. "Taft is so passionate about his projects, and the commitment he's shown me every day that I've known him, in every way, is remarkable. So many shows were wooing him, but I'm the lucky girl who succeeded."

Freya winks at the crowd. The journalists can't quote her fast enough, and the cast looks absolutely stink-eyed.

"The *Banshee* story and characters resonated to us creatively, and we both knew this was a project we really wanted to sink our teeth into, and we're so lucky to get to do so in such a new and exciting way in the film, which we can't wait to share with all of you."

There. If Taft wants to toe the party line, play diplomat for his traitorous friends, then she can at least remind everyone that his career is thriving because of his *own* talent, not by just leaning on the past to stay relevant. She hopes her speech underscored the point in red.

"And, of course," says Taft, "while I've had no involvement in the reboot, I wish the cast and crew all the best. I'm excited to watch my friends on-screen again, and hopefully this isn't the last you see of me." He manages to make his wink look cute, cheeky, and cryptic all at once.

Freya's veins ignite.

Taft's been kept out of the loop every step of the way, left out of the fucking family reunion, and he's *still* so even-keeled so nobody loses face. Their treachery doesn't deserve his diplomacy. As much as she loathes their behavior, it doesn't hold a candle to how much she admires his grace under fire.

Chances are good that Freya's the only one who recognizes how much this costs the man beside her. The journalists are eating this up, and Connor looks like he's swallowed something sour.

Pens scratch and scribble across paper, thanks are given to Taft, and the media dissipates to find other celebrities to hound. Most of the cast follows suit, except for Connor and Holly. The powder keg of emotion doesn't lessen with fewer eyes. She waits for Connor to thank Taft for the save, but he just stands there, shuffling his feet. Looking for all the world like he hasn't done anything wrong.

Stunned by the silence, the words rip out of Freya. "Is that it?"

She knows that the real Mandi wouldn't show as much emotion, but all it does is reinforce how much she wants to leap to Taft's defense with daggers drawn. That it's her place to do so. Her utter fucking privilege.

The ferocity of Freya's stare pins Connor in place. "No, I'm sorry," Freya fires off, not actually apologetic at all, "but how do you justify stabbing a friend in the back?"

His nostrils flare. "It's work. It's not personal."

The words are scarcely more than a mumble, and if Connor truly believed his bullshit, he would look Taft in the eye while he said it.

"Mandi, no offense," says Holly. "But this doesn't affect you, so why are you even in this conversation? It's not like Taft's hurting for money or anything."

Holly thinks Taft isn't hurting? *Once Bitten* was a part of Taft's life that meant everything to him, a part that he'll never have again. Do they really think that just because he's become more famous that he doesn't care anymore? This man cares more about everything than *anyone* she's ever known.

"I had to sign a nondisclosure agreement," adds Connor. "I could kill whoever opened their mouth before the press release. You know they're going to think it was *me* now, right?"

His wife nods along in sympathy, but is he callous enough to expect them to be indignant on his behalf, too? Evidently, yes.

Not one of these assholes have ever been gentle with Taft's heart.

"It *should* have been you," Freya hisses. If Taft isn't going to be pissed, she will gladly gather all his grudges and carry them on his behalf. "That was one hell of a sucker punch, bestie."

Connor's eyes flash. "I didn't want it to come out like this."

It's still not an apology.

"You should have trusted him," says Freya. "You don't do friends dirty like this. Even if you didn't want to put anything in writing because of the NDA, you could have, oh, I don't know, had a phone call? Met in person? Except that would involve actually giving a shit, right?"

"Okay, wow." Connor's jaw tightens. "You need to back off. This is between us boys, and he's chill." He throws Taft a *C'mon, man* look, like he wants him to collect his girl and slink away. "You get it, right?"

That you're a prime asshole, yes. A million times, yes.

"I do," Taft says in a neutral voice. "I get it."

Some of Connor's tense energy zaps away. "I knew you would," he says in a hearty voice, reaching out as if to clap him on the shoulder.

Taft sidesteps. "You misunderstand me. You think because I forgive the little slights and make allowances because of our long friendship, that I don't realize where I stand with you."

Connor scowls. "That's not—"

"*I'm speaking.*" Taft's voice slices in a way it never has before. "I'm tired of being your third-tier friend when you've always been my number one." He looks at Freya, and then, without a tremble in his voice, he says, "Let's get out of here."

———

FREYA STICKING UP for him is the single hottest thing a girl has ever done for him. And that includes dirty stuff. He doesn't need an avenging angel to fight his battles for him, but the rush of her *wanting* to . . .

The feeling is unsurpassed.

Striding out of the premiere arm in arm with the most beautiful woman in the room made him feel like a badass, like he was unstoppable. But now that they're actually outside and walking in the direction of his car, he needs to apologize.

"I'm sorry, I know you were looking forward to the after-party," says Taft. He swallows his pride. "Do you still want to—"

"Don't you dare finish that sentence."

The ferocity in her voice makes him turn to look at her, and the scowl of indignant anger on her face almost makes him stumble. Her chest heaves as she says, "After the shitty way they treated you, screw them. Do you really think I wanted to spend the rest of the night with them?"

He's flustered. "I didn't ask whether you wanted to leave. You should have had the choice. It's your first Hollywood premiere, and I kinda yanked you out of there pretty unceremoniously."

Not exactly the behavior of a gentleman, he thinks, but Freya's snort clearly tells him she disagrees.

"Taft," she says, pulling him to a stop. "You're my— You're my friend. Of course I choose you."

Hearing her say that, so matter of fact—like *Hello, is this not obvious?*—Taft is supremely glad his feet aren't moving. He's pretty sure he would have tripped on his own surprise.

"Oh," is all he can manage, a sting building in the back of his throat.

"And as your friend, I am so glad we got the fuck out of there," says

Freya. Her arm is still linked through his, so with her fingers curled around his biceps, she tugs him into motion again.

They don't get more than ten feet before someone across the street leaps out from behind a car with a camera. "Leaving already, Mandi? Another fight with lover boy? You're making my career, sweetie!"

Instinctively, Taft uses his body to shield Freya from view. He knew there might be press outside but had hoped that by leaving early, they'd be able to slip by unnoticed. "Absolute fucking vulture," he says under his breath.

Freya's fingers dig into Taft's arm as she tries to peek around him. "Oh god, he's trying to cross over to us."

As they hustle away, Taft glances back to see a familiar photographer indeed attempting to weave through multiple lanes of traffic. He instantly recognizes the paparazzo who's made stealthily following Mandi his mission for years—Kurt Kane. He was the one who took the picture at the club that sent Freya and Taft viral.

"Please don't panic," starts Taft. "But as invasive as the paparazzi can be, this guy is one of the worst."

Freya sucks in her cheeks. "I *knew* he looked familiar. Oh my god, I think he's even followed us on our walks with Hen."

It wouldn't surprise Taft. He's used to feeling eyes on him, but with a pang of sympathy, he realizes that he'd forgotten how disconcerting it must be for Freya. "Can you run in heels?"

She looks horrified. "What's he going to do if he catches up to us?"

"Get in our faces. Block our way to the car. He filed charges against Mandi's last boyfriend when they got in an altercation outside her apartment. Kurt's pushy and aggressive when it comes to her," Taft admits.

A series of loud honks erupt as traffic is forced to stop for the intrepid photographer.

"I'm never wearing heels again," Freya says decisively. "I don't care if she's an inch taller, apparently from now on I need shoes I can evade stalkers in." She scowls. "*Thanks a lot, Mandi.*"

"I'm sorry we didn't mention him before," says Taft, throwing another look over his shoulder. "Let's go!"

He does his best to tug Freya along with him, but with Kurt gaining on them, it becomes obvious after a few feet she's at risk of twisting her ankle. He can't ask her to shuck off her heels, either, not on these streets.

Without breaking stride, he bends just enough to scoop her into his arms, one arm bracing her back, the other behind her knees. She gasps as she's jostled against him, breasts bumping his chest. Taft tries not to groan; it's the worst possible timing, but she feels so good, all soft curves and warm skin.

Before Taft can sink too into the feeling, Freya yelps, "We won't make it all the way to the car like this!"

She's right, his arms are straining, but it's worth it to carry her bridal style. It's also given them enough of a head start to lose Kurt, but not for long. They're not close enough to the theater to double back, and still too far from the car, so that leaves them with just one option.

The time-honored tradition of a hot-and-heavy pretend make-out.

He ducks into an alley behind a seedy bar. Farther ahead there are a few people idling around trash cans, cigarette butts glowing orange in the dim light.

Freya squirms in his arms. "We're stopping?"

Taft glances down at her and throws away every reason why, even if it's only make-believe, this is a bad idea. He sets her down, heart thumping when he hears her soft gasp as her shoulders meet the rough brick wall behind her. "You okay?"

The alarm hasn't left her face, but her mouth twitches into a smile. "Has this move ever worked?"

He opens his mouth.

"In real life," she adds quickly.

He has no idea. Probably. Definitely. "Mmm," he hums, noncommittal.

Freya's eyes are dead set on him. She's so close he can count every single black eyelash. Long and lush, they graze her skin as she shuts her eyes as he dips his face into her neck. God, she smells incredible. Like the comforting warmth of fresh ink on old paper and the tingling sweetness of summer mint from his herb garden.

Taft settles his hands, only slightly trembling, on her waist loosely. His hip bones brush hers. To any outside observer, they're just two lovers unable to keep their hands off each other.

Freya's arms reach up to clasp behind his neck, eliciting a growl deep in the back of his throat. Her slightest touch and he's a goner. She must have come to the same conclusion, because in unison her thumbs start to leisurely scratch his nape. Involuntarily, he tenses, hips bucking into hers. It's been so long since someone has touched him like that.

She makes a sound that could have been a giggle, and suddenly all he wants to do is look at her.

Dressed as they are in their premiere finery, Taft knows this is the last place Kurt will think to look, but just in case, he keeps his head bent, obscuring his face, and inhales her scent, anchoring himself to this moment. A memory he knows he will revisit in the future, like the way Freya flips the pages of her favorite books.

"This is just like something out of a movie," she whispers, breath tickling the curve of his ear. Her arms tighten around Taft, bringing him closer until their bodies are flush. "Can't lie, it's exciting."

Taft's smiling lips hover above the crook of her neck, feeling the warmth rising from her skin. He wants to close the gap, press open-mouthed kisses as far down as she'll let him. "You're adorable."

Freya tilts her head as if in invitation, giving him better access. "Just adorable?"

Awkwardness lances through him, turning him all of sixteen again. "Uhhh . . ."

Freya's gaze flicks from his eyes to his lips, fastens there for lingering seconds, leaving no doubt as to what she wants.

There are a thousand adjectives on the tip of Taft's tongue to describe her, so he's kicking himself that the one that actually came out of his mouth was "adorable." Hen wearing a party hat is adorable. Photos of his nieces and nephews dressed in football onesies on game day are adorable.

Freya is . . . *his*.

Possessive want flares in his belly. He blinks. That wasn't the word he intended, but he can't take it back or say it out loud because he has *no business* wanting her as much as he does.

"Loyal," Taft says, drawing back to look at her as he says it. "Beautiful. Driven. Courageous. So goddamn sexy. Even when you wake up cranky before coffee and your hair is a mess, sticking up all over the place with the previous night's hair spray. Maybe especially then."

Freya claps her hand over her mouth to contain her giggle, dropping it to mouth *Sorry* for the interruption.

"I've never known anybody like you."

"LA is full of girls like me," says Freya. She seems almost embarrassed. "Everywhere on this planet is full of lost girls struggling to be adults and figuring their shit out, struggling to move on . . . I'm not special."

Unacceptable. The wrongness of this woman thinking she's a dime a dozen needs to be rectified *immediately*. If she talked herself up as much as she talked herself down, Taft is convinced there is nothing she couldn't do.

"You endure, Freya," he says softly. "It's one of my favorite things about you."

Her red lips part and her tongue wets the inner seam of her mouth like she doesn't even realize she's doing it. She has a terrible habit of accidentally eating Dior lipstick, Taft notices fondly.

"But I've caused you so much trouble," she whispers.

"Are you kidding me?" He gives her an incredulous look. "Sweetheart, the trouble was the best part."

Her smile is sweet and tentative, but she doesn't say anything for a long moment. Either she's savoring his declaration or she's mentally writing the line down to reuse in her book later.

Freya bites her lip. "I like when you call me sweetheart."

Taft promptly resolves to use the endearment more often. Every day if she wants. His fingertips brush her jaw, skating up her cheek and slipping into her hair to cradle her face. "Can I kiss you?"

"*Finally.*" Her voice is husky, heavy with want. "What are you waiting for?"

"So demanding," Taft teases, but there's no world in which he doesn't oblige her.

He doesn't start with Freya's lips, like he's sure she expects. The first kiss Taft perches is on her shoulder, a place he's always found tempting. He's rewarded by the shiver that goes through her, followed by the breathy, needy whimper as he drags his mouth up her throat to gently suck at her pulse point.

He's careful not to leave a hickey, since he's not sure how she'd feel about it, but from the way her fingers insistently dig into him, he gets the sense she wouldn't mind. Smiling against her skin, his lips sweep along her jaw, the softness under her chin, and then, the final destination they've both been aching for.

It isn't like the thought of kissing her hasn't been devouring him ever since they first met at Books & Brambles, the barbs flinging from her mouth at such odds with the gentle, almost loving way she smoothed her hands over that corgi wrapping paper. He'd wanted her even more when he realized she was the girl in the red dress, fleeing like Cinderella at the ball.

But now the anticipatory buildup is a crescendo in his chest, the pulse of the city all around them, and Taft knows that this kiss has *nothing* to do with their cover and everything to do with her.

"Taft?" Her whisper is a little unsure. "I . . . I think the photographer's moved on."

"I told you once that when I kiss you, it wouldn't be for anyone else." She nods uncertainly.

Hovering over her lips, Taft murmurs, "Whether or not we're being chased, I want you to know that I want this."

And then he closes what little distance remains between them, capturing her sweetness with a hunger he can't remember ever feeling before. That first taste is like summer lightning on a hot, humid Texan night. Those sultry temperatures have nothing on the heat that's radiating from both of them in this alley, and when Freya squeezes him even closer, like she can't get enough of him, he can't remember why he wasn't kissing her all along.

Her lips are soft and firm, and she knows how to use her tongue, exactly as he remembers from the photo shoot. She coaxes entry into his mouth using the perfect amount of pressure, and when the kiss deepens, she scratches her nails into his scalp, making him hiss with pleasure.

She's nestled into his body so fully that there's no way she doesn't feel his growing erection against her thigh, but she stays where she is.

Like there's nowhere else she'd rather be but here in his arms.

When they part for breath, Taft comes to with slow, languid blinks like he's coming out of a dream.

His thoughts feel fuzzy, but he knows he has to stop before they go any further. Freya deserves better than an alley behind a bar, and even though need rages through him, he wants her in his bed, with sheets and a door and no risk of bystanders. He wants to savor her, give her slow, exquisite pleasure, not the rushed desire of a quickie.

"Let's go back home," says Taft. The smokers in the alleyway have left, and he glances toward the street. "The coast is clear."

Freya doesn't let go as her eyes search his. "You don't regret what just happened, do you?" Her shoulders curl in on herself, bracing for bad news. "Like, we aren't going to go home and you're going to overthink this? Because if you ice me out again, I don't think I can—"

"I'm never going to do that again, Freya," he says before she can finish the sentence. "God, I don't know how I made it through the first time. It killed me to hold myself apart from you."

Taft can tell that these are the words of reassurance she needs to hear when the tension leaves her body and she gives him a shimmering smile he's never seen before.

Freya slips her fingers between his, squeezing their interlocked fingers. "Then let's go home."

CHAPTER NINETEEN

The drive home is a blur. All Freya remembers is that they were there and now they're here, shoving their way into the bedroom, fingers wandering with abandon, both of them breathing erratically as they steal kisses back and forth.

"Bed," Taft groans into her ear.

Her breasts feel heavy and tight, nipples hardening at the tickle of his breath. "You'll need to unzip me," she says, placing his hand on the small of her back.

"Soon." His eyes are dark with promise. "Sit on the edge of the bed first."

She watches him take off his black jacket and drape it over the footboard. A few loose curls flop onto his forehead and with an impatient sound, he rakes them back. He looks sinfully good in his black pants and white dress shirt, no longer crisp, especially when he rolls back the sleeves.

Taft kneels at her feet and places one hand on each of her knees, parting them slow enough that she could stop him if she wanted. "Can I?" he asks, voice losing all trace of authoritativeness and abruptly replaced with a vulnerability that makes her unable to deny him anything.

She can't say she's not nervous, but she nods.

"I need you to say it, Freya," he says gently.

"Yes," she whispers, voice hoarse. "Yes, I want you."

Without taking his eyes from her, he palms her dress up to scrunch at her waist. Her silky nude panties are soaked, and when he takes in a sharp breath, she knows he's seen it. But to her surprise, he doesn't just yank them off. Instead, he leans in to press a soft, lingering kiss behind her knee. His breath is hot and the pressure of his lips just right as he drags his mouth up her inner thighs in nibbling little kisses that make her muscles twitch the closer he gets to her center.

Freya's back hits the mattress as she spreads her legs even farther apart for him, whining when he doesn't stroke her where she *really* wants to be touched.

"Impatient," he says, sounding amused and maybe a little smug, too. "I'm going to take my time with you, sweetheart."

At the first graze of his teeth on her inner thigh, *so* close to where she wants him, she almost snarls her frustration. But then the tip of a finger flirts with her folds and her stomach reflexively tightens. His touch is featherlight, never quite reaching her clit but circling the rest of her until her thighs tremble and her breath quakes.

The same finger dips inside her in shallow exploration before withdrawing and repeating the process, knuckles pushing in farther with each thrust. "Fuck, you're so wet for me," says Taft, voice strangled.

"More," she begs, tossing her head to the side, feeling the blush rise in her breasts. She wants his hands on her, wants him to peel off the dress until there's nothing separating them, but he doesn't seem to want to be rushed.

He adds another finger, curling his fingers just right, and she can feel his eyes on her face when she clenches around him. The sensation feels good, but it's not enough. Only once does the heel of his palm pin her clit as he experimentally rotates his wrist, hitting new angles. He gives her a knowing look when she keens for him but doesn't repeat the move.

It awakens something primal in her, something that wants him inside her *now*. She *aches* to feel full.

He moves in and out of her, building the tension until her clit is throbbing. When he swipes some of her own wetness onto the bud, the friction from the pad of his thumb makes her hips jerk. Only his other arm splayed over her waist keeps her still, which is useful a moment later when his mouth takes over.

Taft's talented tongue knows exactly where to swipe and swirl, coaxing the neediest sounds out of her. Each flick makes her writhe and fist the sheets, thrashing her head with utter abandon. Her limbs melt under his ministrations, every shudder he pulls from her rolling through her body like magma.

Like everything he does, even in this he's thorough and devoted, leaving no part of her untouched.

The teasing abruptly stops and he starts sweeping kisses over her thighs again, tiny butterfly caresses that send tingles down her legs but do little for the tension building inside her.

"Taft," she gasps. "*Please.*"

Whatever he hears in her voice must convince him, because he nuzzles her skin with his nose one final time before using his thumbs to part her folds. His tongue moves against her with new fervor, lapping and feasting until her vision almost shorts out. Eyes tightly closed, she digs her fingers into his hair and pulls him closer. Now both his mouth and his fingers are working her, his tongue circling her pulsing clit while his fingers curl inside her.

"I'm . . . I'm . . . ," she starts to gasp, stomach tightening with a familiar feeling.

"That's it, baby. Let go," he encourages.

His thumb grinds against her clit and she cries out, the crescendo starting to build.

That's when his lips clasp her clit, sucking hard, and just like that,

Freya crests. She comes apart around his mouth, feeling his tongue and his fingers and his teeth stoking her need. His touch calls her back, grounds her to him, even as her body shudders and her toes clench.

"Good girl," he murmurs.

"Me?" Her laugh is strangled. "I should be telling *you* 'Good job.'"

"Tell me, then," Taft says cheekily.

She smirks. "Earn it first."

He gives her a few more thrusts of his fingers, helping her ride it out, and when she falls back to earth with bright eyes and mussed hair and sticky thighs, he gives her a slow grin and wipes his chin with the back of his hand before very deliberately licking his fingers clean.

It's indescribably hot, and even though she feels a bit like jelly, Freya leans forward to cradle his face between her hands. When her lips land on his, she kisses him like a revelation, relishing the stubble along his jaw. She tastes herself in his kiss, especially when their tongues tangle and he moans into her mouth.

She draws him up until he's standing between her legs. But when she reaches for his belt, he shakes his head and moves her hand away.

"I want to make you feel this good, too," she protests.

"Pleasuring you did make me feel good." The way he says it, all deep and throaty, washes her skin with goose bumps. He grins at her reaction before starting to undress, then scoots them both back until their heads are on the pillows.

It seems a bit unfair to Freya, but when he kisses her again—his warm hand drawing down the zip of her dress and then stroking her flushed skin—she decides to temporarily let him think he's won.

Taft peels the dress down her body, kissing her feverishly as she unbuttons his shirt and tugs his pants down his thighs. He kicks them off the rest of the way, making a sound that's half laugh, half groan when they snag around his ankles.

His cock is long and thick, twitching with want, the tip glistening.

She slides down his body, leaving soft, open-mouthed kisses in her wake, before swirling her tongue over his head. His taste is salty and distinctive, not unlike her own, but she doesn't have much chance to return the favor.

"Another time," he rasps, gritting his jaw. His pupils blown wide as he looks down at her. "I need to be inside you, and I won't last five minutes if you keep doing that."

His words bring a heady rush, and she crawls back up to meet him, tasting the desperation in his kiss. He twists so he's on top, her knees brought up on either side of him.

Freya's thighs are still sticky when his hand weaves between them to find her dripping. His fingers are clever and quick, and she hisses at the dance of his touch, nipping at his shoulder as her arousal reignites.

He gives an amused chuckle at her reaction, turning his attention to her breasts. They look extra luminous in the darkness of the bedroom, topped with rosy brown nipples that he seems entranced by. He bends his head to capture one in his searching mouth, teeth toying with a nipple until it pebbles.

She squirms when she feels his teeth drag against the tender skin, not as rough as she'd like, but close. He turns his attention to her other breast, peppering sweet kisses around her areola until this nipple matches the other. She arches against him when he uses the Goldilocks amount of teeth this time, sensation strumming straight to her clit.

"Can I?" he asks, yanking open his nightstand drawer for a condom.

"Yes, please."

Once he rolls it on, Taft gazes into her eyes as he aligns himself with her entrance, groaning at their first contact. She tenses, too, anticipating the stretch and the fill she hasn't been able to stop thinking about, and lets her nails bite into his bare ass.

The wordless encouragement is all he needs. In one solid thrust, he drives into her, sheathing himself fully. Her gasp is swallowed by his mouth, and her hips snap into his. The first time he pulls out, she makes an embarrassingly needy mewl that makes him smirk. The retaliatory swat she intends for his shoulder fizzles halfway and turns into desperate backrubs, aching for his return.

Each subsequent thrust she meets with equal ferocity, both of them losing themselves in the quick pace he sets. He hooks one of her legs over his shoulder, and when the angle changes, his cock hitting her just right, her moan fills the room. Taft's eyes are molten as he brushes hair away from her forehead.

Heat coils low in her belly, and she reaches down to touch herself, when his hand stops her.

"That's my job," he grits out, finding her nub again.

With a two-prong assault on her senses, it doesn't take long before she starts to quiver. His face contorts when he feels her muscles constricting around him, and she knows he's close to the edge, too.

"You feel so good." Taft's thrusts pick up speed. His groan is low and full of desperation as they both chase their climax. "Are you going to come for me again? You first, sweetheart. Come on my cock. You're so close, I can feel you clenching my cock."

The dirty talk is what does it. Freya reaches her peak within seconds, spasming around him until, with a shout, he follows her over the edge.

"That's it, just like that." Taft's voice is rougher than she's ever heard it. He gives her a couple more thrusts, even though he's already softening inside her. "Good girl. Let go."

"That was definitely more than five minutes," Freya murmurs thoughtfully after he pulls her against his sweaty chest and drops a surprisingly chaste kiss to her lips, followed by one on the forehead.

Taft's answering laughter rings around them until the bed starts shaking again.

CHAPTER TWENTY

Freya wakes up half splayed over Taft's chest, one leg thrown high over his hip and her face buried in his neck. Utterly sated and boneless. More well rested than she's been since moving in, for sure, but also, this is the best sleep she's had in forever, even though neither she nor Taft got a whole lot of it.

"Good morning," he murmurs in a sleep-roughened voice. He turns, arms cocooning her and tucking her even more snugly against him. His weight pins her to the mattress, the warmth and scent of his skin lulling her to sleep again. Their bodies are so close that she can't tell whether it's his heartbeat she feels or her own.

"Morning," she whispers back, skating her nails lightly up and down his spine, rewarded with the soft growl in the back of his throat that takes her back to last night. Involuntarily, her hips jerk.

With a laugh, Taft buries his face in her neck. Nimble fingers find their way into her hair, plundering deep to massage her scalp just the way she likes. Her breathy exhale makes his cock twitch, and she smiles, pressing a soft kiss to his temple.

His lips tickle against the crook of her neck as he asks, "How are you feeling?"

She considers. She's sore in the best of ways, but she gets the sense that's not what he means. "Good," she says simply, and it's not because of writer's block or snarl or any other excuse. It's because that one word says it all and says it best.

"Me too." His voice is gravelly and muffled. "I've been thinking about sharing a bed with you for so long. It's been hell on the couch, imagining you in my bed, wanting me as much as I wanted you."

"More," says Freya. "I wanted you more."

His eyes turn molten.

"Honestly, though," she says with a hint of a blush, "I like everything about you. Sometimes, with other people . . . I feel like I have to try? You know? Not like I'm trying to impress them or anything, but that I have to live up to my best self. Someone who I haven't been in years. With you, I just have to exist. You take me as I am. You meet me *where* I am, *who* I am right now."

"I know exactly what you mean," he replies. "I'd like you even if we never played the ten-secrets game. I did, in fact. Like you, that is. When we first met in the bookshop, you were all I could think about. You were the first girl who made me regret my 'relationship' with Mandi, and it killed me when you recognized who I was . . . Because then the fantasy of being just some guy who could flirt with you was over. The truth is, until you, I always felt like a bedside book."

She blinks. "A what?"

"You know. That book that sits on the nightstand of people who'll take forever to read it, and that's only because it's one of those highbrow ones they think they're supposed to read before they die, but they just keep putting it off? It's just . . . there. Waiting to be picked."

The laugh startles out of her. "Oh my god, are you kidding me?" She twists out of his arms, ignoring his whine of protest, to grab something from the nightstand. "A bedside book like *this*?"

She arches an eyebrow as she holds up a thick paperback, spine creased and corners decidedly not crisp, thoroughly tabbed with what looks like at least a hundred neon stickies. When she waves it in front of his face, he stares like he's hypnotized.

"You're the bedside book I would reach for a hundred times over. A five-star favorite I'd reread like I was visiting an old friend or long-lost lover." Freya swallows, throat tight. "For the record, this reader loves a good bedside book."

His mouth is on hers almost before she can finish the sentence.

The kiss is tender and bruising at the same time, and when he snakes a hand up her thigh, she moans into his mouth. Sensation skitters across her chest, stiffening her nipples into hard peaks, and strikes between her legs. The friction from the pads of his fingers is enormously pleasing, but it's not enough.

"I'm not ready to get out of bed just yet," Taft mumbles against her collarbone when the kiss breaks, both breathing heavily. The sensation tickles, making her toes curl the same way they did last night when he crooked his fingers inside her just right. "I don't want you to leave me— my bed."

He covers his slipup quickly, but Freya's heart twinges all the same.

Truthfully, leaving their snuggly, cozy cocoon is the last thing she wants, too, but her manuscript deadline is looming, and she promised Stori she'd come by the store this afternoon. It's just a little past 9:00 a.m. and if she tries, she can get a few hours of writing in first.

Freya's not quite sure what kind of debauchery her aunt thinks they get up to when she's with Taft, but since Stori thinks her shifts at Books & Brambles keep her writing on schedule, she doesn't want to push it. Boss Stori won't "fire" her, but Sister Stori will be worse, all I'm-not-mad-just-disappointed lecture and I-worry-about-you-when-you're-not-here guilt.

"I can give you five minutes before I start writing," she offers, nuzzling into his warmth.

His laugh makes his entire body shake. "Should I be insulted?"

She presses her lips against his pec and tries not to smile, but he can probably feel it, anyway. "Okay, ten." He pokes her in the ribs. "Fifteen?" Another poke. "You are way too easy to tease, you know."

"Mmm," he hums. "I'll remember that."

She leans back to cock her head at him. "Why did that sound like you're promising vengeance?"

No less than an hour later, after he's brought her to the edge three times with just his fingers, he shows her exactly how he's going to tease her.

"This is *incredibly* unfair," she huffs, thrashing her legs. Her hair is matted to the back of her neck, her calves ache deliciously, and whoever invented edging is absolutely going to get a piece of her mind, except that they've probably perished by now from lack of orgasm.

His chuckle is entirely unapologetic, and there's a hint of mischief in his eyes as he brings his middle and forefinger, slick with her wetness, to his mouth.

Freya groans and tosses him a condom to wear. "Okay, okay! You are an unselfish and mind-blowing lover. Your foreplay prowess is unsurpassed, and you have ruined me for all other men. And you definitely aren't a five-minute wonder."

"Was that so hard?" He nudges his painfully erect cock between her legs.

She glares at him. "Fucking *finish* me."

"Well, since you asked so nicely."

And within ten minutes, he takes them both stratospheric, though like the true gentleman he is, Taft makes sure she finishes first.

Later, while he showers, Freya makes breakfast. Cooking for a guy is a new thing for her, and while she's nowhere near good enough to make a habit of it, the one thing she nails every time is her eggs Benedict. Even Stori, who's picky about the doneness of her yolk, loves it.

In New York, it was Freya's favorite going-out-for-brunch food, and she'd sweet-talked the chef into giving her the recipe. Toasted English muffins, crispy Canadian bacon, perfectly poached egg, all smothered in Hollandaise sauce and a confetti of Taft's windowsill dill? Her mouth waters just thinking about it.

While she waits for him, she sends Ava a message.

Freya: GUESS WHO'S OFF FRIEND ISLAND?

Ava:  or

Freya: MInd-blowing

Ava: HOLY MOTHER FORKING SHIRTBALLS

"Did you cook?" Taft's eyes are wide when he comes into the kitchen, sniffing appreciatively.

Freya puts her phone facedown on the table. "It's no avocado on toast, but I hope you like it."

"Okay, I may have been an Angeleno since I was eighteen, but I'm not an avocado evangelist," he says with a grin, sitting down at the table. "More of a beans-on-toast guy."

Freya hands him a knife and fork. "This is so good it'll convert you into an eggs Benedict guy."

Taft cuts into the egg, letting the runny yolk pool. He spears a forkful and sends her a lazy, disarming grin. "You making me breakfast is enough to make me a *Freya* guy for life."

LATER, FREYA'S ARRIVAL at Books & Brambles coincides perfectly with everyone's lunch break, so she has the shop floor more or less to herself. Skye and her wife swing by early in Freya's shift to buy romance books, chide her for missing their barbecue, and slyly congratulate her on the love bite blossoming on her neck.

Freya makes sure to hide it with her hair, air-dried into its nest of messy curls, before she video-calls her dad. "Hi, Dad!" she says brightly when he picks up on the first ring.

His response of "Sweet pea!" is every bit as enthusiastic, but she sees his smile falter just a touch. She's taken aback, too—that endearment was usually reserved for her mom.

"Are you going out?" she asks, taking in the wallet and keys in his free hand. "I can call back."

"Nonsense," Jay Lal says firmly. "It's just some errands. I always have time for you."

It's corny, but it makes her smile. She watches as he takes a seat in his favorite living room armchair before she asks, "How have you been?"

"Honestly, honey, I miss the hell out of you. But I guess I can't blame LA for sweeping you away from boring old Dad," he says with a chuckle.

Freya fixates on the family portrait behind his head. "It's not like that. I needed to be somewhere—"

Else. Somewhere without all the memories that hurt too much right now to remember.

He nods. "I know, hon. I know. And at least you're living with family. Has Stori been a good influence on you? I seem to remember a certain twenty-first birthday in Atlantic City—"

Freya hastily cuts him off. "She's been great. More than great. And I've been great. But you're not off the hook, Dad! You still haven't really told me how *you're* doing."

"Me? I'm great." He can't keep his face straight.

"*Dad.*"

"Saving all your other adjectives for your book?" he teases. "The one Stori tells me is almost done?"

"Interesting segue. Very not suspicious at all," she drawls right back.

"How did that TikTok sound from that animal video you sent me go? 'Don't be suspicious, don't be suspicious.'" His smile is so wide that she can count every single one of his crow's-feet. "Mom would be so proud of you."

Eye contact suddenly gets to be too much. Freya swerves her eyes to the shelves she just rearranged.

"I'm proud of you, too," her dad continues, voice infinitely soft and gentle. "And all jokes aside, I'm doing well. I'm so glad that you are, too. You look happy like I haven't seen in . . . well, a long time. I hated seeing how stressed and lost you were, like all the magic had gone out of the world."

She takes in his words and then she takes in his appearance. His shirt is ironed, the collar crisp. He's less haggard, like he's sleeping through the night and drinking enough water and doing all those other things Freya worried he wasn't taking seriously.

"You look happy, too," she realizes out loud.

She wishes she could tell him about Taft, but there's no way she's ready for a paternal freak-out.

"Freya, there's something else I wanted to talk to you about, too. I met someone at my grief counseling group. Sakura Takahashi, she's an English professor. We've met for coffee a few times. I never thought that after Mom, I would ever . . . But I wanted to make sure that . . ." He hesitates, teeth scraping over his lip. The gesture is so Freya that she suddenly can't remember if he picked up the habit from her or the other way around. "Are you okay with that, sweet pea?"

"Dad, of course. I . . . Mom told me that one day you might want to date again. She wouldn't want you to be alone. I don't, either."

"That's Anjali, all right." He chuckles. "She always knew everything. Knew us better than we knew ourselves. Remember how she said your first book was *the one*?"

"And Mom was always right," says Freya, transported back to her debut novel's signing right here at Books & Brambles.

The proud smile on his face now is the same one he wore in the front row when, just four years ago, they were all here at Stori's bookshop to do a reading of Freya *Anjali* Lal's debut novel—slated to be fall's biggest book according to publishing and Very Important Internet People—to a full house.

If she concentrates, she can still remember the heady scent of pungent Sharpies as her inky signature swirled across the title page in the signature she's been practicing since she was nine and her dad took her to Staples to spiral bind her first manuscript.

"I wish she'd been here with us to celebrate my first book. It feels weird to write the second without her," Freya admits. She stares at Hunka Junk on the counter, still set to the background image of that night. "Sometimes I wonder how many books it'll take before that will fade."

And what if it never does?

"Why don't you tell *me* about it?" her dad suggests.

So Freya does. She talks until she's hoarse, because she still hasn't perfected her two-minute elevator pitch, and fields all his questions, of which there are many, mostly fatherish ones about why she wants to write about murder and is it because he let her watch horror movies as a child.

Suffice it to say, she's more than happy when Stori returns from lunch with a to-go box. "Is that for me?" she asks with a hopeful gesture.

Stori sets it on the counter. "Prawn and cabbage dumplings, yup. Hi, Jay!"

"Hey, sis. Freya, I should let you get back to work."

"Okay, but text me how your date goes," says Freya.

Date? Stori mouths.

Tell you later, Freya communicates with a hand wave.

"Sure thing. Love you, sweet pea."

"You too, Dad."

"He's dating?" Stori asks when Freya ends the video. "Who is she? Does Dad know? Did *you* know?"

"No, but I'm fine with it. I'm proud of him for putting himself out there. Dating is hard. God, even just being a *person* is hard, never mind letting in another person."

Stori nods in understanding. "So . . . that smile you're wearing. I'm not even going to pretend that you're thinking about the gorgeous Manish Dayal or Oscar Isaac. This smile is all on Taft Bamber."

Freya's mouth drops unsubtly open. Is sex glow a real thing? Does Stori have sexdar?

Stori rolls her eyes, reading her easily. "He's coming in. I saw him parking."

True enough, Taft slips through the doors of the bookshop a minute later. "Hey, Stori." He whips off his cap and sunglasses as soon as he sees there's no one else in the store.

"It's a slow day," Stori explains. "I let Cliff and Emma have the afternoon off. So you two can be over here and I'll just be   " She looks between Taft and Freya. "You know what, pretend I'm not here."

Freya watches her aunt leave with a fond smile. "She thinks we're going to jump on each other."

Taft laughs. "I mean, did we rule that out, or . . . ?"

"For now, yes," says Freya. It's taking all her willpower not to lean in, cup his chin, and pull him close for a kiss that will leave his eyes as glazed as they were last night.

But they're in public. She can be strong. She can ignore her instincts because she *has* to. Even though all she wants is to be a girl who kisses her guy without having to worry about anyone watching.

"I missed you," Taft says with an endearingly shy smile even though it's not the first time he's confessed this. "Fuck, Freya. I miss you all the time when you're not there. I've never felt like this before."

And as mind-blowing as their first time together was, this soft admission is even better than sex. This is Taft standing in front of her, telling her his truth without a hint of doubt or embarrassment. This is him knowing he's safe with her—knowing that she's gentle with his heart.

She swallows hard. "It's new for me, too. You are, without doubt, my person, Taft. My . . . home."

His eyes are the Bermuda Triangle, magnetic and mesmerizing, sucking her in. Right now they're a whirlpool of caution and frustration, and she knows he hates having to keep up appearances in case anyone comes in. There are people walking on the sidewalk who could duck into the bookshop at any second.

"When you find a book you want," she says, "I'll gift wrap it for you, if you want. On the house."

"Yeah?" His voice dips, running over her like a caress. "You want an extra couple of minutes with me?"

"Honestly? I want a lot more than that."

He takes a step closer to the counter, enough to invade her senses with his nearness. His spicy aftershave, the faintest whiff of this morning's coffee, and . . . did he try out her bar of goat's milk soap? The thought brings a smile to Freya's face. She'd used some of his body wash before, too, and she likes the idea of her scent on his skin.

"You've got it, baby," says Taft. His eyes blaze. "You can have everything you want."

CHAPTER TWENTY-ONE

"Y̶ou know, I don't think we have any commitments on our schedule today," says Taft. He strokes Freya's calves, which have been draped over his lap for the last hour while, on the opposite end of the couch, he reads the book he just bought from Books & Brambles yesterday. "How do you want to spend it?"

Freya glances up from her typewritten pages, startled to discover how difficult it is to pull herself back into the present. She's cozily reclining, wearing a tee Hero sent that reads I FOUGHT WRITER'S BLOCK AND WON. With some surprise, she realizes it's almost time for lunch.

That morning, she'd extricated herself from the warmth of Taft's arms at 5:00 a.m., but even though she'd shut her office door and tried to type quietly, Taft had woken by six. Freya hadn't realized until she'd smelled the coffee he'd started. Perhaps sensing she was in the zone, he let her work without interruption after thoughtfully bringing her the French press, a ham-and-cheese croissant, and a bowl of cut cantaloupe.

Blink, blink, blink. "Sorry, say again?"

His smile is knowing. "Reading anything good?"

"Five-star excellence," she says with a laugh.

He starts to frown.

"No, seriously," she hastens to tell him. "It's good."

It hadn't taken him long to figure out that self-deprecating statements were part and parcel of authorhood—Freya, at least, confesses that her ego is simultaneously deeply insecure and intolerably confident. It's cute how he makes it a point to protest whenever he thinks she's taking a dig at herself.

"Yeah? The typewriter helped?"

It's impossible to miss his eagerness to be helpful. He doesn't want credit, just the contentedness of doing something for her. It's never in a showy way, either. Despite his leading-man looks, it constantly surprises her how okay he is with being in the background.

A hasty part of Freya wants to hand over her pages and let him see for himself, but she knows that if she does, she'll start second-guessing everything and itch to start over the way she nearly did when he caught a glimpse at her screen last week.

She grins. "I'm so close to writing 'The End.' I just hit seventy thou." Or what she guesstimates is seventy thousand words—it's hard to tell when a typewriter doesn't come with a word counter. She riffles through the pages, still not over how *much* there is, or that she was so engrossed that she almost forgot it was her own writing she'd been reading.

"Freya! That's incredible! Now we *have* to do something to celebrate!"

His shout brings Hen traipsing back into the living room.

Where Freya downplays her pride, Taft displays it for all to see. She smothers a smile, imagining him as the perfect supportive Instagram boyfriend, filming her doing silly promo TikToks and Instagram Reels with her books for the likes. But he'd probably be adamant about staying out of view so he didn't steal her thunder, even though she'd tease him that the whole point of dating a superstar was to capitalize on his face. He'd roll his eyes, make some joke about how—

Taft's hand lands on Freya's knee. "Penny for them?" At her

confused look, he smiles gently and traces shapes against her skin. "Your thoughts."

"Just thinking about you," she tells him. His eyes darken. "My drafting brain is still on. I lost myself for a second, fictionalizing a moment between us a little bit in the future."

"Know me that well, do you?" He continues the soft, lazy touches, this time tickling the back of her knee. It's a place he loves to kiss, especially after he found out it shoots meteor showers down her legs, a fact he derives great pleasure out of exploiting at every opportunity.

She grins. "Well, Google is *very* informative."

"'Google,' she says," he says through a laugh, like he can't believe it. He brings her hand to his lips, turns her wrist to face up, then kisses that shivery spot ardently. "If you have more questions for me, all you need to do is ask."

Freya's face burns and she brings her stack of pages up to hide her face.

Yes, she's keenly aware of the fact that he's seen her sweaty and shrieking his name, but mortification never crossed her mind once during any of their sexy times. But being caught allowing herself to be vulnerable, and asking that of him in return, is a different story.

"You can play with me whenever you want," he says, the double entendre sinking into her until her feet squirm in his lap. But the next thing he says is serious. "Honestly, you have only to ask, Freya. There's pretty much nothing I'd deny you."

"What if I want to spend all weekend with you right here at home? I could keep working, and you could finish reading your book. I could help you run lines for that indie movie audition on Monday."

It's not the first time she'd referred to his place as *home*, but it hits different this time.

This cozy Saturday-morning domesticity allows them to be themselves—Freya and Taft. Anything else means donning a mask again. And that's getting harder and harder to do. She can see from his face that the idea of holing up here holds a certain appeal for him, too.

"We could do that," he agrees. "Or . . . And I know you have a deadline, and all our scheduled appearances have been taking time away from that, but how would you feel about getting out of the house for a little?"

"I thought you said we were free this weekend."

Taft's eyes meet hers steadily. "We are."

"So . . . this would be, like, a date?"

"I wanna show you my world. Mine, Taft's, regular guy. Not Taft, actor."

"And who would I be in this scenario? Freya, regular girl, or—"

"You're the one that I want, Freya," he interrupts. "Be you."

She's always liked how he says her name. The syllables sound like a secret rolling off his tongue, and it's one she wants him to tell her over and over again, because she'll never tire of the cadence of his voice. And now, the way he says it makes it sound like he's choosing her. Risking something for her.

She slides her feet to the floor, heart thumping erratically. "Are you serious?"

He can't be. There's no way. If they're caught, *all* their careers are in jeopardy.

"I'm positive. I wouldn't put you at risk, I know how hard you've worked to get your writing back on track."

"That's sweet, but it's not *me* I'm worried about," she says, hearing her frustration. "You know we can't go out in public together with me looking like myself. It would blow up in our faces, and I don't want to be a liability to you and Mandi again. I promised myself I wouldn't. I'd love a real date . . . but I refuse to be selfish with you."

Especially as he's showing a shocking lack of self-preservation right now, she doesn't add.

Taft's face is indecipherable. "I don't want to compromise anymore."

Connor and the rest of the *Once Bitten* group comes to Freya's mind. "Good. You shouldn't have to."

"That includes *you*. What you said at the bookshop, you were right. You and me, this is real. I don't want to pretend like we're not happening. I *can't*. I want to know everything about you, Freya, but I don't need the ten-secrets game to do it. I don't need to know your secrets to know that I *already* like you."

This is everything she ever wanted him to say.

"I'm not going to let anyone else's idea of my career stop me from spending time with you," says Taft. "Or being with you, or building something real as soon as we can. The only person who gets to dictate my destiny is me."

Freya's heart flies into her throat. This coming from a guy who once let his entire life be mapped out for him, who thought compromising who he was and what he wanted was the only way he would get ahead. His speech throws all that noise out the proverbial window.

"You're making it really hard for a girl to stand her ground," she whispers.

"That's because I want to sweep you off your feet," he says. Before Freya knows what's happening, he's scooped her up behind the legs and pulled her against his chest.

Freya tips her head back to eye him. "That's not a line from one of your shows, is it?"

He dimples boyishly. "I'll have you know that was a Taft Bamber original. Only the best for you." He makes Freya's mind up for her when his nose nuzzles into the ticklish place behind her ear. "Come on, let me show you all my haunts. Be a tourist with me, baby."

TAFT'S IDEA OF *the best* includes bringing her to two of his favorite places in the city: Griffith Park and its iconic observatory overlooking downtown LA and Hollywood, and the indie bookshop Skylight Books.

"A bookshop, Taft? Really?" Freya tips her head back, getting a close-up of his grin as he slings an arm around her shoulder. She pushes her sunglasses higher on her nose. "You do remember where I work?"

They're both trying not to stand out: she's wearing the emerald-green blouse from their almost-kiss at Books & Brambles, thrown her hair into a messy ponytail, and stuck with light day makeup instead of Mandi's full face of products. Taft's casual in an unassuming baseball cap and aviators.

They're standing on a shaded bit of sidewalk next to the Los Feliz 3 movie theater, in front of spotless windows boasting dozens of summer's latest releases and big-name authors' books face out to entice buyers inside. All four of her friends' books are prominently placed, Steph's and Ava's next to each other like the best friends they are.

"It's not just any bookshop. It's a beloved Los Feliz cornerstone. Before Books and Brambles stole my heart, this is where I always came," Taft explains, holding the door open for her. "You'll love it."

"It's the place where books literally live, so that's a given," she teases, humoring him because he's being all cute and earnest, and no self-respecting writer would ever turn down a date at a bookshop.

Inside, she's welcomed home. The crisp smell of pages and familiar covers greet her. It gives her a euphoric rush that rivals the one the view from the observatory gave her. Despite both places' reminder of her own sense of cosmic smallness, she also feels a connection that she hasn't felt before. Not just to this city or her work, but to the man next to her, who, somehow, always gives her what she needs.

"Is that an actual tree?" Freya asks, staring at the ficus growing from the center of the store and disappearing through a skylight in the wood-domed ceiling. Its branches drape over multiple sections of the bookshop. "That is . . . epic."

Taft grins at the astonishment and awe in her voice. He wants her to love it here, Freya realizes.

"You know," Taft says, all casual, "I run into Chris Pine here occasionally."

"And you're only telling me this now?"

She's way too charmed by his casual name dropping to ask him anything else, like is Chris as nice as he seems or is he even nicer? (Personally, she thinks it's the latter.) And Taft just grins, like he's not jealous at all and finds an enthralled Freya equally charming, too.

Freya wanders the store, fingertips trailing over spines in the loving way that only a bibliophile can. Like Books & Brambles, Skylight Books is everything an indie bookshop should be: well stocked but still cozy enough not to lose its neighborhood feel.

She reads handwritten shelf talkers; pores over the sections dedicated to LA poets and staff picks; and slides her eyes up, down, and across shelves to find all the names of her author mutuals on Twitter, squeezing Taft's arm to excitedly point out each of her friends' books.

She hadn't realized how good it would feel to be *herself* again, in a place she loves, with a man she—

Not *loves*, maybe. Not yet. But maybe soon.

"Don't you want anything?" Taft asks after Freya picks up a third book, skims, and puts it back. "Grab whatever you want. My treat."

Flustered, she drops her hand before she reaches for a fourth. "Oh, no, it's fine, I'm just looking—"

"I have a reputation to uphold, you know. I can't walk out of here without buying *at least* five books."

When she bites her lip and doesn't say anything, Taft takes a step closer and lowers his voice. "Freya, let me spoil you."

"I can't accept—"

"Sure you can. Get whatever your heart desires."

What she really desires hits her like lightning, electrifying and all at once: all she wants is his heart.

"What about *you*?"

"Me?" Taft's voice comes out hoarse. His eyes flare and he doesn't blink. Not once. "Oh, I . . . um . . . I don't need anything. I haven't finished the books I already have."

She can't tell if he's being intentionally oblivious or not, so she doesn't push it. "Shhh!" she says instead. "Not so loud! The books will hear you."

They leave Skylight Books twenty minutes later with a heavy tote full of books Taft insisted on paying for, sliding cash across the counter in one smooth motion before she can even reach for her wallet. She bets he even knows how to tip all suave, palming bills to someone like he's the next Bond.

"Oh my god, it's Raft! Mandi! Taft!"

Freya barely has enough time to throw on her oversize sunglasses before they're besieged by a throng of shrieking teenage girls who just can't believe they ran into Hollywood's It Couple while window-shopping on Vermont Avenue. Her heart hammers as she smiles for selfies, hard enough that she's surprised it hasn't cartoonishly popped out of her chest.

The girls hang off Taft, who gamely puts his arms around their shoulders, only the slightest tension around his mouth. It's an invisible little tell to everyone but Freya that he might not be as comfortable with all the casual touching as he looks.

Pushing herself aside in favor of being Mandi—*forgetting Freya*—has never made her feel this sick before. Because today had been one of the best days of her life, and all it had taken was a second for it to be over.

Ava was right, Freya realizes suddenly. She might be playing his decoy girlfriend, but it's just a character. Once upon a time, being Mandi had been like having a comfort character like the ones in her fanfiction.

But now it's just another thing she'll have to give back.

CHAPTER TWENTY-TWO

T-*A-F-T*, Freya types one-handed into the search bar the next day, followed by *B-A-M-B-E-R*.

It's not the first time his name has graced her browser history. Aside from her misspent teenage years trawling the Web for all his mentions, she's kept on top of all the Raft gossip, especially after the close call with fans outside Skylight Books yesterday. Realistically, she knows that she doesn't need to check; if anyone was actually on to them, Moira and Gareth would descend in a blink of an eye.

Balancing a plate of her dinner in one hand—spiced carrot-and-mint couscous topped with a garlicky lemon-butter salmon filet—she hits Enter.

Immediately, millions of Google hits pop up: Taft's Instagram and Twitter, an old headshot without a hint of the silver hairs she's so fond of, IMDb and Wikipedia pages, a handful of semi-spoiler interviews about what to expect on *Banshee of the Baskervilles: The Movie*, *Once Bitten* cast interviews, and profiles on *Us* and *Entertainment Weekly*.

She takes a moment to skim everything, desperately relieved that all the clickbait headlines about his supposed cheating have been buried deep on page three.

"Freya, you do know I have a perfectly usable kitchen table, right?"

"It is a truth universally acknowledged that if there's a sofa to eat on instead . . ."

Taft snorts but joins her anyway. He tucks his feet underneath himself and digs into his own plate. "A less secure person might think you like this couch more than you like me," he says.

She good-naturedly rolls her eyes. It's blatantly untrue, even if she does love his house, and she hopes he knows it.

"Thanks for cooking," she adds, as though he hadn't eagerly scooped up all the cooking responsibilities since day one. She should feel guilty about that, but . . . "Your couscous is delicious."

His answering grin is so proud and so *rare* that she decides then and there that she is going to compliment him every chance she gets. Appreciate him. Love him. Show him what it feels like when someone's *his*.

He fluffs the couscous with his fork, as though it isn't already perfect. "I thought we agreed that we're way past googling each other."

"I wasn't—" she starts to say before catching him nodding meaningfully at the screen. "Okay, I was. But only to see what people were— Wait. 'Each other'? Have *you* been googling *me*?"

"Yes, weeks ago," he admits easily. She blinks at his frankness. "It's been hell making sure I don't reveal anything I know about you that I got from Internet stalking, sweetheart."

She wonders if what he discovered lined up with what he expected. "I wouldn't care. It's not like I haven't stalked you, too. Former fan, remember?"

"This just got very *You*," he says with a faint smile. Then something seems to occur to him, and he dimples mischievously. "I recall you telling me recently that you were *still* a fan."

She swats his arm as best she can without jostling her dinner plate. "New rule. Stop using what I say against me. If I wrote it in a book and you quote it back to me, sexy. Otherwise, nope."

"I thought we weren't making up our own rules anymore?" he counters.

She spears a carrot and shoots him a victorious grin. "Since I'm clearly the exception to your once-ironclad rules, I figure I have the right to make at least one of my own."

He stares at her for a long moment. Under the intensity of his gaze, Freya swallows, but it feels like sucking half-set concrete through a straw.

"Think you're pretty special, don't you?" Taft teases. He tucks a tendril that tumbled free of her loose braid behind her ear. "Well, you'd be right."

Freya can tell from the pleased smile sneaking over his face that her cheeks must be a telltale pink.

"You're blushing," he says, quite unnecessarily, half in surprise, half in wonder.

Any other guy and she'd bristle, peeved that he didn't have the decency to ignore it. But she doesn't mind that Taft sees, that Taft knows *he's* the one who put it there.

"I *am* known for showing and not telling," she informs him as prissily as she can muster.

He laughs, just like she'd hoped for. But then he frowns and cups her chin in his hand, dinner forgotten as his eyes search hers. "As much as I enjoy you singing your own praises for once, has no one ever told you that you're special?"

Freya bites her lip. Is he being serious? People don't go around saying things like that.

"Literally no one has said that to me in the history of ever," she tells him, averting her eyes.

Even her mom—who was her biggest supporter—would have found it corny. And it would have embarrassed Freya too much if her mom had vocalized it, but Freya never doubted that she thought so.

There were so many hollows left in her when her mom died, and one of them is something she's only now starting to get back. *He's* giving her back. Until Taft, she didn't recognize how much of her own confidence came from that kind of support.

Maybe he reads a scrap of her thoughts in her expression, because his frown turns into something else. Sad and thoughtful, and then fierce.

"You're special, too," Freya says, because she thinks she has an idea where this is coming from.

Both his brows shoot up, giving Taft an air of comical surprise.

Before he can go all modest and unpretentious about how amazing he is, she continues. "And it fucking kills me that people in your life don't make sure you know it. I see it, even if those idiot *Once Bitten* showrunners and the network didn't. You *carried* that show."

He makes a sound of protest. "I'm not—"

"Yes, you are," Freya says tenderly, placing her hand over his. "You're hurt, and you don't want to be, but that doesn't mean you're not. You should let yourself feel whatever you need to in order to"—*move on*—"make peace."

His laugh is low and disbelieving. "With Connor? Maybe in the next century."

"Not with him, not if you don't want to. But *you* and your mental health deserve it." She drifts her hand to his temple. "You live in LA. You should know all about precious real estate."

Taft almost cracks a smile, but his next words break Freya's heart. "I loved my time on *Once Bitten* so much. This was everyone's big break. We were like . . . Hell, we *were* a family. If making peace means pretending the show and its people don't mean anything to me anymore, I don't know if I can do it."

She's reminded of their breakfast together the morning after their first appearance. She knows it troubled him that she deleted words that weren't working for her, enough so that he loaned her an actual typewriter to put a stop to it. No wonder he isn't okay with deleting people.

He sighs and leans into her touch, eyes closing. "I know I shouldn't give any of them space in my head"—for a split second, his mouth had formed the word "heart" before he course corrected—"but I can't just *forget*, Freya. When I care, and I know sometimes I care too much, I can't let go. The memories . . . they haunt me. I hate the idea of living my life in distant parallel to people I used to share it with."

Her throat burns like she's just downed six shots.

Once she can swallow again, Freya says gently, "It's not about pretending or forgetting. You can acknowledge that everything you're letting go once meant something to you. But whatever threads tied you to them? They vanished the moment your personal and professional situations changed. Some were cut, others just weakened with time and lack of care. It's not your fault. Sometimes people just outgrow each other."

"I didn't outgrow them," he says automatically, almost defensive.

She gets why he thinks moving on means resigning himself to a haunted house of memories he doesn't know anymore, but she needs him to know it won't always hurt this way.

Freya shakes her head. "It's not a failing, baby. It's . . . it's life. Unscripted, ugly, unpredictable life. You don't always get a reason, closure, whatever. People leave. But sometimes they stay."

And I want to prove myself to you. I want to be someone you can trust to stay, she doesn't allow herself to say, but it lingers in the subtext.

She doesn't know if that's something in her power to promise, anyway, no matter how much she means it. They haven't known each other that long, and any number of things could happen between now and the premiere. It's strange that she lives for romantic slow burns in fiction but craves something faster and more frantic in real life.

He half smiles. "Got any tips about evicting and possibly exorcising *really* shitty emotional ghosts?"

"Actually, yes." Freya meets his eyes. "Don't accept anything less than what you deserve. Better friends will come along. Tell yourself that when it comes to your heart, compromise is never an option. You deserve to have true friends in your life who champion you. Not because they're keeping track of tit-for-tat obligatory reciprocity but because it's important to them to be there for you the way *you're* always there. Having needs doesn't make you needy."

It hurts her heart to see how much Taft gives away to people who treat it like nothing. He goes all out with the people he loves, both with big gestures and quiet consideration, and he doesn't expect it back in return. He's learned to live with so little from others, and that ends *now*.

"You're going to meet someone who is going to be"—Freya's breath catches—"so soft and gentle with your heart. That person is going to make you believe in how much more you deserve. Because you do, Taft. You deserve all the good things. A heart like yours deserves nothing but the best."

There's a caged emotion in Taft's eyes, a little wild and lion bright, like he's never been this seen before and doesn't know what to do with it. He's such a good guy, and it kills Freya that his friendship and loyalty have gone unnoticed and unappreciated all this time. Her chest burns with hot coals. Givers need to set boundaries, because god knows the takers don't have any.

"Experiences can bring you together," she says. "Nothing bonds like-minded people more than going through the same rite of passage together." Being a writer showed her that. "But sometimes, once you don't have those shared, relatable experiences anymore, friendship can take a nosedive."

Writing showed her that, too. Success—or the lack of—often showed you who your real friends were. Those who hung around hoping some of your star power would rub off. Who ditched you once they eclipsed you by some unknown metric that only mattered to them.

With a pang, she realizes how much she lucked out with Steph, Mimi, Ava, and Hero. It wasn't until she met someone so deserving of friendship as Taft that it truly sunk in that she'd taken her friends for granted. That she did them a disservice by not letting them be there for her. Didn't even let them *try*.

"The good outweighs the bad," says Taft. "Sometimes."

"Does it, though?"

He looks wounded in a way she never wants to see on his face again. She doesn't want to be another person who hurts him, and she knows that by being so blunt right now she's taking a battering ram to his already bruised heart, but he's holding on to people who have long let him go. Now it's his turn to walk away.

Biting her lip, she leans in to slant her mouth over his. Soft and teasing. Breaking the kiss before he can deepen it, she scrunches her fingers in his curls and keeps their foreheads together.

"We're used to bit-part friends in our lives turning into headline names, but it can go the other way, too," Freya whispers against his lips, each word moving like a hungry kiss even though they aren't touching. His mouth mirrors hers; she's not even sure he realizes what he's doing. "Sometimes the leading people become cameos ghosting in and out of your universe. Maybe, in the end, so small they don't even get their name in the credits."

"Freya Lal," he states, somber as a sacrament.

A lightning strike zaps down her spine. The moment between them is charged and new. He doesn't usually say her name like that, all pronouncement-like and irrefutable and with a sexy trace of barely-there Texan drawl that he's all but shed.

It's the kind of voice that makes her still with anticipation, quirking a brow as she waits for the rest.

Taft smiles with his eyes. "You'll always be a headline name to me."

———

THE NEXT DAY, as Freya and Taft stand on the sidewalk in front of a French-inspired cake shop in Los Feliz, a bemused Freya crosses her arms across her chest. "I *think* I might be a little underdressed."

In truth, she doesn't mind that she's wearing one of the most casual outfits from Mandi's wardrobe, a white halter crop top and wide-legged flowy pin-striped trousers. But the other couple who just entered the storybook patisserie wore clothing so elegant that they might have just walked off a runway.

Taft, on the other hand, is completely unbothered in his fitted black tee and oatmeal-colored chinos. "They have the best cake, I swear. Connor"—for a second he bites his lip, seeming abashed to mention his former friend's name—"and Holly ordered their wedding cake from here, but this place does an incredible high tea—sweet only, no savory. I thought it would be fun to try someplace I've never been before."

Freya can't help her smile. "Yeah, but . . . high tea?"

"What can I say, I'm an old-fashioned dude," he deadpans. "C'mon, it'll be fun. You deserve it."

"*We* deserve it," she corrects, swallowing the offhand quip about them being a power couple, because *Oh wow, presumptuous much, Freya?*

They're here to celebrate her completing the manuscript *and* Taft getting an offer for an indie movie. Last night, before she even realized it, she reached the end of her novel. A sense of peace and held-back excitement rushed through her, unmatched only until this morning, when Taft heard back about the indie project he auditioned for. He got the part, obviously.

If it was just her, she would have made a Funfetti cake and thrown in extra sprinkles, but Taft loves celebrating everything, especially when it comes to her.

As if to prove his point, he holds out his phone. Tiers of Joy has over eight hundred thousand followers on Instagram. Their grid is full of decadent cakes with work-of-art frosting that it would physically *pain* Freya to cut into.

"I'm determined to expand your palate," says Taft. "I mean, how can you say no to this face?"

Freya steps through the door he holds open for her with a good-natured roll of her eyes. Hand in hand, they cross the black-and-cream bistro-tile floor to be seated by the elegant hostess.

"Hello, my name is Bea, and I'll be taking care of you today," she says, smiling wide as she looks between Taft and Freya. "Is this a special occasion, Mr. Bamber?"

He glances at Freya a bit bashfully before nodding. "Yes, we're celebrating."

"Congratulations!" Bea enthuses as she seats them at an intimate table for two. The backs of the formal white chairs are bow tied with pale pink fabric that matches the linen. She waits until Taft pulls Freya's chair out for her before she says, "We have a set dessert menu, but can I get you started with tea?"

"Darjeeling, please," says Taft.

Bea looks expectantly at Freya.

"I'll have . . ." Freya suspects asking for coffee is a no-no. "The same?"

When Bea bustles away with their order, Freya gets her first real look at her surroundings. Sparkling chandeliers drip from the coffered ceiling, glinting off the antique mirrors framing the chinoiserie-wallpapered walls.

"You know," she says conversationally, only a teensy bit serious, "if this is how I'm rewarded for every book I finish, I'm going to be a lot more productive."

Taft presses his fingertips together under his chin and smirks. "Then my evil plan is working."

"It's not evil if it helps me," she protests.

"It is if I have ulterior motives." His smirk sweetens into a smile. "I get to take you out and spend the whole afternoon with you."

Quickly, Freya sees what he means. When their pastries are wheeled over with a cheery "Bon appétit!" it's obvious that it'll take them the better part of the day to make their way through the small mountain.

"So that's why it's called 'Tiers of Joy,'" she says, ogling the pretty three-tier stand laden with a month's worth of sugar content.

"All their cakes are three tiers, too," says Taft, pouring a cup of tea for Freya from the small white teapot. He winks. "Everything and everyone in LA has a brand."

She wraps her hands around her cup, inhaling the fragrant spiral of steam while she considers the bite-size pastries. Among the many delicacies are lavender macarons, perfect and round and probably every bit as airy as they look; strawberry mini cupcakes topped with pink champagne buttercream as tall as the cake itself; something that smells like lemon-curd cake squares sprinkled with edible violets.

Freya's halfway to reaching for a cupcake when she stops, realizing there's only one of each dainty delight. It's obviously meant for a couple to share. Before she can feel embarrassed, Taft picks up the cupcake and neatly slices it in half, giving her first choice.

"To your indie movie offer," she says.

"To you finishing your book," he counters.

She smiles around a bite, flavor bursting on her tongue. "And to hopefully getting my career back on track."

Taft's eyes drink her in as deeply as the cup of Darjeeling in his hands. "To having someone to share my life with," he murmurs. "When . . . when the movie premieres and the contract is officially over, I'll be free to pursue what I want. Everything I want."

And *who* he wants? Freya's eyes shoot to his. She can't *not* read something into that.

His smile is gentle and knowing and *everything*. It feels like an answer.

The stormy clouds of anxiety circling her head poof into clarity. For the first time in years, she doesn't want to fast-forward her life to some hypothetical save point where everything is okay and adulthood is figured out.

She trusts the timing and she trusts Taft—she is exactly where she needs to be.

CHAPTER TWENTY-THREE

I know you're awake," Taft whispers in Freya's ear when he can't hold out against her early-morning squirming any longer. He finds it adorable that she thinks she's sneaky, when in fact she might quite possibly be the most unsubtle person he knows. It's one of his favorite things about her.

"Shh, I'm sleeping," she mumbles. "Cake hangover."

He laughs and rests his chin on her shoulder, lazily stroking her thigh and hip under the sheet. Sugar crash notwithstanding, she's nowhere near as sleepy as she wants him to think.

"Then I guess I should stop"—he glides his palm over her ribs to cup her breast, rolling the nipple between thumb and forefinger, eliciting a shivery gasp—"this?"

"I changed my mind," Freya says hoarsely. "I'm awake."

He kisses the crook of her neck. Her skin tastes salty, and he can smell himself on her: sex, sweat, and the faintest tickle of his own soap. "You were *always* awake. You were just trying to get my attention."

Her voice hopefully lilts, "Mission accomplished?"

His erection twitches toward his stomach. He had her three times last night, and pleasuring her was still his first and sole thought. Taft lets his hand travel to her other breast, gently flicking Freya's nipple until it perks almost as hard as his cock, still straining in his pajama pants. "What do you think?"

She rolls to face him with a self-satisfied purr. "Glad to see it worked."

"Oh, it worked all right." He flashes her a wicked smile, letting her *feel* just how effectively she's woken him up. The fact she still has the ability to blush after the things they'd done after coming home—from afternoon to dawn—is nothing short of arousing. "Next time, I want to have you on the couch."

Honestly, he's surprised they haven't already. He's only thought about it twice a day since he's met her. Freya, nude and writhing against green velvet, brown eyes full of desire, legs wrapped around his waist to draw him even closer, hair askew and entwined with his fingers as his tongue tangles with hers.

Taft knows she's going to hold him to it from the way her eyes sear into his.

"Yes, please." Freya determinedly pushes at his shoulder until he understands what she wants and rolls onto his back, staring at her wide-eyed.

She's not going to . . . Taft's mouth goes dry with want. *Is she?*

She throws one leg over him, trapping him between her parted legs. "I've never . . . Is this okay?"

Her shins are braced on the mattress, and it's sweet how she tries not to put any weight on him, but he doesn't want her tired before this even begins, so Taft gently urges her down. His fingers settle into the same indents he held her yesterday like they were just waiting to return. At this angle, looking up at her, he can see his marks on her neck, soft blotches where he sucked too hard. God, she's beautiful.

"It's spectacular," he says, then rephrases. "*You're* spectacular."

Her smile is alluringly shy as she wraps her fingers around his cock, both of them inhaling sharply as his hips buck. His fingers dig into her hips, and with a curse of apology, he gentles his grip. "Please tell me if I'm too rough," he says, running his hands up and down her sides.

Freya seems confused by his statement. "You're not. I like everything you do to me." Her hands release him and drift up her stomach, her breasts, and then her neck. "Are you talking about these?"

"I'm sorry." He nods, a little shamefaced. The apex of her thighs is right in his line of view, so he throws his eyes to the ceiling.

"I like *them*, too," she whispers.

His eyes shoot to hers at the, frankly, unexpected confession. "You don't mind hickeys?"

"Not usually, but I like *your* hickeys on me," she corrects. She bites her lower lip, trailing her fingertips back down her body and onto his, gently skimming his clavicle. "You're wearing my marks, too."

With a surprised thrill, he realizes he's a little tender, too, like his shoulders had a *really* good massage. He glances down, cataloging the evidence of her fevered kisses on his own flesh.

When he meets her gaze again, she's already grabbed a condom from his bedside table. She hasn't bothered to close the drawer, as though she thinks they'll need more than one. The thought makes him grin.

After rolling the condom down his length, Freya reaches between them to touch herself and comes away with her fingers glistening. Without any more fanfare, she guides him to her slippery folds. "Teach me what you like?"

Taft hisses through his teeth. "Just like that."

It's exquisite torture the way she sinks onto him, the head of his erection slipping through her entrance, but it's nowhere near enough. He grits his teeth and keeps his hips level, forcing himself not to push his hips up and into the molten heat he's craving. In this position, she's the one in control, and he wants her to set a pace she's comfortable with.

"Keep doing what you were doing before," murmurs Freya, bringing his hands up to her ribs.

He's quick to oblige. She experimentally moves up and down on trembling thighs, taking him in shallow thrusts, in sync with the friction of his palms brushing from the curve of her hips to the swell of her breasts. Finally, eyes closed in rapture, she sinks onto his entire length.

"God, you feel good," Taft groans, fisting the sheets. Her walls are a slick and wet welcome.

Freya pitches forward to halfway lean over him, breasts swaying. She rises off him, not quite enough to slip out, then inches her way back down. "So do"—gasp—"you."

"Kiss me," he demands, tilting up to meet her halfway.

She closes the distance between their mouths, planting her lips possessively over his in a way that makes Taft ache to pull her down, filling her to the hilt. He kisses her back, matching her tongue stroke for stroke. Her kiss, he's sure, is meant to devour him until there's nothing left and he's wholly hers.

Of course he is. There was never any doubt in his mind of *that*.

He will be this gorgeous girl's for as long as she wants him. If he's lucky, he will get to learn her every gasp and shudder. Pinpoint every place that makes her shiver and scream. Perfect the sweet torment of bringing her to the edge of orgasm over and over again until she falls apart in his arms.

"This angle is amazing," Freya says with a soft gasp, starting to rock over him. It doesn't take long before she finds a rhythm that has her tossing her head back and breathing a little erratically.

He can tell she's close, but he knows how to get her there faster. Maybe even more than once.

Taft cups her ass with his left hand, using it as leverage to meet her thrusts. His other hand moves between them to bury his fingers in her damp curls. The pad of his thumb presses against her clit.

"Fuck!" Freya's whole body convulses. Shock waves radiate through her core, muscles squeezing him. A second later, her hips slam against

his, trapping his hand. "I'm not used to a guy paying me so much attention there," she explains breathlessly, looking a little embarrassed.

Taft frowns. Just *who* has she been sleeping with that clitoral stimu-
lation is still so new for her? Scratch that, he doesn't want to know. All
he wants is what *she* needs. "It's okay, you can relax. Let me love you."

He pauses at his own phrasing. "Let me *make* love to you" is what he
meant to say, but what came out is, strangely, exactly what he wants.

Freya's breathing is ragged. "I thought . . ."

He lifts his hips in a halfway thrust, prompting her to continue.

Her muscles give him another involuntary squeeze. "I thought that,
um, in, um, cowgirl . . . I had to do all the work? I mean, not that this is
work. It is exhausting, but that's not what I—" She lets out a short
laugh. "I'm saying this all wrong. I just thought guys were into this?
Lying back and letting the girl ride them?"

He's so fucking charmed by her. "I don't know about 'guys,' but I
love that you wanted to try it. I want your first time on top to be good
for you, too, baby. Just let me make you feel good, okay?" He holds her
tight while he bucks his hips up, driving himself deeper. He rolls his
pelvis up toward her belly button, hitting her sweet spot.

Her hands grab at his shoulders, nails digging in. "That," she says
hoarsely. "Keep doing that."

Taft smirks, ready and willing to play a far more active role now that
she'll let him. Passive participation was fun, but he's far from a lazy lover,
and now he just wants to watch her come all over his dick. "Yes, ma'am."

He gives her slow, measured thrusts that have her biting her lip, eyes
fluttering shut. That won't do. He doesn't want her holding back on
him. Without breaking their rhythm, he uses his elbows to push himself up into a sitting position.

Freya's eyes fly open at the new angle and a low moan, unlike any
he's heard before, escapes her lips. His breathing is labored, but he sucks

her earlobe into his mouth, raking his teeth over her skin until she's clawing at his back.

He sets a punishing pace, one that has her calling his name and burying her face in his neck. Her nibbles are sharp and aggressive, but she makes sure to soothingly sweep her tongue over his skin after.

"Don't stop, don't stop," she chants, snaking her tongue around the whorl of his ear.

His fingers circle her clit. "Wild horses couldn't stop me."

She laughs, breathless and hysterical, like it's the funniest thing she's ever heard. "I don't think sex has ever been this fun for me before."

He knows exactly what she means, and when the friction of his thumb over her clit shatters her, he suspects that it's never been this satisfying for him, either.

"Oh, fuck. Fuck, fuck, FUCK," she half sobs into his neck, her upper body sagging against his. "My legs feel like jelly." She pulls back when he stills inside her. "Keep going. You didn't come."

He tenderly sweeps sweaty tendrils of hair behind her ear. "Are you sure?"

She kisses him hard and swift. "I don't think I'll be able to come again, but yes."

"I'm going to take that as a personal challenge."

For all that she was exhausted a few moments ago, when he continues thrusting, Freya starts grinding down on him, trying to take him deeper. At one point, he thinks he's hit her cervix, but she doesn't stop or slow, intent on chasing her pleasure. Her breathless, honeyed moans are all the encouragement he needs.

"I love the sounds you make," he pants, nibbling along her jawline.

Taft sees the exact moment it happens, when she finds her power and grabs it with both hands. There's no hint of her earlier uncertainty and inexperience in the way she guides his hands to her breasts, encourages him to squeeze and knead and roll her nipples until she's whimpering his name and god's interchangeably.

As their pace quickens, her eyes open. If she's surprised to find him looking straight at her, her face doesn't show it. Her upper chest is flushed and her mouth open, which he takes as an invitation to lean forward to capture her chin. The angle of penetration changes, and she gasps into his mouth as he kisses her, soft and sweet, cradling the back of her head to keep them doubly joined a few seconds longer.

"You feel so good, Freya," he says in soft pants. "So hot and tight. So wet for me."

Even their bodies seem to agree, the wet slap of their joining loud and just a little lewd.

She answers by kissing him again, both hands winding into his hair and scratching his scalp. The sting of her nails coupled with every other sensation makes him growl into her mouth.

As they kiss, he lets his hand slip back to her clit. All it takes is a touch to wrack her body with tremors of pleasure. When she starts to flutter around him, his stomach tightens and begins to reverberate like a just-plucked guitar string. His balls tingle and tighten. His own climax is building, but he refuses to come until she does.

With firm, insistent pressure, he strokes her clit in hard circles, snapping his hips into hers one last time. She comes apart with a cry, the sound swallowed by his mouth. In the aftershocks of her orgasm, her muscles milk his release, and with a low shout that could either be her name or a random string of unintelligible syllables, he comes, filling the condom.

They lay together until their bodies start to cool and their breathing evens out.

"You're perfect," Freya declares, pulling away from his neck to look him in the eyes.

He grins. "Aren't I supposed to tell you that?"

She playfully rolls her eyes and leans in, her kiss electrifying him. "Tell me after I pee and shower?"

Regretfully, Taft slips out of her and watches as she throws on his shirt on her walk to the bathroom. The hem barely covers her ass, and, impossibly, his groin tightens with yearning at the sight of the plump globes just barely peeping out. He swallows—hard.

The imprint of her is still on his skin, and letting her out of his arms makes him feel bereft. Alone. And the idea of being alone in his bed now that he knows what it is to hug her against him doesn't settle well.

He could follow her. He doesn't think she'd mind. But he should give her some space. The last thing he wants is to look needy. Even though, he admits, he is.

Freya hesitates in the bathroom doorway. "Or," she says. "You could join me and tell me now?"

He's out of bed before she even finishes the sentence.

CHAPTER TWENTY-FOUR

Maybe it's the post-sex high, but that morning Freya's in the mood to do all the things she's dragged her heels on before, and what's more, she initiates them.

Look, she's never going to be tea's number one fan, but she can admit that the rooibos tea Taft brews for their breakfast isn't totally terrible. In fact, by the third sip, she even finds it tolerable. Although—and she can't overstate this enough—she remains deeply suspicious of hot beverages that contain no caffeine whatsoever. Taft whips together some delicious banana-nut muffins while wearing nothing but boxers and a KISS THE COOK apron that she chooses to take literally even though she doesn't really need to reach for a *reason* to kiss him any longer.

While the muffins bake, she makes her mom's anda bhurji, a favorite from her childhood and something she's never made for any guy the morning after. Or any guy at all. The soft, spicy Indian scrambled eggs are extra aromatic with finely chopped red chili, onion, and cilantro; a pinch of turmeric and cumin; and lovely soft chunks of tomato, all of it smothered in plenty of butter.

"The onions made me cry," she informs him while he tries—unsuccessfully—not to laugh. "I hope you love it."

He does.

Freya even finds herself scratching Hen behind the ears and suggesting a walk around the neighborhood, which has both man and dog lighting up and leaping for the leash.

"We're lucky no one noticed that I've been mostly the one walking him," Taft says as they step out the door.

"Erm, sorry about that." She bumps her hip against his and tightens her hold on the leash. "But I guess after tomorrow it doesn't matter anymore?"

The premiere has creeped up on them in what feels like a blink, even though they both know they've each been steadily eyeing the calendar.

Maybe he reads something in Freya's voice, because he asks, "This is going to work, right? You and me?"

"If we made it through the last four weeks, figuring out what comes next will be a piece of cake."

She blushes on the last word, remembering her rather wanton behavior that morning but unable to stop herself from reliving the highlights reel. Especially when Taft grins at her like *that*.

"When we get home, want to help me plant my new herbs?" he asks as he pulls her and Sir Henry to the side of the street, allowing a family with four kids to bike past.

"You're out of room on your window box."

"Mmm. Maybe you could help me start a new one."

"Yeah, okay. I'd . . . I'd really like that."

"And then," says Taft, "maybe after Mandi and I 'break up,' there are some other things you and I could do around the house."

"Gotta warn you, I'm not the handiest," Freya says with a laugh. "Unless that was a sex euphemism? In which case, I am very down to be nailed. Or hammered." She tries to think of a third, but blanks. "Okay, that's it, that's all I got."

A bemused smile ghosts across his lips. "I was thinking we'd start out in the bedroom—"

"I knew the DIY was code for sex!" she crows.

"And clean out half the drawers and closet space."

A frown creases Freya's forehead. "What? Why? You don't need to. Won't Mandi move all her stuff out of your closet? You'll have everything to yourself again."

"But what if *your* stuff moved in?"

She stumbles, almost tripping over her own feet, but Taft is there to catch her.

"God, you live in an amazing zip code, why can't they fix these potholes," mutters Freya.

Taft glances up and down the perfect, unblemished asphalt with nary a pothole in sight. "Too fast?"

She doesn't want him to think that she doesn't want to, but his offer is, well, unexpected. And she can't quite untangle what she wants to stay. Her writer's snarl is out in full fucking force.

"Not too fast," she finally settles on. "I mean, we've already gone about everything backward, haven't we? And it's not like we don't know what it's like to live with each other. But . . ."

When he starts to look crestfallen, she grabs his chin. "Hey. No. None of that. I'm not saying no, I'm saying . . . there's going to be a lot of eyes on us. Maybe more than there already are. Are you ready for that?"

"If you're with me, I'm ready for anything."

Twenty minutes of strolling later, they're within sight of home when Taft's phone goes off with a shrill ring. Freya makes a face at the screen when she sees Gareth FaceTiming him. "Ugh, may have spoken too soon."

"It can't be me he wants to speak to," says Taft, looking worried. "He must be trying to get through to Mandi."

"Let's take it together," suggests Freya.

Freya pastes on a bright smile while Taft accepts the call. "Hi, Gareth."

"*WHERE HAVE YOU BEEN?* I've called you three times, Mandi." He makes a rude sound in the back of his throat. "I *detest* being forced to go through other people."

Her blood pressure spikes. If Gareth is so desperate to get in touch with Mandi, it can't be for any good reason.

"*HAVE YOU SEEN IT?*" he demands, not using his inside voice.

Freya's eyes fly to Taft's. "What are you talking about?"

Gareth's exhale is gusty as hell. "The pictures of your loving boyfriend flirting with another girl at a bookshop. Christ, what is it with you two and books." There's a small pause, as though he's double-checking. "Books and Brambles. Familiar?"

Nothing so melodramatic as the earth cracking open beneath her happens, but it *feels* like it.

"Mandi, are you listening to me?" Gareth's voice grates in Freya's ears. "This blurry picture with 'Mystery Girl' has gone viral. My god, the headlines are actually *worse* this time than the goddamn club.

"Nothing to say for yourself, Taft?" Loathing seeps from Gareth's voice. "We need to get out ahead of this. Thank god someone caught you two looking cozy inside the patisserie. The photos should be able to bury this bullshit *he* caused. Why the hell you went somewhere that specialized in *wedding* cakes is beyond me. At least that boy can act. Almost looks like you two are actually . . ." He trails off, then laughs, like the idea that anything developing between Mandi and Taft is inconceivable.

"Gareth, can I—"

"Whoever 'Mystery Girl' is, I hope he let her down easy," continues

Gareth. "The last thing we need is some woman speaking to the gutter press about her 'wild night with a Hollywood star,'" he says with a scoff. "All because your boyfriend couldn't keep it in his pants until the premiere. Jesus. What a fuckup."

Freya glances at Taft.

His arms are crossed, like he's trying to make himself smaller, defensive. His jaw tenses when he catches her looking at him, and his mouth forms an expression that could sort of be mistaken for a smile, but it's more of a grimace.

"Gareth, I need to call you back," Freya says bluntly. She can't listen to him for another second.

She hangs up on his sputters and returns Taft's phone. Suddenly she feels exposed, like photographers could corner them. Like Kurt Kane could pounce any second.

Taft must feel the same, because he quickly says, "Let's hurry back. Moira's texting me that we need to hop on a call ASAP."

The second they get home, they both google the photos. They're all over the Internet. The red-bubble notifications on Mandi's Instagram and Twitter increase by the second as she's tagged and DMed by people all over the world. Media outlets have run with the stories, each one more titillating than the last.

While the photos from Tiers of Joy are getting the most attention, the ones of her sans makeup at Books & Brambles have stirred plenty of controversy. Some people, mostly women who think she should know better and troll accounts without icons, are criticizing Mandi for keeping a cheater in her life, linking back to the viral photo from the club as Exhibit A.

The speculation doesn't stop there, though. People with nothing better to do have started linking Taft to other women he's been in the vicinity of during the last few weeks, making all kinds of vile accusations about whether he's done anything with them on- and off-screen.

Bowen's name is right at the top, along with unnamed "sources" claiming Mandi and Taft left Bowen's premiere early because there were unresolved feelings between the former costars. From there, all it takes is a few clicks to lead Freya to more articles speculating about the real reasons the rest of the cast and Taft aren't buddy-buddy—all boiling down to Taft's apparent insatiable sexual appetite.

GOLDEN BOY'S STAR LOSES HIS SHINE (AND HIS HALO), reads one particularly cruel headline.

"So," Taft says finally. "I better make that call."

Freya tears her gaze away from the damning evidence. "Okay."

His expression softens at the quiver in her voice. "We're going to figure this out."

She exhales. "Yeah. What are we going to do?"

"You mean what are Mandi and I going to do?" asks Taft.

Freya blinks. No? That wasn't what she meant.

"Moira's last text said she's drafting up a statement for me to post online denying all the rumors," Taft says. "She's advising me to stick to the story that the bookshop picture is taken out of context and deny an engagement. I better let Mandi know what's going on, too. She needs to be prepared for this shitstorm."

Freya attempts to find the bright, yet dim, side in all of this. "Okay, well, um, at least I'm not wearing the store name tag in the photo, so they can't trace 'Mystery Girl' back to the real me."

"Yeah, but when you move back home after the premiere and start being there more regularly, it's going to be kind of obvious."

"Right, but I thought—" *I thought this was home.* "What happened to moving in together?"

She feels foolish as soon as she asks the question. Selfish. More than a little nauseous.

"With these new rumors, it's going to be harder for me and Mandi to 'break up' after the premiere like we planned. If you move in right now—officially, I mean—everyone's going to figure out who Mystery Girl is. I know it sucks, but we need to push back our plans. We can't risk the attention right now."

Freya isn't sure which *we* he's talking about: Him and Mandi. Him and her. Both.

"We were caught 'out of character,' and now everything is so messed up," he says with a groan. "People are calling me a cheater. Again. This is my career and Mandi's on the line, and the *Banshee* premiere is tomorrow night. This couldn't have happened at a worse time. I don't want this to be the way our relationship starts. I want to protect you from all of this shit."

Freya bites her lip. "I feel so guilty. I love how romantic you are, but I shouldn't have agreed to all those little dates that were just for us."

"It's not on you, sweetheart. I knew better, too, but not when it comes to you," Taft admits. "I don't think you know what I'd do just to keep you smiling at me the way you did on those days." He takes a deep breath. "I love how you always have the right words to say to me, but I don't think they'll help this time."

She blinks at him for what feels like forever. "Then what can I do?"

"Just . . . just sit tight and try not to worry." He looks like he wants to say something, but in the end he gives her a tight hug, a forehead kiss, and mutters that he'll call Moira from the bedroom.

The silence in Taft's wake presses on Freya's ears as loudly as Gareth's grating voice had a few minutes ago.

So when the group chat erupts in a flurry of messages, she's glad to have something else to focus on.

Mimi: Are you seeing what's trending on Twitter?

Hero: Freya, are you okay?

Steph: The sanctuary's teen volunteers are huge
Banshee fans and they can't stop talking about
what happened. Should we video chat?

Ava: Wait, what did I miss?

Sir Henry looks up at her, and for once, Freya's more scared of something else than she is of him and his teeth and the way she still can't see his eyes. Hen butts his cold nose against Freya's knee and makes a soft *whuff.*

Without thinking about it, she crouches to pet him. Hen rests his head on her shoulder for a moment, as though he knows she needs a hug.

This morning she had been so happy. She'd been looking forward to her next chapter.

Freya's eyes well with the memories of everything she wants so desperately to cling on to but is afraid that, like a dream, is about to drift away.

Freya: I need you four. Call me now.

CHAPTER TWENTY-FIVE

The lavender chiffon Elie Saab gown is easily the most expensive thing Freya's ever worn. She angles herself in the bathroom mirror, watching the sway of the lacy skirt. It's a romantic dress fit for a Disney ball, and at any other time, she would have felt like a princess wearing it, but tonight it just feels wrong.

"You look gorgeous," says Taft from the open doorway.

She hadn't noticed him behind her. Her smile is a little strangled. Even when everything sucks, he's trying to make her feel good. "You look very handsome yourself."

Freya forces herself to stop from licking her Diored lips and tries to calm the clawing in her chest. It doesn't work. The limo is going to pick them up soon, and if Mandi isn't here before then, she'll have to go to the premiere in her place.

"Sorry yesterday was so dramatic, and that today hasn't been much better," says Taft. "I know it can't have been easy for you."

"Don't worry about it. I had my girls. You needed to regroup with Moira and Mandi. It's fine."

Taft closes the distance between them and takes her in his arms without caring about the perfectly pressed lines on his tux or the foundation that could get on it when he squeezes her tight. "It's not fine."

Well, no. Freya hadn't particularly enjoyed spending the night alone on the couch while Taft conducted hushed conversations in the privacy of their—*his*—bedroom. She wanted to help, but she supposes it's sort of hard to be part of the solution when you were one half of the problem.

But it is what it is. And she knows he trusts Moira to advise and look out for his career.

She tips her head back to look at him. "I'm sorry."

"They were my indiscretions," says Taft. "*You* have nothing to be sorry about."

"Are *you* sorry? Do you regret any of it?"

Immediately she wants to take both questions back.

"Don't you dare think that for a second," says Taft. "Of course, I wish those pictures hadn't leaked, but I could never regret you being in my life. You're the best thing that's ever happened to me. You . . . you make me happy." He looks down at her in wonder. "And I think—I hope—that I bring you joy, too."

She smiles and strokes his cheek. "That was never in doubt."

"Mandi's on her way back," says Taft, stroking Freya's cheek.

Her smile falters. When she last spoke with her, Mandi had been so happily holed up in her Airbnb on Rosalie Island that she wasn't planning on coming back for the *Banshee* premiere at all.

And Freya knows how selfish it is that she'd been excited to attend in Mandi's place. That even now, she feels possessive of this life that has never truly been hers. She doesn't care about the clothes or the fame, but she does care about Taft. After everything they've shared, *she* wanted to be the one with him tonight, the one to celebrate his accomplishments. But yesterday had changed everything.

"I guess," Freya says slowly, "I should change, then?"

There's clear regret stamped on his face. He bends his neck, not to kiss her as she first expects but to rest his forehead against hers. Taft feels solid and real, his breath hot against her cheek. His eyes close as he just holds her to him. Anchoring himself.

"I want to kiss you so badly right now," says Taft.

His nearness and the scent of his cologne go to Freya's head like *really* good champagne. She swallows. "It's not like I'm going anywhere."

He peers at her, eyebrows drawn in concern. "Are you upset?"

She releases a gusty exhale. "Yes and no. I do wish I was going with you, but I'm also weirdly relieved that Mandi's going to make it, after all. A red carpet would have been fun, but it wouldn't have been mine."

Taft nods, eyes sympathetic. "I can think of one thing that's all yours," he says softly.

The tension between them triples.

"And what's that?"

He tugs her hand up his chest to cover his heart. It's the same gesture he made at the photo shoot.

Tears spring to Freya's eyes, and oh god, she's suddenly glad she doesn't have to leave the house tonight, because it takes all of two seconds for her makeup to streak, tears dripping down her cheeks and dangling off her chin.

"I don't ask girls to live with me and then take it back," says Taft, using his thumb to catch one. "We're moving forward, Freya. It's just going to take a little longer, after all of this dies down. Putting you in the crosshairs of people like Kurt . . . I won't let you live under a microscope like that. I don't know how we'll find the balance, but I refuse to let you be some juicy bit of gossip people swap like currency. Being with you is worth any price, but I can't let you be the one to pay it. Can you wait for us?"

She takes a wobbly breath. Of course she can. What he's asking isn't unreasonable. And he's only thinking of what's best for her. She appreciates it, but *he's* what's best for her. She doesn't need to be protected; she just needs to be his.

"When you're ready," agrees Freya. Then, cheekily, "It'll give you a chance to miss me."

"I started missing you the second we spent the night apart," he admits.

Her heart feels like it's tripping over itself. Repeatedly. She wants to kiss him, muss him up until he's hers, hers, hers.

"So, for the record, just how many girls have you asked to live with you?" Freya asks, winding her fingers through the soft curls at the nape of his neck.

His irritated look is utterly unconvincing. The outer corners of his eyes crinkle with the force of his smile. "One."

"I wish I could kiss you," she says with a longing sigh.

"Me too. But then it would be impossible to walk out of this house without you."

It's not as bittersweet as she thought to change out of the dress. Not when it's Taft's fingers gliding the zipper down her spine. His lips sweeping across the back of her neck, cock hard against her ass as he helps her step out of it and then neatly hangs it up for her. Him drinking in the sight of her in lingerie, jewelry, and heels.

The air around them smells like need on fire. The heels are next to go, his hot mouth ghosting along her inner thigh until she shivers and clenches her fingers in his hair.

When that happens, he makes a low growl in the back of his throat that goes straight between her legs, and hoists her up on the counter. A tube of lipstick topples into the sink with a sharp sound, but they both ignore it.

Instinctively, she wraps her legs around his waist, bringing him closer to her throbbing center. Her arousal is slick between them, the counter cold under her ass as she perches on the edge and hungrily watches him roll on a condom.

"She's going to come here any second now," Freya whispers into his ear, grazing her teeth along his lobe. "Make me come first."

She's immensely gratified when a shudder goes through him. Her statement doesn't come from a desire to stop but to remind him that she needs him inside her.

There's no slow and tender in the way he takes her, which is exactly how she wants it. How she *needs* it. He feels solid and real inside her, arms bracketing her body, mouth gnashing and possessive as it slants over hers. Pleasure alights in her every single synapse. This coupling is all about the reminder that they're not going anywhere. Seeking refuge in each other like they never want to find their way out.

When she cries out, walls pulsing and gripping him even tighter, he finally lets go and comes with her.

"I know you're all 'Ladies first,' but next time, I'm sucking you off," Freya mumbles against his sweaty neck. "And you're going to be naked. I can't believe you barely got undressed for this."

Taft laughs and rakes his hand through his hair, disheveling it beyond redemption. It's a good look. "Okay, you've got a deal." He nudges her legs and wipes her thighs with a hand towel, cleaning their combined fluids before attending to himself.

Freya's just shimmied herself into a pair of sleep shorts and a soft NYU tee when the doorbell rings.

"I'll get it!" Taft calls, already freshened up. He drops a sweet kiss on her shoulder before leaving.

She scrutinizes herself in the mirror. There's no getting around it—she looks exceedingly well fucked. Flushed cheeks, messy hair, suspiciously bright eyes. With a shrug, she goes out to join them.

Hen looks happier than Freya's ever seen him, tongue lolling and tail vigorously wagging.

"Who's been a good boy?" Mandi coos to the dog, giving him several head rubs before rising from her crouch on the floor. "I've missed you, Sir Henry."

"You just assume he's been a good boy, huh?" asks Taft.

"Uh-huh. Because I sure know you haven't." She grins up at him, then catches sight of Freya and the smile dwindles.

Mandi's dressed in all black, but she's still looks enviably gorgeous in yoga pants, a fitted hoodie, and an Adidas cap pulled low to hide her bare face. She takes it off now, shakes her brown hair out of its ponytail, and sighs. "You two have made a god-awful mess."

Freya opens her mouth, then lets the point stand. It's fair, more or less. "I'm so sorry, Mandi."

She isn't sure how she expected the other woman to react. Pitch a fit, maybe. Yell at her, definitely. But what Freya never suspected in a million years is that Mandi would walk over and put her arms around her. The hug doesn't come naturally to either of them, but Freya squeezes her back all the same.

"It's okay," says Mandi. "It was a good run, wasn't it? And I was always supposed to be back by now, so I guess thanks to you, I'm right on time. At least no one has the full story, right? The engagement rumors we can squash, but it would be pretty shady to explain *you* to the world."

Taft frowns. "She doesn't mean it like that."

"Look, bad choice of words, but admit it, we're all going to look ridiculous if the truth gets out that Freya took my place for the last four weeks," says Mandi. "It'd seem like the worst publicity stunt ever."

"I don't want to make either of you look like a laughingstock," says Freya. She feels pinched and insignificant, about *yea big*, and it takes a sizable effort to make sure her words don't seem that way. "Or make things worse for you with Gareth."

"At least tell me this wasn't just a fling," says Mandi, looking between Freya and Taft.

Freya's breath catches as Taft reaches for her hand, linking them together. "I already said it on the phone, but I'll happily say it again. It absolutely was not just a fling," he asserts, bringing their joined fingers up to his mouth for a kiss. "We're in this together."

Freya didn't know how much she needed to hear it until this moment, and something inside her cracks wide open. The way he's looking at her is more intimate than anything they've just done—than everything they've *ever* done.

Taft's answer seems to satisfy Mandi, too, and she gives them a genuine smile. "Good. Now, I need to get ready. Freya, want to help? I assume you're familiar with my red-carpet look?"

Freya holds up the tube of rescued lipstick in Mandi's signature color. "Do you even need to ask?"

CHAPTER TWENTY-SIX

It's hours later when Taft returns, tiptoeing around like he's doing his best to be quiet. It's cute he's trying not to wake her, so Freya stays still under the sheet, feigning sleep. She'd tried to wait up for him, rereading her old *Once Bitten* fanfic in the dark, but a little after 3:00 a.m. she'd finally succumbed.

Her old writing, she was surprised to discover, wasn't as embarrassing and milquetoast as she'd built it up in her head to be. Maybe only 27 percent garbage fire. In fact, put that way, it's downright decent. Unputdownable, even.

I'll just read the comments to kill time until Taft comes home turned into *Just one more chapter* and then *Just ten more chapters* and *Oops, I finished the whole thing and thank god I didn't abandon this fic because a cliffhanger is actually capable of killing me and this was a* huge *mistake because these characters will live rent-free in my mind until the end of time and I am emotionally fucking wrecked.*

She hasn't read this late into the night since college. It's familiar and comforting, just like the pillow next to her that smells like Taft. But it has nothing on the smell of him when he crawls into his side of the bed, throwing an arm over her waist and tangling his feet with hers. His bare chest warms her back.

Freya inhales his cologne and the alcohol on his breath when he presses his nose into her neck. Underneath it all is the freshness of Irish Spring, the soap he's used since he was a teen, according to an article she'd once read and promptly forgotten about until this moment, when it swarms and stirs her senses.

She grinds her butt gently against him. "Hey, you."

"I knew you weren't asleep," he murmurs into her skin with a warm, open-mouthed kiss. "Missed you. Wanna tell you something. Got good news. Or . . . news. Depending on whether you think it's good."

She rolls in his arms to face him, pleased when he doesn't let her go. "Mmm, sounds cryptic."

When Taft doesn't say anything for a long, achingly suspenseful moment, she brushes her hand over his forehead. His hair has spilled over his face, and he's watching her with languid and sleepy eyes.

"At the after-party, Moira told me and Mandi that we've been green-lit for two sequels in the *Banshee of the Baskervilles* universe."

If he hadn't been holding her, she would have launched straight off the bed. "Oh my god!" she shrieks. "Two sequels?! Already?" Her chest feels fizzy and full. "Congratulations! That's *amazing*."

"The box office numbers are looking good. All the projections are strong, and apparently this was on the table for a long time behind the scenes," says Taft. "Moira just didn't want to raise my hopes in case they didn't make the offer. But apparently all the buzz about me and Mandi worked in our favor."

"Wait, why do you not sound happier? We should be celebrating!"

Freya doesn't care that it's the middle of the night. She'll make that box of Funfetti cake that she got for a just-because occasion and pop open a bottle of wine. Well, except she doesn't think Taft has any wine save for the ancient bottle of red that he only uses for cooking. It's only been open for a couple of weeks, so it should still be drinkable. Possibly. Maybe. She thinks.

The look on his face brings her back down to earth. He looks solemn and a little pained. If she didn't know him as well as she does, it wouldn't even be perceptible.

She bites her lip and lightly pushes at his chest until he lets her sit up. Leaning against the headboard, she runs her eyes over him, making sure he's okay. When she can't find anything overtly amiss, she trails her hands over his shoulders, massaging the tense muscles she finds there. "Talk to me, baby."

Maybe it's the endearment that does it, because Taft finally opens his mouth. "It's going to be at least a two-year commitment I'll have to turn down the indie movie. There's no way I can do both."

"You don't know that for certain. Walk me through it," says Freya, squeezing his shoulders again.

He relaxes into her touch. "It's just . . . I finally thought I had a chance to do something different, and then the universe decided, *Hey, you know what would be fun? Giving you this other incredible opportunity that is the exact opposite of what you want, while still managing to be everything you want.*"

"A good opportunity is only a good opportunity if it's the right one for *you*," she reminds him. "If this step isn't going to help you live the life and do the work that you really want, then maybe it's just an opportunity that isn't the right fit."

Taft's eyes clash with emotion. "Yeah, but . . . who turns down an offer for two movies?"

He mentions a dollar amount so astronomical Freya wonders if she has wax in her ear, until she confirms she heard him right.

"I feel like the biggest asshole," he says, tone unfairly scathing. "I thought I wanted to make great art, but the second something super commercial and career-defining comes along, I'm tempted by success.

And that's not even taking into consideration how many other people this would affect. It's work for *hundreds* of cast and crew if I do this."

"You're not an asshole," she says. "If you were, you would only be thinking of yourself. I respect your commitment to doing right by as many people as possible, but what *you* want doesn't matter any less. If this is how you're feeling, maybe you need to take a second look at the definition of success you're using. Is it money and fame? Or is it doing projects you love?"

Conflict crosses his face. It's visible in the clench of his jaw and the flat line of his lips. She spies it in the knit of his eyebrows, like he's trying to solve for *x* and doesn't want to give up.

"I don't want to be a sellout," he says. "I shouldn't even *be* tempted by the money. But this is the kind of offer that comes along once in a lifetime. How can I walk away? This is everyone's dream."

But is it *his*? She can't answer that for him, and even he doesn't seem to know.

"You're not lesser for admitting that the other stuff matters, too," says Freya. "I spent so long thinking that I wasn't a real writer anymore because I found it so hard, and that was absolutely untrue. *You* helped me realize that. You held my hand while I suffered through all the suck until I made it to the other side. Instead of accepting all my false starts and moving forward, I chased a nonexistent magic formula. Don't be me—run *toward* something. Course correct if you get it wrong. Embrace the suck. But don't deliberately aim for the wrong thing just because it's what 'everyone' wants. 'Everyone' isn't you."

When she finishes what turned out to be an embarrassingly earnest speech, Taft props himself up on his elbow to look at Freya. The corners of his mouth lift with a smile she can already tell she's going to engrave in her mind to keep forever. It makes her heart squish and she can't help but stare openly.

This man is everything she's ever wanted and then some. She wants a lifetime with him, and then, just to be safe, a thousand more.

"Thank you for being my person," he says, and his voice is so achingly tender that Freya can't help but kiss him. It's not a kiss meant to lead to anything. He tastes faintly of booze and the mouthwash she heard him sloshing before coming to bed.

When they part for air, she turns back around so he can spoon her. He's a comforting presence behind her, tucking her close against him. "Go to sleep. It's late," she mumbles. "We can talk more tomorrow."

"I love how you just nooked in there," he whispers into her hair.

"Hmm?"

"You. In the nook of my arms." He nuzzles behind her ear, fingers combing through her hair without hitting a snag. "You're the right fit for me, Freya."

She smiles sleepily and locks her arms over his so she's snuggled even tighter in his embrace. Only when his hand is in hers does she close her eyes. Falling asleep like this is a luxury that she's gotten used to, and several minutes of slow, even breathing pass before she realizes he hasn't fallen asleep yet.

"If I signed on for another two movies . . . my dad might be proud of me." His voice is pitched low, a secret whispered in the black of night. "If he sees how much other people believe in me."

His voice is so quiet and hesitant that just before Freya drifts off, the thought flits through her mind that she isn't even sure she was meant to hear it.

CHAPTER TWENTY-SEVEN

"Taft? Are you sitting down? Trust me, you need to be sitting for this."

He pulls his cell phone away from his ear. Moira isn't usually this screechy, especially not first thing in the morning, so of course his mind immediately whirs with ten thousand terrible possibilities before he remembers to take a breath, shoving that spike of anxiety down. "What's up?"

He slips out of the bedroom before their conversation wakes up Freya. Heart swelling with affection, he lingers in the doorway for just a few seconds, a fond smile on his lips as Freya cuddles onto his side of the bed, reaching for his pillow. Just getting to hold her all night is better than having sex with anyone else.

"So . . ." Moira sounds like she's about to bubble over. "The written offer just came in."

"Uh-huh," Taft says distractedly, spooning Freya's favorite grounds into the coffee machine.

"I had a little chat with Gareth, and we have the leverage to get an even more lucrative counteroffer for you and Mandi."

The new number she tells him makes his hand wobble. Half the coffee grounds land on the counter. "That's . . . great," he says, sweeping the mess into the palm of his hand.

"What, that's it? I know you're not the type to bawl on the phone, but I expected something a little more effusive. At least a thank-you after I spent the night hammering out this contract with that ass of a manager."

Moira really doesn't like working with Gareth more than she has to. But when Taft found out during their last contract negotiation that Mandi was making less than him—despite being number one on the *Banshee* call sheet and a far bigger star—he insisted Moira and Gareth work together to ensure that they would have parity, at a minimum, moving forward. Even if it meant his taking a pay cut. He's all too aware of the pervasive gender inequality in Hollywood, and it's the least he can do to acknowledge his privilege and use it to be an ally and advocate.

"We're already at the contract stage?" Taft can't keep the surprise from his voice. As slow as Freya tells him things move in publishing, they're often even slower in film and television.

Moira hums. "They're really eager to get you both back to Dartmoor as soon as possible for filming."

He dumps the coffee grounds into the filter and turns the machine on. "Um, can I think about it?" The silence stands for so long that Taft thinks the call must have dropped. "Moira? Hello?"

"Do you want me to go back to the table to ask for more money? Because I've gotta tell you, that's a no-go. I thought *I* was a shark, but when Gareth pushes, he is *shameless*." Moira snorts. "Trust me, he tried, and they won't budge."

"God, no," Taft blurts. "The offer is great. It's more than I could have dreamed."

"Okay . . . so what's the hang-up here, exactly? It's not the indie movie we accepted, is it? Because I can get you out of it like"—she snaps her fingers—"*that*."

He wishes he could be as honest with her as he was with Freya, but he knows how hard Moira works for him, getting him the best terms and advising him when to walk away when she can't. The commission on this is going to be enough to pay off all her kids' college tuitions. And Mandi is clearly leaping at the opportunity.

It's the right fit for everyone.

But is it right for *him*? The question has nagged at him since last night and he isn't sure he's any closer to an answer.

"If it means that much to you, I'll renegotiate," says Moira. "Give me the rest of the morning to find spots we can push a little more, and then I'll send you the contract to make sure you're okay with everything. I think I can get us some equity points on the back end and ask for a signing bonus."

"Can I have some time to think about it?"

Her exhale is frustrated, crackling in his ear. "Taft, talk to me. They're literally throwing money at you and you're not saying thank you?"

"Thank you," he says automatically.

She sighs. "Not what I meant. Is there some reason you're not excited that I need to be aware of?"

He gnaws on his lower lip. "This is just all moving really fast."

"There are a lot of moving pieces in play right now. Fast is the only speed we're on. And I know it feels like this all happened overnight—and *yes*, sure, if we're being technical, it did—but you have worked your ass off. Your 'overnight success' was a decade in the making."

"Yeah," he says over the steady *drip, drip, drip* of the coffee machine.

He can't be more eloquent than that when his brain is fast-forwarding through the next few years. If he says yes, what if he can't escape the typecast? What if after the *Banshee* trilogy comes to an end, all the other roles dry up, filled by other actors who have proved their mettle in more prestigious roles?

Can he grow if he stays in his comfort zone, or should he take a chance on himself by pursuing a passion project that he'll be paid a relative pittance for?

"You should know," says Moira. "They want to keep you and Mandi together as a package deal."

Taft grabs two mugs from the cupboard. "You mean as love interests in the movies? That's understandable."

"Not just the movies. They were thrilled with all the great press; one of the producers called me up to offer their congratulations that your showmance turned into true love. Guess they don't know that the engagement rumors are a bunch of baloney." Moira snorts. "If I'm being honest, the relationship is the main reason they agreed to the increased quotes we asked for."

"Wait. Moira. They expect us to continue the showmance for . . . what? *Both movies?* That's got to be at least *two years*!" He doesn't even care that she'll hear the anger in his words.

"It's not like either of you is seeing anyone else. You get along. You've been living together for a month with no problems, right? Come on, this can't have come as a surprise."

"*We had an end date.*"

"Taft, sometimes we have to compromise to get what we want. You know that."

He does. He wishes he doesn't.

"That one is nonnegotiable," says Moira. "Like last time, it's a clause in the contract."

"So if I say no," he says slowly, "they'll recast me?"

Without meaning to, he travels back in time, thinks about *Once Bitten* and not even having a choice about his future on it, and how different this decision is. Because now it's in his hands and his alone.

He doesn't want to walk away from his own series, but . . . His heart is pounding a frantic drumbeat that sounds suspiciously like *Freya,*

288 • LILLIE VALE

Freya, Freya. He doesn't just want stolen moments with her, he wants a *life*.

"No, Taft, they won't recast you." Before the relief can unfurl in his chest, Moira says, "Without you on board, there are no sequels. They'll scrap it."

He can't help it. He thinks of every single person who works on *Banshee* suddenly losing their job because of *one* asshole person who decided they just didn't want to do it anymore—him.

"I can get you the day to think about it," says Moira. "But think long and hard. Have a chat with Mandi. Because it's not just your future at stake here." Her voice softens. "I'm your manager, and I will support you in whatever you want to do. Just make sure whatever that is, you really want it."

Their goodbye doesn't come quick enough. The coffee machine has finally stopped sputtering when he hears soft footfalls padding out to the kitchen.

"Good morning," says Freya through a yawn. "Were you on the phone?"

"Moira had some follow-up points about the sequel offer," he says, handing her a mug prepared just the way she likes it. "Can we ... talk?"

She gives him a few bleary blinks before taking a sip of coffee. "Yeah, of course."

When they both sit down at the table, he says, "I ... I think I'm going to accept it."

"Oh," she says. Just one word.

It encompasses everything and nothing, and yet Taft can't read anything into it. At a loss, he asks, "You don't think I should?"

"No, it's not that." Freya wraps her hands around the mug. "I guess I just didn't realize you'd already made the decision. Last night it seemed like you didn't know where you were leaning. But I guess a good sleep helped clarify things?"

It didn't, but Taft finds himself nodding.

"I'm really happy for you, baby," says Freya. She stands, leaning forward to meet him halfway across the table in a quick peck. "When you were gone last night, I got all packed up to go back to Stori's place. It's so strange, I don't even think of it as 'home,' anymore," she muses.

"Home can be a person."

She smiles shyly, meeting his eyes. "Yeah, exactly. I think so, too. Anyway, I'll be back here soon, right?"

"You're my girl, Freya. Of course you will. Just . . . maybe not as soon as we thought."

The warmth in her face is replaced by worry. "I don't understand. Are you still worried for me? Because, you know, there are a lot of Hollywood couples who manage to keep their relationship on the down low. I even made a list yesterday! I don't know exactly how it works keeping their pictures out of the press, but I'm sure you could ask someone? Moira, maybe?"

"Freya—"

"And I was thinking, who's really going to be *that* interested in me, honestly? Alina's still reading my manuscript, and it might be complete trash and totally unpublishable. Until my next book comes out, there's nothing newsworthy about me, and since I'm *never* going to pretend to be Mandi ever again, there's no reason that someone like Kurt would give a shit."

"*Freya.*"

She takes a breath. "Sorry. I had a lot of time last night to think about this."

He just has to say it. There's no gentle way to ease her into the realization they should have both made last night.

"My 'relationship' with Mandi is the selling point they want to capitalize on," says Taft. "The leaked pictures? Turns out that Moira, Gareth, and the movie publicists were actually able to give the bad optics the right spin, and the only story anyone cares about anymore is what's next for Raft. Everyone wants to announce the sequels with confirmation that we're engaged."

Freya blinks at him. Finishes her coffee without saying a word. Blinks some more.

"Please say something," he implores.

"I don't know what you want me to say. I'm still processing the fact that the guy I was fake dating who I *thought* was going to be my boyfriend is now planning to fake marry another woman. So. That's where I'm at."

Shit, it sounds so bad. He winces. "I'm not ending things. We'll make this work, you and me."

"Oh, okay." Her tone is icy. "So explain it to me. When we do go out in public, will you introduce me as your 'friend' or as the other woman?"

"*What?* No!"

Freya shoves the mug away and fixes him with hard eyes. "So then what?"

"I realize this is a big ask, but what if"—Taft swallows—"we kept our relationship a secret?"

SHIT SHIT SHIT, THAT'S NOT WHAT YOU WANT, YOU KNOW IT'S NOT.

He wishes he could take it back as soon as he says it.

FREYA'S NOT ANGRY. She's disappointed.

The question suspends between them like cheap thread, flimsy and fraying. Taft breaks eye contact first, sucking in a sharp breath like he's a bit horrified at what just came out of his mouth.

"Did you seriously," Freya says slowly, "ask me to keep pretending? Like the last four weeks of it hasn't been enough to last a lifetime?"

She has the wild, fleeting desire to reach out and grab his hand, make sure he's real. That all of this hasn't been an illusion all along. If she concentrates, she can remember the weight of his palm against her hip.

The splintered silence that lingers in the wake of her response is anything but empty—so much hangs in the balance.

"If doing these movies instead of the indie film is what sets your soul on fire right now, I support you," says Freya. "I don't know that it'll give you what you're looking for, but I want for you whatever *you* want for you. I always will. But what I can't do—what I won't do—is compromise on who I am. Not anymore. I can't be fake."

She's never been more sure of it than she is in this moment.

"When I said I was *done* being Mandi Roy, I meant that. I'm ready to be me again. Not the girl I used to be, but the person I've become now. The person I found with you."

Taft looks tortured, but she knows he's listening.

"I *just* found that person," she says quietly. Her words are unscripted, but she knows exactly what she needs to say. "I don't want to hide her to be with you."

"But I don't want to lose you, either," says Taft. "Don't make this an ultimatum, please."

"It isn't one. I'm telling you what's important to me. When the photos of us at Tiers of Joy and Books and Brambles came out, it felt like we'd lost everything because of a couple of mistakes. So maybe hiding us seems like the answer to you, but I'm telling you that it's not. *We're* too important to compromise."

His face flickers with an emotion Freya can't place, but as her heart sinks into her stomach, she's afraid that he's been compromising for so long that he's too scared to find another way.

"I care about you," Taft says, and when has that ever prefaced anything but a *but*? He pauses. "But sometimes we have to compromise to get what we want."

She nods. She had expected it, but it still hurts as though she hadn't.

"Then you are a cheater," she says without any animosity. "You're cheating yourself out of what you *really* want."

He stares into his coffee, likely gone cold. It's hard to tell what he's thinking when he won't even meet her eyes. She waits, hoping he'll say something, say *anything*, but she gets it. She's picked her writing over relationships too many times not to understand.

He sees the choice before him as no true choice at all, and even though her pride still smarts, she can't even blame him for wanting his cake and eating it, too.

"I'm going to call Stori to pick me up," says Freya.

She waits for him to tell her not to, but he simply nods.

That one small, resigned gesture breaks her heart. She was going to leave today, anyway, but going like this makes her want to scream, cry, throw things against the wall.

When Stori arrives, Freya hesitates at the front door, taking everything in one last time. The green couch they never had a chance to christen, the billowing curtains with the shadows of his windowsill herb garden, Sir Henry's empty doggy bed. She never thought she'd say this, but she'll miss Hen, too.

"I'm proud of you, Taft," she says. Her voice doesn't crack. *I'm a better actress than I ever gave myself credit for*, she thinks somewhat abstractly. "And you should be proud of you. When that's enough, I hope you come after me."

And then she's gone.

STORI, UNSURPRISINGLY, MAKES tea. It's the most Stori thing to do, and Freya can't help but love her for it.

She drinks the tea. She loathes it, remembering Darjeeling and cupcakes and *I'll be free to pursue what I want*. She crawls into bed and hopes she doesn't dream.

When Freya wakes up, she can hear Stori's boyfriend, Marcus, in the bedroom next door. His Cuban accent is soft and coaxing while Stori's is hurried and agitated. Without using names, she's explaining that Freya's having boyfriend trouble and is back home to regroup.

It's only midafternoon, so Freya slips downstairs to Books & Brambles to distract herself, takes over the register from Cliff, and thumps Hunka Junk down on the counter. Everything is going back to normal, before cute actors blazed into the bookshop and turned her entire world upside down.

Except . . . From here, she has a vantage point to the stacks where they almost kissed. She glares in that general direction before budging everything ten inches to the left.

She's never felt so out of place.

When her phone rings, her literary agent's name on the screen, Freya latches on to it like a lifeline.

"How are you?" asks Alma. "Because *I'm* doing terrific. My incredible client just wrote a killer book, I can't stop thinking about that last plot twist, and her publisher is going to be very, very happy. I just have a few tiny notes for you that I'll send over tonight and once you address those things, we can send it on to your editor. Sound good?"

It takes Freya a solid ten seconds to realize that it's her, *she's* the client. "You liked it? Really?"

"If you call reading it in one sitting and having to close my laptop about eight million times because I just needed a minute to calm my heart rate down before I perished? I woke my girlfriend up when I squealed on three separate occasions and finally she just stayed up so I could read out all my favorite parts to her, so yeah, safe to say I more than liked it."

"Alma, my brain just short-circuited. Can you, like, just repeat all of that?"

"*Kill to Be You* is my new favorite thing. I will make a thousand

Goodreads accounts just to give it all the five stars it deserves," says Alma, every word enunciated with a melodramatic flourish. "Seriously, where have you been keeping this gold? How did you even come up with this?"

"Uh . . . would you believe me if I said I kinda wrote it like a super AU fanfiction of something that happened to me in real life?"

"Ha! Fine, fine. Keep your secrets," says Alma. "Just have a good story for what inspired you, because your editor will definitely want to know. She's been champing at the bit for your second book, and while this is a huge departure from your debut, I think it's the perfect way to launch you again. Good work, Freya. You're back."

CHAPTER TWENTY-EIGHT

Freya's gone.

It's only been a day, but every trace of her has faded from Taft's house. Colors and flavors seem muted somehow. He can't even look at the couch, where she'd spent so many hours curled against an arm with Hen sprawled next to her, the clicks of keys such sweet background noise. The scent of paper and ink that always trailed after her is gone, too, not even a tickle of it in the air.

He's appalled that she left thinking she was the other woman. Freya Lal is the *only* woman he wants or will ever want. The upward trajectory of his career has always been dictated by the women he's with, but he would happily take a nosedive right now if it meant redeeming himself.

All he's ever wanted is to love and *be* loved, and yet he'd fallen into the trap of compromising once again. She was right—he *had* cheated himself. He'd cheated them both.

"You did what?" Mandi's aghast when he tells her how he and Freya left things. "You just let her go?"

He drums his fingertips against the kitchen table where they're sitting, waiting for their 8:00 a.m. call with their managers. "How could I ask her to stay after what I said?"

It seems like a reasonable question, but when Mandi rolls her eyes into the next dimension, he comes to the conclusion that she, too, thinks he's a gigantic fuck-up.

"Taft, when we agreed to take the offer, I didn't think it meant at all costs. You love her, don't you? How can you bear to let her go for . . . for what, exactly? Something you don't even want?"

He does love Freya, but he once promised himself that he wouldn't be selfish with her, and then he'd gone and done just that. "I never said I didn't want it. You know what *Banshee* means to me."

"Sure, but that doesn't mean you haven't outgrown it. You *are* allowed to move on. You can want other things. You don't owe some random people your loyalty."

But loyalty has always been how Taft has measured everything. Loyalty is the people you choose who choose you back.

Understanding shifts behind her brown eyes. "Wait . . . You think you're doing this to be loyal to *me*?"

"It's your career, too," he says. "If I tell them no, then there's no sequels for you, either."

If he had to put a name to the emotion that darts over her face, he would call it love.

"Thank you for thinking of me," Mandi says in a voice that's surprisingly thick. "But it's your life, Taft. What you want is important, too."

What you want out of a relationship—romantic or platonic—doesn't matter any less than what the other person wants.

"I'm not Connor," says Mandi, and Taft almost snorts, because hello, understatement of the century. Mandi's a better friend than Connor has ever been. "But I hope you think of me as your friend, too."

Taft startles, undignified and wide-eyed and tongue-tied. He didn't know how much he needed to hear it until the words are out there and she doesn't take them back.

Her lips curl. "And not because you're my costar or because we *have* to be friends because of all the secrets we're keeping. You're my closest friend because you give a shit about me, which is more than I can say about the other people in my life. You've always had my back and helped me get what I wanted. This time it's your turn. You have leverage, Taft. Use it."

His brow furrows. What leverage does she think he has?

He's still stuck on it when they join the three-way video chat with Moira and Gareth a minute later. "Hi," he says upon joining the call, still eyeing Mandi.

"Have you reached the right conclusion?" snaps Gareth. "Or are you going to make yet another mistake?"

"I'm going to stop myself from making one," says Taft.

"*Thank you.*" Gareth's voice is heavy with sarcasm.

"We got all the deal points we wanted," says Moira, frowning at Gareth.

Gareth gestures to someone off the screen to bring him his latte. "You should have a DocuSign by now in your email to electronically sign. You don't have to read it, Mandi. It's quite long, and your time is better spent getting a facial. Your skin is looking a bit dull, and don't forget, you're a guest judge on that new Netflix baking show next week."

On the screen, Moira's face clenches before she smooths it into her usual professional calm.

"Actually, we might need to amend it one more time," says Taft.

"You've got to be shitting me," exclaims Gareth.

Taft continues like he didn't hear him. "Moira, about that indie offer? I want to take it. If they want us so badly for the *Banshee* sequels that they agreed to everything we asked for, then I'd say we have enough leverage to ask them to work around other commitments if needed. And Mandi and I—there isn't going to be a Mandi and I."

"Excuse me?" Gareth sputters.

Taft ignores him. "We'll do whatever promo they need, but we aren't going to pretend to be anything more than what we are." He glances at her and smiles. "Best friends."

"You don't speak for my client," says Gareth.

"No, I don't," Taft says easily. "But neither do you."

"Gareth," says Mandi. She takes the phone from Taft and holds it up to her face, staring her manager down. "If you aren't as invested in respecting my well-being as I am, then we need to part ways."

"Mandi, you're not thinking clearly. I have been with you since the beginning. I *made* you."

"No, Gareth, you didn't. I made me. You always tried to make me less myself. I appreciate all the work you've done on the *Banshee* contract, but as soon as this is over please start the process to end our professional relationship. I plan to seek new representation as soon as contractually possible."

He sneers, then exits the call without another word.

"Good for you," says Moira, addressing Mandi. "I have no doubt you'll have plenty of interest, but I'm more than happy to put together introductions for you with any of my colleagues at Lord and Fine."

"I'm not going to rush into a decision this time around," says Mandi, "but thank you, I would appreciate that."

Moira slides her eyes back to Taft. "I'm guessing you meant everything you said, and it wasn't just to piss off Gareth?"

He doesn't use his words lightly. "I meant every word," he confirms. "This is what I want."

Moira studies him for a long moment, like there's something there she's never seen before. "Okay, then. We'll shoot our shot."

FREYA'S BEEN UP since six working on her agent's edit letter, which landed soon after their call. Most of Alma's feedback is micro, line-level stuff. She's also caught a passage where Freya used the same word six times in two sentences, which is *mortifying*, but instead of letting it send her into a spiral, Freya laughs it off and moves on.

While eating comfort Chinese takeout last night, Stori had protested her diving right back into her regular shifts at the bookshop, but when she comes downstairs this morning to see Freya wearing a name tag of her own, with her *actual* name on it, she tears up and keeps the coffee coming to help Freya power through revising.

"Hey, you're actually writing and not just staring off into the distance with your thinking-about-Manny-Jacinto-in-a-rom-com face," says Stori when she comes back to officially open up the bookshop a few hours later.

"Don't worry, I haven't been replaced by a pod person," says Freya, who is on her third Bialetti espresso and chocolate-filled croissant. "I've penciled in my Manny Jacinto time for later."

"Don't forget about Sebastian and Richard. Don't want them to get jealous," Stori tosses over her shoulder.

Freya grins and gets back to work, not paying attention to whoever comes in a few minutes later. From experience, she knows that anyone coming in this early doesn't need help and will know exactly what they're looking for and where to find it.

"Hi, I need a book."

The familiar phrase knocks her off-kilter so quickly that her entire body jerks, her hands almost knocking her laptop off the counter.

Taft Bamber stands in front of her wearing a crisp shirt, a hopeful smile, and an empty tote bag slung on his shoulder. "I'm not in a rush this time."

She rights the laptop, but it's considerably harder to right the rest of her, her heart flinging itself toward Taft the second she sees him. "Are you here because you miss me or because you know what you want?"

Taft tilts his head. "Both." His gaze is intense, like he's drinking in the sight of her even though they were only apart for a day. "I'm sorry. I should never have said what I did. Never have let you leave like that."

"No, you shouldn't have," she says coolly. "But I understand why you did."

"You were right. I don't want to compromise when it comes to how I feel about you."

Hope surges in her chest, but she tamps it back down. She doesn't want him to see how she feels until she knows where *he* stands. "What about the sequels? You told me you were going to take the offer."

"And I am," says Taft. "But on my terms. Let's just say I redlined the contract a lot. Especially one particular clause that, if I'm being honest, I was never too thrilled about and should have pushed back on from the beginning."

"One clause." She lets that sink in. "And it's gone now?"

He nods, coming closer. "So this is me coming to find you."

This early, there are no customers yet, and Stori's still packing up preorders, but that could change any second. The last time they assumed they had privacy here, they were swiftly proven wrong.

"Let's go out to the bookgarten," says Freya. "It's more private."

They seat themselves on one of the white wrought-iron bistro sets. Taft's gaze follows the climbing roses ascending the brick wall before shooting back to her with a fierceness. "I know you're cautious because I've fucked up before. But if you let me, I promise you, I will be gentle with your heart."

"I know you'll try, Taft. But I meant what I said—I don't want to wear a mask ever again. I don't want to hide who I am or who I'm with, and for a minute, that was what you were offering. It's not enough."

"It's not enough for me, either. You were right: we're too important to compromise on. If they want me badly enough, they'll agree to *my* terms."

"And what are those terms?"

He reaches across the table to clasp her hands. "That I'm ready to walk if their offer hinges on continuing a fake relationship with Mandi. She's not my headline name. My red carpet is reserved solely for Freya Lal," he says quietly. "If she'll still have me."

"You're ready to walk?" Her eyes widen. "And Mandi's okay with that?"

"She basically told me what you've been telling me: what I want doesn't matter any less than what someone else wants. But it didn't truly sink in until you left. And when Mandi told me she'd choose my happiness over the movies, I realized . . . wow, how lucky am I? Two of the people I love the most chose me over themselves. Most people don't even get that once, I was a selfish dick, and I will spend every day making it up to you if you can still see a future for—"

"Wait, did you say you love me?" Freya tries not to tremble or show her emotions, but from the absolutely wrecked way he's looking at her, she's sure she's failing abysmally.

"I love you," Taft states simply, leaning in until they're sharing the same breath. No pretty words and no scripted lines make it mean all the more. "There are no dream roles or dream opportunities without my dream girl."

The hint of a question in his eyes makes Freya realize he's waiting for some kind of confirmation.

She's never seen him this unsure.

"Fictionalize the future for me," she says. "Tell me what happens next."

"Next, I'd like to kiss you. Or you can kiss me. I'm not picky," says Taft. "And then I'll get up and make you a coffee because I'll always make my girl a coffee. I'll bring her fresh cups whenever she wants, and I promise not to push a tea agenda."

She cracks a smile at that one.

"And then I'll blow off all those interview requests and spend the rest of the day here with you so you'll know what Moira says as soon as I do. But no matter what message she bears, nothing is going to change for us, Freya. From this moment on, I will always choose you."

She touches her lips to his, traces the planes of his face with her hands. "And then what?"

"I'll tell Moira that I want to be with you and ask her to help us figure it out. She has my back. And then, maybe before the indie film starts shooting, we could go visit your dad? I'd really like to meet him."

Freya smiles against his lips. They aren't playing roles anymore, they're building a *life*.

"But, baby," Taft whispers, his hands catching her face. "None of this is fiction. This is our future. This is me in love with you so goddamn much that I'm not doing what I really want to do right now. We've been apart for a day and I already know I hate not seeing these beautiful brown eyes, not kissing these lips. So the only question left is: Is this a future you could want?"

Her heartbeat quickens. "God, Taft, I . . . You've outlined our story so well, how could I not? Might make a writer out of you, yet."

Taft laughs. "God, no. But speaking of . . . Have you heard from your agent yet?"

"Alma loved the manuscript," Freya confides. "She has some notes I'm working on, but she thinks it's going to be my comeback book."

"I can't wait to read it. But maybe I'll save it for the plane."

"The plane?"

Taft nods. "If they still want me for *Banshee* after my counteroffer, think you could revise on the moors?"

"Wait. Are you asking me to . . . join you?"

"Yes, if that's what you want. It wouldn't be for a few weeks, but I have a *really* comfy trailer that I would love to share with my girlfriend. Or the girl I *hope* will be my girlfriend. I don't want to hide her—I want to show her off. Take her places to eat cake and wander bookshops and dance in clubs."

"Are you sure you're ready for that, Taft?"

"With you, I'm ready for anything." His smile makes her blood sing. "With you, I'm ready for *everything*."

Finally, we're both on the same page. So this is what it feels like to be with a man who wants her as much as she wants him. Who's willing to walk away from fame and fortune for her: Freya Lal, headline name.

"I am starting to love LA, but I'll let you sweep me wherever your next role takes you, Taft. I love you, too," she murmurs. She stands up and takes a step closer to the drinks gazebo. "Now, I think you mentioned something about making your girl as much coffee as she wanted?"

Taft grins, desire and sunshine swirling in his gaze. "That's true. But first, I said I'd kiss you. Or you could kiss me."

Freya is no longer a girl who waits. She doesn't delete, she doesn't go backward. Facing the future together, and all the bad and good that comes with it, is how they have to move on from here.

She kisses him first, arms snaking around his neck to tug him even closer, savoring the heat of his skin and the familiar scent of Irish Spring she loves so much. His smell fills her senses, enveloping her as though she's still in the bedsheets they shared. Her stomach flutters when his teeth catch against her lower lip, sharp and sexy. She makes a bitten-off protest in the back of her throat, unhappy when he doesn't linger to soothe it. Instead, he peppers fervent kisses down her neck, lightly sucking and scraping.

Freya places her hands on his bristly cheeks, his stubble scratching against her palms, and drags him back up to where she wants him. Taft can't get enough of her either, if his ardent response is anything to go by. His mouth is downright magical, firm and insistent and tender all at once, tongue sliding in with sinful wet heat. It feels good. *Exceptionally* good.

God, kissing Taft is like kissing fucking sunshine after living in a world of rainy gray cloud. His arms clasp her tight, but she squirms against him, burrowing even closer. She's ready to crawl out of her skin just to get closer to him.

"I"—"love"—"you." Taft punctuates every word with a kiss.

"Love you," she mumbles against his lips. "I really needed that."

Taft grins. "Me too, sweetheart. But want to know a secret?"

She pretends to think. "Um, always."

He dips his head closer, nose nuzzling into her cheek. "I really, really, really wanted it, too. And someone once told me that what I wanted doesn't matter less than what someone else wants."

"Must have been someone pretty wise, huh?"

"Oh, the *wisest*."

"Lucky for you," whispers Freya, "that we both want the same thing."

"The luckiest," says Taft, wonder in both his eyes and voice. "Believe me, there's no doubt in my mind right now that I am the luckiest guy in LA. In the world. In *all* the worlds."

"Now shut up and kiss me again," demands Freya, although it's really more of a plea and they both know it.

She doesn't have to tell him twice.

ACKNOWLEDGMENTS

As I sit down to write the acknowledgments for my fourth published novel, I'm both incredibly humbled and exceedingly gleeful that I have the best job in the world. And here's a secret: it wouldn't have happened without the people who helped me take the risk.

When I came up with *The Shaadi Set-Up*, the book that would become my first foray into writing for adults, I remember having an anxious phone conversation with my agent, Jessica Watterson. What if this inspiration is just a one-off? Will adult readers love my stories? Am I even grown-up enough for this? And like the wonderful human and excellent agent she is, Jess squashed those Whac-A-Mole worries with endless positivity, support, and faith that now I had the first idea rolling, other ideas would come quick.

Fingers crossed, I thought, silently willing her to be right but also a little terrified she was overestimating me. Reader, I emailed her five hours later with the pitch for *The Decoy Girlfriend*.

The idea of being mistaken for an actress popped into my mind because I'd recently heard the story of my namesake, my great-grandmother, who was often mistaken in the 1930s for a famous leading lady with whom she shared the exact same name. Relatives from far and wide sent telegrams to my great-grandmother's family asking if she was acting in the movies! Talk about mistaken identity!

Working on this book with the spectacular team at Penguin Random House and the Putnam imprint has been, in short, a dream. From day one, I've thanked my lucky stars to be working with such enthusiastic, communicative, and dedicated people. To the star-studded Putnam team, thank you for everything you do to make my books sparkle.

My editor, Gaby Mongelli, makes me feel like a creative superstar, but *she's* the guiding star without whom this book would probably have gone supernova as I grappled with the first draft. She's probably the most *together* person I know in the industry and I'm so grateful for her editorial insights, attention to detail, and love for these characters. Thank you for your patience and grace as I persevered through writing another pandemic book. You always divine what I'm going for and help me get there.

Kristen Bianco, whenever I see an email from you pop up in my inbox, I know there's some stellar publicity news coming. I am endlessly thankful for all you do. To production editor Leah Marsh and copyeditor Erica Ferguson, thank you for taking this book across the finish line with me.

Maybe I'm giving away secrets too readily, but here's another: *The Decoy Girlfriend* has my favorite cover. Thank you to designer Vi-An Nguyen and artist Maria Nguyen for bringing mes bébés Taft and Freya to life in such a stunning, glamorous way. Truly, when I sent over reference pics of Logan Lerman and Ananya Panday, I wasn't prepared for the magic you'd make. I'm still starry eyed! And shoutout to Logan, too, because if it wasn't for those articles about his pandemic hair going viral, I would never have been struck with inspiration and thought, *I'm going to write a book about that man one day*. Or a fictional man with his looks, anyway!

Ali Hazelwood, Alison Cochrun, Mazey Eddings, Ava Wilder, and Lauren Kate, I have nothing but the biggest stars in my eyes for you all! Your luminous words shine bright on this book. Thank you!

Kate Holiday, giver of sound advice and receiver of "Can I be petty for a minute?" messages, you are my light in dark places when all other lights go out. Thank you for your fellowship and for making it through this book without bursting into flames.

Mom and Dad, thank you for encouraging me to aim for the stars and often rearranging your lives to make it so. Like Taft, I've been in too many one-way-street friendships, and this book wouldn't have been as emotionally honest without you telling me that I could dig deep and do this. Mom, thanks for motivating me to write without fear. And also for watching loads of *Love Island* with me while I wrote this book.

To the shooting stars—booksellers, librarians, reviewers, Book-Tubers, BookTokkers, Bookstagrammers—all over the world who love this book, thank you! You're all out of this world! I appreciate your enthusiasm and hard work in shining a light on my work, and ensuring other book lovers continue to find my books for years to come.

You're all walking on *The Decoy Girlfriend*'s red carpet with me <3

DISCUSSION GUIDE

1. In *The Decoy Girlfriend*, protagonist Freya Lal is a perfect doppelgänger for superstar Mandi Roy. If you had the chance to step into a celebrity's shoes, even just for a day or two, would you?

2. At the beginning of the novel, Freya is facing writer's block on her next book. Have you ever hit a hurdle on a creative project? What did you do to overcome it?

3. What did you think of Mandi's plan to have Freya take her place? Did you think it would be successful? Why or why not?

4. The idea of "pretending" is a major theme in *The Decoy Girlfriend*. How do each of the characters pretend in some way? Ultimately, how do these actions impact their relationships? What about their own sense of self?

5. Before the start of the novel, Freya lost her mom, who was one of her biggest advocates. Where else has she developed a support system?

6. Discuss Taft's relationship with Mandi. In what ways do they have trust in each other? Why do you think this is?

7. From the moment Freya and Taft meet, sparks fly. Did you anticipate the turn their relationship took? Why do you think they were so drawn to each other?

8. As Taft's career shifts, he begins to realize that his friendships with his former costars aren't as strong as they once were. Have you ever outgrown a friendship? What happened and how did it impact you?

9. Talk about the way these characters build a sense of home. Is home a physical place, or is it a feeling? Discuss some of the small details that help create a home for Freya and Taft.

10. Who is your favorite celebrity couple, and why?

11. What do you think is next for Freya and Taft? What about Mandi?

PHOTOGRAPH OF THE AUTHOR BY LILLIE VALE

Lillie Vale is the author of *The Shaadi Set-Up* and the young adult novels *Beauty and the Besharam* and *Small Town Hearts*. She writes about secrets and yearning, complicated and ambitious girls who know what they want, the places we call home and people we find our way back to, and the magic we make. Born in Mumbai, she grew up in Mississippi, Texas, and North Dakota, and now lives in an Indiana college town.

VISIT LILLIE VALE ONLINE

LillieLabyrinth.com

🐦 LillieLabyrinth

📷 labyrinthspine